T0366106

Also by Stan E. Hughes aka *Ha-Gue-A-Dees-Sas*

"The Sacred Ceremonial Pipe" (*Awareness* Magazine Jan/Feb 2011)

Medicine Seeker – A Beginner's Walk on the Pathway to Native American Spirituality (NorLightsPress 2010)

Favourite Memories (Noble House – London 2009)

Collected Whispers (International Library of Poetry 2008)

The Best Poems and Poets of 2007 (International Library of Poetry 2007)

Forever Spoken (International Library of Poetry 2007)

Standing in Two Worlds – A Look at American Indian and Alaskan Native Spirituality (Indian Education Center III Press – Gonzaga University 1994)

Chon-TEH Oh-DOH-won (Heart Song) (Ravenswood Publishing 1993)

CHILDREN OF THE BLUEFISH

Written and Illustrated by

STAN E. HUGHES

Aka *Ha-Gue-A-Dees-Sas*

Copyright © 2016 Stan E. Hughes.

All rights reserved. No part of this book may be used or reproduced by any means, graphic, electronic, or mechanical, including photocopying, recording, taping or by any information storage retrieval system without the written permission of the author except in the case of brief quotations embodied in critical articles and reviews.

Archway Publishing books may be ordered through booksellers or by contacting:

Archway Publishing
1663 Liberty Drive
Bloomington, IN 47403
www.archwaypublishing.com
1 (888) 242-5904

Because of the dynamic nature of the Internet, any web addresses or links contained in this book may have changed since publication and may no longer be valid. The views expressed in this work are solely those of the author and do not necessarily reflect the views of the publisher, and the publisher hereby disclaims any responsibility for them.

Any people depicted in stock imagery provided by Thinkstock are models, and such images are being used for illustrative purposes only. Certain stock imagery © Thinkstock.

ISBN: 978-1-4808-2854-4 (sc)
ISBN: 978-1-4808-2855-1 (e)

Library of Congress Control Number: 2016935309

Print information available on the last page.

Archway Publishing rev. date: 04/22/2016

North American Bobcat. Also called "e-H'MOO-to<u>n</u>-kah"

CONTENTS

DEDICATION

To my elder spirit-brother and mentor, Bobby Lake Thom, *Medicine Grizzly Bear,* a proud and upstanding member of the Karuk Indian Tribe of Northern California. He walked into the Spirit World to find my true name,

    Ha-Gue-A-DEES-Sas (Man Seeking His People)

and patiently guides me as I continue to learn how to carry that name.

To my life-long pal, Adam Hudson, *Ee-che-MAH-ne We-CHOSH-teh* (Traveler), who embraced the magic of the Black Hills of South Dakota and taught me to listen to the timeless beating of her heart.

To my children: Heather, Ted, Beth and Cathryn who walk gently on the Earth Mother and give me the hope that my short time here will prove to be, through them, a blessing in the future.

To my little brother, Rod, who heard the enchantress's call of the "Mother of All Waters" (Chesapeake Bay) and learned to love and respect her.

And especially to Phyllis Betts, the heart of my heart and the tender part of my life.

PRELUDE

Like a vast onyx mirror the Chesapeake Bay rested in silent anticipation as the cumbersome longboat labored toward the distant shore ... the only sounds that bitter winter night in the early 1600's were the creak of the oar locks and the muffled and steady dip of the oar blades pulling the huddled occupants toward the first parlay between the Englishmen and the leadership of the *Choptank* Indian tribe. Each member of the seven-man trading delegation was hunkered down against the damp coldness deep in thoughtful trepidation reflecting on life and wondering, "How in all that is holy did we ever come to this ..."

Master Edward M. Wingfield was attired to the 'nines' with his grey combed-wool three-piece suit, bright red cummerbund, and wide-brimmed musketeer hat with large feathers extending half-way down his back. His chest glittered with his medals and honor ribbons. His cape was of maroon velvet with silver braiding and held at the neck with a gold chain. It was not by accident or favoritism that Wingfield was selected as the first president of the Jamestown settlement. His life-long love was the business of business and he excelled in those efforts for the London Company. If there ever was a middle class in 1600's England, the Wingfields could serve as their poster family. They had keen minds and an unusual ability to make the right business decisions. Edward's father, uncles and male cousins all were businessmen and all were very successful in their endeavors. As a young executive Edward would occasionally consider the thought of marrying and starting a family; but he had established specific financial goals during his career climb and was determined to reach them before considering the ties of domestication. Each time he worked his way upward in the organization, he found another plateau to reach before he could consider himself "there." Now, a somewhat slouched-shouldered older man in his 40's with expanding waist line and receding hair line, his dreams of a family were slowly dwindling.

Captain Gabriell Coverdale was in his formal English Navy blue winter uniform with double rows of gold metal buttons and gold braided epaulets on his shoulders. The sleeves of his uniform were covered with gold braiding from wrist to elbow. He wore his matching blue triangular military garrison cap with gold tassel and carried his sword and brass scabbard at his side which added to his imposing appearance. He too, had his chest fraught with medals and ribbons. Because of the lack of contact with the mother country, he did not know that he had been promoted to Commodore. He was a dashing man, always clean-shaven, exceptionally tall, broad in the shoulders and narrow in the waist and hips. His eyes were gentle and a deep, deep brown that melted the hearts of the ladies. Women would quietly comment that he looked more like a Greek god than a human being and many longed to run their fingers through his dark brown and curly hair. The captain descended from a long line of military officers. As far back as his family's oral tradition could remember, there had been a Coverdale in service to the monarchy. The family prided itself in the fact that King Henry VI had given them their surname in the mid 1400's. The family's original name before that honor was lost in the foggy reaches of time. Coverdale was a confirmed bachelor despite his striking appearance and handsome features. He held a deep dark secret that ate at his soul during long and restless nights. At first it started as a special affection for his men in general. He expressed this by his care and consideration which endeared him to all those who ever served with him. But he became obsessed by specific young soldiers restlessly doting on the sculpture of their bodies, the way they would look child-like and trusting at him, the flow of their hair or the fluid ways they carried themselves. He fought the compulsion to embraced them and hold them against his body. The wars Captain Gabriell Coverdale fought for King and Country could not compare to the endless war in his heart. He would be the last of his family's line.

Vicar Robert Hunt, in stark bleakness, was in black from head to toe with his white collar contrasting against his long, crane-like neck. His Adam's apple seemed to have a mind of its own and it would tremble and bulge out for no apparent reason. He was an extremely tall, gangly man, with rich black hair, unusually pallid skin and large knobby unkind hands. When he would endeavor to emphasize a point in his many "Hell Fire and Damnation" sermons, he would extend his bony forefinger at the congregation and stomp his heavily booted foot on the floor. Somewhere in his training and experience, he missed the message of God's love through His son Jesus Christ. Hunt believed that the only way people could get to Paradise was through subservience and fear. Sunday services were required attendance by the exploration party members unless they had specific duties that would exempt them. The men soon grew weary of Hunt's accusatory and guilt-ridden tirades, and would often volunteer for just about any job to avoid attending. He grew up in the wild hillsides of Wales and was the second son of a cold, aloof father who was also a man of the cloth and the second son of a cold, aloof father ... and so on back down the family tree. His mother was a plain, mousey woman who never spoke unless she was spoken to. She was very thin and skeleton-like. Her clothing hung on her body more than it could be said she wore them. He once saw his father scream at his mother "Submit!" as he was mercilessly beating her with a riding crop. This taught Hunt a perverted way to deal with women, which might partially explain why he had never found someone willing to marry him ... his basic personality and appearance notwithstanding.

Sergeant Bartholomew Lusby looked somewhat uncomfort-able in his faded non-commission officer's uniform of red and green. The clothing had been in his keeping for at least fifteen years, and his girth had long outpaced the ability of seamstresses to let out the waistband of the trousers. He had always been a large strong man, and as the years passed the large outpaced the strong part of his appearance. He was an amazing marksman with the firearm of the day, the fusil, and had distinguished himself on the field of battle with his prowess. Not only was he a great shot, but he could shoot, reload, prime, and fire again faster than anybody had ever seen. His upward mobility through the enlisted ranks kept pace with his ability to improve his performance, and he was at one time the youngest sergeant in the British military. Still youthful, he had gone as far as he could in the enlisted ranks; and despite his accomplishments those in command could not envision him as an officer. Lusby had a wife in Manchester that he had not seen for years. There were rumors that he also had wives sprinkled from Essex to Westover, but he would never own up to those rumblings. Sometime during his military career he had learned to read and write, and he surprised people with his ability to discuss a number of cogent issues in an intelligent and genteel fashion. Lusby had 'military' in his blood and would remain in the service until his death.

John Capper, the carpenter, had a love affair with wood. His father and grandfather had worked in this natural medium in their shop in suburban London. They distinguished themselves by their skills and craftsmanship and were always in demand and busy. Capper gladly learned the family trade and maintained the tradition of excellence. He could look at a tree and see chairs, tables, bed headboards, lintel beams, window sashes and any number of other uses for that particular piece of lumber. Even as a small child, the aroma of wood-working pleased him, and it was no less pleasant now that he was an adult. As a teenager he had severed two of the fingers on his left hand with a wood-cutting awl. It was a running joke by the expedition members that Capper could only count to eight. The carpenter knew almost every tree imaginable just by looking at a piece of wood. He would touch it, sometimes taste it, hold it up to the light, take a brief sniff and identify it perfectly. He knew soft wood trees from hard wood trees, and what could be the best use of that specific lumber. Capper was invaluable to the team because of his training and skills and really was held in high esteem by everyone. The carpenter had never found himself in a position to meet the 'right' women and over the years grew weary of the challenge. He had long ago given up the pursuit of the ladies and one of the reasons he had enlisted with the Jamestown expedition was that there would be no females.

Wingfield instructed him to carefully observe how sturdily the different Native structures were built, if there was some form of sanitation system in place, and any other aspects of the village that might afford clues to its strength and defensibility.

Private James Dixon's childhood was painfully similar to many of the poor and destitute children of the loud, squalid and foul cities of 1600's England. His earliest memories were being dragged along by an abusive older brother to see the fly-encrusted severed heads of criminals on pikes along the road to London Bridge and to hear the painful moans of prostitutes being brutally and publicly whipped at well-attended floggings. At age six his father sold him to a furrier in Newcastle named Bartlesby. Dixon's only recollection of his mother was of a heavy woman with large arms and no teeth who seemed to cry all the time. His situation was truly involuntary servitude. Bartlesby had an abject fear of people and never touched other human beings except in anger, so Dixon's growing years were totally devoid of gentleness or affection. The young bondsman would occasionally quietly follow his supervisor home to see what the 'good life' was like. Dixon was on the job seven days a week, was fed one meager meal a day and allowed to sleep in the furrier warehouse. Through the endless nights he would nestle down in the stacks of raw furs and his eyes would fill with tears of loneliness and rejection. He did learn the furrier business and became quite adept at identifying and grading and preserving different animal pelts. This ability assisted in his gaining a place on the roster of those first adventurers traveling to the New Lands. When Dixon was in his early teens, Bartlesby did not come to work one day. Arriving at his apartment he saw the housekeeper unceremoniously salvaging the silk sheets and pillowcases from under the cold lifeless body of his master. The housekeeper was filling the pillow cases with just about everything of value in the apartment before the coroner and legal authorities could arrive to claim the body. Dixon ran back to the furrier shop, knew where Bartlesby had sequestered the cash box, emptied the contents in his pockets and never looked back. When his money ran out, he joined the military and became quite adept with the fusil. As an adult he was understandably cold and distant toward other people and unnecessarily physical and overbearing toward women. It unsettled his acquaintances when he seemed to especially enjoy the blood-lust of battle. If a blast from his fusil might decapitate an enemy, he would laugh hysterically. He too, had distinguished himself as a ferocious warrior and could match Lusby medal for medal. The fact that he was still a Private was directly related to his inability or unwillingness to perform the social expectations associated with higher rank.

Theodore Brooks-Hughes was the progeny of a long line of sea-faring people. Only in his twentieth winter he had traveled farther and seen more of the world than most people twice his age. Every male family member as far back as could be remembered knew that when they were of age, they would sail the world's oceans. There was a family joke that the first Sons of Hugh had helped throw Jonah overboard. As with all the men, Brooks-Hughes started his career as a cabin boy, but he had distinguished himself in a special way. He had developed an affinity for drawing and painting and found himself in the role as the ship's artist. More often than not, he was painting the masts and gunwales of the ship, but he also had an extensive portfolio of drawings and etchings of life at sea and of the development of the expedition's new home in the Western World. Wingfield especially appreciated his talents and had him create extremely accurate portraits of the leading members of his team. The settlement administrator kept this collection and enjoyed viewing the art work in the privacy of the Master's House. The artist had a special young lady back in England and would occasionally pine over the separation. His long-range plan was to return to her and marry. He would never know that his little butterfly had suffered for days until she died of the pox just a few weeks after his departure into the Unknown.

This would be Brooks-Hughes' second of many visits to the Native village and part of the time he could be seen busily sketching in an effort to record the historic events. Those rough penciled sketches would be later finalized in India ink in the comfort of the ship's cabin. His actions were of special interest to the local people, and they were constantly jostling around him to see what he was doing. Brooks-Hughes endeared himself to them and would be the first White Man to actually meet a young *Choptank* Indian woman.

How strange, that in the fullness of time each man's individual and arduous journey through the trials and tribulations of life would bring them to this point where together they would step forth into a most exciting and extraordinary adventure.

CHAPTER I ...
DEPARTURE

The *Phyllis Redoubtable*

In the early-morning hours of that eventful day in 1607, the worthy sailing barque *Phyllis Redoubtable* found a favorable late summer wind from the southeast to fill her sails. She began to ply the uncharted waters of what would sometime later be called Chesapeake Bay by Captain John Smith of the Jamestown Colony.

HMS Phyllis Redoubtable

The experienced mariners knew that the red morning sky could be a harbinger of worsening weather, and indeed, this proved to be true. By midmorning, a gale of frightening force was buffeting the riggings, and a lashing rain swept over the quarterdeck. As if the soul-chilling breath of the hounds of hell themselves were behind her, the small craft, despite the fact that most of her canvas had been wrapped, scudded over the churning whitecaps in an almost due northerly direction. The boiling clouds, low, dark, and angry, combined with the heavy rains to shield the view of the tablelands off to starboard, raising the anxiety of the ship's company. The heart-stopping fear that they were being driven out to sea and would soon be lost in the maelstrom brought fevered prayers to the lips of all hands.

Master Robert Hunt, the expedition's man of the cloth, could be heard above the dreadful moan of the winds as his rich Welsh voice intoned God's deliverance.

Grasping the forward gunwales with all their strength, and fighting to see through the stinging salt spray and enveloping cloud bank, able-bodied seaman Theodore Brooks-Hughes and London Company employee William Cassen peered into the gloom, endeavoring to espy some sign of hope.

Brooks-Hughes pointed at the foaming waters around the sturdy *Phyllis* and cried to Cassen, "The water's murky! My God! The water's murky!"

Both men knew what this implied: for some reason, they were approaching shallow water. He then turned back toward the wheel stand and screamed against the high-pitched whine of the wind, "Wrap sails! Anchor down!"

Obadiah Withams, the ship's navigator, could not believe what he was hearing. "What?"

Brooks-Hughes repeated his plea, this time with panic in his voice. "Wrap sails! Anchor down!"

Something was very strange.

Two topside crewmen rapidly released the anchor, and it splashed heavily through the ecru-colored water. Seamen Jerald Pennyfeather-Grayson and Percy Exum (a topic of conversation among the crew because of the snake tattooed on his lower arm), struggled against the biting wind and rain. They crawled up the mainmast rope ladder and tied down the remaining sails. The *Phyllis* shuddered and slowly swung around as the anchor dragged along the sea bottom.

Ship's officer Lieutenant Edwin Marian, in his breeches and undershirt, emerged from below shouting, "What's wrong? What's happening? Why are we stopping?"

Navigator Withams briefly explained Brooks-Hughes's concern.

Marian responded, "We'd best ride it out here until we can see what we are getting into. When the seas calm, we can take some depth counts." He instructed the seafarers to get the leaded line and returned, already soaking wet, to his cabin to dress against the conditions.

───────────

How quiet the footsteps of time.

Less than twenty-four hours before the terrible storm, embraced by the early autumn sunrise, the worthy *Phyllis Redoubtable* lazily floated southeastward down what cartographers would someday call the James River, toward the tidal lowlands. The red and magenta iridescence of the eastern firmament promised worsening conditions, but at that hour, all was calm.

An important question had yet to be addressed: where to go?

The cabal of 1607 that had forced Master Edward Marie Wingfield, the duly appointed first president of the Virginia Expedition, from his leadership position of the Jamestown Colony still tasted vile in his throat as he surveyed his situation. He felt somewhat betrayed by the fact that the small detachment of military fusiliers—their ranks depleted by illness, death, and injury—had chosen not to get involved in the political in-fighting of the community. However, Wingfield was the sponsor-recognized leader of the expedition, and the crew of the *Phyllis Redoubtable* was charged with following his orders and supporting his requests.

He glanced at his roughly scrawled passenger manifest, reviewing the names of the sixteen London Company men who had chosen to remain loyal to him. Including the three-man military unit and the ship's crew, there were twenty-eight pairs of strong arms at his disposal. Little did he know that the results of his decision to depart Jamestown would be the first step in a great story, one that would extend the lives of most of those who had chosen to honor their commitment to Wingfield. The colonists remaining in Jamestown would suffer terrible hardship, and their numbers would dwindle from 144 in May to 32 by Christmas of the fateful year of 1607.

════════════

As the storm temporarily eased, a hastily formed committee convened. Captain Gabriell Coverdale, the colony's military attaché; ship's officer Lieutenant Edwin Marian; Magistrate Cuthbert Guilford, the legal advisor for the colony; Fusilier Sergeant Bartholomew Lusby; and Wingfield carefully discussed the options.

Guilford, the legal expert of the group, suggested, "We could continue the patent of the London Company but in a different location. Once the new settlement is on its feet, we send the *Phyllis* back to the homeland to inform the partnership of what has occurred and where the new colony has been established."

Ship's Officer Marian, still in a quandary as a result of the turn of events, offered, "We might inventory ship's stores, replenish them from local flora and fauna as much as possible, and endeavor to return to Mother England. If we can avoid marauding Spanish ships, we have a good chance of reaching the English settlements in the Caribbean. From there, we could join a convoy for the voyage across the Atlantic."

Wingfield's preference was to return to Jamestown and wrest back control of the settlement in the name of the company. He was not sure this would be received with any enthusiasm, so he contributed, "We have enough manpower to construct a new community downriver from Jamestown and await the replenishment of supplies from England. We could set watch until the convoy plies past, hail them to shore, and explain the new circumstances. As the legal representatives of the London Company, we would have the rights to those provisions. A taste of starvation might bring the usurpers around."

Magistrate Guilford carefully reviewed the original patent and unscrolled the Settlement and Governance Compact to determine the legalities of the next move.

Neither document clearly addressed the issue at hand, nor could Cuthbert apply a legally written precedent. The phrase "first colony in the southern part of Virginia" was confounding. As the only criterion listed in the patent, it needed further consideration. Now that it had been established, he felt there were no geographical limitations should they choose to rebuild in another location.

After some continuous discussion and weighing options, the original question was now answered. The *Phyllis*

Redoubtable would seek a new and better home in the Western world. The adventurers had seen many of their friends and shipmates die at the Jamestown location. As the weather grew warmer, the flowing brooks and streams became a swampy, fetid landscape that was fraught with snakes and noxious insects. Since they had chosen to remain in the wild lands, the site for their new settlement would have a renewed and extensive list of criteria for acceptability.

As the *Phyllis* restlessly tugged at the anchor near the headlands, Wingfield called a meeting of all hands. He allowed the decision-making committee members to share their feelings and impressions of what the next move would be. Presenting a united decision to continue exploration, the crew and passengers accepted this idea with resolve—and some trepidation.

════════════

Then the heavens opened up! The sturdy *Phyllis* bobbed like a cork in a storm drain, but she was holding her own. Just as it seemed the storm could not get worse, almost magically, the winds abated, and the seas began to smooth out. As the afternoon sun, stretching for the western horizon, broke through the cloud cover, the saturated ship glistened as if it were encrusted with diamonds. Little did they realize that the power of the hurricane had pushed the *Phyllis* nearly ninety nautical miles almost due north, nor did they comprehend that the break in the weather was just the eye of the hurricane and more trouble was on the way. These hardened mariners of the 1600s had braved North Atlantic turbulence, and their prior experiences said that once the storm calmed, things would improve dramatically.

A hum of activity followed, as all hands worked to undo the storm damage on the ship's deck and prepared to get underway. The dim outline of the low-lying eastern shore emerged through the diminishing cloud bank, and it was now clear that landfall was quite close. Pennyfeather-Grayson and Brooks-Hughes began to take depth readings under the watchful eyes of Marian and Withams. As they pulled the leaded line back, one would count the arm-lengths as the other grasped the rope: "Five ... six ... seven ..."

Withams was incredulous. "Seven! We must be almost a league from the shore. How could it be seven? Do it again!"

This time, Pennyfeather-Grayson cast the line, and Brooks-Hughes counted the pulls, "Five ... six ... seven." Subtracting the ship's draught of around ten feet, less than another ten feet of water lay under their keel. It was clear that these were indeed strange waters; the *Phyllis* would have to proceed with due caution.

The homely and unpretentious vessel continued slowly and surely northward, allowing ship's crew to keep taking depth counts in the cocoa-hued water: "Four ... five ... six ..."

"Sixteen? Twenty! I can't find the bottom—and look at the water! It's as blue as a sapphire!"

As seaman Matthew Tasley pulled the roughly woven leaded rope, the normal aroma of saltwater permeating the line was replaced by the heady fragrance of freshwater. The *Phyllis* had encountered the mouth of a very large river flowing westward into the bay. Because it was an ebbing tide, the fresh water was mastering the effluence of salt water and would do so until the neap tide countered the river's flow and pushed salt water upstream. Someday this powerful river would be called the Choptank.

A tree-covered spit of land extended before them on the north and a pleasant bay of navigable water appeared to separate the finger of *terra firma* from the main land body on the east. The ground appeared higher on the starboard which might prove to have more potential for a settlement site than most of the surrounding area ... and there were majestic trees as far as the eyes could see. Ship's officer Marian instructed Withams to head the craft into the estuary and ordered his men to prepare a long boat for going ashore at morning's light. As the evening began to slowly walk her slender feet upon the slumbering lands, Marian and Master Edward Wingfield scanned both shorelines with their spy glasses looking for possible landing sites. Much to their amazement, there appeared to be some sort of rough habitation near the beach on the port side. It seemed prudent at this point to avoid contact with any Indigenous souls peopling that area, so he decided to inspect the more rustic and wilder appearing eastern landfall.

The exploration party had only begun to prepare the skiff for the morrow's adventure when dark and menacing clouds began to envelope the area ... this time hailing from the north! Blessedly, the sheltered basin of what would someday be known as the Tred Avon River diminished the bite of the storm. Still, the hungry waters boiled, the rains in their ferocity pelted the *Phyllis*, and the impelling winds wailed through the riggings like banshees in agony. Though securely tethered, the small craft strained against her anchor chains as the tireless gale endeavored to prod her onto the eastern shoals. As the long and tenuous night slowly passed, ship's company held on and attempted to find some rest before what might prove to be a very trying and exhausting day ahead.

CHAPTER II …
DAY BREAK

The Work Begins

The survey party was led by Captain Gabriell Coverdale and included Fusilier Private James Dixon, John Capper – the carpenter, and the Cassen brothers: William, George and Thomas. With a strong sense of expectation they propelled the skiff shoreward with Coverdale at the tiller scanning the coast line for an appropriate landing site. The nearing beach was rocky and uninviting but appeared to gently join the water which implied any number of locales to make landfall. Obscuring the rapidly shallowing sea bottom, the water was thick with silt and various flotsam from the earlier storms. Suddenly their paddles began to churn up muck, and before the captain could order them to ship oars, the dory shuddered to a stop with a sickening grinding sound. All hands tumbled backwards as Private Dixon was expelled into the water splashing clumsily as he disappeared from sight.

As he thrashed to the surface, he screamed in great panic, "I can't swim!"

"Stand up!" shouted Coverdale.

And Dixon realized he was only partially immersed in less than chest-deep water. Peals of laughter rolled over the calm waters even unto the *Phyllis* as the rowers struggled to right themselves and saw the soldier looking similar to a drowned rat, with a most chagrined expression on his face. In this most unusual fashion Private James Dixon could be considered the first Englishman to set foot upon this pristine ground. Spanish historians credit Juan Menendez de Marques as the first European to explore the area in the 1570's, but there is no account relating that he landed there.

Wading in the shallows, the crew pulled the boat onto the rocky shore and began to unload various tools, weapons and provisions. The sea bottom seemed to crunch under their feet, so George Cassen obtained a shovel and dug into the sandy murk.

"Oysters!" he yelled in glee. There must have been a half-dozen glistening mollusks in the shovelful and a sizeable soft-shell crab scurried off the spade and plopped back into the water. It was at this moment the party realized they had stumbled upon a veritable cornucopia of eatable sea life.

And this has proven to be true even unto modern times.

The exploration team followed the shoreline in an effort to reach the gentle rise seen earlier. The forest and underbrush were so thick that its hungry arms extended toward the stone infested beach and blocked the morning light. As they rounded the headland, they found an open meadow leading toward the land's high point that allowed them to survey the surroundings. The air was crystal clear and the morning early autumn sun was beginning to warm the soil. Wisps of steam rose lazily as the saturated ground began to evaporate. The humidity was oppressive causing the Englishmen to tire more quickly than normal. Looking to the north and east, the travelers spied the *Phyllis* floating gently on the incoming tide. A pastoral lea, grasses still lush and green despite the time of year, meandered to the shoreline offering an acceptable location for the colony and needing very little pre-construction site work. The forest sheltered the meadow from the open water on the west and could also provide safe cover from marauding Spanish ships plying the main bay. Toward the rising sun a small rill tumbled seaward. The fact that it still flowed this late in the season was a good sign indeed. And the trees! Like a vast ocean of green, the forest of Loblolly pine and oak trees extended to all horizons – and beyond. The pine tree trunks were straight and broad and reached skyward with their branches and limbs. The oaks were so large that three men holding hands around the base of these magnificent warriors could not replicate their diameters.

Captain Coverdale, his throat choked with the emotion of the moment murmured, "It's as if the Hand of Providence has carried us here ..."

The ensuing days, though growing shorter as winter approached, were filled with long hours and aching muscles. Master Robert Hunt, the expedition's preacher, determined they should christen their home "New Providence," and all agreed by voice acclaim. The settlement would be constructed at water's edge on the west bank of the small cay that extended southward from the main bay. Even at lowest tide, the estuary would draw enough water to allow the *Phyllis* to rest comfortably in its sheltered arms.

Master's House and Shed at New Providence

Wingfield and Magistrate Cuthbert Guilford organized the men into work details with Ship's Officer Marian's assistance. Two large crews under the direct supervision of carpenters Edward Pising and John Capper would be responsible for felling trees, skinning the branches from their trunks and using them to construct the buildings. The smaller limbs and boughs would be cut and stacked for firewood. Pising and Capper would supervise the actual construction of the domiciles as designed and platted by Wingfield and Guilford. The settlement would eventually consist of the Master's House, a shake shed for making shingles, a small barracks and jail for the fusilier detachment, a combination wood shop and foundry, a large dormitory for the workers including some private rooms for higher ranking expedition members, a dining hall and kitchen, and various sheds and outbuildings for storage, smoking jerky, etc. A rock jetty would be constructed and extend eastward into the cay until it reached deeper water. This would help ease the off-loading of provisions and supplies and would also serve to enhance the lading of products determined to be of value for the return trip to England.

The second phase of construction would include a palisade around the entire compound with gun turrets at the four corners, an infirmary for the ill and injured and a chapel for worship. Additional protection planned was a moat on the landward sides of the village filled with water from a canal dug to intersect with the stream south of the hamlet. The second phase was never undertaken – reasons to be divulged later.

Sergeant Bartholomew Lusby and his soldiers, Dixon and Kenneth Quinby were assigned as hunters and gatherers. Two of the seamen, Percy Exum and Jonas Profit, were somewhat adept with weaponry and were occasionally enlisted when not working elsewhere. Because of the need to save black powder for the *Phyllis'* cannons, the fusils were stored away and the hunters used either long bows or cross bows to bag the plentiful geese, turkeys, whitetail deer and elk. Traps and snares were devised to catch squirrels and rabbits, and an extensive trap line wound its way along deer trails deep into the forest to find the groves of persimmon trees, plum and cherry trees, and hickory, walnut and chestnut trees where small mammals congregated. Ship's cook Oscar Johnson logically became responsible for meal preparation, and he enlisted Thomas Couper – barber and William Love – tailor, as assistant cooks. Surprisingly, the settlers ate extremely well as Johnson varied the menu between fowl, red meat and sea food. There were still provisions from England to round-out each repast.

Surgeon William Wickinson was able to maintain an infirmary aboard the *Phyllis* which proved to be a Godsend.

Little be known in the realm of 1600's leechcraft, he could quarantine ill expedition members and control any outbreak of infectious diseases. The fetid pools of water around Jamestown that provided breeding grounds for mosquitoes, diphtheria, and dysentery were not a part of the New Providence landscape. Their potable water supply was the flowing stream which was as clean and clear as could be found. Wickinson was an accustomed tea drinker and was able to convince Wingfield to allow a daily tea ration of sassafras and blackberry. Again, unbeknown to the leechcraft of those times, this potion also improved the men's probability of maintaining good health.

By December 1607, New Providence was gaining the character of a bustling community. A sense of permanence was growing and many of the colonists were beginning to feel at home. Three expedition members were lost during this construction phase. London Company employee Kellam Throgmorton was crushed when a heavy Loblolly pine lintel beam rolled over him. His broken body was tenderly removed to the *Phyllis* where after a restless and painful night the gloomy morning silence told his shipmates he was gone. Francis Midwinter succumbed from blood poisoning resulting from a relatively minor axe cut on his foot. Surgeon Wickinson tried every medicinal in his apothecary to quell the fever and bring him comfort. All to no avail. Able-bodied seaman Percy Exum left the confines of the village one early morning at low tide to procure a basket of oysters. He just never returned. Many a night in the workers' dormitory crew members mulled over the possibilities: Wild animals? Hostile Indians? Sea Monsters? Most likely, he lost track of the tide changes in his eagerness to fill his basket and was washed away. Only a small handful of expedition members could swim – so the sea was always hungry and posed special dangers.

Contact

The winter arrived ... Not roaring out of the north like an angry slavering meat eater, but silently and menacing like a tom cat creeping toward a preoccupied field mouse. The days grew shorter – the nights grew longer. The slumbering land seemed to wrap itself in blankets of hushed inactivity. The chill and dampness of the air extended its icy fingers through the chinks in the log walls and shake roofs contesting with the fireplaces for the spirits of the colonists. Boredom and depression crawled through the community like a malevolent spider. The rains had come, and no man was exempt from the drenching discomfort. Outside activities such as wood cutting or food gathering were met with a sullen, almost mutinous, attitude. Old animosities among the London Company employees were coming to the fore. Long-forgotten grievance, insults and degradations were suddenly remembered causing tempers to flare. The jail in the fusiliers' barracks was almost always occupied.

Wingfield had experienced this growing sense of dissatisfaction in his men once before, and it eventually resulted in his ousting at Jamestown. He had no wish to re-live that situation. He summoned Magistrate Guilford, Captain Coverdale, Sergeant Lusby and Ship's Officer Marian to the Master's House to determine the appropriate action ... or reaction.

"Let's hang the malcontents," offered Lusby. "Watching two or three of them dancing by the neck from the yardarm would do wonders for their dispositions." A nervous chuckle passed through the committee members somewhat subdued by the thought that Lusby might possibly be serious.

Marian suggested, "Aboard ship we combat boredom by keeping the crew busy. Even make-work has its value. Idle hands … you know."

Coverdale nodded in agreement, but responded pensively, "At sea there is no place else to go. Here, the men could cast us out of the compound and never be held accountable. No one, not even our employers, knows where we are."

A thoughtful silence ensued until Marian responded, "My crew is loyal. With the help of a few of the London Company men we could get the *Phyllis* under way in a matter of hours."

Coverdale stood up. "We didn't come all this way and work so hard to abandon the project. I cannot comprehend fleeing when we have so much to lose and so much to gain."

The only sounds were the rain drumming on the roof, an occasional "drip-splot" of water leaking onto the stone floor, and the crackling of the fire. Each man was wrestling with the issue at hand. They truly were on the horns of a dilemma.

Wingfield and Guilford walked away from the rest of the group and were quietly engaged in an animated discussion. The others watched them knowing an idea was germinating. After some moments they returned and the expedition leader announced, "We are going to make contact with that indigenous encampment we saw on the other shore. We have barrels of trade goods and we need to learn more about them: How do they survive through the winter? Are they hostile or friendly? Are they weak or powerful? Why haven't they tried to contact us?"

He instructed Captain Coverdale to notify the assemblage of a meeting in the dining hall at first light. Ship's bell would be rung at the proper time. He also cautioned the captain to not discuss with the men the topic of the convocation. As the committee members retired to their respective quarters,

Wingfield and Guilford parlayed long into the blustery night working out the details and anticipating contingencies.

Johnson, Couper and Love had roused hours before daybreak and were busily preparing the morning's meal when Wingfield and Guilford arrived in the dining hall to get ready for the meeting. The aroma of warming bread reassured the hard-working Magistrate that the provisions from home were not yet depleted. Cauldrons of salt pork and venison were bubbling happily, and a large metal urn of rain water simmered over the fireplace patiently awaiting that magical transformation into sassafras and blackberry tea. Wingfield watched the three galley-mates scurrying around with fascinating efficiency. They actually looked happy in their work.

Johnson, as head cook, had the sole right to ring the ship's bell calling the men for the two daily meals. In mock deference, Couper and Love stood at attention and saluted Johnson with large wooden spoons. Despite the gravity of the developing situation, both Wingfield and Guilford found themselves chuckling at the comic opera. Murmuring voices and footsteps slogging across the saturated parade ground predicated the arrival of the expedition workers. The tears of the rain gods had lessened to an annoying drizzle; but much improvement over the week-long deluge.

Displaying a show of unity Wingfield and Guilford were joined at the front of the room by Lusby, Coverdale and Marian. One of the crewmen mumbled to those sitting near him, "The last time we saw those five together we ended-up sailing into the buttocks of Hell itself."

"Gentlemen," began Wingfield. And the group fell into an expectant silence. "We feel the necessity to partake in the next aspect of our exploration: Contact with the aboriginal savages of this land." The administrator paused a moment as his words rippled through the assembly. "We have laid out a basic strategy and will need the cooperation of each one of you as we make preparations for this important endeavor."

Coverdale watched the reaction of the men and felt renewed admiration for Wingfield. Regardless of how he presented the plan or regardless of what he was about to request each person to do – he already had their collaboration by asking rather than commanding.

"As soon as the weather clears," the exploration team leader continued, "We will sail the *Phyllis* in full flags, canvas and regalia toward the rude encampment. The one we spotted earlier on the opposing shore. Once we come within hailing distance of the village the fusiliers will fire off their weapons, but without shot. We will follow this with a fuselage from the four cannons; again without shot. Chances are the natives will have never heard such a commotion and they will be both terrified and curious. The fusils and cannon will be immediately reloaded, this time in earnest, in case there is a hostile response from the shore."

Guilford moved into the center of the presentation and continued the plans: Two skiffs would row to the village. Wingfield, in his best ambassadorial attire, would be in one and Coverdale, in full dress uniform, would be in the other. Each craft would have six oarsmen and a man at the tiller, all heavily armed. In each boat would be an assortment of trade goods. These would include glass beads, rolls of brightly colored cloth and ribbon, a cask of rum, tableware and an assortment of simple metal kitchen implements. All these trade goods were readily available either stored on the *Phyllis* or stacked in the various sheds and outhouses. All efforts would be made to make this first encounter peaceful and productive.

The same laborer who had commented earlier muttered, "That's a waste of good grog."

Wingfield, reviewed the contents of *The Articles on Intercourse with Indigenous Peoples* to remind the men that they were Englishmen representing the most powerful king and nation in the world and should conduct themselves accordingly. These heathens must learn to embrace the Christian faith and become loyal subjects of the honorable King James I. He then closed the presentation with a simple statement, "It is reasonable to believe that the savages who inhabit that commonalty on the far shore have experienced countless winters in this area and have developed the skills and knowledge to survive. Hopefully, they can learn from us and we can learn from them."

The expedition team members had only one thought: "Gold!"

The men devoured the victuals set before them, and table conversation was light and exciting. The five leaders huddled together and began to determine who would be on the contact team, who would remain on the *Phyllis*, and who would stay at New Providence to protect the compound. By the time the lists were completed, every single soul had a responsibility in this new adventure.

———

Thankfully, it was not forty days and forty nights, but the weather conditions did eventually improve and the expedition prepared to set sail across the estuary. With the clearing skies came bitter cold. The seamen were busily chipping ice off the deck of their ship with the same red, stinging hands that hoisted the anchor out of the frigid water. Winfield peered briefly at the craft's chronograph. It was 21 February 1608, exactly one year and two months since they had left Mother England.

A raw, steady breeze hailing from the southeast combined with the outgoing tide to help the *Phyllis* slowly move in the direction of the encampment. Marian swept the farther bank with his spy glass and observed strange huts, most looking like amber bee hives and some like large loaves of bread about half-again as tall as a man and obviously constructed of vegetation.

Wigwams in the Choptank Indian village.

The thatched roofs had holes in them, and some were allowing faint smoke to rise into the air from those openings. There was no palisade around the community which implied the inhabitants had the ability to protect themselves. The beach was littered with large overturned sea-going dugout canoes carved out of massive tree trunks, and nets were spread out across the rocky areas of the shore line or suspended from tree limbs. Some of the structures had flat-topped and open-sided canopies also built with reeds or branches. Very large piles of brush and tree limbs dotted the hamlet's open spaces. It appeared these stacks were to be used for firewood; and because of the size of the accumulations the villagers were planning to spend the winter in that location.

But where were the occupants? Marian scanned the village again and again, but no movement could be detected. He handed the telescope to Wingfield saying, "I can't see anyone. Not even any animals! Are your eyes sharper?" The expedition supervisor focused and re-focused the glass ... nothing.

"We'll stay with the strategy," Wingfield replied. "When we fire our weaponry, it should cause some response." By this time the aboriginal settlement was close enough that the workers could see without any visual aides it appeared deserted. Seaman Parksley and Brooks-Hughes dropped the anchor, and the *Phyllis* creaked to a stop.

"Sergeant! Fire your fusils!" barked Captain Coverdale. Three loud "pops" echoed across the water's surface ... nothing. "Fire aft cannon number two!" ordered Marian, and a deafening "B-o-o-o-m" shook the ship and rattled the riggings ... nothing.

The expedition leader grew agitated. Innately he realized something was not right, but he also knew the Englishmen could not discontinue the contact efforts. Seldom patient, but always prudent, Wingfield made a forceful decision. "We will take one long boat to the beach. Each of the crew will have extra weapons at hand. I will hold the tiller and watch for trouble as we close in. Should we find any inhabitants, I will try to communicate with them."

He turned to Marian. "Have all four cannon loaded and ready to fire. We may have to retreat in great speed."

Those left behind watched as the skiff skimmed over the waves toward the bank. A light dusting of snowflakes was descending signaling that more bad weather was on the way. Master Robert Hunt, the preacher, began to recite a prayer of protection which offered little comfort for those who remained aboard. Marian followed the dory's progress with his spy glass and also scanned the tree line and huts for some sign of the native population. The boat crunched softly into the shallows – thick with shucked oyster, clam, and mussel shells. The crew jumped into the icy, knee-deep water and hoisted the skiff onto the shore so quickly that Wingfield almost tumbled off the aft board. Weapons at the ready they formed a human shield around their administrator as he stepped aground.

"Hallo!" he called. He held up a handful of red, gold and blue ribbons … no response. "Check that large hut to the left!" Wingfield ordered Brooks-Hughes and Pennyfeather-Grayson.

Empty.

It did not take long to realize that the Europeans were the only humans in the encampment. A mangy looking dog emerged from one of the huts, growled at the Englishmen, then skulked into the forest. Some of the structures had smoldering ashes in their fire pits, but it was impossible to tell how long it had been since new wood had stoked the flames. Countless footprints were impressed in the earth during the heavy rains and then frozen like fossils when the temperature plummeted. They were rapidly filling with falling snow flakes. Landward from the village, many paths wound into the nearby forest, but the hard ground concealed any signs of recent foot traffic.

Then one of the strangest sights the explorers would ever see unfolded before their eyes: A small, very terrified Indian woman seemed to appear out of thin air.

Elderly Choptank Medicine Woman named "Chop-tah-nk."

She shuffled haltingly toward them with her hands fisted tightly against her mouth. Her hair was as white as the falling snow and endless wrinkles outlined her fearful eyes. She was dressed in animal pelts that dragged on the ground hiding her deerskin footwear. Yet, this tiny forlorn creature had an air of grace; almost regal in nature.

A dry, shrill crackly voice spoke, "*Chop-tah-nk. Chop-tah-nk.*"

"So here is the sacrificial lamb," thought Wingfield.

The English leader had no idea what she was saying, but her words did not sound threatening. He cautiously approached the crone, nodded briefly, and held out the brightly colored ribbons. He inquired, "Where are your people?" and spread his arms and shrugged his shoulders hoping the non-verbal motions would express his confusion.

With startling quickness, the elder snatched the ribbons from his hand and stepped back.

Winfield shuddered, "If she was here to kill me ..."

The withered person began to rub her calloused, gnarled fingers on the ribbons and was so engrossed by their smoothness that she seemed to forget the tall, hairy and very rough-appearing pale men that approached her. She looked at Wingfield and a wide toothless grin seemed to take years off her time-worn countenance. The most musical, joyous laugh the Europeans had ever heard rippled outward from the frail lady warming their hearts and easing their tension

As if by some cosmic intelligent intervention, the snow ceased falling. The forest was suddenly alive with short, stocky, not altogether attractive, brown-skinned people; men, old women and children, similarly dressed like their elder envoy. Their language was totally non-understandable, but their curiosity was clear. The Natives crowded around the White Men causing uncomfortable proximity issues and violating the personal space boundaries of the Europeans. With bird-like fingers, the Indians constantly touched their clothing entranced by the colors, textures and stitching of the fabrics. Some of the Red Men adorned themselves with various feathers looking as much like strutting turkeys as human beings. They did have assorted weaponry: crude bows and arrows, lances with stone points, and an especially nasty looking battle axe consisting of a large, rounded stone attached to a wooden handle by sinew. The men were holding their weapons in their left hands, which was a universal sign that they meant no immediate harm.

It was soon clear who would speak for the encampment. Five older men, imposing by their demeanor and clothing, emerged from the forest as the throng parted and grew silent. The elder men were surrounded by a group of younger men heavily armed and looking menacingly at the strangers.

Wingfield smoothed out his red cummerbund and called for the small barrel of trade goods. He then laid out a long colorful rough cotton tablecloth on the frozen ground. He placed five shiny, decorative porcelain plates on the banner and stepped back. One of the young warriors received an instruction from a chief, inspected the plates carefully, abruptly brushed them aside, and handed the textile to his elder. Later, the visitors would learn that anything that appeared to be associated with food preparation was for women only. The European's actions, though offered in good faith, implied that the tribal leaders were womanly. Only the forbearance of the Native aristocrats kept a very unpleasant event from happening. One of the elders was obviously very pleased with the fabric, so Wingfield collected up the plates and offered four more cloth segments. This was the proper decorum.

The crowd of *Choptanks* and Englishmen flowed back into the village as the tribal leaders motioned for the tall, hairy men to follow them into one of the larger structures near the center of the community.

Marian was closely watching the encounter from the *Phyllis* with his cannons at the ready. It appeared that the visitors were not under duress, but he could not help but worry when they disappeared into the domed hut. Meanwhile, the contact team was enjoying their new found attention. Except for the administrator and Sergeant Lusby, the visitors from across the sea had meandered through their lives with few if any people knowing they were even on the planet or caring if they lived or died. For the first time, they felt special, even valuable ... and this was something to relish and remember.

As the Englishmen entered the building they noticed that it was surprisingly spacious. *"Wig-ah-wum,"* muttered one of the elders as he extended his arms. The Europeans could not determine if the word meant "Come in and sit down" or if the word described the setting.

One of the other white haired women put branches on the smoldering embers and they soon flared up into a comfortable fire. She placed a large, light-brown leaf into the flames and the most pleasant aroma filled the room. Some light was struggling through the smoke hole in the roof and through the open doorway, but the interior of the structure was basically lit by the fire pit. The floor was covered with animal pelts and stacks of decorative baskets woven from reeds or grasses rested against the walls. Hanging from the rafters were bundles of the same light-brown leaves causing the Westerners to consider the headroom that appeared to be just fine for the shorter locals. The Natives sat down knee-to-knee leaving very little room for the visitors to follow suit. Joints cracked and voiced grunted as the gangly White Men assumed the uncomfortable position of their hosts.

Then, possibly the most unusual ritual the Englishmen had ever seen began. One of the elder men, apparently the head chief of the village, mumbled something and was handed an ecru-colored leaf. He began to fold it, and because it was so dry, it popped and cracked softly in his hands. Soon he had formed a long, flat tubular shape and placed one end in the flames. As the tube began to smoke, he placed the cool end in his mouth and inhaled deeply causing the end to glow. Then, as he exhaled the pungent smoke, he passed the leaf to the next person who repeated the procedure. Eventually, the smoking plant reached Master Wingfield. He grasped it gingerly and noticed the saliva on the end. This immediately disgusted him and he hesitated. *"To-bac!"* said the Indian on his right hand. He looked pensively at the other crew members, and they were smiling in impish expectation. Despite his better judgment but unwilling to offend his hosts, he replicated the actions the others had done. As the smoke entered his throat he began to cough uncontrollably. The Native men laughed merrily, as did the Westerners. Lusby sobered mid-laugh when Wingfield handed him the leaf, and it was his turn. The visitors, to a man, had brief coughing fits as the *to-bac* passed from mouth to mouth.

Now it was the visitors' turn to share something. Wingfield found a large tin cup in the trade barrel which was set just inside the doorway and filled it from the rum cask. The Natives watched closely as he opened and then closed the wooden spigot. He took a brief sip then handed it to his men. Despite their desire to drink fully and deeply, they mirrored his actions. "Grog," stated Pennyfeather-Grayson as he handed-off the container. As the rich brown, heady liquor passed from Indian to Indian, it was clear they found it very, very enjoyable. The warming feeling and sweet flavor was so unusual and so pleasant to a people who had never experienced sugar or alcohol before. Wingfield knew there was no way he could take the remainder of the rum back to the boat, which disappointed his team.

Whether it was the calming effects of the tobacco smoke or the comforting sensation of the rum, a growing sense of fellowship was felt and it became evident that both groups would be able to relate to each other. Two of their hosts were still wary and distant, almost hostile, but overall there was a positive tone to the meeting. Wingfield stood up slowly and smiled at the Indians. He nodded briefly and motioned his men to do the same. Clearly, the Natives wanted their guests to remain, so the expedition leader formed a circle with the fingers on his right hand, and swept it from right to left indicating they would return the next day. The cold winter evening was fast approaching and none of the Englishmen felt comfortable with the thought of being in the village after nightfall. It was relatively clear that the porcelain plates, cups and bowls had little immediate trading value and were left outside the *wig-wam*. A loud melee ensued as a group of older Indian women fought over the dishes. More than one of the pieces could be heard smashing on the frozen ground as they struggled for the precious items. Three of the elder chiefs went straight for the rum dispenser.

Preparation and Anticipation

That night on the *Phyllis* was one of tale telling and planning. The landing party crew members shared their impressions of the events of the day. The stories they wove transformed a cold winter's night into something of mystery and awe. Ship's crew kept asking what the women looked like. Private Dixon thought a moment and said, "I don't think I saw any young women or girls. There were plenty of old crones though ... if you're interested." After a brief moment of laughter, the others who had met with the Indigenous population realized that his point was indeed true. This unusual turn of events directed the conversation down a number of roads as the men tried to think of the possibilities.

Seaman Brooks-Hughes commented, "It doesn't make any difference. Remember the *Articles on Intercourse with Indigenous Peoples*. We are representatives of the most remarkable king of the world and should present ourselves accordingly."

The others berated his interjection and continued their "man talk."

Meanwhile, in the captain's cabin a more serious conversation was flowing. Master Robert Hunt, the Preacher, had joined the conclave and was insisting on being an active participant the next time the Westerners and Natives met. This would be his first opportunity for proselytism and his eagerness knew no bounds. Magistrate Guilford asked if the landing party had noticed anything of commercial value, like silver or gold ornamentation or precious gems. Lusby replied that they saw nothing of metal at all. "These people are still in the stone age."

He continued to press the point to determine what the Englishmen might gain by this contact. "How about mink or ermine integuments? Did you notice anything of that nature that might be worth trading?"

Wingfield reflected a moment and then replied, "The floor of the lodge was covered with animal skins. Mostly elk, deer or bear I would imagine, but I think I saw some smaller pelts with rich, luxurious fur. Remember that this was just one short meeting in one location, so it is a bit hasty to draw conclusions about the commercial potential. We might do better to try to acquire the provisions we will need for survival and sustenance through the winter, and consider looking for profitable ventures in the mean."

As important as the "what" was; the "how" of the pending meeting was even more vexing. Should the White Men insist that the parlay be held on the *Phyllis* or should they continue to meet in the village? The Native leaders did seem very interested in the textiles amongst the trade goods and especially favored the rum. Would these prove to be the most effective trade media? The Englishmen had barrels and barrels of glass beads and metal kitchen utensils and tools. Would these have any value? What if they were only interested in the British weaponry? There was no way they could allow fusils, or even crossbows and longbows, to fall into their hands. Clearly, this could be a major bone of contention. Magistrate Guilford reviewed the *Articles* to see if there were any guidelines for the actual face-to-face intercourse with Indigenous Peoples. An Appendix did describe how to communicate in gestures for basic needs, like food and water and shelter. But there was no assistance at all for trade and commerce or how to establish values on commodities. They were on their own.

That evening in the meeting lodge was similar in many ways to the one on the ship. Head-chief *Pemetosusk* parlayed long into the night with the other village leaders as they continued to sip the rum and recount the experiences. What did these strangers want from them? The *Choptanks* had been furtively watching them since they arrived some months before. They were amazed how the implements they used could fall a tree so rapidly and how sturdy their lodges were. It was clear the visitors were planning to stay. How would this effect hunting and gathering? Both were scarce during the cold times. Would there be enough to sustain both people? How could the tribe profit by this encounter? Can they negotiate from a power position or will they be at a subservient level? Lesser chief *Pacowassamuck* was very fearful of the White Men. He still remembered the terrible, loud noises that came from the great canoe as they hid in the forest. The weapons they carried looked cruel and without honor, hard and merciless. *Weesanusks* was most affected by the alcohol and was happily chanting to himself as he wrapped up in some of the furs on the floor and fell asleep.

Tattowin and *Weanchum* were the true thinkers of the group and their words carried special value with *Pemetosusk*. "Speak, my brothers," implored the head-chief. "What do your hearts say?"

These two leaders were exceptionally rare. They were twins and had been held in special regard for the 40 years of their lives, even as children. The usual practice of the tribe was to kill the second twin if it was of the same gender. The *Choptanks* honored the works of "The Creator' whom they called *Wak-KON-ton-kah* and abhorred anything they considered an act by "The Imitator" fearfully named *E-EH-ched-gah-gah*, but never said aloud except in a furtive whisper or to frighten the small ones. The second-born twin was thought to be made by "The Imitator" and was not even allowed to take its first breath before being thrown into the Mother of All Waters. The very night *Tattowin* and *Weanchum* came into the world a cosmic display of such frightening magnitude occurred that the village midwifes were able to convince the chiefs that these two were holy. Had these births occurred in contemporary times, people would have barely noticed the late summer Perseus meteor shower that mystical summer night.

The twins never married nor casually mingled with the other people in the tribe. Despite having two bodies, they seemed to have one mind. Often they would start some activity, stand up or walk off in unison without a word being uttered. Even as children, animals would congregate around them. Imagine their mother's shock when a large black bear lumbered into the village and reclined beside the boys as they rested. Deer and elk had no fear of them and the twins could actually walk up and pet any wild animals without giving it a second thought. Strangely for this tribe of Indians, *Tattowin* and *Weanchum* never ate meat of any kind, yet they seemed able to thrive comfortably on fruit, nuts, vegetables and eatable herbs. No one could remember when the two had ever been ill, and in their young adult years they were as strapping and as strong as other boys which added to the respect felt and displayed by their peers.

Tattowin was the first to reply to *Pemetosusk's* question. As he began to express his intuition, *Weanchum* would nod in silent agreement. His voice was soft and somewhat feminine. "We had a dream about these tall, hard, pale men with faces like *Ha-KAH-sha-nah* the groundhog. We thought they must be devils. Their eyes were white and without mercy. They were surrounded by flashes of light and they carried weapons that hissed and spit like *sin-TEH-h'dah* the snake. Their lances, axes and arrows shone as does the sea in the morning sun, and it hurt our eyes. We had to look away. When we turned back, these strange men were legion upon legion clear unto the horizon. Everywhere was smoke and destruction. Our lodges were in ashes with bones piled waist high. There were no trees, the grasses were brown and dry, and our rivers ran red like blood. The schools of fish were in death thick as white snow, the clams and oysters were black and poisonous. We could hear the anguished cries of our women and children ... The dream was continuing but it was too painful, we awoke in great distress"

Pacowassamuck groaned in grief as he listened to their vision. *Weesanusks* had risen onto one elbow and was jolted back into sobriety by the ramifications of what the twins related. *Pemetosusk* covered his face in despair and a sense of hopelessness crawled into his heart.

The five village leaders pulled their animal skin cloaks around their tired bodies and wearily walked from the meeting lodge to their *wig-wams*. It was a long and troublesome night and each felt especially old and heavy hearted. A cold, unkind wind fraught with moisture out of the northeast was beginning to howl, promising more bad weather before the night was over. *Pemetosusk* looked seaward through the darkness and saw the lights on the strangers' craft bobbing up and down in the choppy waters. He entered his home longing to be someone or someplace else. In his years as head chief, he had always been able to meet the needs of his people and help them flourish and blossom. He was an exceptional leader always being sure his people were safe and settled before he partook in his own comforts. His father shared with him only two thoughts to govern by when the elder gave him the Talking Stick of Leadership, "You are the soul of your people, when they are happy you are happy, when they grieve you grieve."

"And by the way," the elder offered almost in humor, "the chief always eats last."

Now, he had no answers, only many, many more questions.

Entering his welcoming lodge he saw that his wife of many wonderful years, *Watsawasoo*, was waiting patiently for him. For a brief interlude his mind wandered back to when they were young in life and young in love. The first time he saw her at a trading rendezvous, it was as if she were glowing. He couldn't take his eyes off her ... and there was no indication that she even knew he was there. *Choptank* women by stature are as big around as they are tall, and this slim and lovely, willowy princess seemed like some exotic flower. He felt a smile touch his lips as he recalled the two day paddle up the river to the trail leading to the *Chicamacomico* village. It took three young men and a full day of walking to carry the dowry he was willing to offer her father. Even unto this day, he felt he really got a bargain.

"Lay by me, my chief." she offered gently, her long grey and black hair glistening in the light of the fire. *"doh-WON deh hon-YEH-du. Ha-HON-nah Wo-e-YOK-she-cha"* (Tonight we sing. Tomorrow we can be sorrowful.)

The Business of Business

Before the beginning of recorded time, the winters of the mid-Atlantic region of North America have been a strange conundrum. One day the weather conditions can be bitterly cold and inhospitable as the mean winds from the northeast or northwest beat against the landscape ... and later that day or the following day the weather can be calm and almost spring-like. Despite the present cold temperature and indications that prior evening of more bad weather, the first day of actual commercial discourse between the strangers and the locals was relatively pleasant.

The bitter winter night had not yet released its embrace on the upcoming day as the Englishmen were loading the longboat with trade goods and rehashing the strategies to be implemented. The flickering light from the whale-oil lamps provided an eerie orange glow to the eyes of the workers as they went about their duties. It also reflected the resolute set of their faces as they endeavored to be prepared for any situation.

Master Robert Hunt, the preacher, was demanding that he should be allowed to preface the trade talks with Bible verses and a prayer. He had even worked through the night in preparation, earmarking specific passages on his rare Tyndall Bible and practicing his prayer delivery. It did not even occur to Hunt that the Natives might not have the slightest inkling of what he was talking about nor could they understand his language. Captain Coverdale was not exactly sure how to deal with Hunt and handed him off to Wingfield, who was totally engrossed in more earthly matters. A very delicate situation was developing and the expedition leader was irritated by the preacher's badgering.

Surgeon Wickinson observed his distressed manner and intervened quickly. "Master Hunt," commented Wickinson, "The heathen savages are unprepared to accept your worthy efforts. They do not understand our language; nor, I am sure, do they have any spiritual awareness. Your words would fall on ignorant ears, like seed on stony ground. Consider them as bare slates awaiting your precious teachings. Allow President Wingfield and his team to open their eyes to the greatness of our Mother Country, then you can open their hearts. God has waited countless years for these people to be led to Him. I am sure he can wait a while longer."

Hunt, reacting as if he hand been slapped, mulled over Wickinson's words and common sense. It was clear he was not going to be a participant in the landing party unless he could offer something of a more practical nature. He turned back to Winfield, "I would find great value in just getting a look at these pagans and trying to determine wherein the most fertile spiritual fields may lie. Sometimes, to touch a people, one has to first reach the leaders. Sometimes to reach the leaders, one has to determine what they already know and what they value. With your permission I would like to join you only as a casual observer. I am willing to row or to carry – whatever I can do to help."

He gained his seat on the boat.

The King's representatives could see that the village was beginning to also stir as indicated by the motion of firebrands and torches in the darkness. Whenever a *wig-wam* door mat was opened, a bright flash of light from the interior fire pits would stream out to briefly conflict with the darkness. *Watsawasoo* had always served her husband as the tribe's graceful emissary. On occasion, neighboring Indian nations and bands would approach the village to trade, to form alliances against impending warring tribes, or to arrange marriages. The *Chicamacomicos, Ozinies* and *Assowamats* spoke similar dialects as the *Choptanks* and shared common customs and interests. She had no reason to believe that the parlay with the strangers from some distant world would be any different than other councils as she organized the village's elder women to prepare food and basic comforts.

This meeting would be held in the men's lodge, called the *we-CHOSH-tah-pe TE-pe,* located in a dense grove of old-growth Loblolly pine trees a short distance inland from the community itself. Women were found on the premises for only two reasons, to bring food before the business at hand and occasionally to tidy up the interior. Only *Watsawasoo* had permission to be there when the men were in attendance.

In fairness, the women had their own Moon Time lodge that was off limits to the men. The young women of the village, always in loud protest, were cloistered there whenever strangers came to call ... and this would also be the situation each time the White Men visited. It would be some time before this information was made available to the *Ha-KAH-sha-nah* (the *Choptank* description of their guests that meant "ground hog" in their language and that would eventually be the generic reference word for the Englishmen).

The framing of the men's hall was constructed with large skinned tree trunks that were erected in a rectangular shape with a row of trunks down the middle to double the size of the interior. This configuration was unusual for *Choptank* structures that normally had a beehive shaped architecture or appeared to look like large loaves of bread. Apparently, the locals had been in similar lodges while visiting other tribes and appreciated the practical use of space offered. The thatched roof was braced with cross beams of logs. Occasionally, the thatch would blow off during the more

severe storms, but the posts and lintels could withstand just
about any maelstrom. The walls were constructed of the
typical reed and stem mats, but done in multiple thicknesses
and interwoven to keep out the cold in winter and the heat in
summer … and incidentally, to muffle the discussions inside
should curious women be nearby. The standard fire pit with
a smoke hole centered the interior of the structure, but due
to its size, there were settings for torches at intervals along
the risers. As in all *wig-wams*, the earthen floor was covered
with animal skins which insulated the participants from the
hard and frozen ground. Bundles of the light brown *to-bac*
leaves hung upside down from the rafters, and weapons
and other utensils were cluttered like wheat sheaves in no
particular order. Parallel to both of the two longer walls were
low tables end-to-end that might be considered primitive
efforts at rattan. On each of these tables were piles of animal
pelts as well as rows and rows of various sized clay pots and
woven baskets. In a somewhat familiar way, the interior of
the lodge would remind the White Men of an apothecary or
general mercantile back home.

———————

The red morning sun barely peered above the horizon to the
southeast as the longboat neared the village shoreline. The
Natives were eagerly awaiting the arrival of these strange
people with amazing gifts. The elder women standing
together began an almost mesmerizing swaying dance; and
with crystal clear voices, high and feminine, sang a repetitive
chant more nasal than melodious:

> *Ho! Le-ci-YAH ni-CO-pi.*
> *Ho! Le-ci-YAH ni-CO-pi.*

(Come hither, hither, ho! Hither now we summon ye!
Come hither, ho! Hither, ho!)

The lesser chief, *Weesanusks*, and a small delegation of *Choptank* warriors led the Englishmen through the settlement and down the path to the men's retreat. The westerners would later learn that the two reasons for this location were to keep the women folk at bay and to protect their wealth from marauding tribes that plied the coastline in warring fashion.

Weesanusks looked up at Dixon and inquired, "Grog?"

Dixon did not look down but a slight nod of his head communicated the affirmative response. There was no reason to suspect that some skullduggery may be at hand, so the visitors followed with little or no trepidation confident in their weaponry and training. The throng stopped at the edge of the village in deference to the gravity of the meeting and in recognition of the social mores' involved.

Entering the meeting lodge was an amazing sensory experience. If a tribe's success was measured by 'accumulation', the *Choptanks* were wealthy indeed. Fragrances and odors were not major issues to the Englishmen because of the poor sanitary conditions of the cities and villages back home and the questionable personal hygiene of the populace in general. One might even say that the olfactory nerves had long ago shut themselves down. However, in the lodge, the aromas were strong and very, very pleasant. The burning pine wood, the dry grassy country-like smell of the reed and bark wall mats, the piles of clean furs, the aftermath of years of *to-bac* use, the clay pots and woven baskets filled to the brim with herbs and healing remedies, and the fact that the Natives were personally clean and odor-free all combined for a very pleasant first impression.

Wingfield noticed that only three of the village leaders were in attendance, but he had little time to wonder why. In short order, all parties were sitting around the fire pit and the welcoming *to-bac* ritual was beginning. This time, Wingfield, Lusby, Dixon and Brooks-Hughes knew what to expect and were careful in turn to lightly inhale the smoking tube. A most pleasant, calming sensation swam through their bodies. Their eyes glistened in impish expectation as the rolled vegetation passed to Coverdale and then Capper, who both coughed and wheezed loudly.

A very dangerous situation developed when Hunt refused to inhale the smoke and endeavored to pass the *to-bac* to the Indian on his left. As far as he was concerned this was some un-Godly heathen ritual and he had no inclination at all to debase himself with such goings-on. This was a major social affront more serious than the porcelain plate incident the prior day with no chance for forbearance. The young braves observing the situation tensed and reached for their weapons. The village leaders scowled and leaned forward.

Capper spoke quietly to Hunt, "Put the leaf to your lips and pretend to cough. If you don't they will massacre us all."

Hunt's hand was shaking, but he was able to comply. As the others did previously, he inhaled too deeply and began coughing loudly – not in pretense, but from the tight constriction in his throat from a combination of fear and smoke. His white face turned beet red as he fell over onto his back and gasped for air in a high pitched almost-feminine voice. The Indians laughed loud and long, and the White Men soon joined in. The tension in the room took wings.

Watsawasoo appeared, as if by some unnoticed signal, and began to serve the repast. She was wearing a striking white deerskin dress decorated with rows of small shells that rattled and clicked as she moved. Sewn to the shoulders of the dress were layers of beautiful cardinal and bluebird feathers interlaced with ivory seagull feathers. Her graceful motions were almost hypnotic in the firelight as she dealt the large clay bowls to each person in the circle; then followed by filling each, starting with her husband and the other chiefs, of course, with a steaming oyster, crab, shrimp and clam stew laced with corn and seasoned with the most pleasant herbs and roots. The dish was so thick that it plopped and glopped as it filled the bowls. She then made another round passing out wedges of a pleasantly warmed, light and tasty corn bread to each participant. The Englishmen watched their hosts to determine when to start eating. They also were wondering if some form of eating utensil was forthcoming. The *Choptanks* held the bowls to their mouths and began to noisily ingest the concoction, so the visitors did the same. They had to admit it was more fun to eat this way than to comply with normal table decorum. Wingfield ordered the small keg of rum to be opened and this treat was the visitors' contribution to the meal. *Weesanusks* caressed the tin cup as if it were a young woman and took an especially long draught. Wingfield made a mental note that this chief had a special weakness, and he was not above taking advantage of this issue if it furthered the goals of the colony. He looked knowingly at Coverdale who nodded in agreement.

After the banquet *Pemetosusk* looked at the young warriors sitting patiently outside the trading circle and gave them brief instructions. Each then rose to his feet and approached a sitting Englishmen. Apparently, their responsibility would be to go with a specific visitor and to assist as much as possible; but maybe more so their charge included maintaining a closer eye on each stranger. Thievery was not only a European issue. Many of the local tribes the *Choptanks* traded with felt special pride if they could abscond with something of value without having to give something back for it. Some of the villages would send only the most deceptive and the lightest fingered as their trade delegation.

Dixon went straight for the mounds of furs. They were collected in assorted piles but not separated by animal in any noticeable fashion. One might conclude they presented a scene of poetic disarray. Strangely, each pelt included the shape of the legs, the tail and the skull with holes where the eye sockets had been. The outline of each animal was clearly recognizable. He rolled back the first pelt and inspected how it was tanned. The inner skin was as white as snow and as soft as silk. It would be many weeks before he found out that the women processed all the furs and preserved them with human urine. His practiced eyes spotted a mink pelt immediately. *"Dook-SHIN-cha,"* commented his guide. Interspersed in the piles were mink skins light brown and shiny gathered during the summer and bright velvety ivory from winter. Only a trained furrier could tell at a glance they were the same animal. Dixon set those aside and continued to dig through the mounds. He held a beaver pelt against his cheek to determine its freshness. The Indian murmured, *"CHA-pah."* The Englishman was not aware that beaver were not indigenous to the region and their inclusion in the collection was a reflection of the inter-tribal trading processes. Unfortunately for true market value, most of the skins were deer, elk and bear, and had little commercial potential though they might prove to be useful to the expedition as the winter cold took its toll on the clothing from home. Then Dixon spotted 'gold': Buried in a pile was a rather small, but spectacular pelt of the most beautiful iridescent red. *"Shoon-HE-nah,"* pointed the Native. A red fox fur was extremely rare and was held in high value back home. Normally, only royalty had the privilege to wear this marvelous item. Dixon thought that if he could somehow get the locals to put all their efforts into hunting and trapping mink and red fox the expedition could be highly profitable.

As he wandered from pile to pile he suddenly gasped in amazement at what he saw in the torchlight. Attached to the wide end wall of the lodge was the most shocking pelt he had ever seen. The fur was as thick as his forearm and colored a rich brown. One end of it changed from long straight prickly hair to almost black, rough curly bunches. It stretched from floor to ceiling and easily was as wide as two men standing side by side. The four legs were splayed out and disappeared in the darkness and the skull skin was bigger around than he could reach. No White Man had ever seen a bison from the vast central grasslands of North America before, and no story was ever told as to how it got to the *Choptanks*. This was a true testament to the tribe's trading abilities and to the vast informal communication system of American Indian groups.

Wingfield had Sergeant Lusby and Brooks-Hughes bring the barrel of trade goods to where the chiefs were postured. As before, they rolled out a partial bolt of colorful fabric made of durable coarse cotton cloth imported from India and began to place various items in some form of order. The glass beads were in small wooden boxes and separated by color. As Wingfield handed the boxes to the Natives, he soon noticed that they were extremely interested in the glasses of blue and yellow, rather intrigued by the reddish beads – and had almost no interest in the clear ones. They did not seem to place any noticeable difference or value between sizes of the items. The colors were the most important.

Reverting back to his years in business, he found himself using the *Tome of Thrup'pence* to place some comparable value on the trinkets. This guideline stated that similar families of trade goods varied in value by stages of three. If the clear beads were valued at 'one', the red glass would be three times as valuable, the gold and blue nine times. The next item passed around was a cloth bag filled with large iron square-sided nails. The chiefs looked them over politely and passed them on having no idea what they might be used for. The *Choptank* leaders really grew intense as the more recognizable metal paraphernalia was displayed. Far and away the items of most value to the locals was an iron axe head mounted on a wooden handle, the iron splitting wedge and a collection of shiny knife blades. It did not take long for the visitors to realize just how much they could gain from just one axe head or splitting wedge. An entire pile of furs higher than a man could be traded for an axe head. Wingfield made an on the spot decision to offer a gift of a larger blade to *Pemetosusk* and smaller ones to the two lesser chiefs. *Weesanusks* and *Pacowassamuck* carefully picked theirs up and inspected them closely. Not unexpected, *Weesanusks* quickly pricked his finger and put it in his mouth with a dismayed look on his friendly face.

The expedition leader would never know why all five of the chiefs had not attended the important trading parlay, but as time passed the three chiefs that did would become advocates for the westerners as serious questions were posed during the council meetings.

Coverdale, Hunt and Capper roamed the lodge with their respective Indian assistants checking out the clay pots and woven baskets. In their hidden hearts they were hoping to find gold or precious gems. Some of the crockery and basketry had lids, others were open. Apparently roaming spiders, noxious insects, small rodents and ground squirrels had a propensity for some stored items and these were sealed to discourage their participation.

Capper found another form of 'gold' as he inspected a selection of larger ollas stored together in a protected corner of the lodge. Each was filled to the brim with whitish-clear crystals of sea salt about the size of a thumb nail. The Native with Capper smiled and uttered proudly, *"M'ne-SKOO-yah!"* There was no indication at all that the Indians knew salt mining techniques, so the *Choptanks* must have somehow learned to extract this precious element from sea water. *M'ne-SKOO-yah* had long-ago proven to be the main trading medium of the *Choptanks*, and they could get anything their hearts desired from other Indian bands for just a small jar of the valuable commodity.

The woodworker moistened his finger and inserted it into the mound of crystals. As he placed his finger to his lips the intensity of saltiness shocked his mouth. It was overwhelmingly pleasant. "Captain Coverdale!' he croaked. The English military man rushed to Capper and realized the incredible value of the find. If nothing else tradable emerged from this contact with the Indigenous people the salt supply made it all worthwhile.

Meanwhile, Hunt was opening baskets, feeling and smelling the leaves, stems and roots and moving from one to the other. Obviously, there was quite a selection of flora, but each time the local would say, *"Peh-ZHU-tah."* Hunt, in his general distrust of the Indians thought that the man was trying to make a fool of him, so discounted his input. What the Native was trying to tell him was that the contents were 'medicine'. In their simplistic view of the world, the Indigenous people would label a collection of similar things by just one name. The British got into this idea when they found their hosts had an all-inclusive name for animal or human excrement: *Oonk-CHAY*. This became a derogatory word they used on each other to express disappointment or disgust with their fellow Englishmen. More than one fist fight resulted from this curse projected at another.

Occasionally, the *Choptank* brave would murmur to Hunt, *"Wah-PE."* in an effort to point out that the particular contents was a form of tea leaves. A number of open baskets were filled with a variety of cowry shells. Uninterested in women's adornment, Hunt could see absolutely no value in trading for the contents of these baskets. Stacked together was a group of similar covered clay pots, more squat than the others and the only ones with any kind of decorations or markings etched on the outer sides. Hunt opened a lid and a pleasant fragrance of blueberries swam into his nostrils. "*Wah-S'NA,*" commented the Indian as he swept his finger into the concoction of berries and tallow and stuck it in his mouth. Not to be outdone, Hunt did the same and the flavor was sweeter than the wild honey he would occasionally find in the Welsh forests. He tried to determine how he could keep the *pemmican* from the others. This was too good to share.

Pemetosusk motioned to Wingfield to sit beside him and the administrator complied without hesitation. The head chief quietly lifted a decorated leather sack from his clothing and displayed it to the Englishmen. He softly said, "*Hay-YU-ha-ha.*" He untied the bag and exposed the contents in the flickering torchlight. It was filled with a fine grey and white powder. Wingfield smiled and nodded knowingly, but had actually no idea what it was. In ensuing months the westerners would find out that the material was considered an aphrodisiac and consisted of ground-up deer or elk antlers.

As the bonds of trust developed between the races, a number of *Choptank* men would offer *Hay-YU-ha-ha* bags to their White friends. It never occurred to the locals that there would be no women in New Providence. Those Natives who had silently watched the construction of the fort saw a small number of boys in the crew and just naturally assumed that the women were cloistered someplace else during the building of the settlement similar to their young women being hidden away in the Moon Time lodge.

The Englishmen were eager to begin the trading parlay. Their main interests were how they could acquire specific furs and as much sea salt as the tribe would allow. They were uncertain how to begin the process, and equally at a loss as to how to point the process toward some degree of resolution. *Pemetosusk* muttered a command to the Indians who were assisting the westerners and they escorted their visitors back to the fire pit motioning them to sit down. The head chief softly said, *"Watsawasoo"* and his elegant wife appeared carrying a large basket filled with baked duck carcasses with the head and legs still attached. They were still steaming and had an absolutely delicious aroma. Gracefully moving from person to person, she dropped an entire fowl into each bowl, and despite Wingfield's eagerness to get on with business, the repast was so tempting that commerce temporarily took a back seat. The Indians began to tear the carcasses apart noisily crunching the moist and tasty flesh, and the White Men devoured their food with equal enthusiasm.

Weesanusks raised the empty tin cup and asked, "Grog?" It was quickly filled and then re-filled from the small cask and handed from person to person.

Then a most unexpected event occurred. *Pemetosusk* stood up, clasped his hands and extended them toward his guests. He stood there motionless expecting Wingfield to return the gesture. The Englishman had no idea what was transpiring and tried to mask his confusion by not responding in any fashion. After a few awkward moments, the chief motioned to his subordinates and they picked up their knife blades and all quietly walked out!

Surprised and somewhat dismayed, the Englishmen realized that the trading rendezvous was definitely over. The visitors felt belittled and somewhat offended. Hunt growled angrily, "Who do these savages think they are being so rude to the King's representatives? They need to be cut down a notch or two!"

Brooks-Hughes and Lusby somewhat bewildered by what had occurred began to gather up the trade goods and packed them in the barrel. Dixon looked longingly at the mound of furs he had set aside and wondered if he would ever possess them. Wingfield realized that at least at this point the expedition would be bartering from a lesser position, and he was not at all pleased with this turn of events. There would need to be a change in strategy, but he was not sure exactly how to bring this about.

Capper silently mulled over the situation as the Englishmen were led back up the path to the village. Hunt's comment about cutting down their hosts germinated a most pleasing idea. As they reached the village, the throng of Natives emerged from their *wig-wams* to see the entourage. The chiefs were nowhere in sight. Capper removed the axe from the trade barrel, selected a softwood pine tree about the width of a man's waist and about 40 feet tall and began to effortlessly chop it down. He was a strong man, well experienced in cutting trees and the axe was very sharp. Not one stroke was wasted. The woodsman knew how to angle each cut so it would dig deep into the tree trunk and the chips flew in all directions. Once he had cut about half-way through, he began to chop the opposite side. At the appropriate time he inserted the iron splitting wedge, whacked it with a loud metallic 'ping' which stung the ears of the locals. The tree groaned and cracked, then fell noisily onto the frozen ground exactly where Capper had intended it to. Compared to the stone axes of the *Choptanks*, the tree was dropped in amazing quickness. The silence of the wide-eyed villagers as they watched Capper was deafening. Not a word was spoken, but the visitors could be ensured that the message would get to the leaders. These strange white men had a special magic beyond the value of anything the locals had ever seen.

As the longboat reached the gunwales of the *Phyllis*, the ship's crew could see that their delegation had returned empty-handed. This could not be good and disappointment was evident. Retrieving the skiff and helping the traders get aboard, questions flew constantly and rapidly. All Wingfield would say was, "Let us return to New Providence."

A biting wind out of the northwest seemed that much colder because of the events of the day, but fortunately it was blowing in the general direction of home. This combined conveniently with the flow of the neap tide to propel the vessel southeasterly and it was a brief sailing back to the protected estuary. Those left behind at the fort gathered on the jetty to survey the booty and were equally disappointed when nothing was unloaded. The silence of the team who had met with the Indians only added to the sense of failure. As the men who participated in the parlay returned to the barracks, groups formed around them to hear what had occurred at the village.

Each discourse ended with, "We don't know what will happen next."

Separation and Misunderstanding

N ew Providence hunkered down for the remaining days of a cold and dark winter in a dreary rut of survival and sustenance.

Woodworker John Capper had formed a small crew that labored long hours in the wood shop making furniture and bed frames. Surgeon Wickinson was positive the main reason for the rash of colds and nasal problems was that the men's beds apprised of mats on the cold rock floors of the barracks. For a 1600's leech purveyor he had a remarkable ability for preventative medicine. Once their sleeping materials were on bed frames there was a noticeable improvement in the basic health of the expedition's compliment.

Sergeant Lusby, Privates Dixon and Kenneth Quinby worked in the foundry during the worse winter weather conditions making shot for their fusils. Some grumbled that they were the only ones of the exploration team that stayed warm during those miserable times. Melting lead bars and turning them into fusil balls was hot work, best accomplished during the cold months. The bore of their fusils was as large around as a person's wrist, so the bullet looked like a mini-cannon ball and was extremely deadly at close range. Also smaller shot could be loaded and discharged similar to a modern day scatter gun expanding the kill zone. Lusby knew that the fusiliers had more shot than powder, but there wasn't much else to do except walking the trap lines and the daily hunting trips. Game was still plentiful and the sea continued its bounty, so the men ate reasonably well despite the redundancy of their meals.

As the hunters brought the game back for meals the pelts of the deer and elk were almost sensuous as the animal's hair thickened for surviving the long winter. Using traditional English preservation methods Dixon was able to provide a continuous supply of furs making them available as replacements for the tattered and worn-out blankets of the men and officers. Despite the unpleasant odor of the chemicals, the expedition workers soon preferred the skins for evening warmth. He also formed a small group to teach them the tanning process, and in short order tailor William Love had enough raw materials to make breeches and leggings. Despite the effectiveness of the trap lines and the sharp eyes of the hunters, no beaver or mink were ever brought back to the settlement. It was never realized that the habitat of those valuable creatures was not in the geographical region of New Providence and a goodly supply of pelts uncovered in the *Choptank* men's lodge were probably the results of trading with other Native groups.

Eastern Ground Squirrel. Called "ze-CHA."

A serious problem presented itself when rats and ground squirrels began to infest the settlement. These creatures, too, were searching for shelter from the cold weather. They would chew away the mud used to chink the spaces between the wall logs or squeeze in through the gaps in the rough carpentry of the door jambs and window frames seeking the warmth and possibly something eatable inside. Expedition leader Wingfield held a contest to see who could devise the most efficient way to control the vermin. The men really got into the competition and some of the most unusual contraptions were created and put to use. Still, the most successful method was a thrown hammer or other heavy tool. There were crossbows on hand in each building should someone feel compelled to endeavor to shoot one of the critters. Seaman Jonas Profit surprised his peers with his success with the crossbow. He had developed this special skill while helping the fusiliers on their hunting escapades. He really could hit a duck in the eye at 30 paces, so impaling a rat was child's play for him. He was so accurate that his shipmates begin cutting off the heads of the vermin, skewering them onto small stakes and placing them in orderly rows in a bizarre grave yard outside the barracks that they named "Profit's Cemetery."

There was no idle play in the Master's House. Governor Wingfield held regular meetings with his leadership team made up of Captain Coverdale, Magistrate Cuthbert Guilford, Sergeant Lusby, and Ship's Officer Edwin Marian. Three smaller exploration parties were being developed with specific responsibilities and would need to be ready once the weather improved. Marian's team would travel by long boat up river in an effort to map the surrounding area and to initiate a dialog with other Native tribes. Lusby's group would be charged with trying to find the minerals needed to make more gunpowder. There was plenty of charcoal in the settlement, but the chances of finding sulphur and potassium nitrate were anybody's guess. In addition, he was given the responsibility to search the streams and hillsides for precious or semi-precious stones and gold. Obviously, the local inhabitants were not interested in such matters, so the geography should be ripe for the pickings. Coverdale was instructed to hand pick a special cadre to re-institute contact with the *Choptanks*. His squad would be made up of some of the prior trade delegation members and other men with very specific personalities and abilities. Wingfield would have final say in who went and who remained in all instances.

In the village, *Pemetosusk* was confident the visitors would return within a day to two, so he was content at this point to wait until they made their next move. He held council with the lesser chiefs to review what they had observed and to determine future courses of action. Among the Indigenous peoples of the Western World, it was standard trading parlay procedure to share a meal together, inspect the items to be traded, then separate amicably to determine what the value of different items might be and what was worth trading for what before the actual commerce would take place. There were never any clocks to drive the rendezvous or interrelationships, so "on time" was whenever the two groups got together again. He had no idea that the *Ha-KAH-sha-nah* felt miffed when he and the other leaders walked out, and he was especially disappointed that Wingfield had not returned the clasp hands gesture that signified: "See you soon."

Pemetosusk asked the twins for their insight. Their intuition had never been wrong, and the tribe prospered as a result of what they were willing to share. *Tattowin* spoke in slow and

measured terms, "We were with you in spirit the night the
Ha-KAH-sha-nah ate with you. They are as hungry as *Shoong-
TOK-cha* the wolf, but their desire is not food or women. Our
hearts saw an evil glow of avarice around them when they
found the *M'ne-SKOO-ya* (Salt) the Mother of Waters gave
to us. The pale one in black has a stone heart that is cold as
ice, and we must never touch him. The man who caressed
the animal skins carries a deep ache that has to come out. It
is driving him mad and separates him from the rest of his
people. He is covered with blood because of his madness."

Despite the many years of counseling with the twin
chiefs, *Pemetosusk* was still amazed that they would be so
knowledgeable of events, even if they had not been there in
body.

Tattowin reached in his clothing and dropped a handful of
wood chips on the floor. They were picked up where Capper
had cut down the tree. For no explainable reason they began
to glow then disappeared into wisps of smoke. Needless
to say, this shocked the other chiefs. "The man with strong
hands appears as *mah-TOH* the bear, but his heart is warm
and gentle as is the heart of the young one who makes the
beautiful marks on the white leaves. The tall soldier has a
women living in his heart. She looks through his eyes and
touches with his hands. He is a *WIN-yon we-CHOSH-tah,* a
holy man, and has yet to reconcile this reality. Their leader is
forthright and serious. He is the one who wields the power
and we do not believe he intends to harm us. The giant man
in the red and green uniform loves war. He has blood stains
on his hands that will never go away. He may be the one who
best represents who the *Ha-KAH-sha-nah* are as a people, and
this troubles us"

Then both twins lowered their heads and sat in silence. As far as they were concerned, this was the extent of their input.

This always irritated *Pemetosusk*. The two medicine men seldom told the rest of the chiefs **what** to do after they had shared their unique insights. He had always felt the impulse to ask, "And so ..." but he knew the actual decisions would rest with lesser chiefs *Pacowassamuck, Weesanusks* his dear friend and, of course, himself. The *Choptank* leaders realized how important it would be to obtain the tools used to drop the tree so quickly. As tribal leaders, they also supervised the canoe building process and the value of the White Men's tools was obvious for this activity. This sacred ritual was immensely labor intensive. It would easily take a month or more exploring the dense forest to find the right tree, cut it down, drag it to the *wig-wam* sequestered deep in the forest where the actual construction would take place, and then start the process of smoothing the exterior and burning away the interior to make the dugout. *Weesanusks* would personally carve the totem to be attached to the prow of the canoe once it was completed. His art work was so unusual that other tribes could spot a *Choptank* dugout long before they would recognize who was in the craft.

The Native headmen were also very intrigued by the colorful cloth the Englishmen brought forth and were especially interested in the beautiful crystals. The touch of the stones was unlike anything they had ever felt before – so cold and smooth, and they had never seen the colors displayed. Many of the other trinkets and tools were of interest, but of a lesser nature. The chiefs talked long into the night in an effort to determine what they were willing to give up and what they had hoped to gain.

As the days passed, the village wandered into the winter as it had for countless generations. The *Ha-KAH-sha-nah* never returned to continue the trading. All *Pemetosusk* could determine was that whatever his people had, the visitors were not as interested as they had appeared earlier. On occasion, a small group of young braves would stealthily paddle over to the White Men's village to observe the goings-on. They could never see anything any more unusual than the strange things that were happening all the time. They did wonder where the visitors kept their women. At times, the braves would explore the general area around the settlement to find the Moon Time lodges of the English females – to no avail.

CHAPTER III ...
OPENED EYES

A Joyful Reunion

That particular early spring morning was exceptional in every way. During the night, the winds had shifted from a biting northwesterly gale to a gentle southeasterly flow and a remarkable warming trend began. By daybreak, the sky was absolutely clear and the air was fresh and clean. The ground was still frozen and somewhat snow covered, but already moisture was beginning to form in the sunlit areas. Ice was breaking up along the stream south of the compound, and the sound of water trickling over rocks was once again a pleasant aspect of the environment. A variety of small birds had remained over the winter, and their wake-up songs were especially joyous. The aroma of freshly baking biscuits for the morning meal wafted out of the kitchen and seemed to beckon the men to begin their new day.

And then, a most astonishing event occurred that would change the future of New Providence forever ...

The sentry walking the high ground west of the compound came running down the path screaming, "Savages! They're coming! They're coming!" The dozen sea-going canoes were too far out to determine who was approaching, but for all intents and purposes it appeared to be a war party.

A flurry of activity resulted as the Englishmen prepared to defend their settlement. The fusiliers and the company men trained with the fusil acquired their weapons, powder and shot and took up their positions along the jetty. The seamen on duty on the *Phyllis* primed the canons and awaited the command to fire. Those able to perform with the crossbow or long bow armed themselves and stood on the shore line. Every other man-jack found an axe, lance, knife or metal implement in preparation for hand-to-hand combat. The cooking crew ran out of the kitchen with large iron frying pans. Despite the gravity of the situation, nervous laughter rippled through the exploration team. Wingfield and Coverdale raced to the ship and joined Ship's Officer Marian on the poop deck. From this higher vantage point they could get a first look at the invaders. The expedition leaders began to regret that they had not pressed the men to construct the palisade around the village.

Coverdale scanned the nearing craft with his spyglass. He immediately recognized the carved totems on the prows of the dugouts. A smile walked across his stern countenance as he handed the scope to his superior. "It's the *Choptanks*," he commented in great relief.

The canoes were now close enough that Wingfield could more clearly see what their intentions might be. Each craft was piled high with pelts, bundles of *to-bac*, baskets and clay pots. They were so heavily laden that they were floating precariously low in the water. The Englishmen had no idea just how sea worthy the dugouts actually were, for the Natives were in no danger at all of being swamped. Wingfield turned shoreward and shouted, "It's the *Choptanks*! They are coming to trade! Place your weapons in your left hand and join me on the jetty!"

As the 40-foot long canoes approached the shore, a most remarkable chant flowed over the water preceding their arrival:

Oh-YAH-teh-wan.	O ye people, O ye
Oh-YAH-teh-wan	people.
Wash-TEE-kah.	Be ye healed.
Wah-NAH-pi-yah.	Life anew we bring
Wah-kah-GHEL-oh.	to you.
Ah-EH-yo, ah-EH-yo.	Amen, amen.

The strong masculine voices of the Natives rivaled the British military battle songs and stirred the hearts of the foreigners as they were collecting in great anticipation.

Wingfield spied Johnson and his cooking crew, "Quickly ... food! Lots of it! The best we have! We will parlay in the dining hall. They are used to sitting on the floor, so make room near a fireplace. Get Dixon and some of the men that have been working with him to bring as many furs as possible and spread them."

The lead canoe contained four braves rowing smoothly and three of the five village leaders bundled in animal skins and some adorned with feathers. The twin chiefs refused to join the trading party and were totally not in favor of the action. As the craft reached the shallows, a handful of expedition members waded into the freezing water and assisted in pulling it ashore. The other eleven dugouts arrived moments later, and soon they were beached side-by-side appearing like a monstrous herring bone. So many trade goods were on hand that the men who had met the *Choptanks* in the men's lodge were sure they had totally cleaned it out.

The implication was that the Indians were willing to give up everything to acquire the items the Englishmen had to offer. It became clear to Wingfield that a protocol was developing dictating that everything must be accepted, whether it had much value or not. The posing question was what the booty would cost.

Head Chief *Pemetosusk* immediately recognized the expedition leader and Captain Coverdale in the throng of *Ha-KAH-sha-nah* and offered a friendly smile. He then nodded to them to walk with him to the first of the trade canoes as the entourage of Natives followed. Once he approached the craft, he opened the palm of his right hand and swept it the length of the dugout as he walked along the beach and into the shallow water slowly from one end of the canoe to the other end. The settlement leaders stayed with him peering into the craft to get a better look at what was stored there occasionally opening a lid or reaching into a container. They found at least one large jar of salt in their cursory inspection. He then made a chopping motion and held up four fingers. As they were observing his actions he reached into his clothing and extracted a small piece of the colorful cloth they had given him at the first contact. Again he held up four fingers. He followed this by making a motion as if drinking from a cup and held up one finger. The Native leader then appeared somewhat perplexed as he tried to communicate his next request. Wingfield could guess that he wanted the glass beads, but was not sure how to say it. He finally massaged his fingers as if he were holding a handful of pebbles, and then exposed his four fingers again.

So ... for four axe heads or splitting wedges, four sections of cloth, a measure of rum and four boxes of beads an entire canoe of Indian trade goods would be in the expedition leader's possession. Multiply this by the twelve dugouts laded with trading goods, and he had gained an entire ship load in a matter of moments. He almost could not contain his joy. He knew that if he looked at Coverdale he would lose his composure, so he stared gravely at the Indian chief as if not totally pleased by the offer. Always being the businessman and looking for a better deal, he responded by mimicking *Pemetosusk's* chopping motion and held up three fingers then nodded to imply the other requests were acceptable.

Pemetosusk raised his arms and happily cried, *"wash-TEH TOH-ke-yo-peh-yah!"* ("Good trade"). The other Natives erupted with shouts of approval, and the entire group of White Men burst into laughter.

Wingfield asked Magistrate Cuthbert Guilford and Sergeant Lusby to supervise unloading the canoes and storing the treasures. He was confident these two would have things well organized and inventoried in short order. The animal skins and salt ollas would be placed aboard the *Phyllis*, and the remainder of the jars and all the baskets would be placed in the storage sheds, the fusiliers' barracks or the dormitory. The jail floor would be piled high with bundles of *to-bac* until ways could be devised on the ship to hang it like it was done in the men's lodge. Lusby decided it would be best to lock this commodity up until more could be learned about it. Wingfield then motioned the Indians to follow him to the dining hall. Some remained at the canoes to observe and possible assist with the unloading. As they were walking to the compound the expedition leader instructed Captain Coverdale to get a crew together and gather the items that would be going back to the village and bring them to the kitchen. He said to add a few articles that were of little value to the Englishmen, but might prove to be of special interest to their guests. He was thinking of some iron items like chains, flat ware, needles and tools.

As the trading delegation entered the dining hall, all was in readiness. Wingfield felt special pride in the efficiency of his people. The expedition leader and the three *Choptank* dignitaries sat together on the floor in front of the crackling fireplace. The Indians who had followed reposed on the floor in rows behind their chiefs. The Englishmen not involved with unloading the canoes pulled up chairs behind the group on the floor to observe the protocol that would ensue. Wingfield nodded at ship's cook Johnson, and he brought out a platter of freshly baked biscuits still steaming in the cool morning air. Thomas Couper and William Love preceded the chief cook with a handful of small bowls which they rapidly filled with a delightful compote of blackberries and cherries. The jam was still partially frozen from earlier storage but melting rapidly. The Natives were surprised to see men doing kitchen work, but they were swayed by the marvelous fragrance from the food. The supervisor took a biscuit, swept it in the compote and took a healthy bite. He then passed the platter to his guests. They responded in kind, filled their mouths with the concoction and grunted in approval. Johnson brought out another helping expecting it to be passed around to the other locals in attendance. The chiefs kept the additional offerings without reservation, and the lesser ranked *Choptanks* did not seem to expect anything more. Johnson looked helplessly at the Englishmen and quietly promised to give them their share as soon as possible. Love and Couper quickly followed with porcelain cups and bowls and metal soup spoons. Love poured the delightful sassafrass and blackberry tea into the waiting cups as his partner dished out the boiled salt pork. They were somewhat taken aback when the Indians ignored the spoons and noisily gulped down the pork straight from the bowls.

Weesanusks seemed to be looking for something and appeared somewhat distracted from the meal. He finally leaned over to Wingfield and inquired, "Grog?" The administrator could not imagine anyone wanting rum for breakfast, but he complied. Soon a small keg was tapped and the brown magic liquid passed around.

As the meal was progressing toward completion, Coverdale and his helpers entered the dining hall with the barrels of trade goods. He removed the lids and prepared them for inspection. The *Choptanks* had no reason to distrust the foreigners, so *Pacowassamuck* gestured a sign that all was okay and spoke some instructions to his men sitting behind the trading delegation. The braves carefully picked up the containers and carried them to the waiting canoes. The Native trade goods had been unloaded from the dugouts and were piled on the shore as Lusby and Guilford inventoried the treasures and instructed the men as to where they should be stored. The sun had not yet reached its zenith in the morning sky, and commerce was over for the day. A general sense of good feelings swept across everyone involved as the Natives prepared for their return trip across the bay. *Pemetosusk* made a circle with his right hand and swept it from right to left across his body. In one continuous motion he followed this with a 'come' gesture signing that he wished them to visit the village on the morrow.

The sturdy young braves helped their chiefs regain their seats in the near canoe, and with amazing strength forced the heavy craft back into the water. This action replicated itself as the other eleven dugouts were soon afloat. The *Choptanks* sped away happily chanting to the beat of the rowing strokes:
    "Wash-TEH TOH-ke-yo-peh-yah.
    OON-she-kah Ha-KAH-sha-nah."

The Englishmen would have been a bit irate had they understood the words to the chant. The locals were lauding the good trade, were comfortably assuming that the visitors had given away all their treasures, and that now the White Men were "poor."

―――――――――――

That afternoon the leadership team met in the Master's House to select the next delegation to meet with the *Choptanks*. This group would be expected to make repeated visits to the village in an effort to enculturate the savages into good English citizens. The *Articles on Intercourse with Indigenous Peoples* clearly laid out the Crown's expectations, but one issue really put the team on the horns of a dilemma: The charge that the Natives would be molded into Christians. Naturally, Preacher Hunt would expect that this would be his responsibility. However, his heavy-handed methods could easily undo the goodwill that was growing between the cultures. Hunt was very aware of the *Articles* and would soon be knocking on Wingfield's door expecting to go to work.

Ship's Officer Marian saved the day. "I have a suggestion." He interjected. "It is still important that we explore the area upriver and do some mapping as we had previously discussed. I will put Master Hunt on my team and take him along. We will inform him that there are countless tribes and villages needing to be proselytized during this excursion. With any luck we will not run in to any of them, but that will occupy the preacher for quite awhile." There was a moment of strained silence as the other leaders considered his remarks, then a chorus of chuckles echoed in the meeting room.

With that poser out of the way the expedition leaders began to select the next group of representatives to meet with the *Choptanks*. "These are historic times," said Guilford.

"I presume Brooks-Hughes is the most capable one we have for recording them for posterity. I recommend he be on the team."

"We are going to have to allow Surgeon Wickinson to get more involved in the communication. As much as we need him here in the settlement, the *Articles* do direct us to teach the primitive societies modern medical practices and hygienic techniques," added Coverdale.

Marian recommended able-bodied seaman Profit. "Jonas' family is from Plymouth where they built row boats and skiffs. In fact, our longboats came from their factory. He has that trained eye so we can learn more about their canoes and any other water craft. Also, he has developed into quite a hunter and may be able to discover how they pursue and kill animals. I have seen their bows and arrows. I'm surprised they can fall anything larger than a rabbit. They must not be able to shoot over 20 paces with any power or accuracy."

Governor Wingfield turned to Captain Coverdale and Sergeant Lusby and looked at them in a questioning manner, "I am requesting that both of you continue to participate directly in the upcoming intercourse. You have both leadership experience and the continuity of prior contact. I must resume my administrative duties here at New Providence, so your responsibilities will be much more than ever before. These people obviously have survived and prospered in this New Land. We need to learn everything we can, whether they are willing to teach us or not."

The Artist and the Princess

Theodore Brooks-Hughes had previously endeared himself to the *Choptanks* by his gentle demeanor and his magical ability to represent on paper the reality around him. Still a youth, he had not grown the thick heavy beard of many of the other Englishmen, so the Natives found him less frightening. He had decided that if he were given a chance to return to the village, he would produce a comprehensive collection of illustrations of the people as well as their environment in general. He hoped the Natives would be willing to sit for him once they realized his skills. His rough sketches from the prior trip only increased his motivation for this project as he finished them with pen and ink and placed them in a portfolio. When he found out he was one of the team members selected to return he actually jumped for joy! Carpenter Capper had made him a small stool and an easel board with tripod so these were stacked with his knapsack packed tightly with art supplies in preparation for the morrow.

Upon arrival at the village, he found his artist's eye looking for subjects and composition. As the other Englishmen departed with the group of local citizenry that met them at the shore, Brooks-Hughes remained with his easel and stool under his arm and his knapsack draped over his shoulder. Comfortable in the early spring sunshine he roamed into the encampment with two of the younger braves and a small crowd of smiling *Choptank* older women and children around him. They remembered him from before and were eager to see what he would do next. The artist showed them a couple of still life drawings he had finished from the prior trip. The shading, perspective and realism were so evident that the subjects almost leaped from the pages. Their eyes widened in amazement for they had never seen anything quite like this before. It really was magic.

Brooks-Hughes was almost overwhelmed by the myriad possibilities. The village was so unusual and picturesque that a lifetime of sketching and drawing could never completely represent all the qualities of the community. He wandered to the forest edge then turned back to get an overview of his subject. He found a liking for the way the light was cooperating and the way a particular tree limb was adding to the composition of one of the beehive huts, so decided this would be a good place to start. In short order he had his easel board in position and his art supplies at the ready. The Natives respectfully gathered behind him and sat in patient anticipation. As he began his handiwork, he became more and more engrossed in his art and less attuned to his immediate surroundings; and as so often is the case even today, people in general enjoy the finished project much more than watching the process. Good art is very time consuming as it grows from idea to product, and bit by bit the *Choptanks* quietly left the artist to his work. Not so much bored as remembering they had other responsibilities and interests. Brooks-Hughes did not even realize that he was quite alone.

The strangest sound brought him back to reality. At first it was almost like the tinkle of a small silver Christmas bell. Then he realized it was more a giggle or snicker, not so much unlike the musical, joyous laughter he heard when they first met the old lady they called *Chop-tah-nk* that now seemed so long ago. He pretended to continue working, but was actually slowly peering left and right to see who or what was making the sound. Certain he saw a human shadow back in the trees a short distance, he remained facing the easel board and made a friendly "come hither" motion and said softly, "Come and see what I am doing." The person in the trees responded with another musical giggle.

Brooks-Hughes slowly turned, and his heart leapt into his throat. Standing back in the trees a short distance but glowing in the spring sunlight was a young *Choptank* woman. In other times and places he might have not given her more than a second glance, but a year without any woman companionship changes a robust man's perspective. The young girl was rather short, with an almost-boyish round figure. Her animal skin clothing did nothing to add to any kind of attractiveness. It was her face and eyes that transfixed him. Her complexion was a light brown and absolutely flawless. Her shiny black hair tumbled over her shoulders and down her back in traditional *Choptank* fashion. The strands held small shells woven into the tresses and the decorations caressed the sides of her cheeks giving her an angel's face. Her expressive dark brown doe-like eyes were the most beautiful he had ever seen and promised so much. The artist felt his mouth turn to cotton as he tried to say his name feeling himself drowning in an ocean of conflicting emotions.

"I – I – I'm Thee-Theodore …" His voice broke destroying any semblance of manliness. His knees had turned to jelly, so there was no way he could stand up … so he just sat there not unlike the proverbial "bump on a log."

The girl giggled again, rolled her eyes, and clasped her hands in front of her coquettishly.

Brooks-Hughes was totally paralyzed as to what to do next. He could barely breathe, so he did nothing. He had always admired his mariner friend Jerald Pennyfeather-Grayson for his ability to succeed with the ladies. Jerald was never at a loss for words and never out of ideas when it came to women. At that moment, the artist wanted to be like his friend more than anybody else in the world, even the King.

Ironically, Theodore's inability to do anything was exactly the correct response. In *Choptank* society, the men do not denigrate themselves by expressing their affection or interest early in a relationship. It was up to the woman to make "the first move," and that is exactly what happened. The young Indian girl gracefully approached the artist, pointed to herself, and gently said, "*Cah-HON-ke*." Her voice reminded him of spring songbirds, and he could not wait for her to speak again. A fragrance was about her that was so pleasant that it made the young man swoon.

The maiden was the daughter of lesser chief *Weesanusks* and his wife *Wicompo*. She was one of the dozen-or-so girls of marriageable age that were always hustled off to the moon-time lodge whenever strange men came to the village. She never cooperated with this activity graciously and occasionally had to be dragged by the older women kicking and screaming out of the village. Her all-consuming curiosity and gregarious nature would at times motivate her to slip-out of the lodge and sneak back to see what was happening. The elder ladies charged with watching the young girls had long ago given up trying to keep her cloistered with the others.

Cahonke looked past Brooks-Hughes and was quite intrigued by the drawing he had started.

"I have some already finished," he said as he opened his knapsack and pulled out the portfolio cover. He displayed some of his pen and ink work, and she was obviously very impressed. He handed her a completed landscape for a closer look.

She timidly took it from his hand and smiled, "*Pe-DAH-mah-yeh*," ("Thank you.") she murmured. Then she did something that totally shocked him. She turned and merrily ran back down the path into the forest with the drawing.

"I –I just wanted you to look at it!" he stuttered. "*Cahonke! Cahonke!*"

But she was gone and so was his art work. It seemed like a dream. He had been sitting in the warm sunshine for some time and began to think that he may have drifted off. He chuckled to himself and turned back to resume his project. At that point he saw the portfolio lying on the ground at his feet where he had dropped it. It was no dream.

There was no way this young man was going to let that lovely girl out of his life so easily. But he was in a quandary as to what he should do next. Obviously, the Englishmen had no idea about *Choptank* courting etiquette. And there was the important issue of the *Articles on Intercourse with Indigenous Peoples* that clearly forbade any kind of fraternization. He did plan to do a number of portraits of the Natives, and this beautiful butterfly would certainly make an interesting subject. In his heart, he knew he was trying to rationalize ways to see more of her, and he might have found an acceptable reason.

By early afternoon the illustration of the village was completed. Brooks-Hughes gathered up his supplies, and as he ambled back to the settlement he soon had a retinue of children and older people joining him. He stopped and displayed his latest project much to their admiration and inquired about the location of *Weesanusks*. Of the five village leaders, he was confident this one would be the most likely to support his plan. He had no idea that this pleasant Native was the father of the young woman he was so smitten by.

Weesanusks and his wife *Wicompo* warmly welcomed him into their *wig-wam*. The artist had become quite a celebrity and any family would have been honored to offer him the hospitality of their home. They sat by the friendly fire, and Brooks-Hughes began to show them his portfolio. Despite the language barrier the communication between the two cultures flowed comfortably. *Wicompo* had a maid-servant who served a simple meal of corn bread, boiled venison and a very pleasant tea, as the drawings were passed around with great care. *Weesanusks* would identify some aspect of a composition in the local language, and the artist would repeat the word as he identified it within the illustration. In this way he began to develop a basic *Choptank* vocabulary. Once he placed the art work back in the portfolio, he tried to communicate in simple words and gestures that he wanted to illustrate the chief. *Weesanusks* realized the message and was both surprised and flattered. He looked at his dear wife who nodded in agreement. Word would soon reach the other chiefs of the pending plan.

"Theodore … Ho!" He heard Captain Coverdale hailing him. "It is time to return to New Providence!"

The Englishmen were not sure where their artist was, but they were confident he was within ear shot. As Brooks-Hughes emerged from the beehive *wig-wam*, he was surprised to find out how much of the day had passed by. The westering spring sun was already below the tree line and darkness would soon follow. He heard *Wicompo* protesting his departure, and she was motioning him to remain with them.

"They want me to stay!" shouted the young White Man. "What should I do?"

Sergeant Lusby answered gruffly, "Do the sign that says we'll be back on the morrow. We need to get on our way."

That evening Coverdale and Lusby joined Governor Wingfield in the Master's House to review the events of the day, but soon the discussion centered on their artist. Coverdale informed the expedition leader that of the five Englishmen who made the visit, Theodore was the only one invited to remain. Wingfield saw a special opportunity to get closer to *Weesanusks* and also to learn more about the Natives. After all his years doing the business of business he was very aware of how important it was to have the most information. One of his supervisors once told him, "The man with the plan is the man with the power." And any good plan is based on as much information as possible. Lusby did not feel that at this point there was any danger of an Englishmen spending a few nights with the *Choptanks*. He also mentioned that the artist seemed somewhat unhappy by having to leave when he was hailed.

"It's settled then," answered Wingfield. "Inform Brooks-Hughes to be prepared to be a guest of the savages for awhile. That is, of course, if the invitation is offered again."

As the Englishmen reached the village that next day the weather continued to be warm and welcoming. The normal throng of *Choptanks* was there waiting for them. *Weesanusks* was dressed in full regalia and despite his short broad body structure presented a very striking image in his formal attire. He wore a leather vest over his clothing that was alive with small sparkling shells that rattled musically at his every motion. His body-length bear skin cape made him appear as much like a short round mammal as a human. His wife, *Wicompo,* as tall and willowy as her older sister *Watsawasoo* stood at his side obviously very proud. *Pemetosusk* and *Pacowassamuck* were at the shore in full regalia to show their support for this unusual project. As the other visitors went their separate ways with their hosts, Brooks-Hughes motioned *Weesanusks* to stand near the decorative prow of one of the canoes and began to go to work. This effort was more unusual than earlier visits because the artist was doing the representation in oil paints on a stretched canvas. One good thing about being aboard an English sailing vessel was that there was always plenty of extra canvas. The normal group of Natives remained to watch as the illustration developed. The artist had such a good eye for composition and could so realistically mirror life that the observers kept looking at the picture and at the chief wondering what was real and what was art. The young man was very aware how tiring it is to stand still for extended lengths of time, so he and *Weesanusks* broke up their day with visits to the *wig-wam* and short excursions around the village. Despite the cultural and language differences an amazing connection between the two was beginning to develop. The chief had lost two sons over the years, and there was an empty place in his heart. *Choptank* leadership was handed down from father to son, but this friendly Indian's only surviving progeny was his daughter. When he would die his leadership role would pass to another family and this grieved him. Also, he was not sure what would happen to his lovely wife at that occasion. Despite her station, she was always considered an 'outsider' in *Choptank* social circles coming from *Chicamacomico* heritage and was invited to functions only because it was protocol. In response, she remained cold and aloof toward the shorter, stockier local women. She was a queen in her village, and even though not treated as such now, she still expected others to be courteous and at her bidding.

By day's end, it was clear that Brooks-Hughes would be able to join the *Weesanusks* family for the evening meal and his hosts were very happy. The painting was not anywhere near done, but it was developing nicely, was of excellent quality, and both the chief and the artist were very pleased with the results. Unbeknown to the young man and his hosts, the other Englishmen had rowed away for the night aware that Theodore had permission to remain in the village. This action also allowed the young girls to be released from the Moon-time Lodge. As *Wicompo* ordered the evening's repast to be served, a fourth place was set around the fire pit. Theodore assumed that one of the other chiefs would participate in the meal.

Suddenly the woven mat door to the hut was pulled opened and an angel glided through. Brooks-Hughes was both shocked and pleased. "*Cahonke!*" he cried in great joy.

"Tee-ah-dor!" she replied with equal delight.

The silence in the *wig-wam* was deafening. .

Leech Craft and *Peh-ZHU-tah* (Medicine)

Ship's Surgeon William Wickinson was eager to bring the 'modern' medical practices and hygienic techniques of the 1600's to the ignorant savages. He was confident that through his leadership and teaching the *Choptanks* would live long, healthy and happy lives. He fondly peered at his jars of leeches swimming in their own effluent and thought about all the expedition members they had bled. His annelid worms were almost like members of his family and he named them all even though they looked the same to the untrained eye. He checked the condition of his blood-letting tools and impressed himself by the fact that he had been able to keep them from getting rusty and that they were still relatively sharp despite such primitive working conditions at the settlement. His collection of apothecary jars was as comprehensive as one might see anywhere in England.

In an effort to anticipate any possible malady, the doctor carefully packed his medicine bag with a large selection of emetics, diarrheic concoctions, tinctures, balms and salves, ointments, aromatic oils, lotions, sulfur mixtures, powders and salts, and of course potions.

Earlier Wickinson had rummaged through the jars and baskets the Indians had left during the trading session. He would inspect a selection of roots, bark or leaves and detect an unusual aroma or texture, unlike anything he had worked with. Preacher Hunt searching for more *pemmican* happened to join him and mentioned that in the lodge the Native who had assisted him kept calling those strange collections a word that sounded like *Peh-ZHU-tah*. The surgeon's examination revealed nothing that he would consider as useful in his profession, but he had a sense that the locals might have believed the materials had some magical and medicinal or healing value.

As New Providence's doctor prepared to leave the infirmary aboard the *Phyllis* his assistant, Seaman Matthew Tasley, was obviously nervous about being left in charge. There were a handful of expedition members resting in various stages of illness - none critical; but Tasley had no idea what to do if an emergency occurred or if one of the sick men should experience a turn for the worse. Being assistant surgeon was easy duty since Wickinson did everything, but now things were getting serious ... and his boss was taking all the leeches! The doctor eased his concern somewhat by reminding him that he would be back at the end of the day, and he was confident nobody was going to die in that short amount of time. The work of the settlement had become a normal routine, and the chances of injury had been greatly reduced once the first construction phase had ended.

Upon arrival at the *Choptank* village, Wickinson stood on the shore with his paraphernalia wondering what the next step would be. He wanted to doctor somebody so the Natives could see why he had been included with this group of Englishmen. The usual throng of locals had gathered around, so he visually inspected each one hoping to see a facial rash, a contusion or bruise, or hear some coughing or sneezing. They all seemed to be just fine, which disappointed him somewhat. Maybe the sick ones were in some primitive form of infirmary or isolated in their *wig-wams*. He opened his medicine bag, took out some of the apothecary jars, and held them up hoping they would motivate someone to respond.

A dry, shrill crackly voice in the back of the crowd commanded, "*Yu-TOH-kon!*" (Move!), and the throng parted quickly. Wickinson could barely conceal his shock as a very tiny, quite aged, white haired woman approached him. He did not know it, but she was the very same crone that had first greeted the expedition. The visitors had since then referred to her as *Chop-tah-nk.*

No longer fearful of the *Ha-KAH-sha-nah* she approached the surgeon, looked at the jars he was holding, and questioned, *"Peh-ZHU-tah?"*(Medicine?)

There was the word that Preacher Hunt had said. Wilkinson nodded and responded as best he could to mimic her, *"Pay-ZOO-tah."*

The village elder turned and motioned for the doctor to follow her. He gladly complied very relieved that so much was happening so quickly. *Chop-tah-nk* led him past the settlement and down a path into the forest. This made Wilkinson very nervous and he stopped in his tracks. When she realized he had stopped following her, she turned, waved her arm at him, and curtly yelled, *"Yu-TOH-kon we-CHOSH-tah!"*(Move, man!).

At the end of the path was the strangest structure he had ever seen. It was constructed of the reed and bark mats used in the village but its shape was entirely different. He likened it to a large turtle shell or the moon halfway through its phases. At its high point, it was just a bit taller than a man and its diameter was somewhat less than the keel of a standard longboat. Adjacent to the hut was a huge pile of tree limbs and cut wood as well as a number of large clay jars that appeared to be filled with water.

The elderly Indian lady pointed and said, *"E-H'DU-ska-pe won-KEH-yah"* which could best be translated as "Sweat-bath lodge."

Wilkinson had been a surgeon most of his adult life, and he had seen just about everything: Gruesome war injuries; disfiguring poxes and diseases; people in the advanced stages of dying their skin and eyes turning black and coughing blood; men, women and children in excruciating pain ... death in its most ugly clothing. But, nothing had prepared him for what he was about to discover.

Chop-tah-nk held open the door mat and as the light streamed into the hut and hot wet steam flowed out, she said softly, "*Koh-Dee we-CHOSH-tah.*" (Transparent Man).

The interior of the structure was very dark except for the light coming from the doorway and the smoke hole in the roof. The fire in the pit was not much more than embers, but clearly he could see a human figure totally nude and partially propped up against the back wall. Another elder woman seemed to be attending to the person, and she quickly left as Wilkinson slowly entered. The floor of the hut was covered with cedar and pine boughs that felt like silk because of the moist air. He cautiously approached the reclined figure and saw that it was a living man with a tragically emaciated and extremely fragile body, more a skeleton than a human. His hair was beyond shoulder-length and disheveled and hung in wet ringlets past his shoulders. Even more shocking, he had a huge beard that basically concealed his face ... and he was so emaciated the surgeon could easily discern his blood vessels, tendons and muscles under his almost translucent bluish skin.

Wilkinson could not help but let out a gasp. Then he saw the tattoo of the snake on the man's right forearm. "Exum!" he breathed incredulously!

In modern times, there would have been a plausible explanation for what had happened: While gathering oysters, the seaman did lose track of the tide and a large wave washed him away from the shore. He was able to pull himself onto an outcropping of rocks and laid there in the freezing winter air for some time as hypothermia began to set in. He eventually stopped breathing and was brain dead when a canoe of *Choptanks* found him. They bundled him in furs and sped back to the village where he was taken to the sweat lodge. As the months passed, the Indians kept his body alive feeding him a warm broth-like mixture of different kinds of medicinals always in hope that he would revive from the coma. They saw the strange mark on his arm and assumed he was some kind of holy man. His heart was so weak and his respiration so depleted that his lips and body were always the strange translucent blue color, which was sacred to the Natives in the region.

Wilkinson knelt by Exum and opened his medicine bag. He extracted two leeches from a jar, and they quickly attached themselves to each side of his patient's temple. He held his ear to the seaman's chest and heard his faint irregular heartbeat. Despite the hot damp air in the sweat lodge, the wasted Englishman's body was very cold. Realizing that there was some circulation occurring, he unpacked his blood-letting razor and carefully cut a 'vee' shape in the skin of the interior of each wrist. Very little blood seeped out, and it was a dark, dark maroon color. As the doctor rummaged through his bag to find the appropriate apothecary, the sailor's body shuddered slightly then went absolutely limp. His condition was so fragile that the assault on his frail body was the last straw. As was too often the case in 1600's doctoring, the treatment was fine but the patient died.

Wilkinson felt no immediate remorse because of his actions but a sense of doubt about his healing abilities was beginning to rise up in his heart. He could see no sense in informing the men at New Providence about what had just happened. The disappearance of Exum was becoming a folk tale among the men and occupied their thoughts at times during long boring nights.

Chop-tah-nk had been closely observing the surgeon's efforts and was totally disgusted by the cruel and barbaric way he treated the "Transparent Man." She felt tears well-up in her eyes in silent rage. As she prepared to purify the sweat lodge and initiate the death chants, she turned her back on him and pointed her calloused, gnarled finger in the direction of the village, and spat, "*Yu-TOH-kon!*"

Angry and embarrassed, Wilkinson never returned to the *Choptanks*.

Two Nimrods and Two Cultures

J onas Profit was eager to display his new found hunting prowess. He preferred the long bow for its range and for the overall killing power and speed it put behind the arrow. However, he did enjoy the accuracy of the crossbow at close range. It seemed like a good idea to pack several of both for the trip to the village. The metal head of the crossbow quarrel was flush with the shaft of the projectile to allow it to slide easily along the stock groove. At times he was able to impale a rabbit, or in recent cases a rat, with so much power at close range that the dart would go cleanly through the critter's body. This always impressed the other men at New Providence, and he was sure it would do the same for the Natives. On his rat hunts, he would pick up the spent missile, pretend to lick the blood off the feather part of the shaft, and growl menacingly. This always brought loud belly-laughs from his mates. Profit was aware that the *Choptanks* had no metal in their daily lives. The arrows he carried for the longbows were made of honed iron and had the sharp, barbed heads used to fall large animals. He was confident these missiles would seem like magic to the village hunters. He could still recall when he shot his first wolf. The animal tried vainly to pull the arrow from its injured body by biting it and pulling. Its strong jaws snapped the shaft like a piece of straw, but the configuration of the arrow head made it impossible to be extracted. Profit had impaled the suffering animal three more times in quick succession to bring about its demise. The proud animal died in pain and frustration bringing tears of admiration to Jonas' eyes.

Unloading his weapons at the village brought quite a crowd of Indians to his side, all men and boys of course, and their interest and curiosity were very evident. He unrolled a large colorful cloth on the sandy beach and began to lay-out the bows and projectiles in neat rows displaying a certain amount of care and respect. This deeply impressed the locals as they watched silently and they were sure there was some kind of secret power afoot. A robust brave, wearing a necklace made of bear claws, possibly in his 20's and quite handsome and tall for a *Choptank,* edged closer to Profit as the others made room for him without question. One of the older men gestured toward the brave and murmured, "WE-h'ne-s'ah." (Our Hunter).

The Englishman realized the deference the others were showing the man, and he decided this one was worth special attention ... possibly his first disciple. He motioned the brave to come closer so he could watch him position the quarrel on the stock of the crossbow and ratchet the string to a point behind the release lever. Holding the weapon at the ready and looking around for a likely target, the other onlookers ducked and scattered not knowing for sure what was about to happen. A short distance away he noticed the totem on a particular dugout somewhat resembled an animal ... aimed and fired. The dart sped toward the target faster than the eye could follow and the wooden figure exploded into countless small pieces with a resounding crack. After a shocked silence, the *Choptanks* yelled their approval and danced vigorously at the display. To Profit, it was an easy shot at a stationary target; but to the locals it truly was magic. He pointed at one of the Indian boys and then at the spent projectile resting far down the beach and motioned him to fetch it. The boy complied with great joy and felt extremely important as he brought the partially bent quarrel back to the White Man and placed it at his feet.

Profit reloaded the crossbow, but not as tightly as before, and handed it to the one they called "WE-h'ne-s'ah." He cautiously held it, somewhat at a loss as to what to do next. The Englishman was so adroit with the weapon that all the appropriate motions blended together confusing those trying to learn. The Native unknowingly released the sensitive trigger, and the dart ricocheted off the sandy beach and sped directly into the right calf muscle of one of the observers. The poor chap howled and dropped to the ground in pain, kicking and thrashing his leg as he tried to extract the missile. For some strange reason, all the other *Choptanks* broke into raucous laughter totally unsympathetic to their neighbor's plight. The Englishman quickly subdued the injured man and removed the quarrel in one swift move. Fortunately, the dart had lost some of its force as it bounced off the ground and it was only a short way into the man's muscle. Blood squirted out of the open wound as the victim limped back to the village presumably to get aid. The Native shooter carefully laid the empty crossbow on the cloth and stepped back. As far as he was concerned that was the first and last time he would have anything to do with the White Man's magic.

The crowd was suddenly subdued as another *Choptank* appeared and approached Profit. "E-TON-chon WE-h'ne-s'ah" ("Our Master Hunter") muttered the same man who had described the earlier nimrod. This Native was as tall, virile and as handsome but had long beautiful grey hair with mother of pearl trinkets carved into animal designs and woven in strands behind each ear. His clothing and footwear seemed to be made with exceptional care and were obviously of a quality above what most of the tribe wore. His attire was decorated with various designs in blacks and reds which contrasted sharply with the plain animal skin shirts and breeches worn by the other villagers and he wore so many bear claw necklaces that they rattled and clacked as he walked. Profit noticed that the claws on the necklaces were separated by the colorful beads traded earlier at New Providence. The striking villager held his hand to his breast and said, "*Asquash.*"

Profit replicated the motion and replied, "Jonas."

Asquash ignored the crossbows, but was very intrigued by the longbows. Jonas hoped silently that this man would be his new protégé. *Asquash* turned to the crowd, said a few words, and they quietly dispersed leaving the two hunters alone. If there was a New Magic to be had, it was not going to be for everyone. The Englishman began to pack up the crossbows and quarrels, and while doing so handed one of the longbow arrows to his companion. He caressed the missile like it was a woman, inspecting the straightness of the shaft, the symmetry of the feather guides, and mostly admiring the razor sharp metal arrow head that flashed angrily in the morning sunlight. As Jonas put the cross bows and darts back in the longboat, he had no fear that they might not be there later in the day. *Asquash* apparently was extremely powerful among his people and his word was law.

The Native warrior motioned the Englishman to follow and they both walked into the village. Jonas was carrying two of the longbows and had two quiver of arrows draped over his shoulders. As they approached one of the larger bee-hive *wig-wams,* the older man gestured for him to wait a moment as he opened the doorway mat and disappeared inside. Profit could hear a muffled discussion and in short order the Native emerged with a smaller bow and an animal skin sheath filled with arrows. He also carried a large reed basket on his back looking as much like a peddler as a hunter. Jonas was surprised to see a very English metal knife blade protruding from his belt. He did not know that Governor Wingfield had given some knives to the chiefs in an earlier meeting, and apparently one was passed on to *Asquash*.

The morning sun was comfortably warm as the two men ambled away from the village down a well-worn path into the forest. There were still occasional snow drifts resting in the shady areas of the groves of trees, but it was clear their days were numbered. A steady hum of insects informed the world that the Bug People were coming out of their winter sleep and were joyously singing in great expectation. The Indian reached into his clothing and removed two large wedges of corn bread wrapped in a leather napkin and handed one to Profit. The pastry had a very slight tanned aftertaste, but it was moist and delicious. He supposed that the *Choptanks* probably got used to their food tasting like their footwear smelled. The hunters had silently walked for about two hours when the Native stopped, moistened his finger, and held it up to the air. Jonas had seen Sergeant Lusby do the same thing and knew both were checking the wind direction. Once 'down-wind' was determined the older man left the path, careful to avoid the snow drifts, and walked into the forest with the Englishman quietly following. A short while later the nimrods found themselves at the edge of a large sun-lit meadow possible a quarter-mile across. A babbling brook was chattering happily as it flowed out of the trees and across the lea. Jonas saw a small herd of deer near the edge of the forest on the opposite side of the field. The Indian whispered, "*TAH-cha*." Profit would have to somehow get closer if he wanted to guarantee venison for dinner and began to survey the ring of trees outlining the meadow. To approach the herd, he realized he would have to move from down-wind to partial up-wind and chances were the deer would be long gone by the time he got close enough to take a shot.

Then *Asquash* did something that totally amazed Profit. He quietly lowered the cumbersome basket from his back, removed the lid and lifted out a very large and folded buck deer pelt that still had the preserved skull and antlers attached. He smiled at the Englishman, signaled him to remain there and draped the skin over his body letting the head dangle down over his eyes. Holding his small bow in one hand and the quiver of arrows in the other, he began to move slowly in a crouching position in the general direction of the herd. The Indian did not wander directly toward the animals but seemed to be in no hurry, sometimes walking a score or so paces to the left stopping as if to graze awhile, then a few more to the right. He had obviously studied the movements of a deer and mimicked them perfectly. Jonas quietly laughed to himself thinking that if he saw *Asquash* in another setting he would have put a couple arrows in his behind. After a while a young four-point buck from the herd cautiously approached the unusual looking animal curious as to what this stranger might be up to. With amazing speed the hunter threw back the deer skull, place an arrow in the string of his bow and hit the buck directly in the eye. The deer dropped with a heavy thud as the rest of the herd wildly bolted for the protection of the forest. The Indian held up his fist and gave a blood-curdling howl of elation then motioned Profit to join him. In the few minutes it took Jonas to get to the kill site, the older man had the deer field-dressed and was holding its steaming heart. He took a large bite out of the organ and handed it to the Englishman. Against his better judgment, but unwilling to offend his new friend, Jonas did the same. It felt hot and bloody in his mouth but was not a totally unpleasant flavor and somewhat similar to beef liver. It was clear that if he was going to participate in future hunting expeditions with the *Choptanks* he'd best get used to this ritual.

They rolled the carcass onto the tanned deer pelt and began to drag it back to the village. Jonas wanted to show *Asquash* his ability to bring down a large animal, but it appeared this would have to occur at some other time. He knew that if he could demonstrate the power of the longbow, the Native would want to learn more about the weapon. He had ambivalent feelings about getting any of these powerful weapons in the hands of the locals. As long as the Englishmen were the only ones with longbows they held a strategic advantage should trouble erupt.

Just as they reached the path again a loud crackling and rustling in the underbrush a short distance behind them caused them both to stop in their tracks. Something very large was approaching with no stealth at all. Profit undraped one of the longbows and set an arrow in the string holding two other arrows at the ready. The Native replicated the same motion with great dexterity with his bow and arrows.

Eastern Brown Bear. Called "Mah-TOH."

Less than 50 paces back down the trail a young brown bear emerged smelling the deer blood and hungrily expecting to enjoy it. He had probably been hibernating the past few months and was way overdue for a tasty meal.

The Indian shouted, "*Mah-TOH!*"

The Englishman drew back his trusty yew wood bow and the vicious arrow flew toward the animal with alarming speed. It caught the charging beast deep in his breast and he growled in great pain, but kept attacking. Jonas had already released the second arrow and it impaled the bear only a couple inches from the first projectile. As the bear tumbled forward not 20 yards from their feet, Profit released the third arrow striking the animal in the throat directly under his slavering jowls. The metal headed arrow struck with such devastation that it nearly severed the hapless animal's head from the rest of its body. Simultaneously two more arrows impaled the creature from *Asquash's* bow. It shuddered, gave out a quiet moan, coughed black blood and lay still on the path just steps from the two men. Now it was the Englishman's turn to field dress an animal and remove its haslet. As he reached down to turn the animal on its back he felt its rib cage. The poor creature was just skin and bones probably because it had lived through the winter on its own body fat.

He mumbled, "This chap needed the deer more than we did. If the village is expecting bear stew tonight, it will be more stew than bear."

As evening drew near the two hunters returned to the village. Both decided it would look better to be carrying their prey rather than dragging it, so they folded the deer pelt and place it back in the basket, hoisted their respective animals over their shoulders and tried not to look totally exhausted. The emaciated bear was surprisingly light in weight and Profit was very happy about this. The young buck had enjoyed a bountiful winter and weighed much more. However, the Indian's raw-bone strength made the burden much less tiresome than another person might have thought. The *Choptanks* greeted their providers with great honor and accolades confident that they would never go hungry. They looked at Jonas and began chanting, *"Mah-TOH Wah-K'TEH-s'ah!"* From that moment on "Bear Slayer" would be his name as far as the *Choptanks* were concerned.

Welcome Home *AH-bah-nah* *Chon-TEH* (Gentle Heart)

C

aptain Gabriell Coverdale found himself enjoying the visits to the village much more than staying at New Providence. As he grew accustomed to the *Choptank* culture he began to see the simple common sense in their interrelationships. Each family unit consisted of at least three generations and there was mutual respect evident. The elderly were appreciated and useful, the parents industrious and honest, and the children were cared for and polite. He did wonder why there were no girls of marriageable age, but this was a purely academic thought. The closeness of the quarters inside their bee-hive *wig-wams* precluded any chances for privacy, but this did not appear to be a problem. As best he could tell the generations thrived on the proximity and felt safe and warm with their loved ones at hand. They were a spiritual people who held their Creator-God, *Wak-KON-ton-kah*, in great reverence and heartfelt thanks was offered at each meal. The name of their god translated into "The Great Mystery."

As a community, the tribe seemed to be divided into four clans.

One group was called the *"Ho-KU-wah-s'ah"* or sea harvesters. Their bee-hive homes displayed the voracious Bluefish, called *Toh Ho-KU-wah*, as their totem. Someday this ravenous fish would be called the "marine piranha." Each clansperson would wear a fish-shaped mother of pearl talisman somewhere on his or her clothing. They were always busy mending nets, constructing wooden frames out of tree branches that Coverdale would eventually find out were for trapping crab, twisting strips of plant fiber into fishing line and netting, and smoothing and sharpening larger flat rocks to use for scraping up clams, oysters, and muscles from the ocean bottom. Theirs was a year-around job, and their only 'time off' was when storms made it unsafe to approach the bay. The English officer would try to think of ways he could get some of the shovels at the settlement into the hands of this group. Each domicile had a large basket by its front door filled with fish hooks made of animal bone. Lesser chief *Weesanusks* was an offspring of this band.

The second clan of Indians was the *"WE-h'ne-s'ah,"* the huntsmen. Their totem was *Mah-TOH*, the bear, and they could be distinguished by the necklaces made of bear claws or bear teeth that they always wore. The hunters were directly accountable to *Asquash,* and he communicated with the village chiefs in their name. Their homes were in one section of the settlement somewhat separated from the rest of the community. It was not so much that they displayed a degree of aloofness, but the fact that they were either in the field pursuing game or preparing to go into the field. *Asquash* was a difficult task master determined to keep his hunters lean and fierce, and well trained with the bow and arrow, battle axe and lance. He knew that in time of peril, his hunters would also be the tribe's warriors.

The third clan was the *"Ke-WE-dah-yah-s'ah"* the gatherers. Their totem was *TAH-cha*, the gentle deer. The women knew all the indigenous plant life that would help the village to thrive. They were not farmers as such, but they knew where specific flora grew, how and when to harvest it. Generations ago, they learned to keep areas free of weeds and undergrowth to promote profusion of the plants they desired, and they constructed rudimentary fences around growing areas to restrict competition from plant-eating

animals. Every autumn was a constant battle with the Bear
People over harvesting the vast berry crop available. They
counted on the hunters to help control this menace. Of equal
importance was maintaining a constant supply of *Peh-ZHU-
tah* (Medicine) for the health of the people. The men were
the woodsmen who cut the trees and provided a constant
supply of firewood for the village. They were given seven
of the English metal axes for their work – which became so
much easier. The Indian medicine men and women were
esteemed members of this clan. The twin chiefs, *Tattowin* and
Weanchum carried the totem of the gatherers. .

The remaining clan was small and the one seemed to be
held in the highest esteem. The *Choptanks* referred to them
as "*Wah-KON-kon-s'ah*" which might best be translated as
"Magicians." Their totem was *Wom-BLEE* the eagle, and they
were the only ones allowed to wear feathers. The men were
the canoe builders in the cold months and they gained the
use of the remaining English axes procured at the trading
session at New Providence. During the hot months canoe-
building ceased and salt production began. In an estuary
north of the village could be found the vast salt cairns built
generations ago and kept in constant repair. A beautiful
checkerboard of blues and grays as far as the eye could see.
Both activities were extremely important to the prosperity
of the tribe which explained why this clan was held in such
high honor. Two of the chiefs, head man *Pemetosusk* and his
cousin *Pacowassamuck*, were members of this group which
added to the overall prestige of the *Wah-KON-kon-s'ah*.

The tribe's survival and sustenance depended on each clan
sharing its gifts without expectations of getting something
in return. This relationship kept the *Choptanks* strong and
united. They lived in a bountiful land, and although variety
was not always available, there was plenty for everyone.

On this particular spring day, the Englishmen reached the village as they had a number of times before. As usual, groups of *Choptanks* would form and follow their visitors as they went about their business. This day was different. Captain Coverdale suddenly found himself very alone. He realized he was starting to perspire nervously as he fingered the handle of his sword. There was a longbow and quiver of arrows in the boat, and he tried to nonchalantly reach for them as if he were rearranging the paraphernalia the visitors had brought with them. The first tenet of his military training was to reconnoiter the situation and try to anticipate the next move of the enemy. He carefully looked around to see if any Native warriors were lurking near their dugouts or the adjacent *wig-wams*.

Coverdale was relieved to see the twin chiefs coming in his direction with two young boy acolytes walking a few paces behind. None appeared to be carrying weapons. He could never determine who was *Tattowin* and who was *Weanchum*, but as time passed, it really didn't make any difference. They were one person in two bodies. Despite their 40 years walking the earth and premature grey hair they seemed very young. Moving with fluid grace and speaking in soft feminine voice, one of the chiefs held up his right hand as the other welcomed him, "*WO-oh-ke-yeh, Soon-KAH.*" ("Peace, little brother.") He then extended his hands to the captain which startled the acolytes. These two village leaders were often seen walking hand-in-hand, but they never touched other people. As Gabrielle gently clasped the hand he was amazed by how soft and smooth it was, yet it was evident that the surface concealed a vice-like grip. He knew that if the Native had decided to put pressure on the hand shake, he would be on his knees in pain.

Weanchum motioned the Englishman to join them, and they quietly wandered through the village enjoying the warm spring weather. The settlement was busily involved in its daily responsibilities, but the *Choptanks* would always take a moment to acknowledge the group in respectful deference as it passed. The twin chiefs would bless the others with a smile and warm greeting. Clearly these two were held in the highest regard of all, and possibly even a degree of fear. The Natives considered these strange men almost god-like and were resigned to the fact that they resided on a higher spiritual plane. Their questioning looks at Captain Coverdale spoke loudly as they wondered why he was included with such discriminating dignitaries. Up to this point, the twins had avoided any communication with the White Men after the first *to-bac* ceremony and in fact had often voiced their deep concern about any further contact.

The group's relaxed stroll eventually led them down a rarely used pathway into the thick forest. Nestled in a small clearing was the twins own 'sweat-bath lodge.' *Tattowin* gestured at the igloo-like structure constructed with layers of woven reed mats and said, "E-H'DU-ska-pe won-KEH-yah." ("Sweat-bath Lodge").

Earlier, the acolytes had started the fire and placed the water and herb filled clay pots by the flames, so by the time the group arrived, everything was in readiness for the ensuing ritual. The chiefs and their assistants begin to disrobe which intrigued and also embarrassed Coverdale deeply. He was suddenly very uncomfortable and started to turn away. *Weanchum* chuckled and motioned the captain to do the same as the rest of them. His imploring expression communicated that everything would be alright. The Englishman felt a wave of fear wash through him, and he had a strong urge to run. Why he did not, he could never completely understand, and at later times he would occasionally try to analyze those actions and reactions.

The interior of the lodge was so hot and thick with a pleasantly aromatic steam that it initially overwhelmed Coverdale. He found it difficult to breathe and very, very claustrophobic. The space was quite small, and by the time the five had circled the fire and sat down their knees almost touched each other. The two chiefs and their young acolytes did not seem to be in distress, so the captain could not very well run out in panic and still be a proper representative of the King. The floor of the lodge was covered with cedar boughs moist and silky feeling from the steam and smelled wonderful. In one of the hot water jars there appeared to be a large wooden ladle. One of the twins scooped it full of hot water and poured it over the head of the person sitting next to him. Then that person did the same to his neighbor. The ladle was rapidly approaching the Englishman and he began to get nervous. The very hot water washed over his hair and down his neck and face and he bellowed, not so much in pain as in surprise. The *Choptanks* laughed loudly. He did not know it, but his reaction was very common to others who were having their first sweat bath experience. The visitor did enjoy a small degree of satisfaction when he poured the water over the man to his left.

As polite as the Indians always were to strangers, they found most of the White Men very unclean and bad smelling. It was difficult to be near them except outdoors. Some of the mariners like Brooks-Hughes and Jonas Profit had more acceptable personal hygiene habits because of their days at sea, but most of the Europeans seldom changed their footwear and clothing and bathed maybe once every month or two if they thought about it. The chiefs held great expectations for the captain and they wanted to be sure he was approachable.

As the ladle was handed around a number of times more, the twins started to sing and chant strangely beautiful songs. Their voices were at once soft and feminine and also forceful and unusually masculine. One of the acolytes handed Coverdale a small piece of dried root and said, "*KEESH-wah*" as the young man began chewing on a piece he had kept for himself.

KEESH-wah root was an enigma to the Gatherer's Clan. Its leaf and stem were unusual and very distinctive, and it had been an integral aspect of *Choptank* sacred ceremonies beyond memory. Some of the mature bushes could stand as tall as a man's waist and it was forbidden for normal tribal members to harvest it. The twin chiefs seemed to always know where it was growing, and after a thanksgiving prayer they would gently pull on the bush and it would slide out of the earth like a stick in loose sand. Its roots were large and splayed out like a giant spider, yet it seemed to gladly give up its life for the holy men. Fresh *KEESH-wah* roots were deadly poison, and tales were told of renegade Indians being forced to ingest the plant as a humane way to end their murderous lives. Once the root dried, it was an amazing medicinal and hallucinogenic part of the holy men's apothecary. The plant could be smoked or eaten depending on the particular ceremony. One day, *KEESH-wah* would be determined to be a member of the "Angelica" family of plants.

The captain tasted the root and as his saliva moistened the fibers a quite pleasant flavor filled his mouth. In a few brief moments he began to feel a sense of weightlessness and the music and sacred chants seemed to flow through his body. He was both elated and fearful of this new sensation and found himself holding tightly to the cedar boughs covering the floor.

A strange indigo light crawled through his mind, then it grew darker and uncomfortably menacing. He saw a raging thunderstorm and a vast expanse of gray water roiling with white caps. The sea turned an evil blood-red and was completely covered with a plague of black ants riding on pieces of wood. He tried to scream a warning, but his throat was paralyzed ... he did not even realize when he had passed out.

Captain Coverdale awoke to a cacophony of singing crickets and realized it must be almost night time. He was alone in the sweat lodge, but someone had covered him with a deer skin blanket. He felt very cozy and comfortable and finding the ambition to get moving was going to take some effort. Then he realized that the other Englishmen would be looking for him. The longboat always departed the beach before dark. He had left his boots and uniform neatly stacked by the doorway to the lodge, but as he scrambled out, they were nowhere to be found. Where his clothing had been was a white deerskin tunic, decorated vest, breeches, and soft leather moccasins. He thought he would look absolutely ridiculous in this clothing, but he could not go into the village totally naked. A head and shoulders taller than almost all the *Choptanks*, Gabrielle was sure the size of the outfit would add to his comic appearance. As he donned the apparel, he was shocked to realize all of it fit perfectly, even the footwear. Someone had gone to a lot of preparation to gain an English military uniform. As he scanned the small clearing to find the pathway back, he noticed one of the acolytes squatting near the trees watching him silently and also very intently. Only the medicine women who had doctored Percy Exum and those that participated in the recent sweat lodge experience had ever seen a nude White Man. The Indians of eastern North America had very little, if any, body hair. Seeing

Coverdale's thick hairy chest made the acolyte wonder if he were man or beast.

The young man stood up, motioned the captain to follow him and quietly led him back up the path to the village. As they reached the first beehive *wig-wams* a large group of Indians was waiting for them. *"AH-bah-nah Chon-TEH!"* they repeated over and over happily pulling on Coverdale's arms and slapping him on the back. At that moment he realized he was now an official member of the *Choptank* tribe and later he found out he carried the honorable name of "Gentle Heart."

CHAPTER IV ...
TWILIGHT

Spring Fever

That late spring meeting in the Master's House at New Providence was not totally pleasant. Governor Wingfield was beginning to feel he was losing control of the overall situation. The expedition leader was always more comfortable with numbers than with people and had been working long hours to prepare for the first return voyage of the *Phyllis Redoubtable* to England. Double checking the inventory of trade goods from the *Choptanks*, he found discrepancies between the figures and the supplies. He was not sure if it was sloppy bookkeeping or pilfering. The number of bundles of *to-bac* on the ledger was significantly more than the amount stored in the jail. The administrator was also at a loss as to what happened to 17 jars of an unusual entry listed as *"pem-mee-kan."* In fact, he was not sure exactly what pemmican was. He was prepared to ask his leadership team how to address this issue with the rest of the men. Fortunately, two of the most valuable items, furs and salt, seemed to be relatively accurate if not under noted. The kitchen crew had requested access to the salt as they utilized it for daily meals and for production of venison jerky, and Wingfield agreed that this would be appropriate. The jars were no longer completely full, but the number was correct.

His leadership team was down to four people, and he had some major decisions to make before it had dwindled even further. Captain Coverdale had not returned for some time from the *Choptank* village. They knew he was okay, because he would occasionally send messages requesting particular tools or utensils, and it was clear he was in the middle of some major project. His request for shovels implied that he was supervising the improvement of fortifications for the settlement, possibly the construction of some kind of defensive revetment. Ship's officer Edwin Marian was preparing for his expedition up river and would soon be gone for an undetermined amount of time. Sergeant Lusby was not always available when the administrator needed to confer with him. Lusby was deeply involved with efforts to find the minerals needed to make gunpowder. He would be gone for days in a row with a team of *Choptanks* exploring the surrounding geographical area.

Surgeon Wilkinson was the team member that the administrator was most concerned about, and he encouraged Magistrate Guilford to try to determine what the problem was. Ever since his return from the village, he isolated himself from the rest of the expedition members even refusing to join the group at meal time. His assistant, Seaman Tasley who appeared to have taken on more and more of the medical responsibilities, would carry some of the victuals to him on the *Phyllis* where he chose to remain day and night. Because of the positive change in the weather and the lessened need for hard labor, there were never very many men, if any, in the infirmary, so Wilkinson's preoccupation was not because of over work. Guilford reported to the administrator that their doctor, normally cleanly shaven and well-dressed, had lost interest in his personal appearance and was prone to muttering to himself and unable to maintain a normal conversation. In the 1600's, these early stages of insanity were shrugged-off as intellectual peculiarities.

Things were not all bad though. Brooks-Hughes continued to produce excellent art work, and about once a week a portfolio would show up on Wingfield's desk. The artist's request for a roll of sail canvas was still pending. The administrator had no idea what he would want that for since the *Choptank* dugouts did not appear to be sail-worthy. Jonas Profit was very reliable about reporting the events with the Natives. He seldom remained overnight at the village and was available for daily updates should the expedition leader request them. Profit found out he had a special propensity for languages and was quickly learning their tongue. Wingfield was confident that he would be invaluable as future discourse would be occurring and he was comfortable that Coverdale and Brooks-Hughes would also be good resources. On occasion, some of the Indian men would return to New Providence with the contact team or row across the bay in their own crafts and remain for a day or two. They seemed very interested in the goings-on at the fort and eager to learn. Sometimes one of the Englishman demonstrating a technique or trying to explain something would become frustrated because their visitors never showed any enthusiasm or said anything. They would just watch carefully and occasionally nod their heads.

Wingfield was reassured when he checked with his kitchen crew, and they reported that the food supply was continuing and at an adequate rate. The original hunting team of Sergeant Lusby, Private Dixon, Private Kenneth Quinby, and Seamen Jonas Profit and Percy Exum had changed drastically. Dixon was so pre-occupied with tanning and fur preparation that he no longer had time to hunt. Jonas Profit was at the Indian village almost daily, Exum had disappeared some time ago, and Lusby was endeavoring to meet his other responsibilities.

White Tailed Deer. Called "TAH-cha."

The leadership for providing sustenance for the men of New Providence fell on the shoulders of Quinby, and he rose to the occasion in fine fashion. He hand-picked a small group from the main crew and trained them daily with the longbow. His schedule for procuring was sensible and productive, and had he known it, excellent conservation practices. Different days of the week saw a different activity: Two days hunting big game and edible birds, the next two days harvesting what the sea had to offer, and then the two-day outing inspecting the extensive trap line. His crew was always on the look-out for berries and fruit. They could keep track of the ripening process and be there at the appropriate time to pick the bounty before the bears had eaten it all. In an effort to keep the Sabbath, Quinby gave his team Sundays off. He found his people volunteering for guard duty or kitchen clean-up to avoid attending Master Hunt's church services in the dormitory. So, he decided to make it their training day, much to their pleasure. This extra day practicing with the longbow and cross bow brought his men to a degree of proficiency that equaled the prowess of Jonas Profit.

Standing in Two Worlds

Lesser chief *Weesanusks* and his darling wife *Wicompo* were in a quandary. They did not know how Brooks-Hughes and their daughter *Cahonke* had come to know each other, but this unraveled a clew of problems. It was painfully clear that both young people had already connected with each other in some unexplainable fashion. The courting mores' of the *Choptanks* were very clear: If a woman found favor in a man, she had to make the first overtures usually taking food or some gift to his *wig-wam* with the supervision of her sisters, aunts, grandmother and mother. Often there might be a dozen or more in the retinue which could overwhelm the gentleman and remind him that there may be serious repercussions if he gets out of line. There was more than one tale told to the young Indian boys at bedtime about the horrible fate of some brave who took inappropriate liberties with a particular maiden. This impending situation was much more complicated because although the chief and his wife obviously liked the young man, he was a White Man.

The first order was to get Brooks-Hughes out of their home without throwing him out in the unfriendly darkness. Frankly, they had not really thought through what they would do when *Cahonke* returned from the moon-time lodge for the evening. They assumed that after a cordial repast, he would return with the other Englishmen to their settlement. As the four sat comfortably around the fire pit enjoying a satisfying meal of seafood chowder both parents realized that the fact that their daughter arrived for dinner was an indication that the other White Men had departed for the day. *Weesanusks* leaned near his wife and whispered to her what he was going to try to do. The former White Man *AH-bah-nah Chon-TEH* (Captain Coverdale) was now situated in his own lodge. The twin chiefs had the structure built in traditional fashion near their own home and the normal accruements associated with a traditional *wig-wam* were included making the hut quite livable. *Weesanusks* would implore the holy men to allow the young man to reside with the new *Choptank* at least until they could decide how to resolve this very sticky situation. He excused himself and hustled quickly to the *wig-wam* of his fellow village leaders.

In a few brief moments, *Weesanusks* had returned to his hut and joined the dinner party. After all had eaten their fill, he lit a small *to-bac* leaf and shared it with Brooks-Hughes as both men enjoyed the pleasure of full stomachs and relaxed comfort. This was strictly a men's ritual, and the women had long ago accepted this fact. *Wicompo's* maidservant quickly cleared the leftovers and dishes. The mother and her daughter both nodded and smiled briefly, *Cahonke* giving Theodore a very special glance, then exited into the night. The chief quietly rose to his feet, motioned the artist to gather his art supplies and to follow him. Theodore realized that he would not be able to stay with his new friends and was somewhat concerned about his accommodations for the night. Being a seaman all his life, he was not in any way a competent camper and was never comfortable outdoors during nightfall. A short walk through the village brought them to the Captain Coverdale's new home. *Tattowin* and *Weanchum* were standing outside the *wig-wam* with a very tall Native. In the deepening twilight, the artist could not recognize who the person might be. As they approached the group the tall man turned around to face them.

"Ca-Captain Co-Coverdale!" stuttered Brooks-Hughes. He was completely taken aback by seeing an English military officer in stunning white deerskin attire. The scene was so incongruous in nature, but so striking and beautiful.

"I will try to explain," replied Coverdale. "I believe you will be staying with me for a while."

As the Native leaders departed, the captain motioned Brooks-Hughes to follow him into the *wig-wam*. The fire was crackling merrily and the many animal pelts on the ground made it even more warm and comfortable. Both men wearily sat down, and the former military man related some of the life-changing events he had experienced these last few days.

The artist was confused by what he had heard. "But you are still Captain Coverdale," he responded. "*AH-bah-nah Chon-TEH* is not a real person, just a savage's name for a man I have always admired and wanted to be like. When you are in the village, you can be anybody they want you to be, but when you come back home … you are the captain."

Gabrielle looked sadly at the young man understanding his confusion. "I am home. For the first time in my life, I feel like I am where I am supposed to be. No one can understand the turmoil I have felt. Never feeling complete, never feeling adequate, nor feeling capable … All that is gone now. I can truly say I am at peace."

Brooks-Hughes lowered his head wrapped in his own inner war. "I am in love with a *Choptank* girl. It is Chief *Weesanusks'* daughter. She is the most beautiful butterfly I have ever seen. I can't get her out of my mind. I know this is against the laws of the *Articles on Intercourse with Indigenous Peoples*. I know there would be a severe penalty if the others found out … but I can't help it. All I want to be … is with her."

Both men sat silently staring into the fire. Despite the outward calm, their old world and their new world were raging furiously in their souls. As the chasm between the cultures began to get deeper and deeper, both men felt like they were being ripped in two.

Terror Upriver

As the early summer sun rose over the eastern flatlands it was bringing promise of a very hot day. The humid conditions along the coast sapped the ambition of the settlers and they hoped for a cooling sea breeze to ease the discomfort.

The mapping and exploration team had prepared the longboat the previous evening, and all was in readiness for the adventure upriver. Ship's officer Edwin Marian would be the expedition leader, and his crew included London Company employees Ustis Clovill, and the Martin brothers, John and George. Private James Dixon was relieved from his tanning and furrier responsibilities and would serve as the weapons expert should those services be needed. A young *Choptank* brave named *Nehatuckwis* was given permission to participate and serve as a guide and translator. He had little English experience but knew a number of the other Native tongues and dialects. The member there by invitation, but not by popular demand was Preacher Robert Hunt. The plan was to catch the neap tide which would help them head up stream until the river overcame the surge. After mapping this point, the team would continue east for two days or until the river was no longer navigable, which ever came first. Both river banks would be mapped, and notes would be scribed identifying noticeable landmarks and other features. Short hikes would be taken up larger streams in search for gold or other valuable stones on the gravel bottoms. Any contact with the local Indian tribes would be cordial and brief. A barrel of trade goods would be taken and shared as an example of good faith. On the third day, the team would float back down river to New Providence.

Meanwhile Sergeant Lusby and his *Choptank* guides canoed eastward up the deep estuary that formed the southern boundary of the promontory the fort was built upon unknowingly on a path that would intersect with the exploration team. Once they reached the head of the inlet they beached their craft at a location that would someday be called "Patrick Plains." By this time the blazing sun was causing Lusby to tire much more quickly than normal. His woolen uniform was very comfortable in cold weather, but added to his discomfort in the heat and humidity. He unbuttoned his red and green tunic which only exposed more of his skin to the insects, mostly mosquitoes and black flies and a particularly obnoxious critter that he had never seen before, which were swarming and voracious. The Sergeant noticed that his Native crew did not seem to be bothered by this nuisance, but the plague was eating him alive. He signaled for the group to stop and sat down in the shade of a pine tree opening his canteen and taking a long draught of his tepid drinking water. One of the Indians noticed his misery and handed him a small amount of green leaves. He motioned the Englishman to rub the leaves over his face, hands, neck and chest. To the White Man it was a miracle. Whatever odor or moisture contained in the leaves it immediately repelled the insects. And the plants had a very pleasant fragrance as well.

He thought to himself, "We've got to get more of this."

This part of the eastern shore of what would later be named Chesapeake Bay by Captain John Smith of Jamestown was as predictable and redundant as any of the other areas they had explored and did not promise any success in finding the minerals needed to make gunpowder. Discovering sulfur was relatively easy because its unpleasant odor would cover a rather wide area and would lead the team to its source.

At this resting spot all the Sergeant could smell was the fragrance of blooming flowers and lush grasses. Lusby did notice how rich and abundant the soil was and could picture English farms someday taming this wild land.

He was jolted back to reality when one of the *Choptanks* spearheading the group suddenly dropped to the ground and motioned the rest to do the same. He whispered, "*Mitsawoket*."

This was terrible news! The *Mitsawoket* normally roamed the area around present day northern Kent County in the state of Delaware, almost a hundred miles to the east. They were extremely war-like, even blood thirsty. To find them so close to *Choptank* country implied that they had run roughshod over a half-dozen other Native villages to reach this point. They could only be after the *M'ne-SKOO-yah* (salt) that the *Choptanks* knew how to acquire. Salt meant wealth to the Indigenous culture … and looking at the size of the war party they weren't coming to trade.

Sergeant Lusby signaled his guides to remain where they were. He then stealthily crawled closer to reconnoiter the situation. What his eyes befell was a very large, all male group resting on the western shore of the present day Choptank River. It was impossible to estimate the size of the force, but easily in the hundreds. Their tent-like structures and lean-tos covered the meadow that extended westward from the river. The bank itself was thick with bark canoes and wooden dugouts. From the designs and markings on the vessels, they had helped themselves from the tribes they had decimated. The *Mitsawoket* were normally a foot people, so acquiring the water craft could only mean one thing: An attack on the *Choptank* village that could be reached from this area only by water. It was imperative that Lusby's team get back to the canoe and return to spread the warning. He was also concerned that such a large raiding party might also attack New Providence.

As he turned to backtrack the way he had come, he was temporarily blinded by the sun in his eyes. The last thing he saw in this life was the shadow of the vicious battle axe that cleaved his forehead and forced blood out his eye sockets.

═══════════

It was slow going for the exploration and mapping team. By the second morning they had covered less than 20 miles upriver. Hiking the streams that flowed into the main watercourse was proving to be time wasted. These streams meandered in a haphazard fashion, flowed sluggishly, and were as much salt water as fresh water. The bottoms and banks were either muddy or sandy, so there was very little chance that any precious metals or minerals would be found there. The biting insects swarmed wherever they walked tormenting them at every step. Expedition leader Marian was considering calling off the venture until colder weather came and decided to give it one more day.

As the longboat skimmed around a large bend in the river, there spreading out before them on the port side was an extensive Indian encampment that crawled from the shore on up a pleasant meadow and disappeared well into the tree line. Whatever the reason, it was a massive group of people. The canoes and watercraft beached by the camp site spread endlessly on up river well out of sight. On the starboard side a relatively small Native village similar to the *Choptanks* in construction clung to the river bank. Later it was determined the settlement was a *gens* (clan) of the powerful *Nanticoke* nation, possibly the only group of Indigenous people in the area that the *Mitsawokets* were unwilling to challenge. Occasionally canoes could be seen ferrying back and forth laden with items that looked like some form of commerce between the village and the encampment. Marian thought to himself, "Well, this is going to slow us down."

He had no idea!

Preacher Hunt could barely contain himself. This would be his first real opportunity to lead a group of savages out of the darkness of paganism. He urged the rowers to pick up the pace and began looking for a good landing spot he could point out to Marian who was at the tiller. He was standing up in the boat and leaning over the gunwale in his enthusiasm.

The expedition's Native guide, *Nehatuckwis*, moved to the prow of the longboat and peered intently at the settlement. He drew back in fear and shouted, *"Mitsawoket! Mitsawoket! Yu-HOM-ne!"* (Turn around!). Marian was not sure what the *Choptank* was crying, but the fear in his eyes spoke loudly.

The Englishmen could see a flurry of activity in the camp ground as the savages on the shore spotted the longboat. Marian extended his spy glass and saw a chilling sight. One of the warriors was haughtily wearing a red and green tunic over his traditional clothing. There was no doubt it was Sergeant Lusby's. "We're turning!" he screamed. "One of those animals is wearing Lusby's uniform. There is only one way he could have gotten it! Row! Row as if your life depended upon it!"

Marian jerked the tiller a quick 90-degrees as the men with the oars stroked so strongly that the longboat almost lifted out of the water ... and there went Hunt unnoticed over the side and under the water. At the same time a cloud of spent arrows splashed around the skiff causing no harm. A swarm of *Mitsawoket* rushed to the canoes and dugouts and prepared to pursue the longboat. Fortunately, they were not so adroit with the water craft and had some confusion getting under way.

The chase was on, and the Indians were rapidly closing the gap! A dozen strong Native warriors heavily armed and rowing a sleek canoe or dugout could travel much faster than a handful of Englishman propelling a longboat never intended for speed. Even though Marian threw the barrel of trade goods over the side it was clear that the pursuers would soon have their prey.

Private Dixon had brought three fusils with him, and all were at the ready. He loaded the first one with a lead shot bigger around than a baseball then rested it against the aft gunwale of the boat next to Marian. He then waited patiently, even eagerly, until the first canoe was in range. Dixon felt special rage when he saw the closest canoe contained the warrior in Lusby's tunic. That renegade began sending arrows in the direction of the fleeing White Men and had no idea what was about to happen. Dixon sighted carefully on the lead canoe, allowed for the distance and cross wind, and fired. The deafening explosion and blinding flash reached the canoe the same time the fusil ball did. The warrior's body, without a head, trembled and then tumbled back into the canoe. The other Indians, covered with blood, screamed in fear and stopped rowing. The next dugout raced past the slowing craft and right into the kill zone of the next fusil – this one filled with as much small shot as Dixon could tamp into the barrel. Again a deafening explosion and blinding flash, and the dugout and its occupants burst into a thousand pieces splashing all over the river's surface. Dixon did not need to fire the third weapon.

Distressed and totally spent, the Englishmen reached New Providence as the longboat scraped to a stop against the jetty. The entire community was there to meet them and to help their exhausted friends out of the boat. The concern on the faces of the exploration party showed clearly that something was very, very wrong. Ship's officer Marian approached Governor Wingfield and despite his fatigue began to review the events that had just unfolded.

He was interrupted by the questioning voice of Ustis Clovill, "Where's Master Hunt?"

Each member of the party looked at the other in silent confusion. Then Private Dixon responded, "He must have fallen overboard!"

The strangest silence followed his statement as the entire compliment of the fort tried to comprehend what had happened. Then somewhere in the crowd, a quiet chuckle started. It spread like the flu and became a ripple of laughter, then a cascade of belly laughs. The colony had lost one of its leaders … and nobody would ever miss him!

The Indian guide, *Nehatuckwis*, was totally at a loss wondering why they had not gone straight to his people and was completely frustrated trying to communicate his concern. Of course, he could not know that a small handful of the friendly Natives traveling with Lusby had managed to escape the *Mitsawoket* and bring the warning to their own people. *Nehtuckwis's* dugout had been pulled onto the sandy beach and he began to feverishly rock it back into the water. Fortunately, Jonas Profit was at the settlement and had learned enough of the *Choptank* language to determine the basis for his anxiety. Wingfield instructed him to go with the Indian and also ordered the Cassen boys, William, George and Thomas, to help with rowing the dugout the three or four miles back to the village. In no time at all, they were on their way at such a rapid pace a wake formed behind the speeding craft.

War!

Preparations for the upcoming conflict with the renegade *Mitsawokets* were happening at New Providence and at the *Choptank* village simultaneously.

An emergency meeting with the remainder of the leadership team was held at the Master's House, and soon a strategy was developed. The Englishmen had a formidable weapon at their disposal: The *Phyllis* and her four cannon. Also, when Marian related how effective Dixon was with the fusils it was clear that the White Men had a considerable advantage concerning fire power. The ship would sail into the mouth of the bay some distance from the village and in the anticipated path of the war party. If one shot from a fusil could destroy an Indian canoe, a blast of cannon fire could do considerably more damage.

The New Providence personnel would be divided into three groups: Captain Coverdale, Brooks-Hughes, and Jonas Profit would organize the defense of the Indian village. Private Quinby would be in charge of protecting the settlement. He would be assisted by the Cassen brothers, William, George and Thomas who made up his hunting team and would be immediately recalled from the village. These three brothers were deadly with the longbow and crossbow and would be significant contributors to the security of the community. The carpenters, Edward Pising and John Capper, as well as William Love the tailor and Thomas Couper the barber were not very adept at the finer art of waging war, but they were Englishmen and would be willing to do anything to help. Magistrate Guilford would remain with the others and provide whatever leadership support he could offer, and Ustis Clovill would stay at his side for extra protection.

Clearly, the main battle would involve the *Phyllis*, so the lion's share of the people would need to be aboard ship. Lieutenant Marian, obviously, would be in charge with the assistance of Wingfield. His mariners, Eldred Parksley, Obadiah Withams, Matthew Tasley, and Jerald Pennyfeather-Grayson would each supervise one of the four cannon. Private Dixon would be at the ready with his fusils in case any of the *Mitsawoket* canoes or dugouts survived the fuselage from the big guns. For lack of a more appropriate descriptor, George Martin, John Martin, and ship's cook Oscar Johnson would serve as assistant seamen and cannon crew. Because of Surgeon Wickinson's deteriorating condition, nobody expected him to participate in any useful way, but hope was held that should he be needed, he would be able to find himself.

The Native dugout sped across the bay in the direction of the village. The Englishmen were pleasantly surprised how easy it was to propel the craft after their experiences with the cumbersome longboats. As it approached the beach a large number of *Choptanks* could be seen in the late afternoon sunshine gathering up what they could carry from their *wig-wams* in anticipation of fleeing to the protection of the forest. Since time beyond memory this was the defensive posturing of the gentle Natives. Lesser chiefs *Weesanusks* and *Pacowassamuck* were among the throng.

Nehtuckwis had only to yell *"Mitsawokets!"* to verify the earlier news spread by Sergeant Lusby's team that a very serious situation was at hand. As the canoe scraped onto the beach the Native guide and Jonas Profit leaped out in preparation to push the craft back into the water so the Cassen boys could fly back to the fort.

A loud voice stopped them in their tracks, *"He-YAH!"* (No!).

The men from New Providence were so shocked, they were speechless. There before their eyes was Captain Coverdale in his striking white deerskin Native attire. He was holding up his arms to get the attention of the panicked Indians and looked like some floating glowing apparition so much taller and so regal appearing. "We are not going to run this time. We are going to fight!" Standing behind him were the twin chiefs, *Tattowin* and *Weanchum*, in their clothing similar to Coverdale's, and next to them was the other Englishman, Brooks-Hughes, contrasting in his blue navy summer uniform.

The *Choptanks* were completely confused not understanding his language. Jonas Profit found himself repeating Coverdale's words and forcefulness in the local tongue. The captain looked pleasantly surprised then asked the English seaman to tell the Indians to get their warriors and meet him on the beach.

Jonas had gotten over his initial shock and without question replied, "I know who the warriors are, sir. The leader is my hunting friend *Asquash,* and their *wig-wams* are near the western edge of the village." At that moment there was a commotion behind the captain. Profit looked past him and said, "In fact, here come the warriors right now!"

At least 30 muscular young braves were running in the direction of the Englishmen heavily armed with their lances, battle axes, and bows. *Asquash,* in his striking leadership attire, had fire in his eyes and a great smile on his face. He never agreed with the pacifist responses of the village chiefs and felt like a coward when he was ordered to stand-down and retire to the forest until the invaders had departed. By now, almost every soul in the settlement, man, woman and child, was crowded on the shore line. Head chief, *Pemetosusk,* slowly walked toward the Englishmen and lesser chiefs, and the villagers opened a pathway for him in great deference.

The Indian guide who had been with the mapping expedition, quickly brought the village elders on board concerning the events his group had experienced that were leading up to the current crisis. The mapping party had seen the endless rows of canoes and watercraft along the river bank, and this information was dire indeed. For the first time in their leadership lives, the five chiefs had to make an on-the-spot determination about how to respond to the impending invasion. Always before, major decisions that might affect the health and welfare of the people were chewed over, discussed and re-discussed over a period of days. Eventually, a tradition was developed that would drive future responses. The head chief and two of the lesser chiefs were comfortable with the 'fly and hide' routine they had always used.

The twin chiefs felt that something different had to be done this time. They had traveled in spirit to the *Mitsawoket* encampment and knew how malevolent they were, and that the raiders would not be content with burning the village and stealing everything of value. They also sensed the death of Sergeant Lusby and most of the Natives who had left with him knowing sadly they would never return to the village. Traditionally, Many Native groups do not wage war at night time, so obviously, it did not take any foresight or extra sensory perception to realize the enemy would be at hand early the following morning.

Remarkably, the Indian leadership team allowed the transformed Englishman to be part of the decision making. A compromise was reached in very brief order: The elder men, women and children would evacuate the village and melt into the forest as before, but the warriors and younger men would stay under the leadership of Coverdale and *Asquash*. The captain realized the Cassen brothers who had helped row the dugout from New Providence would be needed elsewhere and after determining the defensive posturing of the *Choptanks* and sharing the plan he released them to return to the fort to let Wingfield know what would be happening. It was clear that Jonas Profit's greatest use would be to stay at the village to help translate to the Indians the strategy being developed. Strangely, the captain's plan was almost exactly the same one previously worked out at the Master's House.

Captain Coverdale's military mind began to form a picture of the village's defense. Each clan would have a different responsibility. The *Ho-KU-wah-s'ah* clan who harvested the sea for the tribe was comfortable on the water and would be the first line of defense. They would prepare about half of the seaworthy dugouts with bows and lances and meet the onslaught face to face. After a brief foray only to get the invaders attention, they would quickly return to the village leading the enemy into the jaws of a pincer movement.

Coverdale inspired the usually docile Natives by commanding, "I want you to be as fierce as '*Toh Ho-KU-wah*', the Bluefish."

The fishermen could recall having their fingers bit and part of their catch decimated by that aggressive sea creature. Many times they had landed an edible fish to see part of it missing and a huge U-shape bite taken out of its body.

The *Ke-WE-dah-yah-s'ah* who gathered for the tribe would immediately construct a barricade of thorn bushes and brush along the beach and then soak the obstacle with tree sap and plant oils they had collected to help ignite the fires in the *wig-wams*. Two large gaps would be left opened where the *Mitsawokets* would be inclined to pass through as they attacked. The *Choptanks* would hide in the brush as quiet as their totem *TAH-cha*, the deer, and then close the gaps behind the invaders setting the entire barricade on fire to prevent escape. Because of the large piles of firewood and brush already collected for winter use of the village, it was mainly a matter of relocating the flammable materials, and the clan went right to work. The remaining canoes would be stacked head-high and formed into corrals with the openings connected to the gaps in the barricade. The invaders would be trapped in the pens and cut down by the *WE-h'ne-s'ah* hunters.

Evening was rapidly approaching and massive thunderhead clouds were collecting over the western horizon promising bad weather. As the Cassen brothers rowed furiously back toward New Providence, they were heartened to see the *Phyllis* under full sail plying the waters in their direction. The ship did not stop to pick them up, but instructions were shouted that the brothers should continue to the fort and join Private Quinby and his defense team. Nervously eying the growing clouds, they continued their journey in great urgency. There was no way they wanted to be caught in open water at nighttime, in a storm, especially in a small boat like an Indian dugout.

The *Phyllis* reached a point less than a half-mile off the headlands where the village was located and prepared to weigh anchor for the night. Both fore and aft anchors were used to keep the craft with its port gunwale facing south and its prow pointed toward the approaching storm from the west. Looking landward, the crew could see many torches darting here and there signaling that much activity was also occurring on the shore. The sails were wrapped and the whale oil lamps lit, then the small crew went about preparing for the battle. All four cannon were rolled into position and chained into place. Then the ammunition was collected and sorted. The battle plan ordered that large cannon balls would be used until the enemy got close enough to be within range of the smaller and equally deadly smaller lead balls called "grape shot." It was heavy work, but with the assistance of Marian and Wingfield completed in record time. Private Dixon and his fusils would be available should the *Mitsawokets* try to board the ship. Dixon was in no way going to wait until they got that close and planned a shooting display that the Englishmen would never forget.

The first edges of the storm rippled over the ship's deck as night fell. Now the only thing left to do ... was to wait and try to get some rest.

It was difficult to tell if the hour was early morning or still night time. The storm had darkened the sky and was raising angry white caps on the bay. The neap tide was tugging at the ship's anchors trying to push the craft further into the bay, but she was holding nicely. As morning light seemed to have a bit more success over the storm's darkness, the winds moaned in the ship's riggings and a warm stinging rain began to fall. Marian and Wingfield were on the poop deck searching the southern horizon with the spyglass to get a first glimpse at the marauding renegades.

At first it appeared as a large shadow, then as the undefined mass grew closer through the driving rain and flashing lightening, it was obviously a huge armada of dugouts and canoes, at least two hundred or more. Without the telescope the vision could have been likened to an army of black ants floating on leaves or branches. Marian observed that a number of the water craft seemed to be having trouble negotiating in the stormy winds and occasionally he would see one tip over and dump its occupants into the cold dark, hungry waters.

As the *Mitsawokets* paddled into range of the cannon a bloody massacre ensued. The bay was so thick with canoes and dugouts that every shot was a hit. The frail water craft would explode from the impact of the cannon balls sending pieces of wood and human bodies in all directions. As the wave of humanity grew closer to the *Phyllis,* the projectiles became grape shot that was even more deadly. Its kill zone would expand as the lead balls sped away from the cannon muzzle and as many as four or five dugouts or canoes would be destroyed in one burst of gunpowder. The roiling sea was red from blood and thick with pieces of debris. Some mangled Indians would be able to pull their shattered bodies onto the floating masses and became targets for Dixon's deadly eye or sitting ducks for the *Choptanks* who had rowed out from the village to confront the attackers. The current from the tide also washed a large number of them toward the shore where the *Choptank* braves were wading in knee deep water with their battle axes at the ready. A steady symphony of "thunks," "whacks," and "bonks" not unlike the sounds of a sledge hammer smashing a watermelon could be heard as *Mitsawoket* skulls were crushed.

As the morning sun began to win its own battle with the roiling black clouds, a strange silence settled heavily over the site of the battle, even the storm had moved away. Then a heart-lifting victory chant in strong and robust masculine voices rose from the near shore and flowed outward to the *Phyllis* and beyond:

> *"Nah-DON-pe TOH-kah*
> *WEEN-yon KAH-gah-pe!"*

"Charged the foe,
But I made a woman of him!"

The chant was repeated over and over in a dizzying hypnotic fashion as the village men danced almost to exhaustion, and the joyous words called the *Choptank* elder men, women, and children out of hiding and back to the community. Great shouts of exaltation and relief emerged from the mouths of the families as they rushed to the beach to greet their warriors. The gatherer clan was so excited that they lit the brush barrier anyway and it roared happily into flames from one end to the other.

Never before or since has an Indian nation bested so many of its enemies with no loss of life.

But … all was not well!

The victor's joy was cut short when one of the revelers shouted, "*SHO-tah!*" ("Smoke!") and pointed to the southeast in the direction of New Providence. Even though the English community was almost four miles away the *Choptanks* could see a massive, black billowing cloud of smoke rising up that could signify only one thing, a huge fire was in progress. At that same moment, the *Phyllis* heeled around and opened her sails making haste back to the fort.

Clearly, something was very, very wrong.

Asquash shouted an order to his warriors and also quickly instructed the *Ho-KU-wah-s'ah* boat clan to prepare to shove off. Coverdale, Brooks-Hughes and Profit leaped into the lead canoe and in moments a small flotilla of *Choptank* dugouts was plying the bay at great speed. The strong arms of the Natives and the sleek construction of the dugouts allowed the villagers to overtake the sailing vessel and arrive at the estuary by the fort well in advance of the rest of the Englishmen. As they rowed around the headland, a sickening sight awaited them: New Providence was in flames. The grounds were strewn with the bloody bodies of both renegades and White Men. A vicious hand-to-hand battle must have occurred and there did not appear to be any survivors on either side. Despite ship's officer Marian's assumption, the *Mitsawoket* were indeed aware of the settlement and a small army of them in coordination with the main war party attacked the undermanned fort from the southern arm of the forest.

As the dugouts scraped onto the beach, both *Choptank* and White Men jumped onto the ground, weapons at the ready, and ran to the scene of the disaster. The Englishmen were not scalped, so the invaders must have had to retreat quickly. They didn't even take their dead with them. *Asquash* determined that they may have fled when they saw the canoes coming. An expert tracker because of his years hunting, he surveyed the ground at the edge of the forest and found the trail leading away from the settlement. The wet earth easily displayed their foot prints, and there was a thick trail of blood which implied that some of them were badly injured. He barked out an angry order, waved his arm, and the Natives took off in a dead run in pursuit of the murderers.

The distraught Englishmen began to sadly collect their dead comrades and lay them tenderly on the meadow. Their bodies were defiled with arrows or deep gashes from the war clubs, stone knives and spear points, yet as the warming sun broke through the waning storm clouds and shone on their faces there was a strange peace on their countenances, and they looked like angels.

When they found Private Quinby, there were over two dozen dead *Mitsawoket* warriors strewn on the blood soaked ground in grotesque pieces within his kill zone. The quiver of arrows for this longbow was empty and his fusil was split open. He must have tamped an incredible amount of corned black powder and bird shot into the weapon for his last shot. The three Cassen brothers had formed a protective wall around Quinby and each man's body was hacked and slashed so many times they were almost unrecognizable. The four settlers had tumbled together in death and appeared like a carven monument commemorating the great battle. William Love and Thomas Couper had been cornered near the dining hall and fell together by the kitchen door. Love, with a hideous grimace on his ashen face and an arrow impaled deeply in his right eye, was holding a large blood-stained iron frying pan with a half dozen Indians laying at his feet with their heads or faces smashed in. Couper had swung his weapon with so much force that the iron skillet was impaled in the skull of one of the attackers and the handle was broken off in his cold hand. The savage's mouth had been hit so hard some of his teeth were sticking out the back of his neck.

A painful moan startled the Englishmen, and they ran to the Master's House where it seemed to be coming from. The door was broken in, but the building itself was still relatively intact. Apparently, the raiders had not had time to set it afire before fleeing. Ustiss Clovill was crumpled dead in the doorway with a half dozen arrows all in his back or buttocks imbedded deeply in his body implying they had been shot at close range. He was holding a bloodstained shovel that must have served as his weapon during the massacre. The mangled and dead *Mitsawokets* were piled on the floor and against the walls. Some of them had been decapitated or had arms or hands severed and strewn everywhere. Clovill must have been a raging banshee in his final moments. Sitting on the cold stone floor in a pool of blood was the very weak and dazed Magistrate Cuthbert Guilford an ugly wound above his right ear and his right eye crushed shut. He screamed in fear and covered his face as he saw the shadows of three men enter the doorway.

Captain Coverdale, forgetting that he was still in his *Choptank* attire, knelt down by the shaking White Man. Guilford cried out again then began to choke and cough. His blood-streaked face turned blue and his left eye bulged out. He clutched his chest in excruciating pain and toppled over ... truly frightened to death.

Brooks-Hughes began to cry as he carefully lifted Clovill's battered body out of the doorway. Jonas Profit reached down to help and bellowed a litany of curses on the murderers.

All three Englishmen were shocked when they heard: "Mates?" coming from the closed bedroom of the expedition administrator.

"Who is it?" shouted Coverdale, "Are you well?"

There were sounds of scraping and moving something heavy and then the door slowly opened. Much to the amazement of the three White Men, out limped both carpenters, John Capper and Edward Pising. They were still holding their axes stained with blood and brains and cluttered with tufts of human hair. Both were bloodied and badly injured ... but both were definitely very alive. The end of an arrow was sticking out of Pising's thigh, but he was not about to let that slow him down. All five men embraced each other in unbounded joy.

The carpenters had fought their way to the Master's House and joined Clovill intending to make their last stand there. The door was barricaded shut, and as they smashed it down they found Guilford cowering in fear by the fire place. A large group of *Mitsawokets* had harassed them all the way and poured into the building behind the desperate strangers.

A terrible battle at close quarters ensued with at least a dozen enemies falling to the shovel and axes of the settlers. The losses were not all confined to the invaders. Clovill's death must have been excruciatingly painful, both carpenters were repeatedly slashed and shot, and the Magistrate's last lucid moments ended with a massive battle axe blow alongside his temple.

The two magnificent gentlemen carpenters would be the only survivors on either side.

The *Phyllis* scraped against the jetty and was immediately made secure. Those victorious crew men were angered and saddened by what they saw. They poured off the ship carrying any weapon they could find hungry for revenge. At that same moment the *Choptank* victory song flowed from the forest as *Asquash* and his warriors emerged carrying two large *Mitsawoket* blankets. They shook the blankets open and at least forty severed heads rolled out along the ground bouncing like soccer balls. The village warriors had caught up with the injured and retreating invaders and massacred every one of them leaving their bodies for the creatures of the forest and bringing their heads back like painted, brown, round trophies. *Asquash*, his English knife stained black from invader blood, approached Jonas Profit his eyes glistening with tears. Despite his heady victory he felt great pain and compassion for his English friend, and both strong unflinching men embraced each other in shared silent anguish. Even as a child the *Choptank* warrior had never cried before.

As that dreadful day came to a close, Master Edward Winfield cloistered himself in the ship captain's cabin and quietly entered the names of his lost expedition team members on the obituary ledger after the names of the two who had died during the construction of New Providence. It was his heart's fondest hope that he would not have to add any more names to this page:

London Company Employees:
  Kellam Throgmorton
  Francis Midwinter

  - - -

  Master Cuthbert Guilford – Magistrate
  Master Robert Hunt - Preacher
  Thomas Couper – Barber and Assistant Cook
  William Love – Tailor and Assistant Cook
  William Cassen – Hunter
  George Cassen – Hunter
  Thomas Cassen – Hunter
  Ustis Clovill – Master's House Protector

Fusilier Detachment:
  Sergeant Bartholomew Lusby – Commander and Leadership Team
  Corporal Kenneth Quinby – Senior Hunter

  (He took the liberty to promote Quinby post-humously hoping that if there were any death benefits for his family, they would be increased due to his rank.)

Crew of the *Phyllis Redoubtable*
  Able-bodied Seaman Percy Exum – Missing

Seeing these men's names penned onto the ledger provided him with a tangible image of the deep loss he felt; and he broke down ... privately, quietly, and professionally.

The gruesome activity of disposing of the *Mitsawoket* corpses strewn across the grounds of the fort was given to the *Choptanks* who gladly accepted the responsibility. It was impossible to make an accurate body count, because the fusils had shattered many of them into unrecognizable pieces. But almost 100 Indian invaders could be identified. The Englishmen's peaceful and friendly Native neighbors proved to be shockingly irreverent toward their enemies. The severed heads were piked on spears and inserted into the ground at the edge of the forest, faces turned away from the settlement. Little did they know that this ritual was not so uncommon back in England pertaining to convicted criminals. The bodies of the invaders killed by the White Men were dragged onto the meadow, stacked unceremoniously face-down on a mound of brush and tree limbs, and cremated into a pile of grey ashes.

The culture of the *Choptanks* dictated that their honored dead must be buried in the Mother of All Waters, and this seemed very fitting to the surviving Englishmen, most of whom were mariners and deeply appreciated the burial at sea ceremonies. The most marvelous and amazing funeral soon followed as ship's officer Marian and Governor Wingfield led the Christian ceremony and *Asquash* and his warriors offered up the plaintive death chants of their people. The sea was as calm as glass and the most beautiful sunset the men could remember added to the poignancy of the worship service. As the bodies were respectfully laid into the water a cool and gentle breeze from the west wrapped its arms around the survivors caressing their pain and blowing away their grief. Head chief *Pemetosusk* chanted the plaintive benediction at the closing of the ceremony. If it were translated into English it would have said, "We have walked together in the shadow of a rainbow."

Toh we-CHOSH-tah (The Blue Man)

The last earthly sounds Vicar Robert Hunt, the expedition's Man of the Cloth, heard as he leaned over the gunwale of the longboat during that fateful summer of 1608 was their *Choptank* Indian guide *Nehatuckwis'* fear-laden scream, *"Mitsawokets! Mitsawokets!"*

This band of renegade Indians was the scourge of the central Chesapeake Bay region in the 1600's as they roamed westward from what some day would be called Delaware. From the massive size of their encampment and all the water craft they had stolen from other villages on their raids, it was clear they were out for blood and had the wealth of the *Choptanks* in mind.

The soul-chilling waters of the mighty river reached its hungry arms to pull Master Hunt out of the longboat then deeper and deeper into the waiting darkness. In fear and desperation, he furiously fought to reach the surface and possible salvation. To no avail.

His water-soaked woolen coat, animal skin trousers and blouse, and heavy boots were his anchors of doom. A suffocating sense of helplessness and fatigue stumbled blindly erasing his thoughts ... Silence.

Then ... a bright light – cold and comfortless flowed through his being.

Followed a frighteningly familiar voice, *"Robert! Why are you here?"*

"Father?"

"Robert!" it repeated, this time in remorseless accusation. *"Why are you here!"*

"I-I'm not sure, father." Hunt questioned. "I-I think I drowned or something ... I can't remember."

"It's not your time, you young whelp!" the voice screamed in utter despair. *"There is still hope for you ..."*

Then Robert recognized the form of his abusive long-dead father emerging from the merciless light, holding a heavy iron chain and opened manacle. As he approached, other figures appeared from the mist, shackled in a continuous row, wailing in endless hopelessness and pain. He saw his grandfather stumbling aimlessly behind his father, but the rest of the personages were formless wraiths.

"This is our fate for all eternity," his suffering father choked. *"We were hard and cold to our Fellow Man and our loved ones. We were called to preach the reconciliation of Jesus Christ, yet we spewed guilt, damnation, obedience and prejudice. We drove away the very people we were commanded to save ... this is our punishment!"*

Then ... a long, unbearable silence – broken only by the clanking of iron links.

The baleful figure of his father rose up menacingly, eyes blazing red, as he thrust the end of the chain toward Master Hunt. His terrible voice wailed like an animal in excruciating pain, *"Do you wish to join us?"*

Hunt reeled back feeling more fear than ever before. He covered his eyes unwilling to see what would happen next. "No! No!"

A calm, gentle voice seemed to wash through his trembling soul, *"Then walk another road, my beloved son, you have been given a second chance ..."*

Something grievous and heavy was repeatedly pounding on Master Hunt's back. Strange voices, muffled and unrecognizable manifested a formless shroud around him. Suddenly, unbearable pain flashed through his body as cold salty water burned his lungs and throat and gushed out his mouth and nose ... then blessed darkness.

━━━━━━

Weak and disoriented, Hunt's fevered mind crawled toward reality not knowing if he were dead or alive. His senses seemed to be turned inward with only the slightest awareness of his surroundings. He felt he could open and close his eyes but there was no difference – only blackness deeper than the Heart of Satan. Cold salty tears welled-up as he succumbed to the sense of hopelessness that slowly, but noticeably, crept through his body.

"I'm in Hell," he thought, "For all eternity ... it will be this way. Oh, God, please forgive me ..."

━━━━━━

Master Hunt did indeed drown in the unforgiving Choptank River. Its freezing waters immediately shocked his body into a state of suspended animation. The river's timeless flow rolled his hapless corporal existence toward the nearing shoreline where it came to rest in the rapidly growing shallows. In a cycle almost as old as the Earth itself, the river level surrendered to the ebbing tide unclothing much of her sandy and rocky shoulders until the incoming neap tide would again reclaim its due.

Two *Nanticoke* Indian grandmothers, occasionally looking nervously at the massive *Mitsawoket* encampment on the farther shore, were foraging along the exposed river bank for mussels and stumbled across this strange, dark shape and were shocked to see it was a human being. Strangely dressed and shod and completely motionless, but nevertheless worth investigating. They approached the body and fell back in awe: Its skin was the most sacred color of the tribe: Blue.

One of the elder women spoke softly to her companion, "*Nantaquak*, this must truly be a Sacred Spirit-Man. The village must be notified immediately."

Dead, the *Nanticoke* Medicine People knew the ancient art of mummification and would preserve and honor his corporal remains for all time. Alive, the Blue Man would represent a gift from the Creator of immeasurable value and great luck for the village.

The elder ladies gently, and with deep respect, moved the heavy body onto the grassy beach. One stayed with this strange personage while the other scurried back to the community to get help. The grandmother who remained, for her entire life wise to the ways of River People, rolled the man onto his stomach and began to pound heavily on his back. In both amazement and relief, the cold brackish water gushed out his mouth and nose, and there was an almost imperceptible flicker of life.

The young *Nanticoke* men respectfully carried the remarkable *Toh we-CHOSH-tah* (Blue Man) to the village's *Peh-ZHU-tah won-KEH-yah* (Medicine Lodge) where the elder Medicine Women prepared to minister to their honored guest. They gently laid the cold body on a plush animal robe resting atop the floor of thick loblolly pine boughs and kindled the fire pit in the center of the lodge. The grandmothers who found him on the river bank, gentle *Nantaquak* and her sister *Kuskarawaok*, were allowed to participate in the healing process and began removing his mud-caked and still icily wet clothing and footwear. All gazed in complete amazement as his entire body was an eerie light blue color. They had never seen a White Man before, and the lack of circulation within the body added to the illusion of something unearthly, almost angelic. A strange amulet worn as a necklace increased even more their sense of awe as it sparkled in the fire light. The

Nanticoke people knew nothing of metal or the Christian cross. This was truly a marvelous omen.

━━━━━━━━━

Time had lost all meaning to Master Hunt. There was absolutely no sense of its passing. Again, a vague and excruciatingly painful sense of consciousness. This time he felt heat, unbearable heat that seemed to be feasting on his stinging flesh. His very basic survival instincts screamed for him to move, to get away, but his arms were useless and there was no feeling at all in his legs. He could not even turn his head. For the first time in his life he was completely helpless, and despair consumed his very being. In silent anguish he begged for it all to end.

Then, something was changing …

The total and spirit-draining darkness seemed to give way to a barely perceptible orange glow, and he sensed motion. It was at this point that the worse pain he had experienced in his entire life racked his throat and lungs and seemed to tear him into ragged pieces. Mercifully, he felt himself losing consciousness as his ravaged body sought relief from the terrible onslaught.

He did not hear the strange sound: *"e-YEH ne* … (He lives.)"

━━━━━━━━━

As the fire flared, its warmth and orange light rapidly filled the interior of the small lodge. The Medicine Women scurried around preparing the healing herb baths and wrapping the body in tanned animal skin robes. Heavy river rocks formed a ring around the blaze in the fire pit and soon glowed from the adjacent heat. Some of the herb mixtures were in clay pots and were placed directly in the flames until they began to bubble and steam. When instructed, *Kuskarawaok* carefully ladled the herb liquid over the rocks which immediately transformed into fragrant, but stingingly suffocating steam filling the structure's interior. Despite the many repetitions of this process over the years, the first effects of the super-heated steam caused the Medicine Women to gasp. They knelt by the motionless body and began to bathe it with the hot herb mixtures using their tender hands to cup the liquid and spread it from hair to feet as they chanted their ancient and hypnotic healing song:

> *Tah-ee-vah Nah-mah-Eeyoni.*
> *Tzeh-ee-hoot-zittoo.*
> *Nah-mah-Eeyoni*

> By night I go on my way unseen.
> Then am I holy.
> Then have I power to heal men.

One of the grandmothers seemed to linger overly long in the genital area of the Blue Man causing the others to chuckle lasciviously. Feigning disappointed because of no visible response, she grumbled, *"e-YEH ne? He-YAH."* (He lives? Not at all.)

━━━━━━━━

The concept of "Indian Time," even today, crashes headlong into the values of the White World. "On time" to the traditional Native American was when the task was done or when the people were all together. Vicar Robert Hunt slowly and painfully re-emerged into the corporal world of the early 1600's, but how long it took for this to happen was never measured or even considered an important aspect of the healing process. The devoted Medicine Women knew the doctoring ceremonies and the ancient procedures and worked tirelessly to bring this Holy Spirit-Man, the sacred *Toh We-CHOSH-tah,* (blue man) back to the reality of sound, sight, touch, taste, and smell.

The pain of the return journey was unbearable. Imagine the feeling in your arm or leg when it falls 'asleep' then as the circulation begins to return that grievous almost electric shock as the nerves respond to the previously blocked impulses from the brain and spinal column. Compound this agony over your entire body and over and over again as the nervous system reestablishes itself. Hunt's pitiful groans of anguish echoed through the long village nights bringing tears to the kindly people. But … at least they knew he was still alive.

In the fullness of time, Master Hunt regained the use of his arms and legs. He could sit up in the Medicine Lodge and sip the warm gratifying repast the grandmothers prepared for him. They truly and deeply loved this Blue Man and even a British gentleman such at the Vicar, unloved his entire life, stolid and closed, could sense this feeling of warmth and appreciation. His winding pathway back from Death's Door had broken down many of the walls he had built around his heart, and he felt a newness that brought a sense of happiness and inspiration running lightly through his soul.

The interior of the Medicine Lodge was the entire world of the Englishman. Day and night had no meaning whatsoever in its somber darkness. As awareness removed the shackles of unconsciousness he could see that the shadows hovering around him were not spirits, but real people. Their skin was dark and their shining eyes were like bits of the coal mined from the green hills of his Welsh childhood. The constant pain from his body seeking to regain some level of normalcy tormented him. The effort to breathe was excruciating; but even that was beginning to subside. He tried to talk to his ministers, but his useless throat could only muster a faint and gasping breath. Even if he could talk, the Medicine Women would not have known what he was trying to communicate.

As this realization sank in, for the first time Hunt became a listener and endeavored to translate the strange language that floated in and out of his cognizance. When the gentle women would spoon small portions of the soup-like mixture into his mouth, they would say, "*WO-dah.*" This must mean 'food' or 'eat.' When they were finished bathing him and would wrap him in the luxurious fur blankets, they would say, "*eesh-DE-mah.*" He determined this must mean 'rest' or 'sleep.' So much like a small baby who suddenly perceives that his world is more than his mother's breast, the Vicar became aware of who and what he was. If he could only piece together the 'where' and 'when,' his resurging confidence would help place his feet on the road to recovery.

Eventually, he felt strong enough to venture outside the Medicine Lodge, and his eyes so long in muted darkness, recoiled in shock as the late summer sunlight bathed his pallid features. He stumbled backward against the lodge and felt the strong hands of the grandmothers as they carefully sat him on the ground and waited patiently as he recovered. Eyes squinting, he looked at his arms and torso. Much to his amazement, he was clothed in total Native attire. His tunic was a beautiful soft tan color decorated with small pink and white shells and hand drawn images including a repeated motif consisting of his sacred cross symbol in a connected pattern. His trousers were made of the most marvelous white deerskin, soft and pliable with colorful stitching along the seam lines. His footwear was perfectly fitting moccasins decorated with variegated dyed strands of hand-woven thread.

Despite the incongruity of the garments, he felt a long-missed chuckle grow from his stomach. "And such a fine figure I now cut," he thought. "A proper English Christian gentleman looking like a bloody pagan."

Vicar Robert Hunt's recovery was an event of great celebration for the *Nanticoke* village. Their sacred *Toh we-CHOSH-tah* could walk among them. This was truly the most remarkable blessing the community could ever recall. It did not seem to matter that there were communication problems. Some villagers considered it impudence and sacrilege to even look at his face, no less try to talk with him.

As with every blessing or revelation there is a price to pay, and Robert Hunt's ransom was no different. His booming Welsh voice was now not much more than a strained and rather hoarse whisper. His lungs and throat never totally recovered from the onslaught of the drowning. His complexion, once healthy and so similar to the thousands of other Englishmen of his day was now an ashen white with powder blue undertones. The veins in his face, neck and hands striving to find new pathways bulged against the outer skin layers adding to his unusual appearance. Until the end of his life on earth, he was tormented by nightmares and re-lived over and over the excruciating feelings of fear and suffocation of his drowning. His strange after-death experience with his father was lost in the depths of his tormented soul, but he could not deny that he was no longer the same person that was claimed by the cruel river so long ago.

———————————————

One early autumn day, Master Hunt was resting in the warming sun by the bank of the great river that had tried to claim him. It seemed almost dreamlike as the English longboat emerged from the morning mist and gently scraped onto the sandy beach.

"Master Robert Hunt, I presume?"

Hunt responded with some hesitation, "Captain John Smith?"

Unexplained Actions Offered in Love

The Englishmen roamed around their former home trying to determine what they could salvage from the destruction. The Indian trade goods aboard the *Phyllis*, mainly furs, *to-bac*, and salt, could still be considered as assets, but almost everything not stored in the dormitory or Master's House, except items made of metal or glass, had gone up in smoke. The *Mitsawoket* had only begun to loot the settlement when the *Choptanks* arrived, so some of the European trading materials were strewn about the grounds and could be reclaimed. In fact, the glass beads were everywhere making the common area look like a beautiful sparkling garden.

Governor Wingfield personally tallied what was left and felt confident that one more trading session with their Native friends would put the venture back in the fiscal black. His heart quietly called to him, "Go home." So the next efforts of his faithful expedition team would be directed toward that end.

The men slept aboard the *Phyllis* trying to ignore the stench of burnt bodies and smoldering structure fires. The clean air and healthful living had re-invigorated their olfactory nerves and they were much more attuned to odors and fragrances, and much less tolerant of the hygiene practices of some of the contingent. Meanwhile, the vestiges of Governor Wingfield's leadership team met in the Master's House. It was just himself and ship's officer Marian. The house was still in a shambles, but cleaned up as much as possible concerning the amount of time available. The stained floor and walls would always be a tribute to the events that occurred there that fateful day.

The two expedition leaders took stock in their situation. Wingfield's decision to return to England was accepted by Marian without question. Much preparation would have to be made before departure, and they would need help from the *Choptanks* in procuring enough provisions for the months-long journey. Something unexplainable had happened to Captain Coverdale and he returned to the village in his strange clothing with the Native warriors. It was becoming clear he was not going to join them on the trip home. Marian suggested that the governor enter their military officer on the obituary log as "missing" so there would not be any sort of inquiry when they returned.

They looked over the roster of surviving Englishmen and were heartened that all the mariners were available for the return voyage except the missing Exum. The carpenters and the surgeon could no longer be considered as 'able bodied'. Seaman Tasley had done his best to patch-up the injured men. No leeches! It was clear they had lost enough blood. Removing the arrow from Pising's thigh proved not so difficult because there was no stone head to the arrow. It was just a shaft of wood. He gave the carpenter plenty of rum before the surgery to ease his pain. The brave woodsman was singing a tasteless tavern ballad in his rich Welsh bass voice as the assistant doctor worked on him. This gentle man of the wood craft would never be able to walk normally again and would represent a human testament to the trials and tribulations of trying to establish an English foothold in the Americas.

Of the original crew of the London Company the Martin brothers were the last capable of assisting during the voyage home. Only one of their fusiliers was still alive, Private James Dixon; but his prowess with weaponry made him as formidable as a squad of soldiers. All in all, there would be enough strong arms to make the long and arduous sailing back to England.

The following morning, Wingfield and Marian met with the expedition members and shared their plan. The discussion was met with shouts of joy and anticipation ... except for some unknown reason, Brooks-Hughes. Wingfield instructed Jonas Profit to take the artist with him to the village and arrange for another trading parlay. He was willing to give up every remaining trade item to turn a profit and gain the necessities needed to get back to England.

━━━━━━━━━

The news of the Englishmen's impending departure was not met with a similar joyous reaction by the *Choptank* chiefs. The five village leaders met in *Pemetosusk's* home with a grim sense of uneasiness. The head chief allowed each lesser leader to express his feelings and concerns.

Likeable *Weesanusks* was the first to speak, "It grieves me to think that our good friends will be leaving us. I feel as if they are my brothers. They have saved our village at the expense of their own. No greater love can a people show another." His friendly eyes filled with tears and he turned away ashamedly.

Pacowassamuck who initially was fearful of the *Ha-KAH-sha-nah* echoed his friends concerns, "The White Men are fearless warriors and as ferocious as *Shong-TOK-cha* the wolf in the heart of battle. Already our women sing chants of their great strength. The Creator must have made them from the same tree he made our own. They are the white inner wood and the *Choptanks* are the brown outer wood. No tree can stand without its heart wood or without its skin. We know that sooner or later the *Susquehannock* raiders from the home of the cold winds will be upon us as so many times before.

Each time they burn our village and send our people into the
forest. How long must we endure that shame? Our strange
brothers must not leave."

Tattowin and *Weanchum*, who so many times seemed to
know the right thing to do despite the fact that they seldom
shared it, were the next to speak. "We are still haunted by
our dream. We see the *Ha-KAH-sha-nah* destroying our land
and raping our waters. They swarm everywhere like ants. We
see their heavy black boots crushing the skulls of our infants.
The anguished cries of our women and children still burn in
our hearts. Our clear skies are brown and red with smoke.
There are no trees, just piles of white bones."

Then the twins offered a decision that would change the
lives of the Englishmen and *Choptank*s forever, "They must
not be allowed to return to their Mother Land. They will
tell their people about the richness and bounty that is here.
They will show them the furs and *M'ne-SKOO-yah* (Salt).
They will defile our *to-bac* ceremony. The others will be filled
with greed and will come here and take everything from us.
We now know something of their weapons and fierceness.
It is clear that the *Ha-KAH-sha-nah* in our dream are not
our brothers of the battle, but it is very clear the others are
waiting."

Pemetosusk thought quietly for a moment, then responded,
"They are now very few. I believe that *Asquash* and his
warriors could easily kill them in their sleep. There would
be no pain, and our people would honor them forever."

The four lesser leaders looked at their chief with wide,
incredulous eyes. *Weesanusks,* who had been his friend since
childhood could not believe what he was hearing, "There
must be another way!" he protested. "These White Men are a
part of us and we are a part of them. To destroy them would
be to destroy ourselves!"

Pacowassamuck made a point that was so obvious the others had missed it. "They cannot return to their homeland without their great canoe. Destroy the canoe, and they must remain."

A plan to that end was contrived so cleverly that it was hard to believe such honest and upstanding village leaders could be so devious: A sumptuous meal would be prepared to honor the fallen warriors from New Providence and served in the men's lodge. The young women of the village would be allowed to leave the moon-time lodge and would prepare and serve the food, giving the White Men their first glimpse of the fairest of the tribe. All the Englishmen would be invited to attend with a promise that after the ceremony a protracted trading parlay would follow. Chances are the visitors would sail their large craft to the village to facilitate the off-loading of the English trading goods and the lading of what they would receive from the *Choptanks*. While the visitors were enjoying the hospitality of the tribe, their ship would be burned to the waterline. If for some reason they did not bring their great canoe a group from the *Ho-KU-wah-s'ah* clan would secretly travel to the settlement during the celebration and destroy it at its moorage.

―――――――――――

It was a most beautiful mid-Atlantic autumn evening as the *Phyllis* weighed anchor a short distance off the village shoreline. A gentle breeze from the southeast and the steady flow of the ebbing tide easily coaxed the ship into position. The entire village was there to greet their English friends, and the elder ladies were chanting their pleasant welcoming song:

> *Ho! Le-ci-YAH ni-CO-pi*
> *Ho! Le-ci-YAH ni-CO-pi*

The five chiefs were dressed in their finest regalia, and Captain Coverdale stood head and shoulders above them looking especially striking in his white deerskin attire. His rich black hair had grown to shoulder length and his skin was tastefully tanned from the summer sun. With no beard, it was difficult to tell if he were European or Native.

The two longboats scraped onto the beach and many of the *Choptanks* flocked around them to help their honored guests. There was no reason to keep a sentry on the ship, so all the Englishmen would be able to participate in the feast and ceremony. This was the first time among the Indians for some of the crew, and they were taken aback by the attention and friendliness of the people. Also, they felt some claustrophobia from the throng moving in and out of their comfort zones.

It was a short and congenial walk from the village to the men's lodge, and soon everyone found their places for the meal. After the traditional *to-bac* ceremony, lovely *Watsawasoo* gently clapped her hands just one time, and at least a dozen young Native women emerged from the back of the room carrying everything needed for this great banquet. Despite the fact that *Choptank* women could not necessarily be considered as very attractive, these were as beautiful and as graceful as Grecian statues to the Europeans as they lithely glided from person to person serving the sumptuous and perfectly prepared food. Jonas Profit looked around for his hunting companion, *Asquash,* but he was nowhere to be found. He was soon engaged in the pleasantness of the evening and did not give it another thought.

It was truly an event never to be forgotten. For generations, the *Choptanks* sang of that fateful night.

Asquash accepted the responsibility to scuttle the *Phyllis*. This would be an extremely important and possibly difficult task, and he would not delegate it to anyone else. His resolve was clear that this action must be done, but he also grieved for his English friends. Freedom was the most important aspect of his life, and he knew that the visitors would soon be in a velvet prison never again to see their homes or loved ones.

Members of the *Ho-KU-wah-s'ah* clan quietly rowed the dugout to the side of the ship, and the Indian warrior deftly leapt aboard with the smoldering torch. He worked his way down into the heart of the craft in an effort to determine the best place to start the arson procedure. As he quietly roamed the interior hallway he saw the ship's log resting on the captain's desk. Paper and the strange symbols scribed on it were unknown to the locals and considered magical and almost holy. It would be sacrilege to destroy such a wonderful icon, so he carefully closed it and held it under his arm. Someday this action would come back to haunt the very fibers of the connection between the Natives and the Englishmen.

Then a most shocking event occurred!

He heard a high pitched, maniacal laugh rolling down the aisle way from the prow of the ship. There was not supposed to be anybody aboard that night! As he edged closer to the source he saw the most pitiful sight of his entire life: There in the faint glimmer of a single whale oil lamp was a shell of a man that had once been Surgeon Wickinson lounging on a stack of pelts. Barely human appearing, this wretched creature's months' long growth of hair and beard was filthy and matted. His mucous-thickened cough seemed to rack his frail body and his yellowed teeth were barely perceptible in a mouth that wasn't much more than a hole. The small room was filled with smoke and the floor was littered with partially burned *to-bac* leaves.

The apparition was deeply engrossed in a conversation with someone who existed only in his mind, "Sod you, Exum! I never thought about that … Here have another *to-bac* you scurrilous dog."

As the shell of the leech craft purveyor leaned toward the lamp flame to ignite the rolled leaf, the pile of furs slipped and he tumbled against the wall knocking the fire onto the floor. Burning whale oil splashed everywhere; on the floor, on the furs, and on Wickinson's filthy clothes. In seconds he was engulfed in flames … and he didn't even scream.

His miserable body was only a shadow in the raging fire, his mouth grimacing in a painful grin of death.

Asquash backed away from the terrible scene, turned and ran up the stairway in great haste. In seconds the dugout was speedily plying its way toward the beach. As he looked back in the darkness, the flames were already visible in the ship's port holes. A horrific explosion occurred as the flames found the first barrel of gun powder; and as a massive ball of Hell fire rose into the black sky, the warrior could see the flaming mizzen mast slowly toppling into the sea. The deafening sound reached the men's lodge almost immediately, and after a few seconds of shocked silence, the Englishmen ran back up the path to the village followed closely by their Native hosts. As they reached the beach the scene of devastation was heart breaking. A second barrel exploded sending the near gunwale in thousands of pieces in direction of the shore. The spectators ducked and shouted in pain as the wood splinters and shattered pieces of hot metal showered all around them. One more massive explosion followed, and the sturdy *Phyllis* sighed sadly, and in tongues of all consuming fire keeled-over and disappeared into the Mother of All Waters.

The silence that followed was deafening.

CHAPTER V ...
RESTORATION

As the Phoenix Rises

In voiceless shock, the Englishmen shuffled heavily back to the men's lodge with the Native leaders. The explosions in the night had called every single *Choptank* villager from his or her home, and the throng parted silently and respectfully as the group passed by. A soul-wrenching wail began to rise from the voices of the elder women as they grieved for their new friends. It started low and plaintive then rose to a high crescendo of pain and anguish. The chant repeated itself again and again, and each phrase drove a spike of despair deeper and deeper into the hearts of the perpetrators as well as the aggrieved. Despite the perceived necessity of the action, the chiefs were fraught with guilt and were glad the warm breath of the night hid their reddened eyes and expressions of regret.

Asquash had quietly returned to his *wig-wam* during the turmoil and in its comforting darkness tried to deal with the shame he felt. Granted, he had not actually started the fire; but he was a man of strong character and a trusted friend who would never harm anyone he cared for. He would have caused the destruction if needed, and he was not used to the contradictions of feelings swarming through his thoughts. For the second time in his life the powerful manly Native warrior felt tears well up in his eyes.

"Am I becoming a woman?" he mused.

———

As the men entered the darkening lodge, head chief *Pemetosusk* and Seaman Jonas Profit were quietly engaged in a brief conversation. Wingfield kept hearing the words, *"Mah-TOH Wah-K'TEH-s'ah"* not aware that the *Choptanks* had named the mariner "Bear Slayer." In moments, the village leaders departed leaving their English friends to themselves.

Profit, in an emotionless monotone, explained, "The chief said we can remain here as long as we want to. He will be sure we will be cared for, and he hopes we can find some peace in our loss."

Expedition leader Wingfield motioned for the men to gather around the fire pit; and in the dwindling light of the glowing embers, he looked at the tired faces of each of his treasured friends. In a few brief days he had lost half of his team, all of the potential profits from the venture, and had lost hope of ever returning home. "What now?" he wondered silently.

Captain Gabriell Coverdale had changed so much, Wingfield was not sure he knew him anymore. He was striking in his Native attire and long black hair, but there was an almost feminine quality that the expedition leader had never noticed before. Coverdale's shiny black-leather knee-high military boots had been replaced by soft-appearing low cut moccasins completely changing his stride and the general motion of his body. The two carpenters, John Capper and Edward Pising, were battered and bruised. Capper's left ear was gone, and Pising would never walk comfortably again as a result of the arrow wound, but both seemed stronger and more resolute. The young Martin brothers, John and George, were always very close to each other, but they seemed most distressed about the loss of the *Phyllis*. Surely, their plans for the future never included being abandoned in this strange land for the rest of their lives. They were looking back at him with eyes that were asking him to "make everything right." He felt the pressure of their imploring glances and knew he had better say something constructive, and soon.

Fusilier James Dixon was the last of the detachment of soldiers. Wingfield felt great comfort in knowing such an able warrior was still at his disposal. Dixon was a man who lived in reality and had long ago learned to make the best of whatever life threw his way. No matter how bad things might get, they would always be better than his empty and hopeless growing-up years. The team leader could sense that Dixon's mind was racing as the soldier sized up the situation and contemplated the future.

Dixon would emerge as an important contributing member on the English decision-making team.

The ship's crew was basically intact – except now they had no ship. Wingfield still carried Percy Exum on the roles as "missing," but it was more and more clear that he must be dead. The administrator scanned the mariners, most of whom were engrossed in conversations with each other. There was his fine cook, Oscar Johnson, whose culinary creativity had been an important aspect in the lives of the men at New Providence. Ship's Officer Edwin Marian distinguished himself as a good friend and confidant, and would be very important in the future direction of the expedition. Navigator Withams had lost all his navigation tools in the sinking. His life was the sea, and Wingfield wondered how he would adapt to becoming a land person. The five young seamen were bright and capable. Matthew Tasley had learned the rudimentary aspects of leech craft and would be important to the health and welfare of the remainder of the team. The administrator especially appreciated Jonas Profit's penchant for languages and Brooks-Hughes artistic talents. There was something unusual going on with Brooks-Hughes. He had that glow about him of an adolescent transcending into manhood. A sense of 'fatherliness' swept over the leader as he looked at his artist. Wingfield knew that he should probably be the last person in the world to offer advice about the fair sex to a young man. His own experiences were rare, brief, and basically unsuccessful.

As Wingfield stood up to speak, all other conversations quickly ceased. "It has been a long and very trying night. I feel the best we can do right now is endeavor to get some rest. On the morrow, I would like to meet with Captain Coverdale, Ship's Officer Marian, Private Dixon, and Seaman Profit to discuss our future course of action."

As Private Dixon put more wood in the fire pit, team members began to stack animal pelts to make their bedrolls around the fire. Wingfield was somewhat taken aback to see Coverdale and Brooks-Hughes depart the men's lodge. It just had never occurred to him that they might have a *wig-wam* in the village.

Morning arrives early in the mid-Atlantic region of North America in early autumn. The emotionally exhausted Englishmen awoke to the aroma of freshly baked corn bread and jars of honey and pemmican. Mountains of oysters on the half-shell filled the steaming baskets set on the floor near their end of the lodge, and small clay jars awash with a most pleasant herbal tea rounded out the breakfast meal.

Wingfield marveled at the quality and quantity of victuals made available and realized that the women who prepared the meal must have been at work well before dawn. He was somewhat undone realizing that no one had heard the food being delivered. He recalled his first meeting with the old crone, *Chop-tah-nk*, the winter that now seemed a lifetime ago. Despite her dilapidated appearance she was so quick and furtive, and the thought echoed again, "If she was here to kill me ..."

The new leadership team members, less Captain Coverdale, filled their platters and cups with the pleasant repast and sat together apart from the rest of the expedition team.

Jonas Profit was the first to speak. He could not get the vision out of his mind of a particular young lady that served them during the prior evening's feast. He found out from Brooks-Hughes that her name was *Cah-cookos* and that she was the daughter of lesser chief, *Pacowassamuck* and his wife, *Pencookos*. He found himself hoping he would be able to see more of her. "Chief *Pemetosusk* told me his people would build lodges for us here at the village. You have to realize what an amazing offer that is. The *Choptank* don't easily take outsiders into their hearts like they have us. I would venture to say we are the first in the long history of this tribe to be afforded such an honor,"

"That's an option," replied Ship's Officer Marian with surprising derision in his voice. "Did you see what happened to Captain Coverdale? He was the best example I had ever seen of a proud British military man ... Now, I don't know what he is. Somehow these savages have washed away his past and his heritage. We are Englishmen and duly appointed representatives of the King ... and we will remain Englishmen. We can fend for ourselves as we always have."

Fusilier Dixon interjected some calmness into Marian's diatribe, "Do we know what is salvageable from New Providence? We have the skills and the strong arms to rebuild. Those murderous heathens did not avail themselves to our tools and implements, so if they were not damaged by the fire, we can continue to use them."

Wingfield reflected back on his tour of the compound after the attack, and answered thoughtfully, "The Master's House is battered, but basically in useable condition. Strangely, the dormitory appeared to be untouched. I wonder if it was 'Profit's Cemetery' that kept the renegades at bay. All those vermin skulls on stakes may have made them think the building was evil in some way. We may be able to salvage the wood shop and foundry; but the sheds, fusilier barracks and jail, kitchen and dining hall are ashes." He noticed that his cook was nearby listening to the discussion. "I'm truly sorry about that Mr. Johnson. If we decide to rebuild New Providence, your work station will get first priority."

Sometime during the conversation Captain Coverdale had quietly joined the group. He was dressed in perfectly fitting Native hunting attire with a white deerskin tunic, decorated vest, breeches and soft moccasins. The very same outfit that was waiting for him when he left the sweat lodge that seemingly long-ago magical evening when he became *AH-ban-nah Chon-TEH*, ('Gentle Heart.') He wore multiple strands of beautiful braided necklaces made of the glass beads traded by the Englishmen and the most remarkable shells appearing like the finest porcelain.

Marian felt his face getting red and his neck getting warm. He was not sure when Coverdale joined the circle and hoped the captain had not heard his ranting remarks. Gabrielle looked at Marian kindly then added, "There are two other options not yet discussed. You could rebuild New

Providence, but on this promontory near the village. It would be much more defensible with only one land approach, the one on the east. The proximity to the village would allow you to assist the *Choptanks* in their time of need and they would be there for you in yours."

Despite his spiritual rebirth, Captain Coverdale still had the mind of a military leader. He continued, "The other option would be to return to New Providence in preparation to build a boat that would allow the expedition to return to Jamestown. You have an experienced boat builder in your midst, Mr. Profit, of the highly esteemed Plymouth boat building Profit family. The two longboats are not seaworthy enough to make the journey south nor are the arms of the men strong enough to row for days on end; but with the correct tools and wood, a ketch or yawl is well within the purvey of Mr. Profit; or at the very least a sloop."

The entire compliment had joined the discussion circle as the captain arrived, and his last remark seemed to bring a ray of sunshine into the hearts of the Englishmen. A pall of depression was settling on them as they tried to face the reality of being stranded forever in the New World. Now, the thought of seeing their former friends and workmates at Jamestown combined with the hope of an eventual return to Mother England seemed to bring wings to their hearts. Only Jonas Profit was fraught with ambivalence. Should the New Providence citizenry decide to build a ship, he would be very instrumental in its construction and completion, and chances of seeing *Cah-cookos* would be even more remote.

Wingfield sensed the reaction of his men, and the decision concerning what the next step would be was surprisingly easy to make. He had not considered the idea of constructing another ship and all his efforts and heart ache had been directed at trying to determine how to make life the most bearable in the *Choptank* world. "Until we can determine the livability of our home, we will need to reside here. It won't hurt to be pampered by these kind people for a while."

Cascades of chuckles echoed through the lodge and out into the summer sunshine, as the men responded to their leader's comment. The news of the positive change in spirit of the White Men reached the village elders immediately after their levity resounded into the nearby forest. This was both a good thing, and a source of concern.

Head chief *Pemetosusk* turned to *Weesanusks*, "Please find *Mah-TOH Wah-K'TEH-s'ah* (Bear Slayer) and *AH-ban-nah Chon-TEH* (Gentle Heart) and bring them to us. It is time to talk and to listen."

The Englishmen walked up the path to the village and then on to the shore where the longboats were beached. As before they were greeted warmly and treated as honored guests and heroes. The elder ladies had fashioned necklaces similar to those worn by Captain Coverdale and politely placed them over the heads of their new friends. The *Choptanks* had not forgotten their contribution to the total defeat of the warring *Mitsawokets*. However, something was especially different and immediately noticed by the visitors – the young ladies were now involved in the on-going daily activities of the community and were easily visible among the villagers. Brooks-Hughes unsuccessfully scanned the Natives in hopes of catching sight of *Cahonke*. Many of the young lasses smiled coquettishly at the younger White Men much to the dismay of the *Choptank* boys.

Weesanusks quietly motioned Jonas to come with him. The young mariner turned to Wingfield and gave him a perplexed look. The expedition administrator wordlessly nodded in agreement. They could do without Jonas' contribution at this time at New Providence. The next few days' work would have two dissimilar goals: to sort through the remains of the fort to salvage any usable items to construct some form of watercraft for the return to Jamestown and also to determine what would need to be done to prepare the compound for eventual occupancy. As far as Wingfield was concerned there should be no problem alerting the village leaders to the visitor's plans that were germinating and also communicate that their White friends would need to rely on the hospitality of the *Choptanks* in the meantime.

The emotional roller-coaster ride continued for the Englishmen. Their positive and hopeful attitudes grew somber as they approached what was left of New Providence. A sense of melancholy flowed through each of them as they saw the remains of their hard work. Some of the structures were still smoldering and the memories of the loss of their workmates and friends were still raw on their feelings. They looked with hatred at the severed heads of the *Mitsawokets* that were piked on spears at the edge of the forest and the pile of bones and ashes where their enemy's corpses had been set afire. Some of the piked heads were now gone as scavenging carnivores were gradually helping themselves to the smorgasbord. The Englishmen could not think of a more fitting end for these dreadful murderers. They had done absolutely nothing to provoke such a vicious encounter and they were still shocked by the magnitude of the violence.

Wingfield asked his carpenters to divide the men into two groups. Any salvageable tools, utensils and implements would be removed to the dormitory and any usable trade goods taken to the Master's House. Ship's cook, Oscar Johnson, went straight to the ruins of his kitchen and dining hall. He found one of the large wooden spoons, charred but still usable, that Couper and Love had used to often salute him. He couldn't help but laugh, then the tears flowed unashamedly. Only memories were now his companions as he rummaged through the ruins of the kitchen and began to stack iron pots and pans, tin cups, and flatware on the ground. To any professional cook, his utensils were like close friends, and it was no different for Johnson. Almost everything metal was still usable although soot-stained and badly in need of cleaning. Most of the porcelain plates, bowls and dishes were broken and scattered across the rock floor of the dining area, but he was able to find enough tableware, generally chipped and cracked, to serve the meals to the diminished expedition team. His cast iron stove, tenderly removed from the *Phyllis* for use in the new kitchen, was tipped on its side, but it still stood like a monument in the ruins. He wondered what the Indians must have thought when they saw it. They probably decided it was some strange sacred object and defiled it to add insult to the attack. With the help of the Martin boys, Johnson was able to stand his cook stove back up and soon had a fire going in the tinderbox to heat water for clean-up. The boys eagerly took buckets to the stream and brought back more than enough water for the project. Johnson's burlap sack of a clear crystalline compound and charcoal that he used for all purpose cleaning had been slashed and spilled, but most of it was piled on the rock floor and easily reclaimable.

Private Dixon surveyed the dormitory and decided that it might also serve as a galley and dining area. Even if it was used as a storage area for the salvaged tools, utensils and implements, and places for the beds of the surviving crew, almost half of the large open room was still vacant. With some simple reorganization, a sizeable area could be cleared for other uses. He wandered over to the remains of the fort's kitchen to discuss the idea with Johnson and was amazed to see how much progress had already been done with the cleaning. The Martin boys proved to be able assistants and things were going swimmingly.

Dixon noticed the cook's cleaning compound and inquired, "What are you using to clean the pots and pans? Sulfuric acid? Boy! Is it doing a great job!"

Johnson's reply intrigued the fusilier, "The large crystals are the sea salt we got from the *Choptanks* and the smaller ones are potash or something. It's all around here growing right out of the ground. I found that if I add some of the charcoal from the fireplaces, it makes cleaning quite easy."

Dixon inspected the compound and thought, "Those smaller crystals are potassium nitrate. I would know it anywhere. It is the main ingredient in black powder. And charcoal is one of the other parts of the recipe. If I could find the sulfur, I could make enough fire power to keep my last two fusils operating until Doom's Day." He made a mental note to see if Jonas Profit would be able to communicate his need to the Indians.

Many hands make work light.

The expedition team dove into the reclamation project with optimistic enthusiasm. In a very few days, New Providence was again able to provide a haven for its occupants. It would never be as grand as it was the prior winter, but it was rapidly beginning to look like home.

Seeking a Union of Trust and Friendship

T he tale of head chief *Pemetosusk's* adventure to find his beautiful wife *Watsawasoo* had grown into a *Choptank* legend. In reality, it was a two day trek by canoe and foot to the *Chicamacomico* village, a couple days of horse-trading, and then a very pleasant return trip home. His wife was the daughter of a head chief and always presented herself in a very royal manner. Taller and slimmer than her husband and normal *Choptank* women, she grew use to the admiring glances from both men and women; and despite her lofty position in the tribe, she was always gracious and caring. There was never any doubt about the love and mutual respect between the two characters of the legend which made the fact that they never had any children the sadness and poignancy aspect found in all good stories.

What the legend fails to remember is that *Weesanusks* was also a major participant in the story. He was with *Pemetosusk* step-by-step, and at one point, actually saved his life when they stumbled across an injured bear enraged with pain. *Weesanusks* was also smitten by the exotic *Chicamacomico* women and found his life's love in *Wicompo*. By her people's standards she was in higher station than *Watsawasoo*. She was some years the younger than *Watsawasoo* and in their culture the youngest female sibling inherited all the family wealth. The reason revolved around the idea that the youngest will be able to care for the elder family members for a longer length of time, if only because the older children will die sooner.

Wicompo, too, seemed especially attractive in *Choptank* eyes; but her personality was less pleasant than her older sister's. She grew up knowing that she had power and she wasn't above lording over people. She was very aware that if she returned to her *Chicamacomico* home, she would be treated like a queen; so she had an obnoxious take-it-or-leave-it attitude about the people of her husband. Her deepest hope was that *Weesanusks* would someday be head chief, and when that failed to happen she would on occasion remind him of his inadequacies. They had lost a strapping son in the prime of his youth, so the only surviving child, *Cahonke*, grew into womanhood watching how her parents related to each other. As her personality developed, she became as independent and head-strong as her mother. She was the apple of her father's eye and knew his entire universe revolved around providing everything she could ever want. Had this family lived next door in today's world, it might be said that she was "a spoiled brat."

Cahonke was growing even more impossible to live with. The hormonal wars of puberty were raging inside her and manifested themselves by disobedience and disrespect toward her family and most of the neighbors. She was prone to crying and screaming fits when she was unhappy or unfulfilled in some manner and the *wig-wams* of the *Choptank* were not exactly sound-proof. As always, *Weesanusks* did everything in his power, which was considerable, to try to assuage her temper, basically to no avail. The only time *Cahonke* was tolerable was when the English artist came to their home to work on his portraits of her mother and father. She would sit near him and watch his every move as he performed his magic on the stretched sail canvas. Obviously, Brooks-Hughes enjoyed the attention, and it took only a brief look into his eyes to see the flames of love burning brightly. Due to the reclaiming of New Providence, it had been some weeks since the Englishmen had been to the village. This fact alone was bringing the parent-child relationship to a boiling point, and gentle *Weesanusks* turned to the tribal leaders for advice.

Lesser chief *Pacowassamuck* was the first to respond, "Isolate her to the Moon Time lodge. Find a couple of elder women to discipline her and teach her respect. Some of those old ladies are as tough as oyster shells. They would enjoy the challenge."

Weesanusks shuddered to think of what might happen to his pride and joy in the hands of those sadistic crones.

Head chief *Pemetosusk* was saddened by the turmoil in the heart of his life-long friend. "She is of marriageable age, very attractive, and could fetch quite a handsome dowry," he commented, "The *Ozonies* will be coming to trade before the first frost. It would be a good thing for the trust and friendship between our tribes to arrange a union with one of their warriors."

"Or ..." he thought to himself, "Grounds for out and out war."

The troubled father could not bear the thought of the possibility of never seeing his daughter again. He could not agree to the idea in any way whatsoever.

Lesser chief and Holy Man *Tattowin* offered, "Is there a young man in our village you would deem worthy of the hand of your daughter? Is there any boy among us that she seems to have an interest in?"

The smile on his face implied he already knew the answer and he only wanted to hear it from the lips of *Weesanusks*. This comment was met with a long and nervous silence as the father bowed his head and avoided the eyes of the other chiefs.

The second Holy Man, *Weanchum*, continued the discussion his brother had opened. "You are our greatest of all friends," he said to the tormented father. "We have had a most remarkable vision about you and your family:

> *It was early morning and a beautiful sunrise was painting the Earth Mother in the colors of the flowers in the fields. The only sounds were the calls of Kon-HE, our Brother Raven. We saw your totem, Toh Ho-KU-wah, the ferocious Bluefish, chasing a school of smaller swimmers near the shore. As it leapt out of the Mother of all Waters it was caught by Ha-KAH-sha-nah, the Groundhog, who was wading along the beach in search of an easy meal. As Ha-KAH-sha-nah held the wriggling fish in his claws, it turned into a beautiful young girl and became very quiet and peaceful. Ha-KAH-sha-nah gently placed her under his arm and returned to his den. Then all was silent ... and we felt a great sense of joy in our hearts."*

Both brothers closed their eyes and seemed to drift off into a pleasant serenity.

The three other chiefs looked at the twin Holy Men in wide-eyed clarity. There was absolutely nothing ethereal or mysterious about this vision. Clearly *Toh Ho-KU-wah* the Blue Fish was *Cahonke*, and *Ha-KAH-sha-na* the Groundhog was one of the White Men. Only *Weesanusks* had an inkling of who was in question.

The eyes of *Pemetosusk* and his cousin *Pacowassamuck* peered into their friend's soul. "Is there something we should know?" accused the head chief.

Weesanusks was the most honest and open person they had ever known. He could never keep a secret or hide his emotions. He blurted out everything he knew about the connection between *Cahonke* and Brooks-Hughes the artist, and continued with everything he assumed or perceived. The ramifications of such a union were beyond comprehension. Even if *Cahonke* was accepting of the suggestion and was able to receive the approval and blessing of her mother and the community, both of which were very unlikely, there was no assurance that the White Men would agree to such an idea. Over the months getting to know the visitors, the Natives had never seen any of them in contact with women. The head chief and two of his lesser chiefs finally assumed that their honored friends were a strange new breed of two-legged that they called *"Hin-TOON Hoo-HA-pe"* ("Hairy Skeletons") for lack of a more appropriate descriptor. At this suggestion, *Tattowin* and *Weanchum* both emerged from their reverie and burst into raucous laughter.

"If *AH-bah-nah Chon-TEH* (Captain Coverdale) represents a normal *Ha-KAH-sha-nah*," chuckled *Tattowin*, "They definitely are not lacking in the *Cheh e TAH-pah-peh* (sex equipment). Remember, we were there for his sweat lodge rebirth."

One problem solved.

Pemetosusk looked kindly at his old friend and inquired, "Are you accepting of a union between your daughter and the young Englishman?"

Unwilling to go against the emerging ground swell, *Weesanusks* nodded.

"Are you able to communicate this idea to *Wicompo?*" questioned *Pacowassamuck* with a rather unkind smile on his face. He liked the friendly lesser chief as much as any other villager did, but he did not agree that he should hold a place on the leadership council. Surely their chief hunter and warrior, *Asquash*, was much more deserving of the position. The *WE-h'ne-s'ah* clan was not represented in the chief's *wig-wam* and deserved to be. He was convinced that the only reason *Weesanusks* sat in honor was because he was *Pemetosusk's* life-long friend. He was occasionally heard to say, "If he cannot even keep his own house in order, how can he lead the village."

The gentle Native shuddered at the thought, but again nodded in agreement. There really was not anyone else to do this task. He had spent his entire adult life handling his wife with "kid gloves" trying every way possible to not ruffle her feathers. He loved her more

than anything in the world, but he feared her temper and her sharp tongue.

Pemetosusk turned to *Pacowassamuck*, "I believe the White Man, *Mah-TOH Woh-K'TEH-s'ah*, (Bear Slayer), will be helpful in communicating our plan to their chief, Wingfield. The hunter is staying in the village at *AH-bah-nah Chon-TEH's wig-wam*. I am asking you to travel to the English settlement with him and convey our wishes for this union."

―――――――――――

Jonas Profit was continually amazed by the ability of the *Ho-KU-wah-s'ah* clansmen when it came to seamanship. Their strong arms could maneuver dugout canoes fearlessly through choppy ocean swells without missing a rowing beat and propel their lithe craft with frightening speed over still water. The brief voyage from the village to New Providence was over before *Pacowassamuck* could fully explain the reasons. Because of the need for him remaining at the village to serve as the translator of the Englishmen's needs, Profit had not seen the fort since the *Mitsawoket* massacre and was heartened by the work that had been accomplished. The Master's House and dormitory were cleaned-up and looked in good repair. The foundations of the destroyed buildings were cleared of debris and raked to ground level. Any salvageable logs were cut into firewood and stacked neatly by either of the two buildings. Already, some large tree trunks had been dragged to the site and were being skinned and planed in preparation for the construction of the new kitchen and dining hall – much smaller in dimensions than the original. There were still some piked Indian heads at the edge of the forest, but the flesh had either sloughed off or been nibbled away by flies and other noxious critters, and they were ghastly as eye-less boney skulls. The Englishmen had agreed to leave them there until they turned to dust.

Expedition leader Wingfield warmly received *Pacowassamuck* and the rowers, and soon they were seated on the floor in the Master's House. Cook Johnson had his kitchen up and running in the dormitory, and a pleasant seafood stew was quickly prepared for the guests. With Jonas Profit sitting between the leaders, and the other Natives stoically observing the goings-on and noisily slurping the victuals provided, the unusual discussion progressed.

It soon became quite clear that the chief of the White Men was not going to agree to any co-habitation between his remaining team members and the *Choptanks*. He had already lost Captain Coverdale, and he felt his leadership slowly slipping through his fingers. Brooks-Hughes was an able worker and a masterful artist. He still had many, many projects to complete as the history of the settlement was being recorded. The lesser chief became more and more agitated as he tried to communicate how important this union would be to both parties. Profit became very uncomfortable endeavoring to share the feelings of both of the leaders and still be as politically correct as possible. Wingfield was a 'company man' and would always be … and 'company men' do not break with traditions or regulations. He stood by *The Articles on Intercourse with Indigenous Peoples* which clearly forbade such conduct. In his mind, he would be accountable for the actions of his team once they returned home, and he was not willing to compromise his values and the traditions of the London Company.

Eventually the negotiations were broken off, not too amicably.

Pacowassamuck had really thought he would be returning to the village with the canoe heaped almost to floundering with dowry items and a very happy young Englishman in tow. If *Wicompo* was hesitant about the possible marriage, the wealth offered would make her much more agreeable. It was common village gossip that she coveted material things and loved to flaunt them over other people. Now, the lesser chief would be returning empty handed and deeply embarrassed.

It was too difficult for Profit to translate exactly the reasons why Wingfield would not deign to give his blessings on the marriage. As best *Pacowassamuck* could ascertain the bride-to-be did not measure up to the White chief's expectations. If the visitors were holding-out until the *Choptanks* provided gifts and barter items so they would take the young lady off their hands, they would be sorely disappointed ... or, maybe they really were *Hin-TOON Hoo-HA-pe* (Hairy Skeletons)

M'ne-SKOO-yah and Mah-KAH-ze (Salt and Sulfur)

A s the marriage entourage departed in chilled silence from the Master's House, Private Dixon and Cook Johnson joined the group slowly walking back to the canoe. Dixon quietly talked to Jonas Profit. "It appears that the meeting did not go so well. Can you tell me what it was about?"

Profit replied, "I think it was my fault. I just could not translate Master Wingfield's reasons to the chief. If anything, I made things worse. The *Choptanks* were trying to arrange a marriage between *Weesanusks'* daughter and Theodore."

"Don't ask me to tell Theodore," Dixon responded to Profit. "If he knew what was going on, he would swim all the way to the village. And I don't think he knows how to swim."

Both Englishmen chuckled silently. Dixon continued, "If we could find sulfur, I think I have the ingredients to make black powder. All I have left now is what I kept in the longboats with my fusils and some I was able to salvage from the dormitory storeroom. Do you think you could ask the Indians if they know where any might be?"

Profit saddened, "I don't know the *Choptank* word for 'sulfur'. There might not even be one. I haven't seen any in the village, and I have hunted all around the area and haven't found any."

Dixon reminded, "But you were not looking for it."

"Sulfur stinks to high heaven," answered Jonas. "Whether you are looking for it or not, if it is anywhere within a league of you, you can smell it. But, I will try."

Johnson inquired, "Do you think you could ask them for more salt? I am running out and would like to stock up for the winter. We still have some things to trade, so I am sure we can pay whatever they want for it."

"You may have to work a trade by yourself," said their interpreter. "Let's plan to get you over to the village in the near future, and I'll take you to the *Wah-KON-kon-s'ah* clan. They are the ones in charge of salt. You can always tell one of them. They are the only Natives allowed to wear feathers."

This early autumn in the mid-Atlantic region of North America was extremely hot, but surprisingly dry. The normal ocean breezes from the southeast were replaced by dry merciless off-shore winds that hailed from due west. Even the nights did not cool down, and the pitiful wails of *Choptank* babies crying in discomfort echoed throughout the village. One good thing about the unusual climate, however, was that it was an excellent opportunity to extend the sea salt production season. The *Wah-KON-kon-s'ah* clan worked day and night filling some of the settling pools and scraping the whitish-clear thumb-nail sized salt crystals from the evaporated basins. The filling-then-evaporating system replicated itself over and over for most of the summer months until the crystals were harvestable. Jonas Profit had been able to discuss Cook Johnson's need for more *M'ne-SKOO-yah* (Salt) with head chief *Pemetosusk,* who was not only the leader of the tribe, but also the top ranking member of the salt-making clan. In passing, Profit mentioned that the Englishman would like very much to see the process, and the head chief was agreeable to this idea.

As the hot morning sun rose over the eastern headlands, the longboat scraped onto the village beach and was greeted by *Pemetosusk* and a small group of his clansmen. They were dressed in finest regalia with feathered headpieces, cloaks and vests. A visit to the salt making cairns was equal to walking on Holy Ground to the *Choptanks* and they dressed accordingly. Brooks-Hughes marveled at the sight and his artist's eye made a mental note to draw or paint one of the Natives in their gay profusion. Johnson was very excited about the trip and hoped he had enough barter items to acquire the salt he needed for cooking and cleaning. Captain Coverdale was also in the greeting party in his spectacular white deerskin outfit. He was quickly learning the *Choptank* language, including its nuances and humor, and was willing to help Profit serve as interpreter. As usual, there were a large number of villagers in attendance hoping to catch sight of their strange heroes. However, the numbers had gradually diminished as the locals became used to having the Englishmen in town.

The *Wah-KON-kon-s'ah* led the group slowly through the village, and the visitors noticed how much deference and regard the people held toward this group. In the eyes of the Natives, they truly were 'magicians'. They could make *M'ne-SKOO-yah* (Salt) out of thin air and construct boats that could fly over the water.

The path from the village to the tide flats wound through the thick forest for at least an hour's walk to the north shore of the promontory. As the cluster of men reached the bluff overlooking the bay, there below them laid a most incredible sight. As far as the eye could see was a checkerboard of colors; blues, grays and whites. The entire shore line had been constructed into squared basins and settling pools separated by narrow causeways made of large rounded rocks. The floor of one section might be bare flat rocks fitted so close together that the seams were almost invisible. Another square might be filled to the brim with sea water while a third would be a pale clear whitish color as the salt crystals were beginning to form. Some of the basins were teaming with Natives and looked like anthills. In these, the sea salt crystals were the appropriate size, and the clansmen were working furiously to harvest them before the weather might change. A large selection of clay pots was at the ready on the adjacent dike some filled, but most still empty.

The Englishmen could not wait to get down to the shore and get a closer look at the process. Captain Coverdale viewed the scene with his military eye. He noticed that seawater was let in to a section through an opening in each dike sealed off by a flat stone gate. Apparently, when the neap tide rolled in, the water level was high enough to flow into a particular settling pool if the gate was opened. After the square filled, the gate would be closed and the water trapped until it had totally evaporated. This process would be repeated over and over until the crystals grew to an acceptable size. This entire area of tide flat could also serve as a barrier against possible invasion from the north if the squares were all filled. An enemy would have to sprint from the bay to the shore across the narrow causeways and would be sitting ducks for archers waiting in the forest. He felt a renewed sense of security knowing that the north flank of the village was so easily defensible. The earlier battle with the *Mitsawokets* had flowed entirely from the south making it easy for him to deploy his Native army. He occasionally wondered how he would repel an attack if the enemy came from more than one direction.

Jonas Profit fit well the name *Mah-TOH Woh-K'TEH-s'ah* (Bear Slayer). He was becoming a ferocious hunter who never came back empty handed. His great friend *Asquash* laughingly told him after a particularly successful hunt, "We should call you *DAH-ku-oh-WAH-s'een Woh-K'TEH-s'ah* (Everything Killer)."

Many of the *Choptank* feasts included plates and plates of deliciously baked wild fowl, and Profit wondered how they were able to acquire such a large variety as well as amount. The Native nimrods were very good at finding and dropping big game, but the accuracy and range of their bows and arrows left something to be desired concerning bird hunting. He had often wanted to join a team planning to secure the plentiful ducks and geese found in the estuaries around the village, and at last the opportunity presented itself.

Jonas was surprised to find out he was invited to a special pre-hunting ritual. Always before, he had waited in the village for the *WE-h'ne-s'ah* (Hunters) to collect in the village 'square' and then joined them as they set out for the day's work. The entire group planning to participate in the bird hunt walked single-file on a seldom used trail that entered the thick forest near the part of the village where the clan had built their lodges. The trail was barely a trace as it wove through the giant loblolly pine trees for at least a league until it ended in a clearing quite secluded and divided by a babbling stream. In the center of the open area was the strangest structure the Englishman had seen since arriving in the New World. Nothing in his experience could describe it accurately, but it was similar to a large, rounded turtle shell about as tall as a standing man and possibly ten feet in diameter. *Asquash* pointed and said, *"e-H'DU-ska-pe won-KEH-yah"* (Sweat bath Lodge). The tule mat door was folded back and Profit could see a huge pile of glowing coals blazing in the fire pit and what looked like clouds of steam issuing outward.

The group of warriors began to disrobe, and Jonas, somewhat embarrassed did the same. As he removed his tunic, he noticed his Indian friends staring at him in wonder. Natives have little or no chest and back hair, and in their eyes the White-Skinned Man really did look like *Ma-TOH* – the

Bear. Each in turn entered the lodge and sat in a circle around the fire pit which was filled with extremely hot glowing rocks. When the last man entered he pulled the door closed behind him. One of the hunters had a large jar of water next to him and what appeared to be a wooden ladle in his hand. He would pour a small amount of water on the glowing rocks and it would evaporate into scalding steam with an angry hissing sound. The lodge was rapidly filling with hot and heavy moisture and Profit found it difficult to breathe. He also realized he was sweating profusely from head to toe.

The Native braves began to sing marvelous *Choptank* ceremonial songs and seemed unmoved by the claustrophobic discomfort and oppressive heat. After what seemed like a life time, one of the braves shouted, *"Oh-WAH-s'ee-nah Te-WAH-hay!"*("All my relations!") then tumbled out the doorway. The others laughed, but soon followed the first man in a similar fashion. Profit would have been more than glad to be the first man out, but he was trapped by those sitting between him and the exit. By the time it was his turn, he was feeling faint and not pleased at all by this new experience. As he entered the fresh air, he saw the hunters rolling and splashing in the brook, which even in early autumn must have been bone-chilling cold.

As each man began to don his clothing he rubbed moist green leaves over the exposed skin on his face, arms and legs. This would repel the mosquitoes and biting flies that infested the tidal lowlands during the warm months. Jonas also did this and noticed the pleasant aroma associated with the plants. Someday these leaves would be called 'peppermint', but for now they were simply *wah-PEH-pe* (leaves). Only the most sacred of tribal stories could tell how this marvelous plant had made its way to the eastern shore of Chesapeake Bay and how over the generations it was cultivated and harvested in almost holy fashion. As the Englishmen hoisted his cross-bow and long-bow, he noticed that about half of the *Choptanks* carried extra war clubs and the other half were leaving all their weapons behind in favor of heavy rolls of fine meshed spun-bark netting made by the *Ho-KU-wah-s'ah* clan for fishing purposes and wrapped around quite long spear shafts carried two-by-two on the shoulders of pairs of braves.

Each of the hunters toted a leather back-pack filled with corn bread, water jars, dried meat and other tasty bites, and an animal skin bed roll was looped over their shoulders. It was clear that this hunt was going to last more than just the rest of the day. *Asquash,* correctly assuming that Jonas would not think of doing this prepared a back-pack and bed roll for him also. The hunting party progressed along the north shore of what would someday be called the Tred Avon River often looking skyward for flocks of gathering waterfowl.

This seemed like an appropriate time to ask *Asquash* about the possibility of sulfur deposits in the area. He knew the *Choptank* word for yellow, *"zee,"* and he could demonstrate the sign of something smelling bad, but this might not be enough to communicate his interest. It was worth a try. Walking beside his friend, he said, "We need something to make the fire powder. It is yellow, and it smells terrible. If we mix three things together it becomes fire powder. We have two of them but still need one more. It is yellow and smells terrible."

Asquash looked at the Englishman as if he were two blocks short of an idiot. Along the trail were occasional mounds of animal droppings and some of them "were yellow and smelled terrible." He finally pointed out a small heap with just a hint of disgust. Profit began to laugh and said, "No! It isn't a pile of *oonk-CHAY!*" He reached to the ground and grabbed a small handful of soil. "It is like *mah-KAH* (dirt)!"

Now he was getting somewhere: Something that was yellow, smelled terrible, and looked like dirt.

The entire hunting party yelled out *"Mah-KAH-ze* (Sulfur)!" held their noses, and laughed heartily.

Asquash looked somewhat relieved and answered, "Yes. I know about *Mah-KAH-ze.* I believe we have some back at the men's lodge. We trade for it and use it as *Peh-ZHU-tah* (Medicine). We can check when we return."

Canadian Goose. Called "Mah-GAH."

His conversation was interrupted by the not too distant sound of geese honking. *"Mah-GAH,"* whispered one of the Indians. The hunting party quietly walked around the nearby headland and there before them in the marshy shallows was a massive flock of Canadian geese floating lazily and feasting on the tasty plant life.

Then the strangest hunting technique the Englishman had ever seen unfolded:

The Indians with the rolled nets waded noisily into the shallow water causing a cloud of geese to take flight in a deafening cacophony of flapping wings and honking sounds. Like tumbling dominoes, other flocks of geese took to the air and soon the sun was obscured by thousands of the giant birds circling overhead. Jonas could not stop himself and began shooting cross-bow darts into the mass of soaring water fowl killing at least one on every shot, but those tumbled into the water too distant from the shore line to retrieve. Meanwhile, the *Choptanks* waded waist-deep into the water and began to unroll the nets and spread them out. Each was the width of the long spear shafts, about ten feet, but they extended at least 20 feet. As the nets stretched out, the Englishman noticed that there were small sea shells attached at intervals on the netting allowing it to partially sink into the water. The nets must have been incredibly heavy to carry. Once the dozen or so nets were in place, the hunters on each end covered themselves with plant life and sat comfortably in the water, and waited. The Indians on the shore began to sweat in the heat as they too waited for the flocks to return. Obviously, the hunters held in higher regard got to be in the water.

With the two-leggeds out of sight, the shore line appeared to be safe and the geese circling overhead began to slowly return to the water. This area had been feeding and nesting grounds for the Geese-People since the beginning of time, and they were not about to let some puny land walkers keep them away. As might be expected, quite a large number of them landed near the waiting traps and continued their foraging. There was no prearranged signal, but suddenly one of the braves stood up and raised the spear shaft as high as he could reach. He laughed loudly as he did so. His partner on the other end stood up also, and as the startled birds tried to fly their feet and wings were tangled in the netting. The other pairs of hunters did the same, and after another roar of flapping wings and honking, at least five or six birds were trapped in each net. The *Choptanks* hiding in the trees rushed into the water and began whacking the startled birds with their war clubs. By the time the feathers had settled and the commotion died down, the hunters had easily four or five dozen potential meals at hand, and this was just the first round of trapping and smacking.

As one group of Indians collected the birds and piled them on the sand, the others waded back to the beach and spread out the nets. Most were torn and tattered from the thrashing of the trapped geese and needed to be repaired before they could be used again. Four of the braves divided the catch into equal piles and began to sort each one's share into two bundles. Once they were done, they threw the bound creatures over their shoulders and lit back in the direction of the village. It was prudent not to have such a massive amount of dead creatures in the camp site with carnivores on the prowl seeking the aroma of blood. The remaining Natives set to work re-tying the netting and adding shells where others had been lost. Evening was fast approaching and the repairs were proving to be quite a time-consuming process. There would be no more trapping and killing geese this day.

Jonas thought that there must be a more efficient way to accomplish the same results, until he realized the true purpose of the hunting expedition that warm night as the hunting party placed their bedrolls around the campfire. As the Indians ate the food that had been packed for them and exchanged stories of present and past experiences it became clear this was more a time for the men to get away from

their wives and families than to bring home great amounts
of game birds. There was much comradeship and laughter as
the men talked about things men from sea-to-sea and even
unto these days discuss together.

At some point in every outing, *Asquash* would be asked
to tell a story. He was famous among the *WE-h'ne-s'ah* for
the tales he could weave, and this absolutely clear and starry
night was no different. Even though the story was related in
the Native tongue, Jonas was adept enough to understand
the gist of the tale.

"This is a Holy Song," he began.

> *"On the banks of a thickly wooded stream, a tribe of The
> People seeking a home set up their camp for the night, and
> there came to them a Holy Man who said, 'Give me of your
> women's bracelets and necklaces and in return I will do so
> much for you that you shall feel no sickness as long as my
> own life shall endure.'*

> *"They gave him bracelets and necklaces, both of shells,
> stones and animal hair, and then the Holy Man told them
> to help him build a sweat-lodge, such as the people call 'new
> life' because the person that comes out of it feels as if made
> anew. When the Holy Man had purified himself in solitude
> he dug a shallow depression in the earth and lined it with a
> beautifully tanned deer hide that was painted red.*

> *Then he instructed one of the young men, called simply
> "Hok-SHE-nah (Boy)" to walk throughout the camp and
> call for all the sick to gather around and place an offering of
> to-bac in the hole. Then came forth the Holy Man, and he
> set a wooden cup on the ground and began to sing this song:*

> > *'O ye people, be ye healed;*
> > *Life anew I bring unto you.*

Through the Father over all
Do I thus.
Life anew I bring unto you'

While he chanted his litany he tapped a rhythm on the ground and the depression began to slowly fill with water. He dipped the cup in the water and said, "We-CHO-ne m'nee" (The Waters of Life) and gave the cup to the sick, and they all drank of the water and were healed, yet the well was never empty. And when they had all drunk, he sent everyone to their lodges and bade them rest until evening.

When the sun was down the entire tribe gathered again about the well, and the Holy Man cleared a space upon the ground and sang again and drew strange designs with his finger in the dust. The Holy Man looked upon the ground and said, 'The spirits of the fathers tell me that all is indeed well with these people.

They are good hearted and kind to the Earth Mother. They are blessed to be a blessing and shall be called Choptank (The People).

They will soon find a home and prosper for many generations to come.'

"The people began to sing in great joy and they felt as if they had set down a heavy burden. Then the Holy Man smiled upon them and said, 'Now shall I go back to my own place.' And before their eyes, he turned to smoke. This I say unto you is true."

Jonas was deeply moved by *Asquash's* story and for some unexplained reason felt tears well-up in his eyes. The legend was the *Choptank's* creation story and was indeed a "Holy Song." He looked around the campfire at his Indian friends and almost all of them had drifted off to sleep. He remembered hearing stories of a 'fountain of youth' long sought after by adventurers. It seemed pleasantly comforting that there may actually be fountains of youth and his Native friends had included one of them in the history of their culture. He rolled over and relived the story until he fell asleep.

The only sounds were the Bug People of the night and their cousins the Frog People singing their own "Holy Songs."

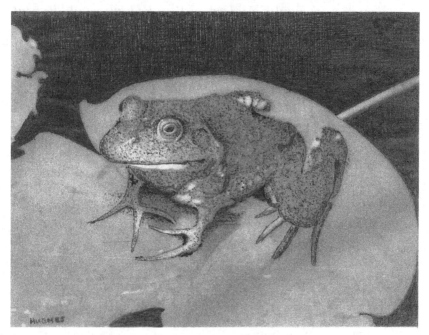

Bull Frog. Called "h-nah-SH'KAH."

Love's Prices Paid

The English artist, Brooks-Hughes, was working on the portrait of *Wicompo* and quite pleased with how it was progressing. She was a fabulous subject to paint; very attractive, dressed in her people's finest regalia, and willing to remain still for extended lengths of time without complaining. However, something seemed different. He felt a degree of tension, even anger, in her demeanor toward him and this represented itself by the slightest change in her mouth and forehead. Anybody else would not have noticed this nuance, but Theodore's artist's eye was trained to see even the smallest of details. Honestly he did not know why she was feeling this way and it distressed him considerably. He felt great affection for this regal lady and her kind husband and in his heart hoped that he would be part of their family someday. His command of the *Choptank* language was improving almost daily, but he still did not have the confidence to try to engage in a serious conversation with any of the villagers, especially *Wicompo*.

And where was *Cahonke*? She was always nearby when he painted, and this day she was nowhere to be seen. It was not his choice to be remanded to the fort for the many days he was absent from his Native friends, and he was happy to be able to return to the village and continue his art. His heart ached to see her again, and he felt a strong sense of melancholy because of her absence. His feelings of rejection continued when he approached Captain Coverdale in hopes of being able to share his *wig-wam* as he did during past visits to the village. At this point, the only other options were to return to the fort or sleep under the stars, so his former commander consented but not with the warm graciousness formerly extended. The young acolyte assigned to the captain prepared the evening repast and made the Englishman comfortable as before, but this time he was embarrassingly affectionate toward Coverdale, and Brooks-Hughes felt as if he was somehow intruding.

After the meal, the Englishmen were left alone in the lodge, and the artist discussed the situation earlier in the day during the painting session. The captain began to explain what had happened between Master Wingfield and lesser chief *Pacowassamuck* at New Providence. Even *Wicompo* had finally consented to the union between the two young people. The Natives were sure this would be the most difficult hurdle to get over. Obviously, Brooks-Hughes had somehow really impressed the lesser chief's very discriminating wife, and a sense of great joy was growing in the community in anticipation of this most amazing event. A wedding of this stature came once in a lifetime, and great preparations were already underway, when they were so insensitively ended. Brooks-Hughes was astounded. His fondest dream had come so close then evaporated so abruptly because of the decision of one person. He blurted out angrily, "I am not Master Wingfield's lackey. I am an able bodied seaman in the English Navy. It is Lieutenant Marian's decision as to whether or not I can marry."

Coverdale sat upright.

What the incensed young man said was completely true. The events of the last year or so had blended the London Company employees and the Ship's Crew so completely that their origins had been clouded. With the loss of the *Phyllis* there wasn't much need for a navy any longer, but that did not imply the crewmen had somehow ceased being British mariners. Coverdale had to find out if Wingfield's rebuff meant the wedding was now off in the eyes of the

Choptanks. He lithely rose to his feet, put on his moccasins, and commented to the artist, "Please remain here and try not to worry. I've got to talk to some people. I'll return as soon as I can and let you know what's happening."

The captain's first visit was at *Pemetosusk's* lodge. This was the safest beginning because the head chief had not actually been directly insulted by the decision of Wingfield. His gracious wife, *Watsawasoo,* welcomed him warmly and brought him to the glowing fire pit. Despite Coverdale's eagerness to get on with the program, *Choptank* protocol always demanded that the parties sit together, possibly enjoy some *to-bac* and a snack, and share small talk before getting to a particular issue at hand. On occasion, this slow walk irritated the captain when he was trying to reach a quick decision, but he soon learned that if he wanted to get something accomplished, he would have to do it the "Indian way." The Englishman had become quite adept at the Native language and most conversations could now be held in *Choptank* without the delays of an interpreter.

The head chief was pleased with the progress of *M'ne-SKOO-yah* (Salt) production and the *Ho-KU-wah-s'ah* clan was enjoying an especially successful harvest of shell fish. Both of these were goods signs that the upcoming winter would be easy on the village. Eventually, Gabrielle was able to bring the conversation around to the issue on his mind. As far as *Pemetosusk* was concerned the wedding could continue if Brooks-Hughes could obtain permission from his own chief.

It seemed prudent at this point to visit *Weesanusks* and *Wicompo* and find out their opinion about this new information. When the two Englishmen and head chief reached the lodge, neither was welcomed with what might be called warm affection. *Weesanusks,* as always, was congenial toward the three visitors, invited them to the fire pit, and instructed the servant to prepare a small meal for everyone. *Wicompo* never handled food or did basic house work; after all, she was a queen to her own people; so *Weesanusks* was one of the few *Choptanks* that had a servant for the daily menial tasks. Their lovely daughter sat in the conversation circle but did not participate. She seemed preoccupied sewing an especially attractive article of apparel. *Wicompo* was civil and deferent toward *Pemetosusk*. She did respect his power if not the man, but she harbored deep resentment that he sat as head chief and her husband did not. The lesser chief's wife was completely disgusted with all White Men because of Wingfield's decision, and some of those feelings flowed over onto Brooks-Hughes despite her special affection for him. As in the head chief's lodge, the food was soon served and small talk stole part of the night away. *Pemetosusk* was able to steer the conversation in the needed direction, and the comments to Captain Coverdale by the artist about who had the final decision piqued the interest of all three family members.

Never one to "hold her peace," *Cahonke* asked the captain, "Do you know this 'Loo-ten-ten Mar-ee-ann'? Is he good to Tee-ah-dore?"

"He is very good to Theodore," responded Coverdale as he turned to the parents. "He is a reasonable man and a great warrior. I hold him in very high regard and respect his opinion at all times." A sense of optimism seemed to rise in the lodge. "With your permission I will approach him about our concerns."

The next step toward the union of two cultures would be even more difficult to take. Captain Coverdale's entire adult life as a military man was based on honoring the chain of command and respect for one's superiors. In a very obvious way, he was going behind the back of Administrator Wingfield to seek Ship's Officer Marian's approval. When he was assigned to the Jamestown Expedition by the British Army, he pledged in writing and in his heart to be loyal and supportive toward the Company and its leaders. His "new life" experience in the sweat lodge had softened his heart and calmed his anxious spirit, but his heredity and life-long military environment were important building blocks in his character and personality.

Still … he knew this may not be the proper thing to do, but it was the right thing to do.

Pemetosusk called for the warrior *Nehatuckwis* and instructed him to canoe to the fort and request that the New Providence leaders come to the village to plan for the nearing winter. This warrior was the guide for the mapping party that first encountered the *Mitsawokets*, and over the ensuing months Ship's Officer Marian and he had become close friends. They were both trying to learn each other's language and having a very enjoyable time doing so. *Nehatuckwis* was wise to the forest and its creatures, and he always had helpful suggestions to improve the Englishmen's chances for comfort and survival as the weather was starting to turn. There was a chance that Master Wingfield would select himself to represent the White Men, but there was a better chance he would send Marian. The expedition leader had seldom visited the village anymore. He was growing more and more depressed and introspective as he continually looked over the losses written in the business ledgers of the expedition and the list of dead team members. His only way to cope with his sense of failure was to be embraced by an environment familiar and predictable. Should he come for the parlay, he would leave Marian in charge of the fort – so either way, Captain Coverdale and Brooks-Hughes would have some private time to discuss their wishes concerning the possible union of cultures.

There was frost on the ground as the Englishmen prepared to take their longboat to the village for the meeting with the *Choptank* leaders. The sun was bright and promised a nice day, but the air was very cold with a chill wind chopping up the waters of the bay. Administrator Wingfield had selected a team consisting of Ship's Officer Marian, the carpenter John Capper, and navigator Obadiah Withams to represent New Providence in the negotiations. Capper's prowess with an axe and the fact that he had lost an ear in the attack by the *Mitsawokets* made him one of the most popular White Men in the eyes of the Natives. Whenever he visited the village, there was always a large crowd of children walking proudly with him begging to touch the cavity where the ear once had been. He would bend down and laugh while they fingered the rough flesh and cringed. He would be a great asset in the negotiating. The Martin brothers, and two mariners, Jerald Pennyfeather-Grayson and Eldred Parksley would assist with the rowing.

Jonas Profit was becoming more and more scarce at the partially rebuilt New Providence, but he would be available as interpreter during the parlay. It was later determined that the Natives had constructed a very capable lodge for the use of the Englishmen when they were in the village. Profit and Brooks-Hughes had moved in immediately which took some of the discomfort and lack of privacy off the shoulders of Captain Coverdale.

Private Dixon was heartened by the cold snap assuming correctly that it would help decrease the insect nuisance that annoyed him every time he went hunting. He gathered up Cook Johnson and they departed right after the morning meal to check the trap lines and possible scare up some big game. Carpenter Edward Pising could not make much progress on the construction of the new kitchen and dining hall without the help of the other men, and he was not in the frame of mind to cut firewood. His injured leg, always painful, made him a detriment to any hunting trip, so he decided to take a basket and shovel and find a nice selection of shellfish for the evening meal.

Master Wingfield found the motivation to break away from his bookkeeping and to take a quiet walk around the compound. The sun was well into the sky, and the cold wind had abated somewhat, so it might prove to be a rather pleasant outing. He had cloistered himself for a number of days, joining the compliment of men only at meal time, and realized the need to reconnect with his team. The normal busy hum of rebuilding activity was replaced by an eerie silence with only the occasional whistle of the wind in the roof shingles of the dormitory. He entered the building to find the large barracks area completely empty and quite uninviting. The fire in the hearth had gone out, and had the door to the kitchen area not been left open, it would have been completely dark. A faint light shown under the door of one of the private rooms, and as Wingfield approached he called softly, "Halloo."

Seaman Matthew Tasley answered immediately and as he opened the door for the administrator, Wingfield could see that the young man had organized quite an interesting apothecary and doctor's office. Over the months of Surgeon Wickinson's pitiful deterioration, Tasley had gradually moved the sick bay from the *Phyllis* to this room in the dormitory which proved to be very prudent considering the sinking of the craft. He had medical books stacked neatly in every corner and was ravenously reading each one in an effort to learn all he could about the magic of leech-craft. The carpenters had built shelving and a very nice closet for Tasley to store the many jars of ointments, salves, and concoctions, and of course leeches, used in the profession. They also crafted a very comfortable chair and matching table that he used constantly. Wingfield was flooded with memories when he noticed Surgeon Wickinson's large leather medical bag filled with the most amazing medicines on the floor by the chair.

"Very impressive," Winfield commented. "With your permission, I would like to promote you to expedition surgeon. I will enter this information in the log book, and you will be eligible for surgeon's pay as of this date."

Tasley was absolutely elated. It just did not occur to him that he might become the actual surgeon of the group. Whatever surgeon's pay was, it had to be better than seaman's. "Y-your honor," he stammered. "Th-thank you for your confidence. I p-promise I will not let you down."

Wingfield left the happy young man to his studies, ambled comfortably through the deserted dormitory and stepped back out into the winter sun light. He felt personally uplifted and like a leader again. As he looked at the western sky he noted dark, angry fingers of clouds reaching to declare war on the sunshine. He thought to himself, "It looks like a bad storm is on its way."

Deep in thought and unnoticing of his surroundings, his reverie was cruelly jolted back to reality as he felt the shocking pain of a spear being driven deeply into his back! Blood rushed into his mouth and throat and he was unable to call for help. The pain grew more and more excruciating as he looked unbelieving at the crimson stone spear point protruding from his abdomen. As his eyes glazed over his head fell back, he took two awkward steps and fell heavily to the ground. The simple word "Why?" emerged as a gurgled whisper from his lips. In total bewilderment he felt his heart slowing down and the life forces ebbing away. His last earthly thought was of a flaxen-haired young lady back in Mother England who he had neglected to tell of his affection. Tears formed, and all went black.

Standing over the body was a miserable looking Native; obviously a renegade rejected and abhorred by man and beast. He was filthy and hungry and represented the very lowest dregs of humanity. His hair was dirty and matted and crawling with head lice. His yellow crusted eyes were cruelly peering from a face so boney that it was as much a skull. In his empty and pointless travels, he had stumbled across the fort and was foraging for something to eat. It was only the most terrible of coincidences that he and Wingfield met at that particular moment in time. Hated and hateful, the Indian's first and only reaction to seeing the White Man was to kill it. He had no idea that the dead man might have a gentle heart and might have been willing to provide him food and shelter.

The beastly man cautiously looked into the darkened kitchen to see if there were other people about. His only weapon, his spear, was impaled in his victim, and as he tried to extract it the crudely built implement snapped in two with a loud "Crack!" The building appeared to be empty, and his flaring nostrils sensed the presence of corn bread. He saw a large metal pan half filled, quietly removed it from the table, and drooling on his bare chest squatted in the doorway and began to hungrily gorge himself. He looked questioningly at the pan as it began to fill with blood not even realizing that the other White Man had crept up from behind and smashed his skull with a shovel. The pitiful creature toppled over still caressing the baking pan in deserved death.

Tasley was totally devastated. No book or miracle of leech-craft could save the fallen administrator. He tenderly swept back the hair from his master's face and realized his true affection for this man. His tears fell onto Wingfield's countenance and the glistening droplets seemed to turn to gold. His confidence in the healing arts evaporated in that moment of time, and he accepted the reality that he was and would always be only a seaman.

He heard a muffled scream and looked up to see Pising limping with amazing quickness to his side. The scene told the entire story.

"Oh no ... oh no ..." was all the carpenter could say with his voice choked with anguish. He was flooded with the irony of the situation. He and Capper had survived an attack by hundreds of blood-thirsty savages, yet their master was felled by one miserable murderer.

Tasley and Pising gently wrapped Wingfield in an especially beautiful animal pelt and respectfully lifted him onto one of the beds in the dormitory. Had another walked in at that time, he would have thought that the administrator was merely sleeping. Private Dixon and Cook Johnson were expected later that evening and would know what to do next. The group parlaying with the *Choptanks* was scheduled to be gone at least three days. Neither the seaman nor the carpenter was confident the two of them could manage a full length longboat well enough to make the voyage to the village before the other two returned from their hunting trip.

The two Englishmen turned to the issue of removing the murderer's body from the doorway of the kitchen, and both stopped in amazement. The wretch was wearing Sergeant Lusby's tunic! It was tattered, stained with new and old blood, disgustingly unclean and badly faded, but there was no doubt whose shirt it was. They shuddered to think how he might have acquired it. How strange that this most important emblem of the *Phyllis'* adventure into the New World would somehow find its way back home. They tearfully removed it, folded it with great respect and placed it near Wingfield's body. Then they roughly grabbed the miserable Indian by his filthy and boney ankles, and dragged his body face-down to the edge of the forest in hopes that the animals or the worms would erase him from the world's memory.

CHAPTER VI ...
DIASPORA

So Many Farewells

The touching and somber funeral of Master Edward Marie Wingfield would never be forgotten by the *Choptanks* or the Englishmen. It was a union of both cultures expressing a deep and abiding respect for someone of great value. In the eyes of the Indians, the administrator of New Providence was considered equal to their head chief *Pemetosusk,* and an ancient and holy rite was to be performed. Each of the tribe's clans took part, and each grieved in its own personal way.

The *Wah-KON-kon-s'ah* boat builders had a dugout canoe that had never been afloat. It was stored in a special lodge in the forest near the sweat house of the twin chiefs, *Tattowin* and *Weanchum.* The canoe had been painstakingly hand crafted over the period of many months with every effort a labor of love. It was beautifully decorated with the totems and designs of the tribe and was more like a work or art than a utensil. In reality, it was being preserved for the time *Pemetosusk* would be sent to his ancestors. The clansmen agreed unanimously that the chief of the White Men was worthy of its use and carried it on their shoulders to the village beach singing a sorrowful death chant in their rich baritone voices. *Weesanusks* had at some time before carved a beautiful eagle with wings extended that would be attached to the prow of the dugout when needed for the head chief's funeral. He gladly offered it as a token of his admiration for Wingfield. The administrator's body would be placed in the canoe and set adrift until the Mother of All Waters took her child home.

The hunting clan, the *WE-h'ne-s'ah*, placed bear teeth and claw garlands around Wingfield's neck in the belief that their totem, *Mah-TOH* – the Bear, would protect his spirit as it sought the path back to the Creator. This group of Natives did a most amazing and memorable thing that truly touched the hearts of both the villagers and the Englishmen: They took the giant animal skin down from the back wall of the men's lodge, folded it into a soft blanket, and gently laid it in the bottom of the canoe. The weather was turning quite cold and they wanted to be sure the man could stay warm on his journey. Even folded, it was so large that when the White Man's body was placed upon it, he could clearly be seen above the gunwales of the dugout. This animal skin was one of the most prized possessions held by the tribe. Only history knows how it came to the *Choptanks*. To make such a sacred object an offering to their friends' chief was a costly and precious gesture.

The gatherer clan, *Ke-WE-dah-yah-s'ah*, filled the canoe with jars and baskets of every possible edible on the menu as they passed by in a long line and sang their melancholy death song. Their tradition reminds that the journey from Mother Earth to the Creator is long and arduous, and the traveler will need nourishment on his way.

In every funeral a large jar of pemmican is included. Everyone knows that *Wa-KON-ton-kah* (The Great Spirit) loves the treat and receives with favor those who bring it to Him.

The contribution from the *Ho-KU-wah-s'ah* sea harvesters included the most beautiful shells, stones and bones formed in bracelets and necklaces which would serve as offerings so the Creator would see how devoted and generous the traveler was. They attached torches along the sides of the canoe which would help the deceased find his way in the darkness. The dugout would be launched at sunset and the torches lit as it was released into the current.

The Englishmen had respectfully dressed Wingfield's body in his finest clothing, and he looked elegant in the eyes of his men and the villagers. His grievous wounds were hidden by his tunic and grey wool suit as much to provide a lasting memory of a whole person as to shield the ignoble cause of death. His personal items, ledger books, medals and ribbons and other artifacts were placed in the canoe which deeply impressed the Natives. This man was going to the next world with what appeared to be great wealth. Because of Preacher Hunt's demise, Ship's Officer Marian would be responsible for performing the Last Rites of the Christian ceremony. During his service career, he had buried some of his crewmen at sea, so he had the prior experiences to draw upon and did a marvelous and tasteful job of bringing Wingfield's life to closure. The remaining members of the expedition sang or hummed the doleful Christian dirges associated with funerals back in the Mother Country of the 1600's.

As the early winter sun dropped steadily and silently into the bay and darkness walked her slender feet across the lands, the Indian tribal council and the last of the London

Company employees gently slid the canoe into the water. The finality of this gesture touched everyone, and the elder Native women began their heartbreaking wail of pain and sadness. *Asquash* himself lit the torches, and despite the bitter cold, not one person left the shore until the flickering lights gradually disappeared in the blackness. An icy, unkind night wind began to make the trees talk and wet unpleasant snowflakes were beginning to fall.

The people slowly and introspectively returned to their lodges.

Marian said without emotion, "Gentlemen, let us retire to the men's lodge." And the visitors from across the Great Waters silently and sadly followed their new leader.

The *Choptank* tribe's time of mourning was one phase of the moon. So for the next 20-some days there were no celebrations or rites of passage; and of course, no weddings. The announcing of the engagement between *Cahonke* and the English artist would have to wait, and then the marriage ceremony would have to occur an acceptable time after that. Needless to say, Brooks-Hughes was slowly going out of his mind. He was completely obsessed by the thought of the beautiful Princess and was unable to draw or paint or even think. He became so irritable and petty that Jonas Profit was ready to throw him out of their lodge into the nearest snow bank.

The situation was not much better in the *wig-wam* of *Weesanusks* and *Wicompo*. The wedding dress was completed, and there wasn't an inch of white deerskin left without a shell, stone or other decoration attached. Normally, during the time a *Choptank* mother and daughter fashioned the attire for the ceremony they would have that long chat about the relationship between men and women. Long before the dress was completed, *Wicompo* could not think of anything else to say, and the conversation between the two women continually deteriorate into arguments to the point that if the mother did not leave the lodge for some moments of solitude, the daughter might end up needing repairs in the *Peh-ZHU-tah* (Medicine) Lodge.

It was clear that now two *alpha* females were living in the same *wig-wam*.

Cahonke was not about to let a tired old tradition keep her from what she wanted, and she began to devise a plot to speed up the process. *Pacowassamuck's* daughter, *Cah-cookos*, was her best of all friends their entire lives, and she ran through the blizzard to their lodge to tell her what was about to happen. Soon the two teen-age girls were sitting in the back of the *wig-wam* giggling incessantly. *Cahonke* never had a plan fail, and she was confident the trend would continue. It would involve the assistance of some of the boys, but she could count on them without question. She was the tallest, strongest, and smartest child of her generation and any doubt of that was squelched when she fought the bully of the village, held him face-down in the sand, and would have smothered him to death if the adults had not intervened. After that, her word was law among the children. She was adored by her cohorts, but also feared.

Much later that evening, the storm grew more and more fierce, and the entire village hunkered down for the night. The fire pit in the Englishmen's lodge had dwindled to glowing embers, but the interior was still quite comfortable. Brooks-Hughes and Profit had talked long into the night about what the next steps for the visitors might be since their leader was no longer with them. They intended to catch up with the other White Men in the morning hoping that group also had time to determine a course of action. As they drifted off to sleep, the only sound was the wind whistling around the lodge and the gentle voices of the nearby trees.

As the stormy night walked across the headlands a sudden rush of bone-chilling cold crashed through the reed mat door of the White Men's *wig-wam* and dark figures entered boldly. Both men were roughly rolled over onto their faces, and before they could fully wake up and respond, strong hands were pulling their arms behind their backs and tying them so tightly that their fingers began to tingle! Not one word was spoken by the attackers, but Profit could see in the dim fire light that there were at least a half-dozen Indians involved. He also noticed their faces were covered with war paint and their teeth had an eerie orange glow in the waning ember light.

Brooks-Hughes called to Profit, "What is it! What's going on?"

Profit yelled, *"Wash-TEH-cha-kah! Wash-TEH-cha-kah!"*("We are friendly!"). But the silhouettes laughed derisively and proceeded to put cloth ties over their mouths and eyes.

Then the Englishmen felt their feet being pushed into their boots as they were lifted into the standing position. Brooks-Hughes' distress was magnified by the fact that his foot ware were on the wrong feet. Animal skin robes were wrapped around the clothing they always slept in, and they were unkindly pulled outside and ordered, *"MAH-ne!"*("Walk!").

Sometime in the night while they were sleeping, the wind had somewhat died down, and the only sound was the crunch of footsteps in the snow and the heavy breathing of the attackers and the White Men. An occasional hand guided the blindfolded men as the group made its way ...

somewhere. They eventually stopped and the Englishmen were rudely pushed forward as the attackers laughed heartily.

Brooks-Hughes thought, "Well, this is it. Jonas and I are the next ones ..."

As the victims stumbled, they realized they had been pushed into a lodge of some kind. The air was hot but inviting compared to the chill outside. Soft warm hands took each by the arms and seemed to be leading them further into the *wig-wam*. Suddenly, both men felt their legs being rudely kicked out from under them and they tumbled on their backs onto a bed of animal skins. The next sound was so out of context, that Brooks-Hughes and Profit were not sure they were still alive. If this was death's 'sting', it had been highly overstated. It was the sound of girls giggling.

Brooks-Hughes felt his tunic being pulled away from his body then heard the sound of metal hungrily sawing through cloth. He realized the irony that his demise would probably result from the metal knife blades the Englishmen had given the Indians as gifts of friendship. Surely the weapon could easily penetrate cloth ... why were they exposing his bare skin?

He had on occasion wondered what it would feel like to have a Spaniard's sword invade his body: Would it feel hot ... cold ... or anything at all? The blade rapidly splayed his shirt and he was aware that very strong hands were wielding the implement of his destruction. Profit groaned helplessly, and Theodore knew the same fate was befalling his dear friend. Tears welled up in his eyes as he was overwhelmed by sadness for the young Englishman at his side.

The indignation continued as the White Men had their boots roughly removed and their trousers cut away. They were so tightly bound that resistance would be truly futile and both were resigned to face their end as stolid British gentlemen.

Profit's voice was surprisingly even and strong, "Theodore, we'll be together on the Other Side. Try not to despair."

Despite the dreadful feeling that was washing over his body, Brooks-Hughes felt calm and resigned to his fate. He began to shiver more likely as a result of stress than the air temperature, as another totally out of context event happened: Uncomfortably hot water was poured from the top of his head to his feet and toes. This was repeated over and over as women's laughter grew with each baptism. The perpetrator seemed to linger in his personal area as if especially enjoying tormenting the victim.

"How strange their murder rituals are," thought Profit. "These savages want to be sure we are clean before they kill us."

They felt the gags and blindfolds being removed and as their eyes adjusted to the dim light, *"Cahonke!"* … *"Cah-cookos!"*

Standing over the very wet, prone and basically nude Englishmen were the two *Choptank* princesses. Both began to slowly and alluringly disrobe in the faint light of the fire pit. Their dance of desire was the most graceful and beautiful thing the men had ever seen as the two lovely young women slowly exposed their bodies. The young White Men were both still tied up, but this did not seem to matter … at all.

It may have been the dead of winter in *Choptank* country, but that night in the lodge was springtime.

———————————————

Ship's Officer Marian piled wood on the fire pit in the men's lodge and thought about the Englishmen that were still alive. Of the 17 London Company employees that left Jamestown, only five were among the living. Captain Coverdale was seldom involved with the issues of New Providence anymore, so there were actually only four available. Since the carpenters, Pising and Capper, had been injured in the attack, only two of those, the Martin boys, could be considered completely able-bodied. His ship's crew had fared considerably better, even though his ship itself had not. Nine members of the British Royal Navy were the heart of the *Phyllis Redoubtable,* and only Percy Exum was missing and presumed dead. And then there was Private Dixon, the last of the Fusiliers. Marian could not help but chuckle thinking of this amazing warrior. He was in every way a one-man army and every Englishman thanked the gods for him being there.

The expedition members had talked long into the night trying to determine what the next move would be. They were truly on the horns of a dilemma because there were not enough men to satisfactorily defend the fort, and most of the Englishmen could not accept living with the *Choptanks* the rest of their lives. As the exhausted Europeans retired for the night they had developed a plan acceptable to everyone: Each longboat would be refitted with a sail and the prow of each craft would be covered with canvas to provide shelter from the elements. Jamestown would be their destination. The weather was terrible and the waters were dangerous, but British mariners have a built-in confidence that they can best anything the sea can throw at them. The mean winds hailed from the north, which was the appropriate direction to push the longboats southerly. And they were confident their hosts would help them fit-out the crafts for the journey.

Leaving behind New Providence was a source of angst to the group. Each man had in such a personal way been a part of the great experiment. His sweat, hard work and commitment had helped develop a part of these Empty Lands into what could have been one day a "New England,"

and it was not easy to turn their backs on such an honorable
endeavor. However, totally oblivious to the hardships that
had decimated the retinue at Jamestown, there was hope that
after some reorganizing, a new group could return from that
location and continue the New Providence project.

Marian wrestled with how to deal with those that may
not want to leave the *Choptanks*. Every London Company
employee was contracted to remain with the expedition,
and although it was in his purvey to honorably discharge
members of the Royal Navy, he was not sure he could allow
himself to do so. The ship was gone, but there would be new
ships; and he did not want to lose a well-trained and tight-
knit crew.

At that moment, some of the women of the village
brought the morning meal and spread it out by the fire pit.
It was the standard corn bread with honey, pemmican, and
a sea food stew that had been served before, but it smelled
delicious. Marian, making a gathering motion, said *"Ha-
KAH-sha-na"* (Indian term for the White Men) to one of
the ladies who nodded implying she understood, and soon
Captain Coverdale, Brooks-Hughes and Jonas Profit trundled
through the snow to join the group. The two young seamen
ate voraciously as if they hadn't had a meal in weeks. They
seemed very content and relaxed and talked quietly to each
other, often breaking into laughter. Of course, the others
wanted to know what happened ... and of course they got
no information out of the two young men.

This could very well be the last time that the entire group
of surviving Englishmen would ever again be together,
and as the realization of this fact began to sink in, it was a
very sobering situation. This unlikely combination of older
men, young men and boys from varied backgrounds and
often different values had survived incredible hardship and

peril ... and emerged better for it. They had forged a team with a unified purpose and had become closer than brothers. The impending separation would be painful for everyone and despite the growing hope that some would reconnect with other expedition members when they reached Jamestown, nobody wanted to think about what the actual departure would be like.

As the men finished their meal, Ship's Officer Edwin Marian stood up to address the group. He had reached a conclusion that would be satisfactory to everyone, and his unique ability to address a problem and bring it to an appropriate solution would pay off for him in future years. One day he would become the highest ranking fleet officer in the British Royal Navy and a national hero of many future campaigns.

"Gentlemen," he began. And the room grew completely quiet. "I believe it is in the best interest of our nation and king to keep some of you here in the *Choptank* village as ambassadors for His Royal Majesty. You will remain on the payroll of the London Company or the Royal Navy and will be expected to present yourselves at all time as upstanding English gentlemen." Quiet chuckles rippled through the group, and a quick scowl from Marian brought back their previous undivided attention.

"As the commander of the expedition each of you will accept the assignment I am intending to give to you, and I will hold you personally accountable that you fulfill your duties. Captain Coverdale, you will be the officer in charge of the group that remains with the *Choptanks*. You will serve as the King's personal liaison to the village leadership council and will have the power to sign agreements and establish commercial ventures in the name of the London Company."

"Seaman Jonas Profit, it will be your responsibility to delve deeply into the Indian culture. I will expect you to become highly proficient in the spoken language and also to be astute to the non-verbal communication methods they use. I want you to be especially knowledgeable of the processes they use to trade and barter within the village and with other indigenous groups."

"Private James Dixon, I am assigning you as military advisor to the tribe. You will train a cadre of *Choptanks* in the methods used by the Royal Marines. When I return to the village, I will expect to see a smartly attired military unit that the king would be proud to claim. Try to salvage whatever you can from New Providence to make your men the best equipped and most effective fighting force in this part of the New World." He then looked at Dixon sternly, "I will accept no less than excellence from you in this endeavor."

Then Marian turned to Theodore, and if someone would have been standing closer he might have noticed a small tear forming in the officer's eyes. "Seaman Brooks-Hughes, as best I can determine, your future has been decided for you. In no way can we insult the tribal council by not endorsing the marriage between you and *Weesanusks'* daughter. As much as I have always admired Master Wingfield, I do not think he realized how close we came to war when he refused to allow the union the *Choptanks* were expecting. Our relationship with the Natives in this region must be kept on a sound and positive footing. You will return to the fort and select the items you feel would make an acceptable dowry. I am asking you to make this sacrifice for King and country, and you have my eternal admiration should you chose to accept this commission."

Brooks-Hughes nodded gravely, "Captain Marian, I accept this commission for king and country." He was afraid to look at Jonas for he knew he would burst out in joyous laughter at the impish look coming his way from his friend.

But greatest of all … his heart took flight.

Two Great Journeys

T he new-fallen snow had the countryside looking like a fairy wonderland. The air was uncomfortably cold, but the bright sunshine made the landscape look like it was encrusted with sparkling jewels. Everything was covered with perfect white cake frosting that rounded off the sharp edges of the world and subdued the sounds of human interruptions.

As the Englishmen walked through the village most of the people were in the warmth of their lodges. Those outdoors smiled warmly and called, "*Ha-KAH-sha-na!*" their term of endearment for their friends. Jonas Profit left the group as it passed by *Pemetosusk's* lodge to inform the chief of the plan the Europeans were about to embark upon. He did not know that the scheme of action was totally opposite of what the *Choptanks* had in mind for their Pale-skinned brothers. In no way were they going to let the expedition members return to the White World and bring back a host of others into their own bountiful and sacred land.

The sea was very calm, and had the air not been so frigid, the voyage back to New Providence would have been idyllic in every way. The longboats plied the estuary with relative ease, and each Englishmen felt a new sense of optimism and hope. Ship's Officer Marian rested his arm on the tiller and almost dozed off as he was guiding the craft. Then he sat upright and his eyes widened as he realized there was no canvas for the sails or for wrapping the prow of the dories. All the sail cloth had gone down with the *Phyllis*. He remembered that the artist Brooks-Hughes had been given a roll for his painting projects, but that was not near enough to meet their impending needs.

In great effort to calm his voice, he asked, "Does anybody have an idea what we could use to make the sails?"

The rowers looked up, and a most unusual reaction occurred: They laughed! And they laughed until the sound of their levity rolled across the water to the other longboat.

Navigator Obadiah Withams guiding the other craft called, "What are we missing?"

Carpenter John Capper replied loudly, "We are going to have to sew our breeches together to make the foresails! When we get to Jamestown our buttocks will be as blue as the sea!" The others began to laugh as they pictured the situation, and the laughter continued all the way to New Providence.

Even unto today it is called "British Ingenuity." As the Englishmen sat around the fireplace in the dormitory and Cook Johnson began to prepare the evening meal many ideas flowed in an effort to resolve the issues at hand. Pising and Capper were sure they could use the undamaged machines that were in the burned-out shake mill to fashion strips of wood for the top for the longboats. These would be even sturdier than canvas, and the laths could be pieced together so tightly as to be waterproof. Granted, the main propulsion for the longboats would be arm strength of the men, so any kind of sail would only be a source of additional speed. The spars for the sails would be cut from smaller tree trunks, smoothed out with the manual planer machine, and then bolted to the bottom of each craft. They could not be too tall or they would topple the boats, maybe at best 10-feet in height above the gunwales. A pulley system with buntlines could be devised to raise and lower the yardarms that the sails would be attached to.

Now ... how to make the foresails.

Jerald Pennyfeather-Grayson was often the 'clown' of the ship's crew. He was always happy-go-lucky never taking anything too seriously. His mates held special affection for him, because they knew he could always find the bright side of any situation. "I've got a great idea!" he commented. "Master Wingfield had large linen sheets on his bed. I know this because I laundered them for him at times. If we reinforce them with stitching, they might just do the trick."

The others broke into laughter at the suggestion remembering that the sheets were faded shades of color rather than manly white or gray, but Navigator Withams seriously considered the suggestion. "A single sheet would tear at the first sign of wind, but if we double or triple the cloth and reinforced the bunting, it might be worth a try. Seaman Parksley, you take Jerald with you and see just how much bedding is still in the Master's House. If there is any, bring it to the dormitory."

The optimism felt at New Providence was not the tone of the meeting in *Pemetosusk's* lodge. Jonas Profit's visit was both good and bad news. The tribal council was very pleased with the Englishmen who were being allowed to remain in the village, and especially happy that the wedding would be held after the proper mourning time. But the thought of the other visitors returning to their own people was quite troubling ... and this time there was no ship to burn.

The terrible dream that the twin chief's had about a plague of *Ha-KAH-sha-nah* (White Men) destroying everything the *Choptanks* held dear was manifesting itself again in even more and more vivid imagery. In its clarity, they saw their own lodges shredded in the cold wind and choked with weeds and thorns ... and absolutely nobody still alive.

Shoong-TOK-cha – The Wolf, so hungry that his bones were showing through his fur, was pacing through the remains of the snowy dream village looking for something to eat. He stopped at the shoreline by a dugout canoe blackened with soot, smashed and useless, and howled so mournfully that the twins began to cry. As the vision faded, the Earth Mother opened her heart and all the Red People in the world fell in: Men, women and children, screaming and trying to hold on to each other. It was truly a nightmare beyond any they had ever experienced in their lives.

Pacowassamuck asked sadly, "Is it what it will be ... or what it might be?"

Tattowin turned away and replied, "We have never had a vision repeat itself so many times and be so real. The only question we have is ... When?"

Weesanusks brightened, "Then the nightmare could be way off in the future, and it might have nothing to do with our friends. None of us has ever felt that our *Ha-KAH-sha-nah* were the only ones like them on the Earth Mother. We have learned much about them, and we have found them to be strong and good hearted, if not too intelligent."

Despite the gravity of the meeting, *Weesanusks'* summing-up of the Englishmen brought gentle chuckles among the others. "Let us rest on this problem," responded *Pemetosusk*. "We have a wedding to plan."

Cahonke nestled her head in her mother's lap and enjoyed the comfort and reassurance. The flames in her heart and body were quelled and she felt like a fulfilled woman. Sewing the bridal gown was complete, so that bone-of-contention was out of the way. The lodge was warm and cozy, and the animal skin bedding felt absolutely luxurious. *Wicompo* gently ran her fingers through her only surviving child's shiny black hair and looked at her with loving eyes. Her little girl had blossomed into a very beautiful woman and the mother was trying to see something familiar in her. Of course, it was her eyes. Those dark flashing limpid pools of mischief had always mirrored the soul of a free spirit, eager to challenge authority and willing to accept the consequences. She asked, without criticism or judgment, "Have you sung with the Englishman?"

Cahonke smiled, stretched like a pampered cat, then answered with blunt honesty, "Yes, mother. I fell in love with that strange man the moment I saw him. From that time on, all I wanted was to be in his arms."

Wicompo felt tears welling up in her eyes. Her life's plan for her daughter was to marry a handsome young warrior from a very rich and powerful tribe who would be the chief someday. She realized that as a young woman, this was her personal hope also … and it just never came to be. *Weesanusks*, her husband, was a kind and caring person, not at all unattractive as a young brave, but somehow lacked the drive and ambition to become what she had hoped for. She knew what the other *Choptank* women felt about her – jealous, petty and gossipy – but she always felt she was above their barely disguised scorn. This unhappy woman could not even count the nights she tearfully lay awake wishing to be back with her *Chicamacomico* people where she would be treated like a queen; honored, respected and feared by everyone. The *Choptank* community was a small-minded village, and if the women were not aware that her daughter had flaunted the sexual mores' of the tribe, it was just a matter of time.

Suddenly, she was determined that her daughter would not have to live like she did. She gently placed her daughter's head on the bed cloaks and whispered, "I will be back soon."

She wrapped her winter attire around her shoulders and ran out into the waiting night.

Brooks-Hughes and Jonas Profit were resting by the warming fire in their lodge and were trying to determine how to best maintain the relationship with their *Choptank* girls as *Wicompo* pushed aside the tule mat door and stepped boldly into their sanctum. The artist's heart leaped into his throat knowing immediately what must have happened, but not knowing what would happen next. For the millionth time, and for another ten million times more, the mother of a besmirched girl was about to hold the offending boy accountable. She did not speak the language of the White Man, but she knew that Profit could translate her every whim. She loomed over the reclining men, looked at Jonas and said flatly, "Tell him everything I am about to say ... and do not change one thing."

The young interpreter felt the hair rise on the back of his neck. What if *Cahonke* also told her about *Cah-cookos*. Then a most unexpected thing happened: *Wicompo* knelt down by the men and began to cry, deeply and mournfully; her sobbing shaking her shoulders. The young Englishmen felt terrible and their hearts went out to the woman. Without hesitation, they were willing to do anything to assuage her grief. Before the visit was over, both men had told her everything – much more than she even suspected. Quietly satisfied that every possible sin had been exposed, she carefully explained her plan to the White Men. Painfully aware that they had no choice, but also realizing this could be the adventure of a lifetime, they eagerly agreed to support her in every way possible.

Wicompo invited *Cahonke* and *Cah-cookos* to join her in the moon time lodge. The woman servant had prepared a sumptuous meal in both flavors and variety then retired to the back of the *wig-wam* awaiting further instructions. "We must leave the village," the mother stated without emotion. "There is nothing for us here any longer. When the people find out about your relationships with the White Men, they will shun you the rest of your lives. The tribal council may even banish you."

Cahonke felt the anger rise up in her throat. "I don't care what the people think about me! I never did before and I don't intend to care now!"

Wicompo touched her arm gently but firmly, "But I do. And I also care what they think about *Cah-cookos*. You are both wonderful and beautiful women and you deserve to be treated like queens … and I know how to bring that about."

———

The evening was clear and cold as the young couples prepared to secretly leave the *Choptank* village. *Wicompo* and her maidservant quietly exited the *wig-wam* as gentle *Weesanusks* snored loudly enjoying a most pleasant dream. The village had never felt it necessary to post night guards or sentries. In fact once the evening came there was very little, actually nothing, going on outside the *wig-wams*. The Indigenous people of the Western World refused to wage war during the nighttime fearful that if they were killed the Creator would be unable to find their souls in the darkness. The small cluster of refugees deserting the village were the only two-leggeds roaming the shoreline that time of night.

The winter winds were completely still and the obsidian waters were like glass. The full moon glistened brightly providing so much light that they could easily see their way. Brooks-Hughes was in the front of the dugout canoe paddling easily and silently. *Cahonke* was resting against his lap snuggled under an animal skin robe and the two lovers were enjoying the nearness of their bodies. Jonas Profit was in the back of the sea-going craft matching his friend stroke-for-stroke and also enjoying his heart's delight, *Cah-cookos*, near him. *Wicompo* and her servant were bundled up in the center of the canoe dozing quietly. The industrious helper had been instructed to quietly begin to hoard food for the journey and in a few short days had acquired so much that all six people had enough to eat for a month if needed. Somehow, she had managed to also acquire two large jars of *M'ne-SKOO-yah* (Salt), a king's ransom indeed. Before the long trek up river, they would need to stop at New Providence to select the dowry items now to be used to impress *Wicompo's* people. She was by inheritance a queen, and it was extremely important that she return home with wealth and status after her many years with the *Choptanks*. The metal tools and utensils of the Englishmen as well as the bolts of colorful cloth that had survived the *Mitsawokets* raid along with the sparkling glass beads stored in the dormitory would make fine gifts and offerings to the *Chicamacomico* leadership. It was agreed that the actual purpose of this visit would remain in the hearts of those on the journey and not be shared with the *Ha-KAH-sha-nah*. Ship's Officer Marian might decide to rescind his commands if he found out the Indigenous tribe that Brooks-Hughes and Profit would be residing with was no longer the *Choptanks*.

The embarkation date for the expedition members to begin their long trek back to Jamestown was just a few days away, so Master Marian had no concerns whatsoever about tallying the dowry items that Brooks-Hughes and Jonas were preparing to load into the dugout. The two English longboats had little storage space, so every square inch would be used for the salvaged trade goods acquired from the *Choptanks*, survival essentials and weapons. He was confident that at some point in the future an entire new expedition would return to New Providence, so tools and items left behind would be there waiting until they were needed again. Despite the failures of this honorable venture, the second attempt to tame this wild land would be so much easier because of the pathway they had already established.

The ship's officer could not understand why the young lady, *Cah-cookos,* was with the others. There was some logic for *Cahonke* and *Wicompo's* participation. They would certainly know what a dowry should include, and under the dim light of the whale-oil lamps were actively involved in pointing out to the servant, the artist and the interpreter what should be loaded and what left behind.

Brooks-Hughes explained her presence, "*Cah-cookos* is *Cahonke's* best friend and will be her bride's maid. She asked to join us and was willing to help select the gifts for the tribal council. Her father is *Pacowassamuck.*"

This made sense to Marian and he did not give it a second thought. Later, in passing, he would wonder why they came during a cold late winter night.

The night was still young as the two Englishmen and their passengers were climbing back into the well-loaded dugout canoe. The remaining members of the original team that had sailed on the *Phyllis Redoubtable* not so long ago were there to see them off and some waded into the water to help get the craft underway. As the travelers paddled into the bright moonlight, Jonas looked back and waved.

This would be the last time any White Man would ever see them again.

———————

How strange the fickle hands of Fate had folded and twisted the lives of these men. It seemed like only a heartbeat ago 29 refugees from the Jamestown Colony had sought a new life. Now there were fourteen left, and only 10 of those would endeavor to return to the beginning of their adventure ...

The longboats were ready and were pulling impatiently on their tethers. Master Marian was waiting for the flow of the ebbing tide to begin which would be a great help getting them out of the estuary and into the main waters. Their 'ships' were the strangest looking crafts the Englishmen had ever seen. The front third of each one was tightly covered with a roof made of strips of wood that gave an impression of decking. Provisions were stored there, and animal skins were organized to make a bed that would stay relatively dry. The men jokingly called the spar "the mizzenmast" even though it was basically a 10-foot pole with a mechanism attached to raise and lower the foresail. The sails themselves were truly a sight to behold. They consisted of the bed cloths of Master Wingfield, doubled and tripled in thickness, then sewed and re-sewed to reinforce the linen cloth. When fully unfurled they formed a respectable eight foot by ten foot rectangle and were surprisingly sturdy. Indeed, they were not a bad example of a homemade fore-skysail. Actually, by British standards they were quite colorful too, and in a few moments the mariners would know if they could serve their purpose.

The men were no less impatient to begin their journey. Each longboat would have a crew of five with Master Marian at the tiller of one and Navigator Withams the other. Marian had to feel rather discounted by the size of his crew and the 'ship'. He had been an officer on some of the finest two- and three-masted vessels in the navy. Now, there wasn't even a category to classify his latest command. By late morning the elements were cooperating as best could be expected for a mid-Atlantic winter day, and the world's smallest British Fleet set sail on a new adventure. As they rowed to join the tidal flow, Marian ordered Seaman Parksley to "set sails," then he laughed and said, "Set <u>sail</u>!" It worked! The small craft gently lurched forward, and Marian had his 'crew' ship their oars. Maybe they would not have to row all the way to Jamestown after all.

Homecoming Heartbreak

Wicompo had taken the journey back to her people in her mind and in her heart a thousand times over the past 17 years with the *Choptanks*, but her homesickness was not to the point that she felt she could try to return on her own. She could visualize every landmark, hillock and pathway right to her parent's front door … and now it was becoming a reality. The anticipation of taking her rightful place as the queen of the tribe made her anxious to get there, and she was aggravated that the young couples did not feel the same urgency. In fact, they considered the trip a 'honeymoon' and were just glad to be 'almost-alone' together.

The itinerary included rowing on into the night upriver until a safe distance from the village could be determined. At that point, a camp would be set up to provide an escape from the elements. A few hours rest would bring safer travel on the unknown river. *Wicompo* was confident she would recognize the trailhead to her village. A half-day hike overland from the river bank on a well-worn path would bring the refugees to the village located in higher country where many artesian springs sprouted life for a number of small streams and brooks that flowed southwestward to the bay.

Generations ago, the *Chicamacomico* had found the place their Garden of Eden. They constructed their *ho-gans* of wood and mud with heavily thatched roofs, and they were built to last. It was a land of plenty and had provided subsistence for the tribe in comfort. They were hunters, fisher people and might also be classified as the very first 'farmers' in this part of the New World. If a traveler would happen to approach their village during the warm months, he would be welcomed and refreshed, and he would see large cleared areas where a cornucopia of edible plant life was dressed, tilled and kept. Also, the tribe had somehow imported living beaver to make dams to obstruct the flow of some of the streams. Those ponds would serve as their idea of fish hatcheries and also swimming holes for the children. About the only items they lacked were *M'ne-SKOO-yah* (Salt) and some diet variety that the sea might provide, so this brought about the occasional contact with the coast people. It had been many years since the last rendezvous between the two tribes, so *Wicompo* had no recent news of the village or her family.

Jonas Profit had learned how to make temporary shelters as a result of the many hunting trips he took with the *WE-h'ne-s'ah* clan. The winter nights at this latitude are always cold, but not necessarily bitterly uncomfortable. These structures would allow at least a modicum of comfort. Brooks-Hughes helped him gather the small trees and limbs that would serve as the lean-to frameworks, then they covered the interior floor and the roof and walls with the animal skins packed in the canoe. Each couple had their own 'tent' and *Wicompo* and her servant claimed the third. The openings faced each other and tightly encircled the campfire, so the warmth from the flames also warmed the shelters. The servant immediately began to prepare the evening meal, and soon each person was enjoying a surprisingly tasty repast sitting in their *'wig-wams'* toasting their feet by the fire.

Cahonke looked across the dying flames at her mother and asked, "Mother will you tell me my favorite story? I think *Jo-NAH-sus* can translate the story to *Tee-AH-dor.*"

Wicompo was surprised and pleased. Her daughter had not asked her to tell a story for years. She began:

> *"A mother sin-TEH-sh'dah (Mouse) had found a home for her three babies under a tree that had fallen so long ago it was covered with moss. She made a comfortable bed of dried*

grasses, and the little ones were as safe as could be in their warm and cozy den.

"She would have to leave her children to forage for food, so she especially worried about the little girl. She was very curious and would not always mind her mother."

Wicompo paused and looked knowingly at her daughter.

"On occasion other mice would drop by and discuss the difficulties and dangers they had to face to keep alive. The hawks and ravens would circle in the sky looking to pounce on them, and many of the hungry four-leggeds were always nearby ready for a quick meal.

"After a particularly troubling day of foraging, the mother mouse returned home to find her two little boys asleep and the young girl eager to find out what her day was like. She became very annoying with her questions and antics, especially when she asked, 'Mother, what is the sky?' She was tired and in no mood to explain anything, so she just pointed upward and replied, 'All you need to know is that it is up there.'

"The little girl mouse settled down, and when she looked up, all she could see was the bottom of the fallen tree. 'So that is the sky,' she thought. 'I wonder if I could touch the sky.' She stretched as tall as she could, but her fingers could not quite reach the tree trunk. So she crouched down then jumped with all her might, and her fingers barely swept across the rotting bark overhead. When she landed, she tumbled onto her back, and with a wide smile began to sing:

Yah-kee Oh-Oh-Oh
Moh-zha nah lay.
A-a-a-a.

Pay Zhay Nah Keesh-kay
Sha-nah Neek Nah-Zhee.
Ka-a-a-y.
Moh-zha nah lay.

"Which means in Chicamacomico: 'I am the most wonderful
Creature of the Earth Mother ... I can touch the sky."

Brooks-Hughes and Jonas Profit both chuckled at the pleasant tale. As the artist looked at his heart of hearts sleeping soundly at his side, he gently caressed the warm and totally flawless brown skin of her shoulders and nestled his face against her clean, shiny black hair that felt like the most marvelous spun silk from far off Cathay. Its fragrance was more pleasant than the most beautiful spring flowers. He felt so much love for her at that moment that he could hardly breathe. Indeed, the life ahead was going to be fabulous.

When the party reached the snow covered trailhead by the riverbank, it was choked with undergrowth and difficult to find. *Wicompo* was positive this was the right location. The nearby rocky outcropping rare in this part of the country had always been an easy-to-find marker, and it was still there. She decided that over the past 17 years, a better trail must have been blazed, and the one she remembered was probably forgotten and outdated. She considered having the group continue upriver to find the new outlet, but decided that even in its rough condition, she was more confident that it would lead them to their destination.

"Let us not overload ourselves for the walk ahead," she suggested. "When we get to the village, we can send some of the braves back to collect everything we leave behind. Each of us should take some food and a sample of gifts and barter items we brought with us."

Jonas had stowed three of the excellent back packs the Hunting clan used on their outings, and they were soon filled with a king's ransom of colorful glass beads, smaller metal goods, samples of cloth, and of course culinary delights. It would be about a ten mile or so hike to the village, mostly uphill, so the men and the servant each hoisted a tote bag allowing the women to carry whatever they wished. Both White Men also shouldered a fine quality long bow and a quiver of metal tipped arrows as much for 'show' as for protection. Normally, the trek would take about five or six hours, but the snowy conditions and the poor quality of the trail added more time before their arrival. Brooks-Hughes would lead for a while tramping down the snow and cutting any overhanging limbs or brush that might obstruct their progress. When he tired, Jonas would take over. Fortunately, the trail wound across many open areas, and the actual 'trail blazing' was not too difficult a task. *Wicompo* keep peering ahead in hopes of seeing rising fire pit smoke that would indicate the nearness of their destination. She became anxious feeling that they should be there any minute.

When they finally sighted the village, *Wicompo* cried out in dismay. Her beautiful and prosperous hometown was almost completely destroyed! Most of the *ho-gans* were merely snow-covered piles of ruin. The few that remained somewhat intact had caved-in roofs and the doors torn off. Their interiors were weed-infested and the fire pits were merely cold black chunks of charcoal and ash. There were actually no signs that any habitation had occurred there in any recent time. Whatever had happened to the village must have occurred so long ago that the Earth Mother was well along in reclaiming her land.

Timber Wolf. Called "shoong-TOK-cha."

There were absolutely no human beings, and the only sign of life was a strong looking raw-boned wolf that slunk out of one of the doorways and turned toward the nearby forest. The frightened creature had not taken two steps before he felt the sting of Jonas' arrow as it buried itself to the feathers in his neck. He let out a painful yelp, coughed black blood, and tumbled dead in the snow.

The proud queen had finally returned home to find no subjects to worship her and no realm to rule over.

Reweaving the Ties that Bind

As winter slowly released her grip on the land, the shocking reverberations of the elopement of the young women and the Englishmen gradually subsided. Still, not one person in the village could forgive *Wicompo's* involvement. They were convinced the lesser chief's wife had somehow enticed the young men to abscond with the girls, probably even against their will. Where they had gone was anybody's guess, but *Pemetosusk's* wife *Watsawasoo* rightly presumed they had returned to her people. She feared to say anything lest the *Choptanks* pursue the kidnappers and kill the offending parties, including her younger sister.

Most of the villagers were sure the group had fled to New Providence, and when two canoes of warriors voyaged to the fort, they were surprised to find it completely abandoned.

Lesser chief *Weesanusks* suffered the most. He had lost his life's love and also the apple of his eye. The two people he cared the most about were gone forever leaving a giant hole in his heart and a deep blackness in his soul. *Pacowassamuck* wanted his pound of flesh for the loss of his daughter and he got it. The tribal leadership council agreed to remove *Wessanusks* from their august body because of the embarrassment the event had caused. This grieved the head chief deeply, because he had never brought pain to his best friend before, and it was his responsibility to tell the kind man and also the village. The position was filled by the honorable *Asquash*, the greatest of all *Choptank* hunters, who begrudgingly accepted the appointment. The *WE-h'ne-s'ah* warrior clan finally had representation at the chief's side and *Pacowassamuck* got what he had always hoped for.

The lodge of *Weesanusks* was cold and empty. He seldom took the time to kindle a warming fire and spent most of his days in painful depression wrapped in the animal skin blankets. He would be seen late at night standing on the beach looking out into the darkness softly calling the names of his family and hopelessly wishing to see the missing pieces of his heart coming back. Some of the elder women of the community would prepare food for him and leave it at the door of his *wig-wam*, but more times than not, it had not been touched.

Springtime is the season of life. The slumbering Earth Mother opens her sleepy eyes and all her peoples, the swimmers, the flyers, the two-leggeds and the four-leggeds, stretch and yawn, then venture out into the newly cleansed world. It was so ironic that on such a pleasant night woeful *Weesanusks* slowly walked down to the shore line, quietly fell into the gentle arms of the Mother of All Waters and began his long journey to his ancestors.

━━━━━━━━

The last of the expedition fusiliers, Private James Dixon, had moved into the vacated lodge of Profit and Brooks-Hughes. He took his assignment to develop an Indian militia unit very seriously, and counted on Captain Coverdale to communicate his needs and expectations as he himself endeavored to learn the *Choptank* language and teach the village warriors as much English as possible. He found it difficult to look past the changes in the only other White Man in his world. The former English military officer insisted he be addressed as *AH-ban-nah Chon-TEH* (the Native name for "Gentle Heart"), and his magnificent British uniform had long ago vanished from his wardrobe.

Dixon surveyed the military equipment he still had at his disposal. Piled all around the men's lodge were longbows and crossbows with more arrows and quarrels than he had imagined were available. Also there were two large barrels filled with metal arrow heads of all sizes and configurations. Yew wood spears and pikes taller than a man were bundled together and would need some attention before they could be usable. The two fusils that had been stowed in the longboats were left in his keeping as well as two more that had been stored in the dormitory at New Providence. He had an ample supply of fusil bullets, both the large baseball size, and the smaller scatter-gun shot. He also had salvaged the lead ingots and the molds from the fort. The problem would be gunpowder. A large bag of corned powder accompanied each fusil in the boats, and he had a small barrel of black powder in need of being corned that had been stored in the Master's House. There was an ample supply of charcoal available and Cook Johnson had showed him where he found the potassium nitrate that had extruded from the soil; but the third ingredient to make more 'fire powder' (sulfur), had not been located. He was not aware that Jonas Profit had found out that a supply of *Mah-KAH-zee* was right under his nose in the Men's Lodge considered by the *Choptanks* as a form of *Peh-ZHU-tah* (Medicine). It was tightly sealed in clay pots, so the noxious aroma was not readily noticeable.

That evening, the warrior, and now lesser chief *Asquash*, and Captain Coverdale met with Dixon to discuss the possibilities of molding *Choptank* braves into the military ways of the British. Dixon's vision included six men trained to use the fusils and another dozen taught to be proficient with the crossbows and longbows. He could not determine in any way how he could find or have made a semblance of a standard British Marine uniform, so he settled on the idea that they would be identified by wearing red dyed leather leggings and wrist covers and red fox headwear. *Asquash* would determine which of the *WE-h'ne-s'ah* clan members would be selected to participate in the training and would be directly involved in the progress of the experiment to the degree he saw fit. Dixon hoped that Captain Coverdale would diagram the maneuvers and strategies to make the unit as efficient as possible. He had a brilliant military mind and a special affinity for getting the most out of the resources at hand.

Much to Dixon's dismay, *Asquash* was not the slightest bit interested in his warriors being trained in the ways of the White Men. He was confident they were already superb fighters and hunters; strong, fierce and totally fearless in the face of adversity. It made no sense to try to change them into anything less. He appreciated the power and accuracy of the English longbow and crossbow, and he deeply respected their 'fire powder', but he saw no value in trying to make his clansmen into something they were not. The discussion had reached a critical point where expectations were as far apart as the sun and the moon. Dixon felt embarrassed and devalued. His adult life had been the British military which he was convinced was the most powerful fighting force in the world. He was willing to share his knowledge and experiences with a group of people that he considered ignorant toward the ways of proper battle techniques and actually not overly intelligent.

The room was silent as both men crossed their arms over their chests and postured their resolve against each other's ideas.

Captain Coverdale turned to *Asquash* and spoke to him in perfect *Choptank*. "Private Dixon is our most honored warrior. Even *Shoong-TOK-cha* – The Wolf becomes a *Poo-SEE-chin-cha* (kitten) in his presence. His enemies tremble and cover their ears just from the sound of his name. When he approaches them, they cast down their weapons and plead for mercy. I have seen him rip the arms off a man and eat them before the victim's very eyes. In battle with the 'fire powder' he once killed eight men with one shot, then he stomped on the pieces of their flesh. It would be good not to anger him."

Asquash looked at Gabrielle with just the faintest raising of his eyebrows. Lying and exaggeration were not a part of the *Choptank* culture, so he had no reason to think the captain was trying to pull the wool over his eyes. He thought a moment and replied, "The White Warrior may train all the *WE-h'ne-s'ah* in the use of the 'fire powder'. It will be the choice of each of them as to whether or not they want to learn more about the longbow and crossbow. Our attire is the totem of our clan and will not be changed."

He then turned to Private Dixon with a more gentle look on his face, extended his arms toward him and stated, "*Ska Zoo-YAH-we-CHOSH-tah*" From that moment on the *Choptank* would know him as "White Warrior."

After *Asquash* left the lodge, Captain Coverdale explained what the warrior leader would agree to. Dixon, always a practical man, realized this would be the best that could be done and consented with little regret. Then he asked, "What did you say to him?"

Coverdale answered as he exited the doorway, "I just said you held him in great respect and would be willing to accept any decision he thought was appropriate."

———————

The two refitted longboats slowly plied the waters of what would be called Chesapeake Bay by Jamestown's Captain John Smith. Ship's Officer Marian was confident that if they could keep the coast line to starboard they would eventually find the mouth of the river flowing from the west that would take them home. The distance from New Providence to Jamestown was deceptive because their first voyage on these waters was under the power of a hurricane which collapsed both time and distance, and they had no idea how far they had traveled before finding the *Choptanks*. Navigator Withams no longer had the instruments to do some actual navigation, so they were truly proceeding by the seat of their pants.

Other issues added to the confusion. They were not aware that four large rivers found the bay from the mainland before what would be called the James River by the English settlers could be located. Their northerly journey paralleled the eastern shore, much of which was obstructed by the storm. Even when the visibility improved any landmarks they might have remembered were out of eye sight from the western reaches. And much of the coastal terrain of the mid-Atlantic region of North America is redundantly similar. This last issue alone added many days to a voyage that in modern time could be accomplished in a few good days' sailing.

Fortunately, the weather cooperated, which was a double-edged sword. The winds were normally calm so the sun was able to maintain mastery over the chilly aspects of moving air, and when the evening off-shore breezes began, they were in a favorable direction. However, much of the progress depended on rowing rather than blowing.

The gritty Englishmen were continually frustrated by traveling upstream on the wrong rivers. After ten days afloat they had barely covered 90 miles of true direction and their provisions were beginning to dwindle ... which meant hunting expeditions that slowed their progress even more.

After two days struggling against the flow of the river of the *Rappahannocks*, the exhausted White Men again floated seaward discouraged and wondering if they would ever find the Jamestown Colony again. Maybe it had been destroyed by marauding Indians even more than New Providence, and they had traveled right past it not knowing. If this were true, there would never be an end to their quest until they all died of old age. The river coaxed their longboats out into the bay until it succumbed to the power of the salt water and left them at their own propelling devices.

Tumbling deeper into the depths of despair, the Englishmen were drowsily resting in the early late winter sunshine. Seaman Tasley was at the tiller when he saw something so shocking he could only croak, "A sail!" The others sat up and looked toward the eastern sky line. Indeed, it was a sail, but the craft was so far away that the curvature of the horizon hid its main proportions.

The first impression of the expedition members was to close the distance as quickly as possible. At last, they were rescued!

The men grabbed their oars and began stroking rapidly and strongly. Marian and Withams took over the tillers and guided the boats in as straight a line as possible. Their makeshift 'sails' were unfurled and the small crafts seem to gain good speed. Then Marian, studying the nearing vessel in his spyglass gasped, "Spaniards!" There before them approached a massive Spanish galleon, three decks high with three massive masts reaching for the sky. The top two decks had gun ports with canon peering like angry black eyes through the openings. These swarthy people were bitter enemies of the English. The disastrous venture of the Spanish Armada in 1588 left a vile taste in their mouths and they plied the seven seas in search of revenge.

"Turn! Turn!" screamed Marian. "Maybe they haven't seen us yet! If we can make it to the shore, we can hide!"

Wasted words.

The Spaniards had been watching the small boats through their long range spyglasses for some time endeavoring to determine just exactly what they were. No one aboard had ever seen such a strange pair before. In fact, they were laughing at the configuration of the dories and their unusual sails. When the boats began to turn about, the galleon's armament officer ordered a shot across their bows. The blinding flash and deafening roar predicated a giant ball of iron speeding in their direction. It hit the sea some distance from the boats, but the huge splash filled the smaller boats with stinging salt water almost capsizing both of them. It was painfully clear they would not be able to escape ...

"I am Admiral Juan Menendez de Marques," sneered the galleon's captain.

The Englishmen drew back as a wizened, slouch shouldered wretch of a man approached them wagging his boney finger in their faces. This legendary Spanish sea man had dwindled in stature and mind after his many years on the world's oceans. His scraggly grey hair plummeted below his ornate captain's cap and entwined into his equally unkempt beard. "You are trespassers on the sacred waters of our most marvelous King Phillip II. And clearly, you are Englishmen. Prepare to meet your doom."

The hapless men were immediately put into chains and irons and roughly taken below to the dark and musty brig. They huddled together in complete misery and were overtaken by the irony of their lives. They had escaped a prison of open air and friendly people and ended up in a prison so much worse. The ten Englishmen languished away in their confinement. It was as if the Spaniards had forgotten all about them. Their only way to relieve themselves was a hole in the floor, and the only way they could tell if it were day or night was a poorly sealed porthole in the wall.

Eventually, the cell door was opened and two large, well-armed Spanish mariners entered. Each Englishman was certain that his time had come. One of the sailors spoke broken English, "Who is your *cap-ee-tan?*" In an effort to save Marian one of the young Martin boys stood up and raised his hand. The Spaniard laughed derisively, hit him rudely in the chest with the butt of his fusil and asked again, "Who is your *cap-ee-tan?*"

Marian could not allow another man to be injured. "I am Admiral Edwin Marian, commander of the English Naval fleet in the New World." Unmoved by the title, the two men roughly grabbed his arms and dragged him out the doorway while another locked the others in.

Marian was taken before Menendez de Marques and the questioning began. Each time the Englishman gave an answer the Spaniard did not like he was severely beaten until his front teeth were on the floor and his shattered mouth was bleeding profusely. Even when Marian tried to tell the truth, he was not believed. Then he realized what the Spaniard wanted to hear.

"I am Admiral Edwin Marian," he slurred through his bloodied mouth, "commander of the English Naval fleet in the New World. We have hundreds of vessels; brigantines, ketches, yawls, man-o-wars hidden along the coast line. As soon as we refill our water reservoirs and replenish our food supplies we will be raiding all the Spanish settlements in the Caribbean area."

Menendez de Marques smiled evilly. Now he really had a victory of great proportion. The massive British fleet would be without their leader if he kept the Englishman in bondage. He was totally confused by the boats his captives had been traveling in ... but after all, the English are not very intelligent.

The galleon continued its voyage northward along the western shore line for another two months traveling deeper into the bay exploring rivers and estuaries as well as sending out groups on land to see if they could find gold or precious gems. Menendez de Marques had sailed the area some years before but had not determined if the waterway separated a large island from the mainland; and even more important, if this was the long-sought way to the Orient. He kept his captives barely alive feeding them bread crawling with weevils and brackish water ... but he did keep them alive. At last, it became clear that this was not the way to China and he turned his massive craft back southward.

"What shall we do with the English dogs?" asked one of the officers. "Shall we keel-haul them until they are dead? It would be a fitting end to all the scurvy curs."

Menendez de Marques liked that idea, but he was also a shrewd businessman. He was always looking for a way to make a profit. "We could hold them for ransom. But by the time it could be worked out, they would probably all be dead. Englishmen are very weak you know."

If only there was a way to get some value out of them. Then the greatest idea he felt he had in years presented itself. It was so simple he was surprised he had not thought of it sooner. "I think I will sell them as slaves to one of the Los Indios tribes. Who knows what they would be willing to barter for these strange White people? They might buy them just to eat them."

Then the thought seemed so humorous to him and his officers that they laughed and laughed ...

The massive galleon rounded the lower headland on the port side. Not too far up the estuary was a rather large Indian village. They could not approach too closely because the titanic ship needed so much draught to stay afloat. To keep safe from running aground, the leviathan anchored about a league from the shore, and a trading delegation continued to the settlement in smaller longboats with the Englishmen crowded together in the bottom of the craft. The entire village was there to greet the Spaniards who were surprised to be met so warmly.

It was the *Choptanks!*

A barely perceived signal by head chief *Pemetosusk* instructed the villagers to remain silent.

The ten dirty and bedraggled Englishmen were chained together as one group. Their hair and beards were long, matted and filthy; and the aroma of their personal hygiene was offensive to even the most insensitive observer. Apparently, it was going to be an 'all or nothing' deal. The Indians were not sure what had happened, but they realized that if they showed any signs of knowing the men, then the captors would become suspicious, and possibly even depart without any negotiating. The Britons were also aware of the sensitive nature of the parlay and kept their eyes lowered and their mouths shut.

Captain Coverdale, dressed in his striking white deerskin clothing approached the strangers; and in perfect Spanish, welcomed them with great aplomb and deference. This, of course, pleased the captors. They did not even notice his skin was somewhat lighter than the other locals and were confident a trade could be worked out. Wrapped in their own egos, they did not feel it was unusual at all for a savage to be able to talk in their language. The entire world should be able to converse in the tongue of the most powerful empire in the world!

Pemetosusk's heart went out to his bedraggled brothers. He recalled when the tribal council had derisively called them *Hin-TOON Hoo-HA-pe* (Hairy Skeletons) in their ignorance and insensitivity. Now, they truly looked like that descriptor.

Coverdale inspected the prisoners, shook his head and looked rather disgusted. He pulled up Ship's Officer Marian's sleeve and inspected his boney arm. Then he roughly opened the mariner's mouth and saw the missing teeth. He turned to the Spaniards and commented, with an impish glint in his eye, "I don't think they are worth very much." He knew that later he would hear from Marian about that comment, but he felt special satisfaction knowing he had gotten away with it, even if only for a short while.

The story of the sale of the Englishmen and the happy reunion would find its way into the *Choptank's* verbal history and culture. As time went by the tale got more and more marvelous, but the facts still remained. The Spaniards were taken to the lodge previously built for Books-Hughes and Jonas Profit and treated like kings as the negotiations proceeded. The Natives were careful not to expose their new guests to the wealth they had stored in the Men's Lodge. The Indians pretended to be stupid traders giving up much more than the White Men had expected for ten very emaciated and probably useless Englishmen. The months on bread and water had caused every one of them to be not much more than skin and bones, and the captors wondered just how much of a meal they would make … even if they had all been cooked together. Eventually, the Spaniards resumed their voyage southward, and the Englishmen were taken-in, once again, by their most marvelous friends, and nursed back to good health.

A New Home and a Bright Future

The only thing crystal clear about the eloper's situation in the destroyed *Chicamacomico* village was that there was no turning back. The small group of refugees felt they had only two alternatives: Remain there and try to put together a new life or venture onward and throw themselves at the mercy of some tribe they might stumble across. Returning to the *Choptank* village was totally out of the question. *Wicompo* was completely devastated and unable to make any decision. She wandered through the remains of her realm trying to find something of value to hold on to.

There was nothing.

Jonas and Brooks-Hughes were practical "first things first" people and realized some immediate action would have to be taken if they were to survive. The *ho-gan* that needed the least repair was selected to be their temporary home, and they set about making it livable. As they cleared the earthen floor of debris and dried undergrowth, the servant and the young girls gathered firewood. Once the warmth of the flames began to make the lodge feel more hospitable, the men trudged back to the dugout canoe to carry other needed items to the village. Their marvelous collection of barter items and trade goods paled in significance to the value of the food and the animal skin bedding.

They knew that the canoe would be like an arrow pointing out their location to possible pursuers; so with a strong sense of regret, they salvaged the items needed to rebuild, chopped a series of holes in the dugout and pushed it back into the river. As the current pulled the craft toward the center of the stream it slowly filled with water and sank from view taking a king's ransom of marvelous trade goods to the murky depths.

Profit had learned from the Hunting clan to use one of the pelts as a skid to pile other items upon, so the two Englishmen could drag a very large amount of necessities across the snow. In just one trip, they relocated everything useable from the canoe. Daylight was quickly retiring when they returned, and the servant went right to work spreading the furs in a comfortable circle around the fire pit and preparing some semblance of a meal. The men collected branches and small bushes to fill the doorway in case other animals might try to join them during the night.

The next weeks at the *Chicamacomico* village were filled with hard work and a growing pioneering spirit among the young people. Jonas was a most skillful hunter and could find game in the most desolate places. The refugees never went for want, although diet variety was limited. The servant was an amazing cook and could concoct the tastiest meals with the very least resources. Brooks-Hughes proved to be a surprisingly capable carpenter and with the tools salvaged from New Providence was able to repair three of the *ho-gan;* one for his love and himself, one for Jonas and *Cah-cookos*, and the largest one for *Wicompo* and her servant. The young girls were surprisingly hard workers with good attitudes and positive spirits. They adored their young Englishmen – and the feeling was definitely mutual. The honored mother was the least useful of the group never having to do hard work or menial tasks. But, she was an accomplished organizer and supervisor, and her suggestions made the entire survival process much more efficient and effective. Although she had been away seventeen years, she still remembered the locations of fresh water springs and where medicinal and other useful plants had long grown. There was a possibility that the winter's snows may have protected some of the greenery needed. In her youth she had explored all the country around the village and knew where the deer would bed down for the night and where the dens of the bob cats and red foxes were located.

Because the valley was situated in the higher country, spring walked in a bit later than it had elsewhere ... but it did arrive. As the earth warmed and the Plant People peeked out of the ground, the two-leggeds were amazed by the variety of edibles growing around the village, and their diet improved almost daily.

The *CHA-pah* (Beaver) families were actively repairing their dams and paid little heed to the people. The ponds had been their homes for many generations and it is not unbelievable that the beaver elders told tales of the two-leggeds living among them with interest and even affection to their little ones. The human children had played in their pools and their fathers had caught fish there for many years, and they actually seemed glad to have them back again. This area was truly a Garden of Eden in every way. Had the small party of exiles traveled their entire lives, they could not have found a better place to start again.

One warm early summer night a most amazing sound echoed across the valley. It was the distressed crying of a new born child. *Cahonke* had brought forth the next generation, and the line of the *Chicamacomico* would not be broken after all. A sturdy and robust boy child entered the world, and just like his grandmother, expected everything to revolve around his comforts and fondest wishes. In the tradition of the tribe, the eldest woman had the right to name the child. She held the handsome baby in her arms and looked deeply into his beautiful dark eyes. She saw her most beloved daughter in them and was very, very pleased.

"You shall be named, "*Tah-TEH Shoong-TOK-cha* (Wind Wolf). You will be a ferocious warrior, strong and wise, and someday you will bring the *Chicamacomico* people back to their former glory."

Books-Hughes smiled warmly. He liked that name and the promise *Wicompo* made to his first born son. "However," he thought to himself. "I will call you 'James'."

CHAPTER VII ...
STORM CLOUDS

War! Once Again

The recovery of the imprisoned Englishmen was rapid both physically and spiritually. Clearly, their hopes of returning to the White World would have to wait for some unexpected event to occur sometime in the future. Heeding Captain Coverdale's earlier advice, they decided to build their new home east of the *Choptank* village. It took a number of trips to the remains of New Providence to salvage the tools and equipment needed for a major building project, but eventually the work was accomplished. The new settlement would include a kitchen and dining hall, a dormitory of all private rooms, a carpentry shed and foundry all constructed in a square pattern with no outward facing windows. The spaces between the larger buildings would be sealed off by an eight-foot high palisade that also enclosed an open space planned for a garden. A gate facing the Indian settlement was intended to be left open forever, unless there was another attack. The men thought about a name for their new community, and after some discussion decided to call it "Wingfield."

Private Dixon set about training the *WE-h'ne-s'ah* clansmen in the effective use of English weaponry. With the assistance of Seamen Parksley and Pennyfeather-Grayson, the task went quite smoothly. The *Choptank* warriors were not stupid at all and were eager to improve their fighting skills. During one of the training sessions, a warrior was accidentally shot with a crossbow quarrel. Dixon and one of his trainees carried him quickly to the *Peh-ZHU-tah* (Medicine) Lodge where a couple of elder medicine women went right to work on him. Before they sealed the wound, they sprinkled a yellow powder on the injured area. Dixon saw immediately that it was sulfur. They called it *Mah-KAH-zee*. He soon found out that there was a large supply stored in covered stone jars in the men's lodge. At last, he had the missing ingredient to make gun powder … And he did … great amounts of it!

The *Ho-KU-wah-s'ah* sea harvesters were having a difficult time keeping their nets intact as they fished off the beach of the village. This particular area was not overly deep and had always been rich in sea life. It was especially appreciated for the bounty it produced as well as the fact that it was very handy. They had never had such trouble with their nets there before, so something was different. Dixon had a secret hope that he might know what was causing the problem. When the *Phyllis* exploded and sank, the force of one of the largest explosions was directed toward the beach. He remembered that night when the people standing on the shore were pelted by shards of wood and pieces of metal. If it were God's will, the obstruction might be one of the cannon. If not, it would be somebody's desk or a bunk or some other large piece of the ship, or possibly a useless sunken log. He organized a group of ten canoes to row back and forth in that area dragging nets behind. Eventually, one shuddered to a stop and the back tilted down toward the water. They had snagged the obstacle. The others paddled to the area and let their nets droop into the water until they, too, had tangled in whatever was below. Then the tensile strength of the combined nets and the strong arms of the Indians began to slowly drag the heavy item along the sea bottom. It was one of the cannon! Many young men jumped into the water to help force the metal leviathan onto dry land.

The armaments of the *Choptank* village had suddenly become a thousand times more deadly.

Dixon found carpenters Pising and Capper making furniture at the fort. He told them about the marvelous find, and instructed them to get the foundry going to make as many baseball-sized lead cannon balls as the ingots and molds could produce. He had the cannon mounted on a base of large flat stones at the headland about 50 yards west of the village so its kill zone had a 90-degree span and it could protect most of the curving shoreline. Three of the British mariners, Parksley, Tasley, and Pennyfeather-Grayson were well-trained cannoneers, so they became the gun crew. Their practice sessions were so spectacular that the entire village came out to watch. They would usually have one of the older canoes anchored in the estuary, then they would ignite the cannon and blow the craft to pieces with one shot.

The *Choptanks* sang and danced extolling the prowess of their special *Ha-KAH-sha-nah* (term of endearment for the White Men).

━━━━━━━━━━━━━

The history of the relationship between the Englishmen and their Red brothers seemed to be an ongoing trail of hills and valleys. And this time was no different. The mid-Atlantic early summer weather was especially pleasant, hunting and fishing were bountiful, and the two cultures were blending smoothly in every way. Then disaster was afoot. Early one morning, a bruised and bloodied *Matapeake* brave from what would someday be called Kent Island, rowed his canoe onto the beach and collapsed in the sand. The friendly *Choptanks* rushed to his side and began to provide aid. He looked at them with reddened and bleary eyes and gasped, "*Susquehannock!*"

The *Susquehannock* nation was evil incarnate to the peace-loving Indians of the region. Their villages were located on the northwestern mainland of the bay and along a large river that flowed strongly and widely from the mountains on the west. They truly were blood-thirsty and fierce. Stories portrayed them as cannibals, and this could very well have been true. They killed without compulsion or compassion, and if they wanted something – they took it; women, children … anything. They had raided the *Choptanks* every few years burning the village to the ground and absconding with anything of value. Always before when they appeared on the horizon, the entire village would flee to the forest and hide until they left. The tribal council would leave valuable items and trade goods where they could find them, so normally the raiders would depart feeling satisfied with their efforts. Of course, the most important item was *M'ne-SKOO-yah* (Salt). Usually four or five large jars of the mineral would please them, and they would eventually leave for other conquests.

But this time would be different.

Captain Coverdale called a war council in *Pemetosusk's* lodge. He had long ago thought through the defenses of the village, and now was the time to put his plans into action. He was so confident and organized that everyone in the meeting was relieved and optimistic. His ability to speak the *Choptank* language made him even more valuable, and not one member of the war council had any doubt as to what each person's responsibilities would entail. Ship's Officer Marian would protect the eastern flank with the Englishmen residing there. Fort Wingfield would be easy to defend because of its tight construction and palisades. If any of the raiders tried to attack from that direction, they would be in for quite a surprise. The last time they had come to *Choptank* country, there was no fort there.

He turned to *Pacowassamuck* and requested that he take the *Wah-KON-kon-s'ah* clan and immediately flood all the settling pools at the salt-making site even if it might involve smashing down the outer rock walls to allow the sea water to flow in. Then he addressed *Asquash* with polite deference and requested he lead a contingency of hunters and warriors to protect the north approach to the village at that location. The great hunter appreciated the assignment but relegated it to *Nehatuckwis.* He wanted to remain with the group that would protect the village from any attack from the south and west. He knew that in the past the main thrust of the *Susquehannock* would be from that direction, as had been the sortie with the *Mitsawokets* when they endeavored to destroy the settlement. Captain Coverdale felt especially gratified to know such a marvelous warrior would be at his side.

The women, children, and elderly men would be led into the forest and would stay in the vicinity of the hunter's sweat lodge until they were allowed to return. This lodge was so secluded that someone could walk within a hundred paces of it and not even know it was there. The elderly men were given spears and pikes just in case they were discovered by the raiders. For the first time in years they felt important and useful.

Then the actual defenses quickly solidified. The cannon crew stacked some bushes in front of their weapon so it was camouflaged from view. They had a small handful of *Choptanks* with them to help load the shot; and should the enemy try to rush the gun site, the Natives would be there to help protect the weapon and its firing team. Private Dixon had his fusils primed and ready. He set up his sniper post behind a beached canoe, and the three warriors most capable with the weapon were there to keep reloading and to keep him firing. This was the first time he did not have to do it all himself, so he felt extremely important and effective.

For this battle, there would be no *Ho-KU-wah-s'ah* clansmen in canoes to lead the *Susquehannock* into a trap. Everything had to look the same as always before or the enemy might sense that something was afoot. The village must look deserted and appear as easy pickings for the raiders. Every available man was given some weapon and was instructed to hide in the lodges until a signal called them to attack. The *WE-h'ne-s'ah* warriors trained with the crossbow and longbow were instructed to quietly lie in the canoes or hide behind the trees along the shoreline until the enemy was in range, then a rain of death would be propelled in that direction.

Coverdale and *Asquash* hiked the short distance from the village to the northwestern end of the promontory to watch for the attackers. Three young and very swift runners were with them to take the news to the three areas of defense once they were ordered to do so. The five men settled down under the trees on the bluff overlooking the bay and waited for something to happen. *Asquash* reached in a bag attached to his belt and pulled out two large pieces of deer jerky meat. He handed one to the captain and began munching on the other. Coverdale was amazed that he could be so calm under such dire circumstances. The aroma of the treat was very pleasant and despite his feelings of anxiety, he too began to eat. The English military man had saved his spy glass from his former life, and the ability to see the attackers a farther distance away would extend the amount of lead time to prepare before the actual onslaught.

And as surely as the sun rises, here came the *Susquehannock* flotilla. It was massive. There must have been hundreds of war canoes confidently plying the Mother of Waters in the direction of the *Choptank* village. Always before, this raid was far and away the easiest and the most prosperous. Coverdale ordered the runners off then observed the oncoming plague. Strangely, a group of canoes moved away from the main force and headed easterly toward the area where the salt pools were. Apparently, they were not going to allow the people to flee the village this time. They intended to land on the north shore and pinch the fleeing population between them. They were hungry for slaves and blood.

Once their strategy was clear, Gabrielle and *Asquash* hurried back down the path to the village to take up their positions as battlefield generals.

What a surprise was in store for the attackers!

The main force of war canoes rounded the headlands and the *Choptank* defenders could hear them singing their battle song. It was confident and arrogant. The enemies could see that the village appeared again to be deserted, and they actually drooled in anticipation of collecting the booty. Also, they knew that this time they would also add people to their list of conquests. They could not wait to murder the young men and rape the young women.

It seemed so incongruous that such a warm, sunny and absolutely early summer day could turn into a bloody massacre.

The *Susquehannock* canoes quickly closed into range of the cannon. The first blast of cannon shot hit the lead canoes squarely in the sides and a half-dozen were suddenly pieces of wood and human flesh. The lead canoes contained the raider aristocracy and tribal chiefs, since they wanted to have first chance at the spoils, and that one shot wiped every one of them away forever. It was impossible to stop the next flight of canoes before another volley of cannon balls destroyed more of the hapless Indians. They were shocked and bewildered by the carnage, and then the blood lust of battle flowed through their pulsing veins and a great mass of canoes neared the shore. The war canoes were heavy with booty, weapons and attackers and floated low in the water, so they shuddered to a stop some distance from the beach. A deluge of battle tested warriors leaped into the water and began to wade toward the village.

Even if the *Choptanks* had ten cannons, it would not have been enough to keep the attackers from landing. The war party was just too large.

Dixon had already gone to work with his deadly fusils. He had loaded smaller grape shot into the barrels and they swept away groups of renegades time and again. The *WE-h'ne-s'ah* bowmen had sent a cloud of arrows tipped with the cutting metal points the English had provided into the attacking mass, and screams of pain and death rolled over the water. The signal was given, and the other *Choptank* men poured out of the lodges like swarming ants carrying cruel looking war clubs, spears, pikes, knives and any other hand held weaponry. The attackers looked with dismay as they realized their normal easy pickings would now mean their demise.

The battle quickly deteriorated into fierce hand-to-hand combat in the shallow water and along the shoreline. The beach was littered with broken bodies and bashed skulls and it ran red with human blood. *Choptanks* and *Susquehannck* were locked in mortal combat. The villagers were fighting for their homes and their families. The attackers were fighting for their lives.

Strangely, the *Choptank* warriors in the water broke off the combat and began to quickly wade back toward the beach. They could see a frighteningly malevolent site behind the attackers: The evil black dorsal fins of a huge pack of Bull Sharks showed that the voracious carnivores famished from recent spawning had rapidly closed the distance to the battle scene. Able to sense even the smallest amount of blood in the water, the sharks hungrily rushed into the melee attacking every motion. One hapless *Susquehannock,* flushed with a sudden sense of victory at the retreat, turned in time to see a two-foot high fin almost upon him as a 500 pound predator snapped his body in two. Screams of pain and shock came from other invaders in the water as they lost their feet and legs to the dreadful creatures' razor-sharp teeth. The murky, blood-filled waters churned madly as the sharks, some up to eleven feet long became a feeding frenzy. Even in just knee-deep water, the Bull Sharks could ravage and maim. The raiders that managed to reach the beach were unmercifully pummeled by the angry villagers.

Eventually, everything grew deathly quiet. The only sounds were the heavy breathing of the *Choptank* defenders, the pitiful moans of the wounded, and the thrashing in the water as the Bull Sharks finished up the remains of the *Susquehannaock* and fought among themselves for the spoils.

This battle was not as neat and clean as the encounter with the *Mitsawokets.* Only a miserable handful of the war party was still alive, and none were unscathed. So many attackers had been killed that their bodies were stacked three and four high, their death masks echoing the pain and shock of the village's ferocious defenses. Littered among the vile dead were many young *Choptank* men and boys who would never again enjoy the warmth of their lodges or the arms of their mothers, wives or lovers.

The surviving attackers crawled or limped together and dropped to their knees to beg for mercy.

Captain Coverdale left his command post and joined the throng. He was flushed with the sense of victory and so proud of his warriors. At that point he realized that *Asquash* had left his side sometime earlier and joined in the battle. In heart pounding distress the White Man began turning over bodies looking for his great friend. He heard a tired laugh and looked up to see the hunter leaning against a canoe holding his hand over his right eye. In the heat of the fight one of the villagers had swung a battle axe at one of the attackers, missed and hit the *Choptank* warrior right below the eye. In modern times this might have been called "friendly fire." From that day until his death many years later, he would be known far and wide as *"Won-ZE e-SH'DAH-su"* (One Eyeball).

At that moment the *Choptank* battle song could be heard echoing from the forest behind the village:

> *"Nah-DON-pe TOH-kah*
> *WEEN-yon KAH-gah-pe"*

> ("Charged the foe,
> But I made a woman of him.")

Captain Coverdale's strategy for the defense of the north shore had worked perfectly. The *Susquehannock* had beached their war canoes on the stone causeways surrounding the settling basins, and as they ran toward the shore, they were picked off like mechanical ducks in a shooting gallery. Almost no attacker made it past the hail of arrows and crossbow quarrels. Private Dixon's training had paid off handsomely.

The *Choptank* archers were deadly accurate and would forever be confident in their abilities with the English weapons.

The hearty battle song faded away as the warriors saw the carnage on the beach below the village. They realized that they had got the best part of the defensive strategy, and that many of their friends and family would no long be able to sing with them.

Not long after the arrival of the north flank defenders, the Englishmen from Fort Wingfield heard the victory song and joined the others. There had been no assault from the east, and the few stragglers from the attack that tried to escape inland had been killed by the archery abilities of the White Men.

Captain Coverdale instructed some of the braves who were not completely exhausted to go to the hunter's lodge and recall the women, children, and elderly men.

That warm early summer night was filled with the mournful songs of the elderly women who sang to help their dead warriors find the long, difficult path to *Wak-KON-ton-kah,* the great god who loves all the creature of the Earth … even the *Susquehannock.*

The few surviving attackers were allowed to leave, battered and bloodied, in the last usable canoe and told to never return. They were so ashamed by their defeat that when they got out into the deep water of the bay, they jumped overboard.

As always, the *Choptanks* were extremely disrespectful toward their dead enemies. They decided to collect as many heads as they could find, pile them in a canoe and tow them northward so the other tribes could celebrate the victory and know that once and for all the threat from the *Susquehannock* was over. They had planned to take the canoe all the way to their enemies' villages; but after a week, the odor of decaying flesh and oozing brains was so strong they cut the canoe loose and let the Mother of All Waters decide what should be done next.

Homeward Bound

Deep in their own private contemplations, Captain
Coverdale, called *AH-ban-nah Chon-TEH* (Gentle
Heart) by the Natives, and Ship's Officer Edwin
Marian, who no longer had a ship since the scuttling of *The
Phyllis Redoubtable*, walked side-by-side along the sandy beach
away from the bustling *Choptank* village. Marian's trials with
the Spanish had left him rawboned with his jaw somewhat
askew presenting a fierce image despite his basic tender
nature. Coverdale's devoted acolyte, labeled by some as his
own personal worshiper, was always nearby but remained
a courteous distance from the two Englishmen. Both White
Men had seen the grotesque and leering mask of death too
many times as they contemplated their experiences as young
warriors ready and willing to plant the cross of Calvary and
St. Andrew in every soil from sun to sun. Now weary and
heartsick from the bloodshed and slaughter of the recent
battle, they only felt an emptiness and bone-deep fatigue.

Those similar feelings of loss were also felt in the village.
Many young and vibrant men and boys had lost their lives
during the bloody confrontation with the *Susquehannock*
renegades. Almost every Native family was affected in
some way and the month-long period of mourning would
impact each person deeply and personally. The slow solemn
drumming and heart-rending chanting rippled over the quiet
bay announcing to the world that the *Choptank* people still
lived and walked the Earth Mother for at least one more day.

With the assistance of the welcoming arms of the
eternal tides, the women of the *Ke-WE-dah-yah-s'ah* clan (the
Gatherers) had scoured clean the beach of the carnage and
there were very few ciphers left of the terrible struggle that

had occurred only a few short days before. Many seasons after, there remained a barely perceptible odor of the blood and gore that had seemed to permeate the very soil, bushes and trees of the shoreline. It was as if the Earth herself was trying to cleanse herself by crying. And even stranger, warriors walking that sacred ground as the seasons passed would relate they could sense an indescribable feeling of melancholy and loss as if countless souls were in eternal torment and pain.

Captain Coverdale sent a kind look in the direction of his friend and seemed to be struggling with something he was trying to say. He stopped walking and gently said, "Edwin, I was in the men's lodge that morning so long ago after the *Phyllis* was lost. I heard your diatribe against the *Choptanks* and what you thought they must have done to me."

The Ship's Officer could feel the heat of embarrassment crawl up his throat recounting all the events of that fateful experience. His hasty words of anger returned from the inner reaches of his mind as if said only yesterday:

"...did you see what happened to Captain Coverdale? He was the best example I had ever seen of a proud British military man ... now,
I don't know what he is. Somehow the Barbarians have washed away
his past and his heritage ..."

Coverdale placed his hand on Marian's arm aware of the uncomfortable feelings he was experiencing and continued, "I sensed that you felt you had lost a friend as well as a ship, so I did not call you to task for your comments. Since then, I have tried many times over to find the way to explain what has happened to me."

He slowly turned away in an effort to mask the tears that were glistening in his eyes. "I will always be your friend whether I am *AH-ban-nah Chon-TEH* or Gabriell. I did not realize that I had been hopelessly spending my life trying to find 'home' … until I found it here with these gentle people. This is where I want to live the rest of my days and this is who it seems right for me to become. I feel that we soon will be stepping onto separate life pathways, and I wanted to try to explain myself before time and distance made it impossible."

Edwin looked up at this tall, handsome man who had changed so much. His image of Coverdale was always the immaculate in every way British officer; and this reality of long hair, Native clothing and footwear, and a gentle almost ethereal nature still seemed so foreign. He felt a sense of relief when he looked into his eyes and recognized the reflection of his best of friends. "It would be good to stay here in this Garden of Eden, but I feel a stirring inside that there is a larger plan for my life waiting for me and time is running out. I ache for the rolling green hills of Holyrood and a bowl of my wife's boiled mutton. My heart will always beat for England, and I have to find a way to return."

The Englishmen at Ft. Wingfield felt deep sympathy for their Native friends, but they knew they experienced the better outcome of the battle with the *Susquehannock*. Their responsibility was to guard the east flank of the village and to confront any raiders who might try to attack the settlement from that landward direction. The pincer movement by the renegades closed from the north and south and the only conflict around the fort was from enemy warriors trying to flee the arrows and lances of the pursuing townspeople.

The White Men made short work of these hapless souls and stacked their bodies by the fort gate for the Natives to desecrate, as they did all their fallen enemies.

That following evening ship's cook Oscar Johnson prepared a marvelous feast for the men in celebration. The striped bass had moved into the tidelands for spawning and the water was thick with their love dances. Johnson easily netted as many fish as he could carry and after de-boning and frying the luscious fillets, the repast was ready to serve. He also had learned how to bake corn bread in the rock oven constructed on the fort's grounds by some of the elder *Choptank* ladies ... and its fragrance was mouth-watering. The last touch was a boiling cauldron of raspberry and sassafras tea. By miraculous fortune and foresight, mariner Eldred Parksley had found a small cask of rum in the ruins of New Providence and had furtively stashed it away these many months. He could not think of a better time to break the seal, and all the Englishmen roared their approval. Needless to say, the tea continued bubbling on the stove, unnoticed.

These nine marvelous gentlemen sat at the table in the dining hall and greatly enjoyed each other's companionship. Former navigator of the *Phyllis*, Obadiah Withams, looked at his friends with a great sense of fondness. This motley crew of British mariners and London Company employees had meshed together into a family closer to each other than any 'real' family could ever become. They had struggled together through and survived so much that they would always consider themselves a Band of Brothers.

It was becoming more and more clear that most of the surviving expedition members ached in their hearts to return to their homes and families. They seemed to know innately that their work here was done. The *Ha-KAH-sha-nah* were held in high regard, almost worshiped, by their

Native friends; but they still longed for the familiarity of life in Mother England. After the successful battle with the *Susquehannock,* there was a sense of 'completeness' concerning the mission compounded with the ongoing need to reconnect the Ties that Bind hearts and minds. Private James Dixon was a British soldier through and through, and he liked it that way. Despite his accomplishments with his Native army, he longed for the discipline and routine of military life in the civilized world. He felt his friend-in-arms and fellow warrior, *Asquash,* and he had trained the young men well enough that they were able to defend their village without further help, and this was an enormously freeing sensation. But more than anything, he wanted, like so many of the others, to get back to his own world.

Seventeen London Company employees had left Jamestown that autumn of 1607, and now only four survivors were left to tell the tale of the great adventure. The two carpenters, Edward Pising and John Capper, would forever wear the scars of their experiences. Pising's leg, impaled by the *Mitsawoket* arrow during the destruction of New Providence, never did heal to the point where he could be considered able-bodied. The grievous wound was constantly seeping blood, and he would walk with a painful limp the rest of his life. Capper's missing ear was less a detriment to his wellbeing and he considered it a Badge of Courage; in fact, as mentioned before, the wound proved to be an attraction to the *Choptank* children during his time with them and a source of awe and respect.

The remaining two company survivors were the young brothers John and George Martin. Still in their teens, they had experienced the high roads and very lowest roads of life. They had seen strong men tremble in the face of death and other humans reduced to mere bloody pieces and smashed bones. They experienced the shock and dismay of knowing people they admired had been murdered and mutilated. Yet, in a mature and almost genteel fashion way beyond their years they somehow weathered the occurrences no young person should ever have seen. Tumbling into the prime of their lives, they were smitten by two graceful and becoming *Choptank* sisters, *Secowuks* and *Signucks*. Innately aware of how fleeting life can be the young couples held each other in a love, shameless and unbounded. These lovely young ladies were not princesses or daughters of chiefs, but they were children of a well-regarded Native family of good bearing and social standing in the community. As the summer gently meandered toward the autumn months, the two cultures mingled together in peace and harmony traveling the well-beaten path from the village to Ft. Wingfield in both directions and often. It was only natural that these young English boys of exceptional worth and character would eventually find wonderful, but unfortunately short lived, futures in the arms of these delightful *Choptank* girls.

Ship's Officer Marian could see Seaman Matthew Tasley's abiding interest in the healing arts was rapidly becoming the bliss of his life. After the inglorious and untimely death of Governor Wingfield at the rebuilt New Providence, Tasley faced his humanity and the reality that no matter how much he wanted to or how hard he tried, he would never be able to heal all those he cared about. In his disappointment and depression he resolved to forget medicine and return to being an ordinary British seaman. Observing how the villagers maintained their good health practices and how they successfully dealt with injuries and ailments common to the times, he regained his confidence and eagerly sought the knowledge and training to be able to perform such marvelous miracles.

Marian realized the best place for Tasley at this stage in his life was with the *Choptanks*. He sat down with the young mariner and offered a proposal that would change the course of this young man's life forever. "Matthew, you seem to have a special gift for the healing arts. I believe that the training you received from Surgeon Wickinson before his untimely demise and the special abilities the *Choptank* healers are sharing with you would combine to make you a valuable and necessary member of the Royal Navy Surgeon Corps. With your permission, I would like to designate a new assignment for you. I want you to remain with the Natives for an extended period of time to learn all they know and also to share our modern medical practices with them. In due time, we will come for you and designate you as a Fleet Surgeon."

Tasley was beside himself in joy. The best of both worlds was opening to him, and he leaped at the chance. "I accept this responsibility," he responded. "To the best of my capacity, I will endeavor to gain the knowledge to perform my future duties. I will not let you down, Captain."

The elder healer, *Chop-tah-nk*, who was totally disgusted with White Man's leech-craft, took Tasley under her wing and taught him the secrets of her profession. Sometime during the learning process the leeches disappeared and were replaced by marvelous herbs and other natural practices and remedies. As he matured into a skillful and confident Medicine Man, he was eventually adopted into the *Ke-WE-dah-yah-s'ah* clan and unaware that he would have to wait for the rest of his life in hopes of rejoining the Royal Navy.

━━━━━━━━

One early summer evening the *Choptank* tribal council met to resolve the most important issue they would ever have to face: Could they allow the Englishmen to leave. These tall hairy men were like brothers and were loved by everyone. After much discussion and hand-wringing by all participants, it was agreed that the Natives would assist their *Ha-KAH-sha-na* friends in finding the pathway back to their homes. The decision was shared with Captain Coverdale, and he ran to Ft. Wingfield to spread the news. In unbounded joy, the visitors began the process of closing down the fort and preparing for the next step in their great adventure.

The most gorgeous summer morning of the year provided a backdrop for the saddest farewell anyone could ever remember. The *Choptanks* were sure they would never see their friends again. These men were legendary and were tightly woven into the fabric of the village.

The twin chiefs stood by their great friends and spoke softly in broken English for the first and last time, repeating the heart rending words offered when Master Wingfield was put to rest, "We have walked together in the shadow of a rainbow."

As the five large sea-going canoes rowed by the *Ho-KU-wah-s'ah* clan carefully moved away from the shoreline, the elder Indian women sang their plaintive and haunting good-bye songs. Three of the dugouts were piled high with trading goods given *gratis* to their White Brothers. There were no dry eyes on the beach and none in the canoes.

Ship's Officer Marian, later lovingly called "Old Ivory" because of the two false front teeth he would eventually wear, looked in a fatherly way at the men in his canoe and then turned to see those in the other craft. He realized that he still had a crew and felt very gratified by what his men had accomplished. There would be a future for each of them. They had grown mentally and spiritually and had become fine people. Then he felt tears welling up in his eyes as he remembered those who were not with them. Deep in thought his eyes caught sight of a beautifully decorated and rectangular back pack resting among some of the gifts given by the grateful *Choptanks*. As he untied it he felt an unpleasant shock ripple through his body: It was the ship's log of the *Phyllis Redoubtable*. His eyes widened as he tried to determine how the Natives had acquired it. It was not water soaked or partially burned, so they must have gotten it before the sinking of their ship. Were they the ones that had destroyed their hopes of returning home? He nervously thumbed to the page where he had made the last entry and sat back in wonder and confusion. It said simply:

> *August 20 … Sailing to the village for a marvelous celebration. Crew anticipating it will be a night to remember.*

Only *Asquash* knew that he had purloined the magic white leaves with the sacred runes just before their great canoe was destroyed. Confident that it was a holy relic, *Asquash* could not bear the thought that his English friends would be without its great 'medicine' on their journey back to their home land. He had sequestered it in his *wigwam* over the ensuing months and there would never be another opportunity to return it to its rightful owners.

As the canoes rounded the southern headlands near where New Providence had once stood, Jerald Pennyfeather-Grayson looked eastward with the faintest glimmer of hope that his dear friend and ship mate Theodore Brooks-Hughes might be standing on the shore waiting to join them. The *Choptank* canoes sped southward and soon the promontory was out of sight. Turning back to the others, he mumbled softly, "Let's go home."

Return to Jamestown

The cannon ball moaned menacingly above the five sea-going canoes and crashed into the water some distance behind the flotilla with a tremendous "swo-o-o-o-sh!"
Fists clenched in the air and face red with unbridled rage, the bear-like and heavily bearded Englishman stood up in the dugout and screamed toward the shore, his words caroming off the surface of the water like a British Man O' War broadside, "You scurrilous dogs! If you don't stow that second round, I'll shove that ball up your bloody arses!"

"Jesus, Mary and Joseph! It's Dixon!"

"Who the hell's Dixon?"

———————

The London Company employees and the mariners who had sailed from Jamestown that summer of 1607 on *The Phyllis Redoubtable* had no way of knowing about the many changes that had occurred at their former home, and the Jamestown colonists still alive that remembered their departure assumed they had returned to England and continued on with their separate lives. Of the original 144 men and boys that landed in the New World filled with hope and optimism, barely more than 30 had survived that first winter, and the winter of 1608 was almost as deadly although two new groups from the Mother-land and their supplies and provisions had arrived up to that point. The return of the *Ha-KAH-sha-nah* (*Choptank* term of endearment for their British brothers and translates as "ground hog") was as astounding as it was unexpected. Very few of the current Jamestown occupants even knew about this group, and it was nothing short of a miracle that there was someone in the cannon squads that knew Dixon and could order the others to cease fire. As far as the Jamestown defensemen were concerned, five war canoes filled with Natives were bearing down on the fort and this could bring about no good. The eight White Men in the canoes had long ago worn out their clothing from home and now were attired in a similar fashion as the Indians.

The word that there were Englishmen in the retinue, as well as mounds of trade goods, quickly reached the village headquarters, and Captains John Smith and John Ratliffe were soon at the shore line scanning the nearing water craft with their spy glasses and waiting to greet the visitors. Both were especially pleased to see their former comrade, Ship's Officer Edwin Marian, among the group and were eager to find out what had happened over the past few years or so.

The two Native dug-outs with the refugees from New Providence shuddered against the sandy river bank and were quickly pulled ashore by the townspeople. The three other water craft loaded with treasures remained some distance out in the stream wary that they might be overcome and the gifts taken by force. Eight unusual Englishmen, dressed in exquisitely tanned and decorated hand-sewn deer skin trousers and tunics were quite a sight to behold, and in a very short time every single inhabitant of Jamestown was on the scene to enjoy the spectacle.

Captain Smith, dressed in his best military fashion, served as the spokesman inviting the auspicious group to join him in the dining hall for a 'real meal' and conversation. He then addressed the citizenry warning them to not molest the Natives and to not off-load their cargo until it could be inventoried. Marian motioned to the canoes that it would be okay for them to land, but Fusilier Private James Dixon, and the two carpenters, Edward Pising and John Capper, elected to remain on the beach to communicate that they were not going to allow any trouble to occur after the administrators left the scene. The carpenters held their axes at the ready, Capper especially ferocious looking with his missing ear. All the imposing Dixon had to do was scowl at anyone he felt was coming too close.

The aroma from the dining area smelled heavenly to the Englishmen and their minds were flooded with memories of home. They had not enjoyed boiled salt pork for what seemed like a lifetime, and the fragrance from freshly baked wheat flour biscuits put even the very best prepared *Choptank* corn bread to shame as far as they were concerned. Huge pewter bowls of the food swimming in thick gravy were set before them, and they could not wait to dig in.

Looking up with his mouth so full the words almost barely understandable, Mariner Eldred Parksley commented, "Shouldn't we get some of this to Dixon and the carpenters?"

His shipmate, Jerald Pennyfeather-Grayson, gave Parksley a side-long glance that said without words, "Are you crazy?"

"Bad idea," Eldred mumbled; and they all ate their fill with great gusto in complete non-gentlemanly fashion.

Captain Ratliffe tried to bring the returnees up to date as best he could. "That winter after you departed, we lost almost our entire assemblage. Surgeon Thomas Wotton, you may recall him a man of good nature and infinite wit, worked day and night trying to save the ill and injured. He determined they were suffering from cholera, dysentery and diphtheria not to mention ague (malaria) and influenza. His obituary book was filled with the names and causes of death of many, many of our good friends and acquaintances. His leeches and apothecary were ill equipped to stop the spread of anguish and death. He, himself, succumbed early that January and missed the arrival of Councilman Matthew Scrivner and 80 more souls. We were elated to see that they had brought more provisions and also tools and implement we would be able to use to procure our own food once the spring came. I must enlighten you that I have never known such severe hunger or deprivation. We tried to obtain stores from the local Natives, but they were hostile and uncooperative. I never found out if they only had enough for their own purposes, or if they were hoping we would all starve to death. When the food from home was gone we ate our horses and dogs. I sent out teams of hunters, but they often returned empty handed."

Ratliffe stopped and seemed to be reflecting on what he had said. It was clear that recounting the experience opened many old wounds of pain and despair. Then he continued, "I will admit that our situation did improve through the spring and summer of '08, and that autumn we received our second supply of men under the command of Captains Peter Winne and Richard Waldo and many more provisions and needed supplies."

He turned to Ship's Officer Marian, and inquired, "And you?"

Marian prepared to respond, then his eyes opened wide with amazement, and even some fear. There standing in the doorway was a tall, pale man that he knew all too well and had been on the scene at his demise.

His shocked silence caused the other Englishmen to turn in the direction he was staring. Ship's Cook Oscar Johnson rose to his feet and uttered in total disbelief, "Master Hunt?"

It was indeed their former Man of the Cloth who had fallen overboard into the cold unforgiving river waters that fateful morning the mapping crew stumbled across the renegade *Mitsawokets'* war camp.

Hunt seemed to enjoy the reaction of his former mates, as he responded in his hoarse, whispery voice, "I, too, have quite a tale to tell. My Native redeemers called me *Toh We-CHOSH-tah*." (Blue Man).

The trade goods and gifts from the gentle *Choptanks* were stacked on the river shore, and the settlement's quartermasters were busily inventorying the many items. Some of the items, like the pots of pemmican and the baskets of herbs and medicinals, were unidentifiable to the English, so they listed them as 'unknown' or endeavored to describe their appearances or aromas. What they did recognize and realize the incredible worth of were the red fox and mink pelts and the jars of rock salt. These items were greatly sought after, and the bookkeepers were eager to share the news with the Company's executives.

The Jamestown people endeavored to communicate to the Natives that they were welcomed to remain with them, at least through the night, but they politely refused. The goodbyes between the *Choptanks* and their English family were protracted and heartfelt. Not so long ago these similar emotions had flowed through the two cultures when their *Ha-KAH-sha-nah* White Brothers left the village for the many-day sailing southward. Those draining feelings, replicated so soon from before, were especially painful. The onlookers were somewhat embarrassed to see the tears and expressions of affection between the groups and wondered just what had happened to the normally stolid and aloof British gentlemen. The townspeople and their new visitors quietly stood on the bank and watched until the canoes had rounded the river bend and melted out of sight into the open arms of the forested hill sides. The water-people *Ho-KU-wah-s'ah* clansmen were unable to communicate to their friends that the unclean and unkempt people of Jamestown, the murky and defiled waters around the fort, and the sprawling community itself smelled so bad their senses were reeling and they needed to get away from the squalid environment. As they rowed away, they could see the rotting carcasses and molding bones of animal remains carelessly thrown into the stream. They saw White Men bathing and even urinating and defecating in the same water others were drinking from. Truly ... who really were the barbarians?

The small cluster of surviving crewmen of *The Phyllis Redoubtable* were given their own quarters in a well-built log structure whose outer walls were coated with a mixture of lime and mud similar to the construction of most of the other buildings in the community. It was a short distance downriver from the main settlement which proved to be more a blessing than a hardship. Its furnishings consisted of a stone fireplace, a small iron cook stove, two rough-hewn tables with accompanying chairs, and a half-dozen wooden bed frames stacked against the back wall. When they opened the sturdy wooden door a family of ground squirrels squeaked in fear and scurried into the sunlight and off into the nearby forest. The cabin looked more like a storehouse than a residence, but it would have to do. The visitors would have to procure their own bedding from the settlement's supply building which would, of course, be ill smelling and flea infested. There was an actual glass window in the west wall that allowed the setting sun to paint the cabin interior with warm colors of oranges and reds. Despite its cold and stark interior, there was a sense that they could make it some sort of a home.

Ship's Cook Oscar Johnson, still shaken after seeing Master Hunt, had befriended the culinary staff in the dining hall and was allowed to bring a large pan of biscuits soaked with salt pork and gravy to feed the carpenters who had missed the earlier meal while protecting the trade goods. There was also enough to feed the other crewmen who were still hungry. He built a roaring fire in the cook stove, and soon the pan was bubbling merrily releasing very pleasant aromas into the room. Setting six wooden bowls on the table and dropping the tin ladle in the stew, he bellowed, "Soup's on!"

Ship's Officer Marian was encouraged to join the others in the barracks of the community's officers and administrators. He welcomed the opportunity to rub elbows with people of like minds and experiences. He suddenly felt out of place in his Native attire, and the other occupants had a ready solution. Folded on a table in the back of the room were piles of uniforms that had once been the wardrobes of other officers who died over the prior two years. All of them were Captain's livery, and some obviously had never been worn before the owners passed on to the next world.

Marian found an ensemble that fit reasonably well and thought, "Well, how about that? I've been promoted. Ten years in the Royal Navy, and now I'm a captain."

Private James Dixon chose to room with the detachment of Fusiliers some of whom he had known or fought with during prior campaigns. They were surprised that he had rejoined the settlement and were very pleased to have him in their company. His reputation as a fierce warrior had preceded him, and the other soldiers were looking forward to hearing about his latest adventures. His roommates expected him to discard his animal skin clothing and don a uniform like everyone else, and he was agreeable to this request. As in the officers' barracks, there was plenty of military garb available. Dixon's girth had greatly increased as a result of the 'good life' with the *Choptanks* and it was not going to be easy to find something that would fit comfortably. As he picked through the clothing, he noticed a faded woolen green

and red sergeant's tunic and was immediately attracted to
it. Holding it against his chest, it was reassuring to note that
there was plenty of material and even room for some future
growth. An identification name was penned in Indian ink
under the collar that made him stop short and take a deep
breath. It read "Lusby." This simple shirt had once belonged
to the man Dixon admired beyond words and still quietly
mourned over. Sergeant Bartholomew Lusby had been his
superior officer during the travail at New Providence and a
comrade-in-arms during those difficult days. His vicious and
totally undeserved demise at the hands of the *Mitsowokets*
truly undid Dixon. If he ever knew a person in his long and
lonely life who might have served as a 'father figure', it was
Lusby. Dixon knew beyond a doubt that this giant of a man
walked onward to the Next Life carrying the well-earned
credentials of entry. Dixon vowed in silence to honor his
name and to wear that shirt well.

Part of the structure of the Fusilier's quarters was the
community jail where two ne'er-do-wells were sleeping
fitfully on the stone floor. Dixon walked over to the cell
bars and held them trying to remember the feeling of good
English iron. At that moment he realized that the entire time
the White Men lived with the *Choptanks* there was never a
need for a jail ... or even any crime. He wondered what magic
they had found to make people so congenial and honest
toward each other.

The gifts and trade goods were carted from the riverside
to the imposing, and unfortunately, rather empty supply and
storage building. As the settlement's provisions dwindled,
more space became available for items much less needed. It
appeared more like a haberdasher's place of business than
anything else. When a person would die, his clothing and
footwear would be salvaged and stored in that location.

There were scores of pairs of boots, brogans and oxfords resting side-by-side against the walls. Leather belts and suspenders were casually piled helter-skelter. Cotton tunics and woolen trousers were stacked as high as a man's head. This presented a strange and depressing monument to the deceased Englishmen who had come to the Wild Lands to make themselves a new life. The odor was overwhelming and nobody cared to linger in the building any longer than was necessary.

That first night back in 'civilization' was uncomfortable and oppressive for the travelers. The stench of the brackish and polluted river crawled its way up the bank and into their confines and there was no way to ignore it. This far inland, there were no cool bay breezes to temper the heat and humidity of a mid-summer night causing sleep to be fitful and fleeting. Tormented by voracious mosquitoes and an army of fleas in their bedding the men tossed and turned and scratched until some wanted to scream in frustration. Then the worse of all happened: They had not eaten thick, poorly cooked foods saturated with globules of animal fat and tallow for a very long time. Their stomachs were unprepared for the onslaught and rebelled furiously. All six men found themselves running for the nearby forest with terrible diarrhea or vomiting ... or both.

Clearly, there would be no rest for the Englishmen this night.

———————————————

Johnson the Cook arose with the breaking morning sun and surveyed the stores and cooking utensils he had been issued from the quartermasters. His mates had finally been able to fall asleep mainly from exhaustion and the fact that the gorged mosquitoes had returned to their environs. He had a bag of unbleached wheat flour, crawling with weevils, naturally; part of a barrel of salt pork that was beginning to spoil; a selection of withered leeks and other roots and bulbs that had either been carried from England or dug from the nearby forest; and a brace of conies trapped sometime earlier and now starting to smell bad, their eyes sunken in and the fur beginning to mottle. He wondered if the purveyors had skimmed off the worst of everything and given it for his men. Sometime later he found out this was common fare for all the community members except the administrators. It was poor vittles compared to the choices he enjoyed at New Providence or living with the *Choptanks:* No fresh venison nor mountains of shellfish and crab, and despite the nearby river absolutely no fish of any kind.

The cook walked down to the river with an oaken bucket to obtain water for the meal preparation and stopped at the river's edge. The water was warm and stagnant, so cloudy and thick it looked more like mud, and it gave off a putrid aroma. As he peered at what could be called 'water' for lack of any other descriptor, he could see the white shape of an animal skull resting against some rocks covered with a black, floating willowy form of plant life. The brook near New Providence was cool and fresh, and the water sources of his former Native friends were as clear as glass. He just couldn't dip the bucket into that swill. This posed a problem because he needed water for almost every aspect of his meal preparation. In hopes of finding better water, he walked along the bank away from Jamestown and soon stumbled across a small and rather shallow rill trickling out of the forest on his left. It did not compare in quality to what he was used to, but it was mountains better than the river itself.

When he returned to the cabin with the bucket of water, the others were already up and had stacked their mattresses in the cleared area near the front door. One of the men had taken a partially smoldering stick from the fireplace and ignited the entire pile. It burst into flames and soon was shedding light and warmth on everyone. The men cheered loudly, and Navigator Obadiah Withams shouted, "Death to our tormentors! We send you fleas back to Hell from whence you came!"

All the men, including the cook, were covered with small red marks and welts from their night's pandemonium. Obviously the bugs had had a smorgasbord for their enjoyment. The mosquito bites were swollen with infection and ugly looking adding to the miserable itching condition of their exposed skin. Mariner Jerald Pennyfeather-Grayson had received a nasty sting near his right eye and it was partially swollen shut. In no way did the men want to endure another night of this, and something had to be done. The White Men now needed some form of bedding for the frames and after sleeping on animal skins for a number of years, they knew lying on the pelts seemed to keep them cool on hot nights and lying under them served very comfortably on the winter nights. A plan was devised to visit the storage building and lay claim to some of the less precious animal furs given to them by the *Choptanks*. The Englishmen were not aware that generations ago the Natives had learned that the mild acrid aroma of the tanning process served as a bug repellant and all their bedding and clothing met this purpose in a natural and effective fashion.

John Capper, the one-eared carpenter, started to walk down to the river's edge, and said to nobody in particular, "I need a drink of water."

Johnson felt a bolt of fear course through him wondering what would happen to his mates if they drank the filthy water. No leechcraft of the day could know that the unfit water was the source of many of the terrible diseases that had decimated the population of Jamestown. The cook just had a feeling that something was not right, and he was determined to keep his friends away from it as much as possible. "I have already brought some water," he explained, showing the bucket. "Help yourself."

After an acceptable breakfast, the plans for the day were determined. Withams, Pennyfeather-Grayson and Parksley would return to Jamestown proper, obtain the animal pelts needed for bedding, track down Ship's Officer Marian and Private Dixon, and would also find out what the Jamestown administration had in mind for them. The cook and the carpenters would walk down to the stream Johnson had discovered and try to determine how it could be put to their use.

By the end of the day a number of questions had been answered. All eight of the newly arrived Englishmen were instructed to report to the administrative building at five p.m. sharp for a common meal and a special meeting. They looked at each other in confusion since nobody had any way to tell what time it was. Clocks and 'time' were unimportant to the *Choptanks* and the *Ha-KAH-sha-nah* were naturally wrapped into that mind set during those idyllic days. The concept of 'on time' for the Natives was when everyone finally arrived or a particular task was eventually completed. The message bearer from the settlement eased their concerns when he mentioned that a canon was fired every afternoon at that time. Once they heard its report, they should find their way to the meeting location.

As a result of the gathering, Each Englishman was given a clothing allowance so they could put their Native attire to rest. The garments could be procured from the storehouse at their convenience. Marian and Dixon had already dealt with the clothing situation, so this action was appropriate for the other six men only. One of the accountants had determined how much back pay the military men had coming, and a cloth bag of sovereigns, shillings and pence was prepared for each of them and dispensed during the meeting. The Royal Navy and the King's Guard had given the colony a strong box of money for the use and purposes of its mariners and soldiers and it was appropriate to mete some of it out at this time. Private Dixon, Withams, Pennyfeather-Grayson, Parksley, Cook Johnson and Ship's Officer Marian were pleased and surprised by this outcome. The paymaster noticed Dixon in sergeant's attire and determined his rank had been erroneously entered on the docket pages. He promised to recalculate what he had coming and Dixon was in no way going to endeavor to correct him. Then the problem with the generosity became very apparent:

There wasn't anything to do with the money!

The only place to spend it was the commissary, and it was totally empty of any items to sell. All six returned their pay bags to the bookkeepers and asked them to keep them in a safe place until they could find passage back to England. Information was shared that another group of colonists were expected to arrive sometime in August on nine ships under the leadership of Captain Newport. The craft were to bring George Somers and Thomas Gates as governor and deputy governor to provide new direction for the colony. The return to the Homeland would soon follow once all items of value were loaded on the boats. Gratefully, many of the things to be sent back to England came from the *Choptank* gifts and trade goods. The Royal Navy men would be more than welcomed to join the return voyage. Nothing was said outright, but the Jamestown administration had plans for Dixon.

What to do with the employees of the London Company was another problem. The business corporation had been reorganized into the Virginia Company, and it was unclear how prior expectations and commitments would now be honored. The accountants were wringing their hands in dismay since the two carpenters were affected by this situation. The answers to all the Company's problems could be found in its by-laws and organizational procedures. This situation was not covered on any page. Both employees were not overly concerned by the issue and assumed that something would be worked out at some future date. Pising and Capper were eager to get back to the business of wood and had little concern for whom they might be working for or working with.

That night in the cabin was much more pleasant. The men's bedding was flea-free and the mild aroma from the tanning process seemed to keep the mosquitoes at bay. A mid-summer thunderstorm was rolling in during the night from the western hills bringing a much needed cooling trend for the men as well as the entire colony. The next morning as the red sun climbed above the eastern tree line, Johnson and the carpenters took the other men down to the small stream previously discovered. Moving rocks and relocating small downed trees and branches, the Englishmen soon had constructed a reasonable example of a dam that formed a shallow pond of significantly cooler and cleaner water than available to the main community. They made a pact to keep this pleasant diversion a secret from the rest of the settlement, and enjoyed it as long as they resided in Jamestown.

Seek and Ye Shall Find

The warm days of spring and autumn in the mid-Atlantic region of North America have always been the 'gentle times', and the 1610's was no different. The *Chicamacomico* village was slowly being rebuilt from the ashes of unknown winters, and the small community was filled with hope and optimism. English mariners, Theodore Brooks-Hughes and Jonas Profit, had proven to be superb providers and clever craftsmen. They were efficient, even deadly hunters, and with the implements salvaged from the canoe used for the elopement trip up-river could build almost anything. Theodore and *Cahonke's* baby boy, Wind Wolf, was strong and active. He seemed to already know that he would someday be a prince, and his cries of impatience were the most remarkable songs his grandmother *Wicompo* had heard since her own child-bearing years. Lovely *Cah-cookos* and Jonas were deeply in love and anticipating another addition to the *Chicamacomico* clan. The elder queen-mother had recovered from the depression that consumed her after seeing her realm desolate and abandoned, and she was developing a plan to bring it once again to a point of prosperity and prominence in inter-Tribal commerce.

Earlier that fateful winter the young Englishmen had demonstrated the foresight to remove all the tools and survival equipment and as many of the trading goods they could carry from the dugout before scuttling it and pushing it out into the river current. Even though they salvaged a handsome supply of the valuables, they wished now that they had taken the time to find a way to cache all the trading goods. Easily, a king's ransom succumbed to the waiting arms of the hungry waters as their *Choptank* watercraft sighed sadly and disappeared in a trail of bubbles. They knew that if the canoe would be found, the pursuing Natives would eventually track down the elopers and return them to the village under dire consequences. As they stacked the booty they saved on the river bank, they were shocked to see how much had been accumulated. *Wicompo,* was determined to return to her people with almost 20 years of accrued wealth, and it bordered on extravagant. It took a number of exhausting trips from the river to the village through the snow and slush to relocate everything, but the men were confident that almost every item would be needed at some point either for trading or survival purposes. Brushing away the last vestiges of footprints in the snow behind them after their final trip, they realized it was a symbolic gesture emphasizing there would be no turning back. The winter snows began to softly fall onto the frozen earth placing a cold white exclamation point on the conclusion of their former lives.

As the morning springtime sun shone gaily through the graceful trees, the small village was once again blossoming into a true Garden of Eden. Generations ago, this clan of the *Chicamacomico* nation had migrated north to find a new home away from the windblown and unkind outer banks of what would someday be called North Carolina. They ventured into Chesapeake Bay, found a small inviting river uninhabited by the indigenous *Nanticoke* tribe, followed it upland to the flowing springs and clear brooks that formed its headwaters and found 'paradise.' Over the years, the Natives constructed a bustling settlement with sturdy lodges and *ho-gans*, extensive garden cultivation, and all the accoutrements of a prosperous community. The village became an important stop-over on the inter-Tribal trading routes and the envy of many visiting groups. The reasons for the destruction and abandonment of such a beautiful place and just exactly when this terrible event occurred was a secret now held only by the Earth Mother herself.

During the months since the new people arrived, Theodore and Jonas had reconstructed three of the lodges and they proved to be warm, safe and comfortable. They had recently finished a fourth structure that was intended to serve as a storehouse. The young girls took it upon themselves to reclaim the over-grown and weed-infested gardens, and their first 'crop' was already well on its way toward harvesting. *Wicompo*, spending most of her adult life regal and aloof from the daily drudgery of sustenance provision, drew upon her prior experiences in the village to direct the rebuilding efforts and to share what she knew about cultivation and hunting. As a young girl, despite her royal bearing, she was eager to learn about everything, and even-though seldom invited, joined the hunters and gatherers in their pursuits. Swept off to the *Choptank* village as a chief's wife, she never soiled her hands or got her moccasins muddy again. Only now did she realize how much she missed the satisfaction of being a productive member of a community.

There was never a more perfect summer evening as the beaver splashed happily in the ponds they had built near the village and the crickets sang their timeless love songs. Somewhere in their genetic memories the comical animals knew that the two-leggeds were their brothers and would again be at hand to keep away the wolves and bears that tore at their lodges in an effort to feast on the young ones. The fragrances from the milkweed and spiceberry bushes were more pleasant than the most expensive French perfumes. The new people of the *Chicamacomico* entered the queen-mother's lodge for a gathering that would change the futures of each of them … forever. In long-standing *Choptank* tradition, a pleasant repast, this one of venison stew augmented with the first pickings from the garden, was served by the woman servant, and then idle talk permeated the night before the actual purpose of the meeting was to be made known. This always irritated the Englishmen eager to 'get to the point' and then continue on with their individual devices.

With only the slightest raising of her head, the others grew quiet in anticipation of what *Wicompo* was preparing to communicate. There was an air of seriousness and determination about her that captivated the others into silent assent. She quietly clapped her hands together, and her handmaiden emerged from the back of the *ho-gan* ready to do her mistress's bidding. As regal as any ruler on the planet, she motioned the woman to enter the circle, and the confused servant hesitated wondering if she understood the signal. Many tribes had a caste system, and those of the lower classes were never allowed to sit with the rest of the family.

"Yes, my dear," responded the queen-mother. "I want you to join us."

The elder looked at the younger woman and asked kindly, "What is your name?"

Tears formed in her eyes as she tried to respond. She had been taken into slavery as a very young child and sold or traded from tribe to tribe until she found herself with the gentle *Choptanks*. Her memories were filled with the hopelessness of being bullied and beaten for not meeting the impossible expectations of her masters or mistresses. For her entire life, she had not been addressed by name only by abusive and unkind descriptors … so she honestly no longer knew if she even had a name. Her earliest beginnings were cloudy memories of formless shapes and unfamiliar sounds. She did not know her mother or her tribe … she just … was.

Ashamed and embarrassed, the servant lowered her eyes and mumbled, "I do not know, mistress."

Wicompo hesitated a moment, then responded, "It does no longer matter. From now on, you will be known as *Sco-seh-WE-toh*. In our language it means 'Survivor.' You will carry this name until you are an old woman ... like me." She chuckled.

The others murmured their approval happy to realize they now had another sister in their growing family. The levity quietly died down as *Wicompo* looked sternly at Theodore and Jonas. "I have a mission of utmost importance for both of you ... and if you fail, do not come back."

The *Choptank* girls' loud protests were quelled by just the raising of the queen's hand. "My people have been murdered or taken into slavery," she continued. "I am charging you both with the responsibility of finding those who are still alive and bringing them home. Creator God made a promise to his people that no matter how hopeless or dire the situations might be a 'remnant' would always remain. It is your burden to find that 'remnant'."

The ensuing silence was truly deafening.

The queen-mother resumed her instructions. It was obvious that she had given the idea considerable thought and there was no room for input or discussion. "We can only assume that those who were still alive after the village was destroyed were bound into slavery. It would seem logical that the captors would prefer to sell them rather than take them back to their homelands ... which very well could have been beyond the setting sun. *Tee-ah-dore* and *Jo-nas-sus*, you will prepare for a journey to the *Assateague*, the *Accomac*, the *Accohannock*, the *Netegro*, and of course, the *Nanticoke*. You will carry as many trading goods as possible ... and naturally your marvelous weapons. Make every effort to barter for my people rather than trying to steal them. We do not need a war on our hands."

As the gravity of the quest began to make itself known, *Wicompo* leaned forward to emphasize the continuation of her directions. "The nearby nations have traded for slaves from many other tribes, so we must have some way of guaranteeing the ones returned are truly *Chicamacomico*. There are five words I want you to say to the people you are considering bringing back to us. If they display an understanding of those words ... they are my people. Listen carefully. The first word is *WO-oh-ke-yeh*. It means "peace." Say it with me, *WO-oh-ke-yeh*."

Even the girls repeated the word. Its lilting sound seemed strange on their tongues, so they were learning something new also. Each in its turn, the queen-mother taught her subjects *"Hok-SHE-oh-pah"* (Child), *"Ko-DAH"* (Friend), *"e-NAH"* (Mother), and the most important word of all: *"Te-YAH-dah"* (Home).

The elder woman could see the concern in the eyes of the young Englishmen assuming correctly that they were worried about leaving their loved ones alone at mercy of the elements and without protection. In complete confidence she asserted, "I have three daughters now. Each one is strong, fearless and intelligent. We will be just fine until you return ... May Creator God, the 'Great Mystery', walk at your side."

The morning of Theodore and Jonas' departure was cloudy and threatening rain. Even the weather seemed to reflect the feelings of the young people as they quietly stood together contemplating the event that swept them up and seemed to callously brush aside their plans for the future. Baby Wind Wolf seemed to sense the tension and sadness and he began to wail incessantly adding to the stress of the departure. It was always understood that the word of the queen-mother was 'law', but somehow this thought paled when measured against the possible ramifications of her dictates. There was no guarantee that the Englishmen would find any surviving *Chicamacomico*. Did this mean they could never return? Not much was known about the demeanor of the tribes they were about to visit, and even less was known about just where their villages were now constructed. All the named tribes, except the *Nanticoke*, were somewhat nomadic and they established their communities in different areas of the landscape depending on the seasons and the hunting and gathering taking place. Two young White Men, even armed with the latest British weaponry of long bows, crossbows, and metal tipped arrows and quarrels, would not be able to match up very successfully with a clan of hostile Native warriors.

The trading goods were personally selected by *Wicompo*, and she had picked out so many items that a rough *travois* had to be constructed just to carry them. This would slow them down considerably and make progress through the thick underbrush that seemed to be everywhere tiresome and frustrating.

As a young princess, *Wicompo* once went with a trading delegation to the massive *Nanticoke* village, so she had a general recollection of the way the men would have to travel. She remembered it was more than a day's walk in the direction where the autumn storms give birth to the most destructive weather of the year. Once they reach a very large river, they should follow the shoreline downstream toward the great Mother of All Waters. At that time, the *Nanticoke* settlement was so vast that the smoke from their lodges could be seen well before the travelers would actually arrive. At last reckoning, this nation was friendly and always agreeable to parlaying with its neighbors. The trade goods collected by

Wicompo, especially the colored cloth and metal implements, were of great value to the Indigenous people of the area and would be usable to purchase almost anything.

A last embrace and a kiss on the forehead of the fussing baby signaled the men's departure. As they left the village clearing and entered the thick forest, the unhappy cries of the young child and the distant rumble of approaching thunder added a sense of gloom to their adventure.

━━━━━━━━━━━━

The *travois* was heavy and clumsy, and the Englishmen had great difficulty making headway through the thickly forested hillsides. On more than one occasion a section of trading goods would slide off causing them to stop and have to reorganize their load. Since the beginning of time, and even up to today, the humidity preceding mid-Atlantic storms was suffocating adding even more frustration and discomfort to the journey. Their first day's progress was discouraging and tiring and their first night in the wilds was uncomfortable and depressing. Jonas began to remove his tunic and was immediately the focus of a swirling swarm of biting flies and mosquitoes. He reached into his backpack, and after extracting a small leather bag, pulled out a handful of moist green leaves. He began to rub them over his exposed skin which took on an eerie greenish tinge as the foliage disintegrated from the pressure of his fingers, and like magic the swarm removed itself and directed its attentions to Theodore.

The young Englishman began ducking and weaving and waving his arms wildly. He implored, "Whatever you have, give me some of it quickly! I'm being eaten alive!"

Jonas could not help but laugh at his friend's predicament as he pulled another handful of the pungent leaves from the bag and began rubbing them on Theodore's neck, face and hands. "Be careful to keep them away from your eyes." He instructed.

It truly was conjury. The voracious insects seemed to lose interest in the men and soon evaporated into their own environs. Someday, the leaves would be called 'peppermint', but for now ... suffice to say it was magic. This particular plant was not indigenous to the eastern shore of the bay, but it proved to be a trading commodity almost as precious as the *Choptank's* own *M'ne-SKOO-yah* (salt).

The fingers of rain began to caress the earth as the men scrambled down the last ridge to the very large river predicted by the queen-mother. Fortunately, the tide was ebbing making the shoreline flat and sandy allowing for much better progress. As instructed, the two young Englishmen continued the trek downstream hoping that their destination could be reached before nightfall. Thankfully, the rain was gentle and cooling, and under other circumstances might even have been considered pleasant. In a very short time, the precipitation ceased eliciting a sigh of contentment from the refreshed soil. Again, the queen-mother was completely accurate in her recollections: A whitish-gray cloud of wood smoke was resting against the shoreline just around a long sweeping bend of the widening river. It was almost certain they were approaching the *Nanticoke* settlement. Countless lodges, *ho-gans* and *wig-wams* had stoked their fire pits to ease the dampness and discomfort of the rain and had this situation occurred in modern times, it might have been described as 'smog.'

Both men had military minds and felt it would be prudent to do some reconnoitering before barging into a possibly dangerous situation. They pulled the *travois* into a thicket adjacent the river bank, and after removing their backpacks and hoisting their longbows and quivers of arrows approached the village under the cover of the thick forest. The sight they beheld would never be forgotten!

Wigwams of the Nanticoke community.

The *Nanticoke* community seemed endless! It extended along the river bank farther than their eyes could see with fingers of lodges, and any number of smaller and larger structures crawling up the adjacent hillsides. In the center of the community was an open area leading down to the water's edge where a flotilla of sea-going canoes perched on the bank offering the appearance of the world's biggest hair comb. At the landward side of the clearing stood a building longer, wider and taller than any other they had seen in the New World. It was not an imposing English cathedral, but in its own right was spectacular. There was no palisade around the town or clusters of warrior-guards on duty. Obviously these people had no fear of marauding groups of renegades or concerned themselves with wild animals wandering onto their pathways. The English mariners were taken aback by the implied sense of permanence and power. This was really going to change things.

———————————

Theodore and Jonas sat down in the tall grasses and looked helplessly at each other. Each assumed the *Nanticoke* settlement would be similar in many ways to the homey and personable village of the *Choptanks*. What extended before them was the New World's example of a true city teeming with humanity. Uncomfortably resting on the horns of their dilemma, they had to make their presence known to the community's leadership without appearing to be threatening and without some Native warriors overwhelming them and taking only their severed heads or scalps to the chiefs.

Theodore suddenly stood up and offered a solution to their predicament that was so bizarre that it just might work. "When we first met with the *Choptanks* it was unclear if they were willing to trade with us or even to acknowledge we were there. Our carpenter, John Capper, did something that appeared so remarkable to the Natives that they practically fell over each other to get to know us and to get their hands on our trade goods. If you will recall, he chopped down a tree while the villagers looked on. The *Choptanks* had never seen a metal axe before, and Capper's efforts seemed like magic. I think it is safe to assume the *Nanticoke* are also in the 'stone-age' and would be very impressed by what we may have to offer. What do you think?"

Jonas looked at Theodore like he had lost his mind. "Are you saying we should take a couple axes, walk into the *Nanticoke* city and start cutting down a tree? I acknowledge that the past few days have been cold and cloudy, but I think you have been out in the sun too long."

Theodore chuckled as he pictured what might happen. "Why not?"

Why not, indeed.

The Englishmen decided to strip down to breeches and moccasins. Head and shoulders taller than the locals and slim and muscular from the hard work rebuilding the *Chicamacomico* village, they presented images of powerful men. More peppermint leaves were rubbed on their exposed skin leaving a slight greenish tinge from head to waist, which added to their mystical appearance. Jonas was very adept with the *Choptank* language and assumed correctly that it was probably an understandable dialect of a broader language family that the *Nanticoke* could comprehend.

What happened next gave birth to a legend that found itself repeated around Native fire pits for countless generations:

Not so long ago, according to an earlier tale, at one of the smaller *Nanticoke* villages on the *Wah-ZE-yah-tah wok-PAH* (North River, later known as the Choptank River) the *Toh we-CHOSH-tah* (Blue Man) was allowed to reside with its people as an offering of gratitude by the Mother of All Waters for their stewardship of her swimmers and flyers. This Holy Man had blessed that village for 'many moons' until one sad day he disappeared into the autumn mist and returned to his Mother. (They did not know that Vicar Robert Hunt had connected with Captain John Smith and returned to his duties at Jamestown).

The people of the capitol city were always envious of that event, and at last they had their own legend, even more spectacular: The *Wah-TOH-toh We-CHOSH-tah-pe* (The Green Men).

Theodore and Jonas ambled, half-naked, right into the heart of the settlement with their axes over their shoulders. Jonas repeatedly called out, *"Oh-YAH-teh, Oh-YAH-teh"*

(People! People!). Needless to say, a large group of Natives flocked to them to see the spectacle. The word of their arrival swept through the city like wild fire. Most held back in fear that these beings were either evil or sacred, but their curiosity kept them transfixed on the giant, green men. Jonas found a sturdy oak tree with a trunk about the girth of a men's waists. He motioned the crowd to come closer and murmured, "*Ke-WE-dah-yah*" (Gather around). Laughing, he winked at Theodore, and both raised their axes and began to chop at the tree. The metal axe heads ate the tree trunk like a starving bear gorging himself on his first spring kill. In a matter of moments, the stately tree creaked as if resigned to its fate then resolutely laid itself onto the river bank. The crowd retreated to avoid being crushed by the limbs and branches, then stared at the tree and the men in total disbelief. Theodore had been correct that the *Nanticokes* used stone axe heads for tree falling … and this was even more magical than the men themselves.

Jonas looked at the nearest people in the crowd and with a friendly wave of his hand invited them to check out the tree trunk. Acknowledging his simple and friendly "*Won-YAH-kah.*" (Come and see), some of the men carefully approached the fallen giant and had to touch its mortal wound to prove they had not been dreaming. The cut area was still warm from the bite of the axes, and they flinched in discomfort. Another carefully picked up a chip of the cut wood and held it like a sacred icon. Then the others swarmed forward eager for a souvenir and for a chance to touch the Green Men. There had never been a real 'riot' in the history of the *Nanticoke* nation, but this amazing event was rapidly deteriorating in a noisy and confusing melee.

From somewhere in the back of the unruly crowd a forceful "*Ah-NOP-tah!*" (Stop!) flooded over the group, and in an instant they all fell silent and stood completely still. A section of the people parted like the Red Sea for Moses, and a group of heavily armed and very serious looking warriors approached the Englishmen protecting a distinguished and obviously very important elderly man.

"Now we're getting someplace," thought Theodore.

Theodore and Jonas stood side-by-side next to their trophy tree, their axe heads on the ground and the handles firmly in the grasps of their strong hands. The *Nanticoke* warriors silently surrounded the two Englishmen fearful of these two green giants but willing to perform their duties at any cost.

"Put your axe in your left hand," whispered Jonas knowing this was the universal sign of non-aggression. As soon as the two men did this, there was a perceptible easing of tension.

The elderly Native respectfully approached the English mariners, and in perfect *Choptank* inquired what the *Nanticoke* people could do for such auspicious guests. Jonas was relieved there would be little or no problem in communication between the two parties. Always graceful and condescending toward any elderly person he inquired about the health and fortunes of his host and commented on the weather and other subjects of small talk. The elderly man was visibly relieved that the *Wah-TOH-toh We-CHOSH-tah* (Green Man) was cognizant of acceptable social courtesies and tastefully led the conversation back to his original question, "What could the *Nanticoke* people do for such auspicious guests?"

Jonas was pleased that the gentleman was as willing to get to the point as the Englishmen were. The *Choptank* tradition of taking the winding trail to 'the point' always irritated him. He responded with one simple word, "*Wah-YAH-kah-pe*."(Slaves).

The crowd murmured its approval. Of course, gods would be seeking more worshipers.

The representative of the community, with appropriate deference, invited the Green Men to join him in the guest lodge for a meal and parlay. Theodore reminded Jonas that their cache of trading goods was stashed in a thicket near the boundary of the city, so Jonas realized they needed to buy some time to reclaim their booty. Unsure how to communicate this without appearing as simple merchants trying to get the best deal, he was in a quandary and decided it would be best to wait until nightfall then quietly fetch the items needed to make the trade under the cover of darkness. He would appear aloof and disinterested and at some point convince the locals the trading should be postponed until the next day.

The guest lodge was very pleasant in every way. The floor was covered with fresh-cut loblolly pine boughs and the fragrance was marvelous. They were still moist from the recent rain and felt like the purest silk from Cathay. A friendly fire had been stoked in the pit and gave off a welcoming light. Strangely, some of the supporting beams had flaming torches allowing even more light to fill the interior. Around the fire pit a sumptuous meal had been prepared and was waiting for their indulgence. Both Englishmen stopped in total shock! The *travois* used to tote the trade goods was propped against one of the wooden pillars and all their treasures were neatly organized and stacked against the lodge walls. The *Nanticoke* were extremely honest and would never consider pilfering property of others.

Their gentlemanly host chuckled as he noticed their reaction and motioned them to sit by the fire. "We are the mighty *Nanticoke*, and we have been watching you most of the day. We were wondering how you would make yourselves known to us and were pleased and entertained by the creative way you came into our city. Our people will always know you as *Wah-TOH-toh We-CHOSH-tah-pe* (Green Men) and we have no intention of letting them know you are merely *Ska We-CHOSH-tah-pe.* (White Men). The exploits of your people's marvelous years with the *Choptanks* have traveled the trading routes from lips to ears, and we longed to meet you. In many ways you have become like giants to the Natives of this area. I cannot tell you appropriately how pleased I am to be knee-to-knee with you."

Theodore was not sure exactly what the *Nanticoke* representative was saying. He knew a useable amount of the local language, but still had not mastered normal conversation techniques. Seeing Jonas' mouth again drop open in complete surprise told him that something very important had been shared.

"What is it?" he whispered.

"We're buggered!" Jonas responded.

The meeting to buy slaves was to be held the next morning in the guest lodge. In preparation for the event, the *Nanticokes* began to identify a number of possible subjects for the transaction. As might be expected, the locals selected slaves who were argumentative, passive aggressive, past their prime as good workers or simply un-trainable. This was a rare opportunity to clear out the ones they had purchased or traded for previously that turned out not to be such good deals after all. By the time the negotiations were to begin, about 20 or 30 slaves crowded into the guest lodge and sat sullenly against the interior walls. The elderly gentleman they had met the prior day was in attendance as well as a small group of very important-looking Natives. A large crowd had gathered outside the lodge, but the warriors kept them at a distance so they could only wonder what was taking place inside. Following standard hospitality procedures, some of the elder *Nanticoke* women prepared and served a fine meal of seafood stew, a pleasant and aromatic corn bread, fresh roots and herbs and a very pleasant tea sweetened with wild bee honey.

The *Nanticoke* representatives motioned Theodore and Jonas to inspect the slaves to see if any were of interest to them. Theodore whispered to his friend, "What do we do? I've never even considered buying another person before."

Jonas replied, "Well, what do people do when they are in the market for horses or cattle? They check their teeth, feel their legs, inspect their hooves, and listen to see if they pass gas."

The other Englishman responded too loudly, "Pass Gas?"

Jonas chuckled and was very pleased that he had consternated his friend. "Well, feel their stomachs to see if they are bound up. And don't forget the special words."

If the observing Natives had not known the histories of their guests, they would have assumed these two had often bartered for slaves. Each man went from person to person not caring if they were male or female, young or old. They pried open the mouths of the slaves, patted them on their exposed stomachs and while doing so whispered "*WO-oh-ke-yeh.*"(Peace).

None of the prospects seem to acknowledge the words until they found two Natives cowering in the back of the lodge trying not to be noticed. One was a woman who might have been considered attractive except for the obvious impressions of a very hard life. It was difficult to determine her age but maybe in her early twenties or thirties, and the other a smaller woman clearly younger but also worn and tired looking. They crouched together holding hands and seemed in abject terror. It was apparent they either were sisters or close friends. Theodore knelt down pretending to inspect them while whispering the opening contact word. Both looked wide-eyed in total bewilderment at the tall man still with a green tinge on his face and hands. He repeated the next three words quietly and as concisely as he could, *"Hok-SHE-oh-pah"*(Child) … *"Ko-DAH"* (Friend) … *"e-NAH"* (Mother). When he said the last word, *"Te-YAH-dah"* (Home), both girls fell into each other's arms and began to cry. At that moment the Englishman did not care if he would have to give up every single item of trading goods. He was going to take these two refugees home. They must have been captured at what have must have seen like 'forever' ago and lived in fear and helplessness from that moment on.

Jonas had wandered into another group of slaves and replicated the process done by Theodore. Again, there was basically no response from those poor souls. An older man, somewhat withered and disheveled, turned away from the Englishman as if fearing he was about to be beaten. Jonas whispered the first contact word, *"WO-oh-ke-yeh."* The man dropped his head and covered his ears. This seemed to be a strange reaction compared to the others, so he continued with the other four key words.

The sitting man refused to look at Jonas, but inquired in a quiet frightened voice in perfect *Chicamacomico*, still recognizable to the *Choptank* tongue the young Englishman was so adept with, "What do you want with me?"

The Englishman replied simply and directly, "I want to take you back to your people."

He took the man's arm, helped him to his feet and stated, *"Deh Won-ZE."* (This one.)

Jonas continued his inspection and found a very strong looking man probably in his late thirties or early forties. It was difficult to accurately ascertain his age. Clearly his hard life had taken its toll on his younger years. The Native's head was completely shaven, which was a sign of punishment, and he had many scars on his bare chest and shoulders indicating he had been flogged numerous times during his life as a slave. His face was deeply pock-marked from neglect and disease. Jonas felt immediate pity for the man, but the glare of silent rage sent his way not unlike the baleful stare of a caged animal made the Englishman decide to walk past him. For some reason he could never explain, he stopped and reconsidered, returned to the man and whispered, "*WO-oh-ke-yeh.*"

The man looked away and muttered, "I have never known peace."

He turned his back to Jonas and it was crisscrossed over and over with the ugly white scars of so many beatings that the regular brown skin was almost non-existent.

"I want to take you home. *Te-YAH-dah.*"

The HA-sah-pah-pe (Black Men)

An unseasonably cold and damp wind from the mainland enticed tired sighs from the trees around the Native settlement and reminded the inhabitants that puny two-leggeds would always be at the mercy of the elements. The early morning sky was a malevolent grey with heavy, moisture-laden clouds scudding eastward toward the distant Atlantic. The silence in the community was abruptly broken by the terrified cries of a young *Choptank* boy as he ran wildly from the shore to the village screaming over and over again, *"WE-dah-wah-dah! WE-dah-wah-dah!"* ("A ship! A ship!").

Captain Coverdale, now known as *AH-ban-nah Chon-TEH* (Gentle Heart), emerged from his *wig-wam* wiping the sleep from his eyes and caught the trembling boy by his arm and commanded, *"TOH-kee-yah?"* ("Where?") The lad pointed off the headland west of the village. There a few miles distant was indeed a large sailing vessel emerging from the low hanging clouds. It was not much more than a dark apparition in the early morning light, but it definitely was of European design.

At that moment, village leaders *Pemetosusk* and *Pacowassamuck* arrived on the scene, and the three men went into immediate action. The young women were rousted from their beds and hustled off to the moon time lodge in the forest some distance inland. The head chief's lovely wife, *Watsawasoo*, was instructed to gather the older women and prepare a welcoming feast to be served in the men's lodge. The warrior leader, *Asquash*, knew to gather the *WE-h'ne-s'ah* clan and make them ready in case the visitors had hostile intent. Lesser chiefs *Tattowin* and *Weanchum* sent runners to each *wig-wam* informing the villagers to gather up what they might need to survive for a few days and hide in the nearby forest until the danger of the situation could be determined. Coverdale was deeply impressed how organized the village was. Each person accepted his responsibility quickly and gracefully, and in a matter of moments the community was prepared for any eventuality.

The English former military man, now comfortable in his Native attire, and *Pemetosusk* peered furtively out of the shoreline undergrowth to get a better look at the vessel. With his telescope, the captain could see that the craft was of Dutch design and flew the flags and pennants of the European Low Countries. He handed his spy glass to the chief and felt a wave of relief that the visitors were not Spanish. It was common knowledge that the mariners from Iberia were more inclined to rob and pillage than to trade.

In hopes they were communicating that the village was friendly, the two men walked down to the beach and waved to the ship assuming that the Dutch were also looking with their spyglasses inland. Coverdale scanned the nearby brush and forest and could see that the hiding warriors, armed and prepared, were at the ready. This brought a degree of comfort knowing that if there was going to be trouble … the *Choptanks* would spring the trap.

Uninvited, but accepted without question, the elder medicine woman, *Chop-tah-nk*, approached the two men on the shoreline and stood beside them silently. Her presence would only reinforce the point that the village was friendly. If hostilities were about to happen, no woman would be on the scene.

The monotonous wind out of the west brought a most unpleasant odor toward the village as it swept across the Dutch vessel. Despite the fact that the craft was at least a

half-mile away, something was dreadfully wrong. Captain
Coverdale had experienced that disgusting stench more than
one time during his military career. It was the sickening
reek from piles of rotting, fly-encrusted human bodies ... the
tragic aftermath of so many fields of battle. He had forgotten
those unpleasant moments, and they returned like a rushing
tide through his heart. He sensed his blood going cold and
shivered in the muted early morning light. *Pemetosusk* looked
up at his friend and felt a deep concern for this gentle man.

A massive longboat was lowered from the Dutch three-
master and began to ply the rough waters shoreward. There
appeared to be about a dozen occupants but only four of
them were rowing. As it approached the beach an unusual
metallic clanking sound was discernable. Coverdale knew it
immediately: The sound of chains and irons.

A small group of *WE-h'ne-s'ah* emerged from the forest
and waded into the water to assist the landing of the craft.

A pitiful sight was beheld by the villagers. There were
four bearded White Men, pale of skin and noticeably unclean
in clothing, hair and footwear. When they opened their
mouths, it was too obvious that their teeth were either long
gone or just blackened stumps. Between them were eight of
the most miserable looking human beings the *Choptanks* had
ever encountered. Their skin was as black as night but was
dull and covered with open sores. Despite the cold winds
they wore only loin cloths, so their ribs could be easily seen
dominating the torsos of their bodies. Their legs and thighs
were mostly bones, and the iron rings around their ankles
had worn bloody wounds that had to be excruciatingly
painful as they were continually scraped open by the metal
bonds. Their hair was disheveled and crawling with lice as it
hung limply over their shoulders. Their coal black eyes were
dull and were silently praying for death.

Coverdale felt a wave of pity sweep through his soul and tears formed in his eyes. He looked down at *Pemetosusk* and saw his friend was reacting in a similar fashion.

"Eight scurvy animals!" roared one of the White Men in common Dutch. "What will you give for them?"

"These are the last of the lot," added another with a heartless laugh. "We'll make you a good deal."

Coverdale knew enough of their language to understand the discourse and could respond with some degree of efficiency. He remembered the times when the soldiers from the Continent's Low Countries had come to England to learn proper military techniques, and he was involved with their training.

Cruelly and without even the least modicum of compassion, the White Men pulled the eight dark humans out of the skiff by their irons and pushed them toward the beach. The ankle chains were as heavy as painful as the poor creatures stumbled and crawled out of the unkind water collecting on the rocky shore shivering uncontrollably. One of the men fell limp and was carried by two others. He had died before their very eyes.

The grieving *HA-sah-pah-pe* (Black Men) began their heart-breaking death chant once again. For endless months, they had wrung out their souls in despair and hopelessness as friends, family and other miserable captives perished on the wretched journey to the New World. This loss seemed especially painful to the dwindling survivors because there was a faint glimmer of hope that their travail might come to an end. The word *"Ajali"* was repeated over and over in their despondency. The *Choptanks* assumed it was the name of the hapless creature, which later proved to be true, and meant "destiny."

The Dutch had been plying the slave trade between Africa and the New World for a number of years. In the eyes of many Englishmen, they were the scum of the earth trying to profit by human misery. Coverdale knew that when the ship left the jungle coast, it was heavily laden with humanity. Always, their first stop was the Caribbean Islands where most of the slaves were sold. The Indigenous peoples of those locations had died off early in the years of contact with the White Men as a result of disease and deprivation. Now a new population of slaves was being offered. It was very unusual for the slavers to come this far north. They must have been blown off course by a storm. He did not even want to imagine how many had died and were thrown into the sea during the sailing. It was clear that the stench of death still permeated the ship and implied that there might still be cadavers rotting in the cells and in need of disposal.

The English captain turned to *Pemetosusk* with an inquiring glance. The Head chief nodded briefly allowing Gabrielle to proceed with the negotiations. "We are the powerful *Choptank* people," he began in acceptable Dutch. "Our enemies cry out just at the sound of our name and cover their ears in fear. They fall to their knees and beg for mercy even before our women and children. They break their weapons and lay them at our feet in total supplication. The Mother of All Waters swims with the bodies of those we have slain. We have all the slaves we need or want. Why should we trade with you for these miserable creatures?"

The slaver negotiator was taken aback by Coverdale's tirade and the fact that he spoke the language so well. He was quick to realize that this was no ignorant savage before him. The captain, dressed in his white deerskin clothing, towered over the visitor adding to his air of supremacy.

"W-well," he stammered, "What would you give for them? We have made a fine profit this trip and do not need the going standard."

"Nothing!" replied Coverdale with obvious disgust and derision in his voice.

"Sold!" yelled the Dutchman relieved to be rid of the last of his sickly cargo. He turned to the other three White Men. "Let's get out of here!"

The villagers were summoned from the forest and slowly gathered on the beach around the wretched Black Men. *Chop-tah-nk* quickly surveyed the condition of the visitors and called for the *Ke-WE-dah-yah-s'ah* healer women who began to minister to these wretched humans putting medicinal salves on their open sores and covering them with deerskin blankets. Captain Coverdale acquired a splitting awl and metal scraper and began to remove the clamps from their wounded ankles. The only word spoken by the suffering travelers was *"Asante"* ("Thank you"), but the looks of gratitude in the slaves' sad eyes spoke volumes.

The ancient medicine woman pointed at a number of the village young men and ordered, *"E-H'DU-ska-pe won-KEH-yah!"*("To the medicine sweat lodge!"). Without question or second thoughts the men paired up and gently carried their wasted guests to the place of healing. Each was so emaciated that one brave could have easily assumed his burden with little effort.

During the weeks since their arrival, the medicine women had been working hard to nurse their strange guests back to health. The twin village leaders had visited the Medicine Lodge often to observe the healing. Each time, the Africans would prostrate themselves at the feet of the sacrosanct men quietly chanting *"Darweshi"* (Holy), knowing innately that these two were almost god-like in bearing and stature.

An amazing testimonial to the strength and resolve of the seven emaciated Black Men's determination to live was the fact that they were improving and regaining their strength. They would never talk to the healers or to each other when the Natives were nearby, but they were completely compliant and accepting of any kindness. It did not even occur to the *Choptanks* that at least one of the men was from a different tribe and location on the Dark Continent and was unable to communicate with the others. The surviving *HA-sah-pah-pe* would soon be well enough to leave the medicine lodge and it seemed logical to allow them to live in the village's bartering lodge until a plan could be put in to effect.

───────────

The tribal council of the *Choptanks* met in the comfortable *wigwam* of head chief *Pemetosusk*. His lovely wife, *Watsawasoo*, had prepared a sumptuous meal of oyster stew and vegetables, warm corn bread, and a pleasant tea made from the recipe that the English cook, Johnson, had shared with her what seemed like a lifetime ago. The combination of sassafras and raspberry with a touch of wild bee honey had become the chief's favorite, and she served it as often as possible, especially during important occasions when the council met or when visiting tribes came to discuss trading and finding wives. Once the council members were served and eagerly devouring the repast, *Watsawasoo* gracefully exited. The head chief watched this marvelous woman as she turned and flashed him a most promising smile. He felt a flow of love warm his heart and wished to follow her. But, important decision-making had always been the sole responsibility of the men of the tribe and this time was no exception.

Lesser chief *Pacowassamuck* sat next to *Asquash,* the great warrior with one eye. He had tried for years to get a member of the *WE-h'ne-s'ah* clan on the council, and after the suicide of gentle *Weesanusks* his wish became a reality. *Asquash* was still uncomfortable with his new responsibilities. He was a hunter and a fighter, more at ease following orders and cracking heads than making major decisions for the entire village. The twin lesser chiefs, *Tattowin* and *Weanchum,* sat at their places of honor and seemed to be deep in their own private thoughts. As always, the discussion started with small talk and the relating of minor happenings since the prior meeting. *Choptank* tradition dictated that it would be rude to go directly to 'the point' of the gathering until a tone of congeniality had been established and previous issues had been recounted.

At the appropriate moment, *Pemetosusk,* barely lifted his hand and all conversation ceased. He began, "The trading season will soon be upon us. The Mother of All Waters has been especially gracious. Our *M'ne-SKOO-yah* (salt) production has been the best in a generation. Our marvelous victory over the *Susquehannock* has made us the envy of the tribes and nations who have heard our great story. They want to be our friends and want others to know that they are our friends. We are in a position of strength when it comes to trading and should do very well indeed."

The council members were pleased to hear these words, but this was not new information worthy of a meeting at this time. Clearly, their chief had an important decision to make and he was not exactly taking the straight path to the issue on his mind. *Pemetosusk* studied the comfortable animal skins he was sitting on and began stroking the thick, rich fur. He stated quietly, almost in an embarrassed fashion, "It's the *HA-sah-pah-pe*. Our esteemed Medicine Woman, *Chop-tah-nk,* has informed me that they are now in good health. She has found them pacing in their confines and arguing with each other as if they were in cages. She senses that they want to be free and they are seen looking longingly at the forest around their lodging. She feels they are tree people and want to get back to their roots."

Pemetosusk turned to the twin chiefs and asked them if they had any visions to share. Despite the many years they had served on the leadership council, he was still amazed how they seemed to be one person in two bodies. There was never a delay when one stopped talking and the other started in. Their soft almost feminine voices were exactly the same and the inflection of their words identical. He remembered closing his eyes one time and trying to determine who was speaking and when. There was absolutely no difference. This continuity added to the sense of mystery around them, and the head chief was especially deferent and grateful he had them as part of his team.

Tattowin began, and *Weanchum's* mind seemed to drift into some other level of consciousness:

"The *HA-sah-pah-pe* are people of the forest. They are proud and strong and very spiritual.

They know the voices of the swimmers, the flyers and the four-leggeds.

They have lived in peace and harmony with their world far beyond the recollection of the Earth Mother.

Their path to us was one of great anguish and misery. We saw a great water everywhere covered with blood and dead bodies.

One of them was an honored chief to his people. He was revered and powerful and known through his land for gentle compassion and intelligence. His family; wives, parents and children; have left this world in unbearable pain and misery and he longs to be with them.

The only reason he clings to life is that one of our *HA-sah-pah* is his only surviving son.

They have become orphans in this New World, but the Mother of All has not forgotten her sweet children despite their anguish.

Creator-God has made a promise to all His people that no matter how painful and hopeless life might become, there will always be survivors to carry on.

There is a place for them."

He then closed his eyes and bowed his head in silence. *Pemetosusk* waited for *Tattowin* to continue, which did not happen. He turned to *Weanchum* expecting more, which again did not happen.

After a short pause, the village leader continued, "I do not doubt that they would make fine *Wah-YAH-kah-pe* (slaves). They are strong and seem to be wise to the ways of the Earth Mother. Any of our village families would be proud to have them in their *wig-wam* or we would trade well if we offered them to other tribes." He paused and looked at *Asquash*. "They might even learn to be good warriors."

Not one of the council members entered the discussion almost certain that the head chief had already decided the future course of action.

Pemetosusk rose to his feet, which he seldom did unless he was about communicate a difficult decision he had made, "The Great Mystery must have a plan for the *HA-sah-pah-pe* since He allowed them to survive their endless travail. It is my opinion that we should take them to the West-lands and free them to their destinies."

As he sat down, the others began rapidly talking with each other. Even the ethereal twin chiefs seem to be jolted from their reverie and joined in the discussion. Not one of them asked "why?" The cruxes of the conversations were "how" and of equal importance "when."

Tattowin and *Weanchum* were given the responsibility to communicate with the *HA-sah-pah-pe* that they would soon be freed. They had often visited the Men's Lodge and were recognizable to their guests. Also the visitors had sensed early that these two were deeply spiritual and were especially deferent toward them.

Later that day, the twin chiefs reclined by the fire pit in the bartering lodge and motioned their Dark Brothers to join them. Indeed these seven men had greatly improved in strength and presence. The older one called *Akida Khalfani* seemed to be especially respected and the others allowed him to sit closest to the two Natives. *Tattowin* smiled warmly and using traditional sign language motioned that in three days the men would be allowed to leave the lodge and would be taken by water to the big land where the sun slept. He noticed them dropping their eyes and a sense of sadness seemed to flow around the circle. The Black Men assumed that they would be sold or traded into slavery to a people probably not nearly as kind and considerate as their hosts. Still smiling,

Tattowin clasped his hands together then opened his arms in a gesture that meant the same anywhere on the planet: Freedom.

———————

The entire village turned out that late summer afternoon to get the *HA-sah-pah-pe* on their way. Most had not seen their guests since their arrival some time before and were pleased, almost amazed, to see how well they had recovered. Their miserable loin cloths had been discarded long ago and each was dressed in sand-colored tanned deerskin clothing decorated with runes and cowry shells. They were shod with well-fitting and expertly sewn moccasins. Their dark skin contrasted sharply with their outfits and they looked handsome and in excellent form. One of their guests, called *Zuberi*, stood head and shoulders above the others and even towered over Captain Coverdale. He was an especially fine specimen, and a number of villagers wondered why he was not kept around. Four canoes were at the ready and two of the smaller ones were empty except for the paddles and supplies and would be towed by the manned crafts. After all, the *Choptanks* could not leave their Black Brothers on the mainland without any form of transportation.

As the grateful former slaves prepared to climb aboard the water craft, they stopped, turned around and then prostrated themselves on the beach before the villagers. They began to sing the most marvelous and ancient 'thank you' song that conjured up visions of a magical sunlit forest, green and untouched, that blessed a clean and gentle land of harmony and peace. Even though the Natives could not understand the beautiful words, their deepest heart-felt feelings of gratitude touched them all and many had tears in their eyes.

Not to be outdone, the elderly *Choptank* women began their goodbye songs, this time filled with joy and optimism. Their voices blended into a beautiful symphony that sent their guests off with light and happy hearts. Indeed, the future was looking very bright.

━━━━━━━━━━━━

The *Ho-KU-wah-s'ah* water people pulled their paddles deep into the waters of the bay and the sea-going canoes sped away from the village directly into the setting sun. The Mother of All Waters was especially calm offering a sense of support for the decision of the village leaders. Well out of sight of land, a Native in the lead canoe raised his arm, and the others stop rowing. He turned around and instructed his clansmen to give the paddles to the *HA-sah-pah-pe*. It was time for a short training session in handling water craft. The laughter of the *Choptanks* was infectious, and soon their guests were also laughing as they clumsily endeavored to get the canoes to go in the proper direction. It did take some time, but eventually they got a reasonable sense of this ancient art and the small flotilla was back on the correct compass direction. The visitors were so strong and paddling so well that the locals sat back, and for the first time in their lives, enjoyed the ride.

The plan was to reach the mainland by nightfall. This land was part of the *Susquehannock* nation, and the *Choptanks* were unwilling to take the chance that some vendetta would be waiting for them after the decisive victory against their massive war party. Since the *HA-sah-pah-pe* had not even been in the village at that time, the Natives were confident they would not be associated with the battle or even be able to communicate to any of the mainlanders just who exactly had given them refuge

Eastern Hoot Owl. Called "he-NAH-kah-gah."

The beautiful sandy beach glowed in the rising moonlight. The ground was so flat that there was no sense of anything beyond the tree line a short distance from the water's edge.

The night was completely still and comfortably warm. Somewhere in the deepening darkness an owl whispered his welcoming greeting. It was, without a doubt, a perfect welcome to a new kind of man walking on this strange land for the first time. The canoes were quickly off-loaded and the Natives helped the Black Men carry their gear into the cover of the thick forest. The *Choptanks* motioned that the two smaller canoes should probably also be pulled into the undergrowth and this was taken care of in quick dispatch.

One of *HA-sah-pah*, called *Betoto* the Owl, touched the nearest tree and wrapped his arms around it as if it were an old friend. He sniffed at the bark and touched it with his tongue. "It is different ... but it is clean and noble. We could do well here."

The night insects were singing their joyous welcoming songs to the new people as each man unrolled a tanned deer hide in the tall grasses and tumbled into its glorious softness. They looked up at the clear night sky and saw a kaleidoscope of stars for the first time since they had been taken into custody and packed into the miserable Dutch slave ship. *Sabra,* the saddest and most wretched of this small band of refugees was afraid to even dream that such a night would someday come. His eyes filled with tears and he quietly chanted the name of his younger brother who had died just as they were saved by the *Choptanks,* "*Ajali ... Ajali ... Ajali.*"

The Hounds of Hell

"H*e-YAH! He-YAH!"* (No! No!)
Lesser chief *Tattowin* sat up in his bedding his body shaking and covered with sweat. His twin brother *Weanchum* touched his arm and spoke softly, "It's the dream again, is it not?"

"The dream" was a terrible nightmare that both brothers experienced often as of late. In their mind's eye they saw their village completely devastated. The people's *wig-wams* were flattened and the sturdy lodges looked like animal skeletons completely devoid of walls or roofs. Black angry smoke was everywhere blotting out the sun and turning all the colors of nature into a depressing dull grey. The waters were as red as blood with white carcasses of dead fish covered with flies and fouling the shore line. The beautiful loblolly pine and oak trees that graced the outskirts of the community were merely shattered sticks reaching fruitlessly toward the sky imploring the Earth Mother to tell them "Why?" The anguished cries of women and children as they prostrated themselves over the mounds of dead bodies completed the weaving of the tapestry of what truly was Hell on earth.

Tattowin stoked the fire in the pit to push away the night's black heart and pulled an animal robe around his shivering body. He felt as if icy fingers were walking up and down his spine. "We must convene a meeting of the council and share our vision. I do not understand the message, but I am confident we need to tell the leadership."

The late-summer's morning sun was slowly pulling itself above the eastern sky line as the twin chiefs sent their acolytes to the homes of the village leaders asking them to meet in the bartering lodge as soon as possible. *Weanchum* felt that Captain Coverdale should also be in attendance even though he was not officially a member of the tribal council. His insights were always appreciated and often proved to be of great value.

The twins were still deeply bothered by the nightmare and had some difficulty relating what they had seen. Neither could express the entire dream without the help of the other. Head chief *Pemetosusk* listened intently trying to interpret the imagery. Was the dream a premonition of the physical destruction of the village or was it a symbolic way of warning the leadership about the moral or cultural demise of the tribe? Was another terrible war looming on the horizon – this time bringing about the end of the *Choptank* nation? It is the season when the Great Winds from the South occasionally crawled their way through the land, but in his entire lifetime the destruction implied by the holy men's dream was beyond his experiences and he had never heard about such a thing from the elders who trained him for his role in life.

Lesser chief, *Pacowassamuck,* had always been the realist of the group and occasionally took the messages from the twin chiefs with less than rapt attention. He appreciated their contributions and never doubted that they should be on the tribe's leadership team, but many times their input was wispy or wandered in and out of the business at hand without any real assistance toward solving a particular problem. Sometimes he wondered if they were *Hay-YO-kah-pe* (clowns) and were messing with the heads of the other leaders. He did feel in this instance he needed to respond, so after some thought he contributed, "Since we do not understand the meaning of the dream we are at a loss as to how to deal with its message. I am confident that the esteemed *Asquash* and his warriors could protect us from any renegade invasion. If the Mother-of-All *Wah-M'NE-oh-m'ne-pe* (hurricanes) is on the way it appears there is very little we can do to prepare for it. And, of course, the dream might merely be a reoccurring nightmare, which we all have had. So there is not much reason for concern at this time. Do you all agree?"

His comments were little comfort to the other council members, but there was an indisputable modicum of sensibility to them. In traditional *Choptank* fashion, the issue was 'tabled' until a future meeting. The decision-making process of the tribe never included any procedures for immediate resolution. This greatly distressed the twin chiefs, but they were only two voices and had done all they could to communicate their feelings of a sense of urgency.

After the meeting the great one-eyed warrior, *Asquash*, and Captain Coverdale deep in thought walked together and found themselves at the water's edge. They turned and scanned the beautiful village behind them. By now the busy hum of daily activity was pushing away any thoughts of destruction and ruin. Each of the four clans was meeting its specific responsibilities. The worthy *Ho-KU-wah-s'ah* water people were loading the crab traps before the incoming tide brought about the crustacean feeding frenzy. The *Ke-WE-dah-yah-s'ah* gatherers were forming teams to harvest the bounty that grew in the nearby forest. The *Wah-KON-kon-s'ah* magicians had already left for the salt cairns on the north bank of the promontory eager to see how the crystals were forming and wondering if they were ready to harvest. They also had a canoe partially built and intended to work on it until nightfall. The warrior clan, the *WE-h'ne-s'ah*, was making final preparations for an over-night deer hunt and some were calling to *Asquash* to join them.

Asquash's heart was always with his men, and he enjoyed the excitement of the hunt as much if not more than the younger braves. He looked up at his English friend, so imposing and almost regal in his white deer-skin ensemble, and inquired, "What do you think we should do?"

Captain Coverdale had transformed into *AH-ban-nah Chon-TEH* (Gentle Heart) many months ago and he felt he knew much more about the Native spirit and the longings of his great friend. "You are needed with the hunters. There are still some that must learn more before they can become successful contributors to the welfare of the village. Your skills and experience are the greatest of all teachers. I will think about this problem. Maybe do some looking around so when you return hopefully I will have a plan to talk over."

―――――

The Englishman enjoyed the sense of reinvigoration resulting from his walks in the forest with his devoted acolyte. They had explored most of the area around the community and despite the metaphysical changes in the former British officer, he still looked at the area with his military eye. He would note 'the high ground' and determine locations that might be difficult to defend … mentally constructing bunkers and revetments. He would notice a small gully or depression that might provide cover for invaders sneaking up on the village and think about having the Gatherer Clan clear it of underbrush. For no special reason they found themselves on the path to the abandoned Ft. Wingfield a short distance east of the village. This monument to the European friends of the *Choptanks* had been deactivated when the last of the crew and passengers of *The Phyllis Redoubtable* longing to return to Jamestown had departed southward in the *Ho-KU-wah-s'ah* canoes.

With the assistance of his young admirer they were able to pull the gate open enough to enter the compound and saw it was still in surprisingly good condition. It was indeed a worthy testament to the construction abilities of the Englishmen. With a minimum amount of repair and tidying it might easily serve its original purpose. He walked around the grounds listening to the voices of the wind in the dry grasses and the mild gusts buffeting the roof shingles. It seemed like a soft gentle symphony ... almost a lullaby. Standing silently in the warm sun he began to realize just how tired he was and felt himself drifting into a strangely pleasant reverie barely cognizant of the temporal world around him. As he closed his eyes, a frightening premonition crawled into his mind! There was a roaring sound louder and more malevolent than the worse reverberations of the bloodiest and cruelest battles he had ever engaged in. Cold, wind-driven rain was pelting his face and eyes in the most painful and maddening fashion. He tried to turn away from the maelstrom and felt the driving wind literally pick him up off the ground and smash him against a groaning tree ...

Coverdale was jolted back into reality and looked around, sweat was pouring from his forehead. Except for his acolyte, he was totally alone. "Did you hear anything?" he asked the young man.

The aide looked at his master with dismay and responded, "No, my lord."

The Captain leaned against the fort's palisade wall to steady himself. Ever since his epiphany in the twin chief's Sweat Bath Lodge a lifetime ago when Gabriell Coverdale became an honored member of the *Choptank* tribe as *AH-ban-nah Chon-TEH*, his spiritual and psychic selves had been growing stronger. He recalled the vision in the lodge while under the effects of the *KEESH-wah* root. He had seen a hoard of black ants floating on oak tree leaves in a roiling sea of blood. The later attack of the vicious *Mitsawoket* renegades as they approached the village across the storm tossed estuary brought that vision into a stark and frightening reality. It was only the first of a growing series of extra-sensory happenings over the ensuing months. It was becoming clear to those he talked to about his visions that Creator-God was grooming him to become the 'forth-teller' of the village, and he was well on his way to fulfilling that role.

Tattowin and *Weanchum* were waiting at the edge of the village when the Englishman and his servant emerged from the forest. In many ways Coverdale had become the spiritual brother of these two holy men and they were often in a strange and even ethereal communication with each other. The twin chiefs had been meditating in their *wig-wam* when they experienced the same sense of foreboding and fear that washed through their White friend. Without any wasted words or cordialities, *Tattowin* said simply, "What now?" Any sense of 'maybe' about the coming storm was a moot point. The issues were ...when will it happen and how can they prepare the community?

Another meeting with the tribal council was organized that same evening. *Asquash* was on the hunting trip with his clansmen, but head chief *Pemetosusk* and his cousin, lesser chief *Pacowassamuck*, sensed the urgency in the twins and their English friend and were prepared to listen to their concerns and recommendations. The five parlayed late into the night and by morning's light a framework for a crisis management plan was agreed to. In an effort not to alarm the villagers, since there really was no tangible proof that a disaster was on the way, the responses were gradual and sensible. Non-perishable foods and other supplies were carried to Ft. Wingfield and stored in the sturdy log structures around the compound. Because of the previous bountiful seasons there was an overabundance of both, and the village was beginning to experience storage problems. This was a logical procedure to ease this issue.

The villagers were encouraged to inspect the construction of their *wig-wams* and lodges and to make any needed repairs. A large supply of reed and branch mats were woven by the *Ke-WE-dah-yah-s'ah* clanswomen and given out to any family who wanted to reinforce their present walls. The few who wondered why this step was taken were told that the extra thicknesses would improve the insulating properties of each structure. The Gatherer Clansmen were instructed to widen the pathway from the village to the fort and to be sure it was well marked for day or night passage. Many of the *Choptank* families had never been to the former home of their English brothers. The village leaders were encouraging them to walk the trail and all were amazed by its imposing appearance and the sense of permanence it provided. This same group of clansmen also were delegated the responsibility to clear away a ring of trees around the Men's Lodge and also the women's Moon time Lodge. The marvelous metal axes received from the White Men made this short, and even enjoyable, work.

The suggestion was offered to the *Ho-KU-wah-s'ah* water people to pull their canoes well up onto dry land when they returned from gathering the bounty of the Mother of All Waters. Usually, the craft were half in-and-out of the water for easier launching. Also, they were reminded to keep the beach as clear as possible of their oars, nets, crab pots and other paraphernalia of their trade. The tribal leadership could not share the reason that if a massive hurricane was an eventuality these items might become missiles of death as they slammed into the huts and *wig-wams* of the villagers.

It was early morning as a deathly sense of forboding seemed to crawl menacingly through the *Choptank* village. The normally cooling and friendly breeze off the bay was replaced by a stifling heavy stillness. Clearly something was wrong.

The village pets became restless and began pacing the interiors of the lodges and *wig-wams*. They began to whine and yap and pull at the clothing of their sleeping masters and mistresses. The drowsy *Choptanks* were irritated by the behavior and either let their four-legged companions out or ordered them to quiet down. Those creatures still inside the homes continued whining and scratching at the door mats until they were also freed. The Natives who stood in the open doorways watched the dogs run back and forth in the village plaza and heard them barking furiously. Then the strangest thing of all happened; the animals high-tailed it into the forest away from the bay.

As the Indians looked at each other in confusion one of the elder women added another piece to the mystery, "Where are the seagulls?" Every morning the voracious birds would circle over the village and strut along the beach looking for handouts and left-overs from cleaning the crab, oysters, and fish that had been harvested. There were absolutely none to be seen or heard …

The first signs of danger came creeping over the southeastern horizon.

The morning sun had still not risen high enough to present itself, but wispy clouds were quietly marching northward. They were the most marvelous iridescent pinks and reds the villagers had ever seen. The word passed from *wig-wam* to *wig-wam*, and soon many of the people were standing in their doorways, rubbing the sleep from their eyes and gazing at the sky in awe. Captain Coverdale remembered a similar sky that fateful day the terrible storm blew *The Phyllis Redoubtable* deep into Chesapeake Bay and felt a wave of fear that made his mouth dry and his hands begin to sweat.

At the same time some of the *Ho-KU-wah-s'ah* clansmen pointed at the bay and there was a sight never seen before also. The ebb tide had gone out so far that the sand and rock sea bed extended to the crab feeding areas. The sea harvesters laughed in glee and began running down to the edge of the water with their baskets planning to 'pick' crab like they were berries on a bush. As they waded into the shallows filling their baskets, the winds started to moan and small white caps began to march toward them. Knowledgeable of how quickly the Mother of All Waters can change her mind, they ceased their activity and began to return to the normal shoreline. The Natives had barely reached the village when the wind velocity picked up and began to howl around the trees and buildings. It had a strange salty aroma and was filled with moisture.

Father Sun emerged over the eastern horizon and was the deepest red anyone could remember. Moments later fingers of blackness reached out and seemed to hungrily devour what little light and warmth he had offered the Earth Mother. A ridge of thunderheads was looming northward that was so black and so high that it seemed like night had decided to overpower day and rule the world ... and the winds evolved into a ceaseless gale with the first tastes of rain.

Then came a distant rumbling roar and the ground began to tremble. Captain Coverdale withdrew his telescope from its case and while scanning southward through the pelting rain drops saw a massive storm surge pushed by the driving monsoon and flowing around the southern headlands straight toward the townspeople. He screamed with all his might in hopes his words would be heard above the howling wind, *"Ah-KE-che-dah-oh-YON-keh!* (To the fort! To the fort!)

Some of the frightened Natives ran blindly into the forest, others obeyed their Captain and headed toward the path of possible safety. Still others were too old, too infirmed, or too slow to escape the inevitable. When the first waves crashed onto the village's beach the crests were as high as three men standing on each other's shoulders. The power of the mountain of water picked up the grounded canoes like match sticks and hurled them directly into the heart of the village. The lodges and *wig-wams* collapsed and crumbled like flower blossoms in a wind storm. Those who had sought shelter in their homes were laid bare and washed along the ground like clumps of grass screaming and trying to reach anything to hold on to. As the greedy waves reached their apex and began to recede, the backward flow tumbled the bodies of the dead and deposited huge mounds of debris along the beach and into the nearby water.

And the winds howled louder and louder and the rains grew more and more fierce. Everything was cold … saturated … and black as midnight.

The Natives who had been able to find shelter in the nearby forest endeavored to return to what remained of their community, but the driving maelstrom made progress almost impossible. The baleful noises were a crescendo of screaming winds and cracking thunder. The blackness was occasionally shattered by flashes of lightning reflecting the distorted faces of the deceased and presenting brief glimpses of total destruction. Those who were able to crawl into the teeth of the wind emerged from hiding and began to call out the names of their missing loved ones. Their cries of pain and anguish flew into the face of the storm and were drowned out by the laughing voices of the Hounds of Hell. Some found their drowned family members, their bodies bruised and twisted into grotesque semblances of human beings. Their tears of despair and shock were washed away by the driving rain and the heartless winds.

How could it get any worse?

But it did. The hurricane winds continued to increase in intensity, and the beautiful forest was the next to pay its due. Huge pine trees were torn up by their roots and crashed against their brothers whom they had stood beside for hundreds of years. The marvelous oak trees held their ground but began to lose their limbs and branches with shattering cracks and painful moans. And it rained, and it rained, and it rained.

It truly was the Mother-of-All *Wah-M'NE-oh-m'ne-pe* (hurricanes).

Sometime during actual night a restless calm carefully walked over the darkened land. A pale and distant moon tried her best to bring some light to the survivors through the thick clouds. The fortunate *Choptanks* who had reached shelter in the fort were huddled together paralyzed by shock and dismay. The rains were now a continuous downpour but had eased considerably. The winds abated into occasional zephyrs making their final efforts to bring misery to the hapless people. Head chief *Pemetosusk* and his wife stepped out of one of the storage buildings carrying blazing torches. He called to his villagers to crowd into the cabins and structures still standing as best they could to get out of the weather and try to find a warm and dry place to remain until daybreak.

The only sounds were the falling rain, the moaning wind, and the pitiful cries of the people ...

Morning came, as it always has since the beginning of time.
The rains had ceased altogether and the first fingers of sun
light were reaching into the fort. The gate had been completely
torn off and was nowhere to be seen. *Pemetosusk* had not slept
the entire night, and emerging from the cabin found lesser
chief *Pacowassamuck* wandering in a daze near the trail head.
They peered out of the fort and saw the massive desolation
that stretched out before them. Their beautiful forest was
now clumps of shattered branches and split tree trunks. It
appeared as if every leaf or needle had been ripped from its
limbs and consumed by some ravenous animal. The pathway
to the village was choked with debris and downed trees and
was completely impassable.

Wiping the tears from his eyes, *Pemetosusk* returned to the
cabin and found his beautiful wife *Watsawasoo*. He asked her
to find some of the other women and do their best to prepare
some kind of meal for the surviving villagers. An ample
amount of supplies and foodstuffs had been stored in the fort
and the small stream that flowed nearby was clogged with
shattered pines and oaks, but appeared to still be usable for
their purposes. The marvelous ladies, always so creative and
willing, soon had salted venison boiling in the iron pot of the
fort's dining hall and were digging through baskets and clay
jars to supplement the meal.

The two village leaders organized a small group of men
to work their way back to the settlement and to reconnoiter
the situation. The others were to remain at the fort and
to wait until further instructions would be forthcoming.
Picking their way through the blow-down, the scouting party
reached the village site. The emotions resulting from what
their eyes beheld could only be expressed by cries of dismay
and anguish. Every canoe had been smashed and shattered.
Not one structure was still in usable condition. Some of the

lodges constructed of skinned tree trunks and long straight limbs were recognizable, but every *wig-wam* was completely gone, their presence marked only by their cluttered fire pits. Some of the village dogs had returned and were resting by the bloated bodies of their masters and mistresses moaning and crying pitifully. And circling above the vestiges of a once bustling community were clouds of buzzards trying to get the nerve to participate in the macabre feast awaiting them.

At that moment a commotion arose from the massive pile of debris to the north of the village. *Asquash* and the *WE-h'ne-s'ah* hunters who had been on their men's outing emerged climbing over downed trees and skirting the barren branches screaming their anger and consternation. They had been camping deep in the forest and the brunt of the storm had been quelled by the time it reached their repose.

The young men went to work immediately using the mounds of rubble to reconstruct one of the lodges. Then they respectfully began to collect the dead and place them in the structure. Many of the deceased were their friends and even their relatives, so it was a sad and heartbreaking responsibility that had to be done to keep the flying scavengers at bay.

Pemetosusk sat down on the broken skeleton of a shattered canoe and recalled something the twin chiefs had said when the council was endeavoring to determine the future of the *HA-sah-pah-pe* (African slaves):

> *"...they have become orphans in this New World; but the Mother of All has not forgotten her sweet children despite their anguish, and Creator-God has made a promise to His people that no matter how painful and hopeless life might become, there will always be a remnant to carry on ..."*

Those sage words crawled out of his broken heart and brought about the smallest amount of hope for the future. He looked at his friend of many years and the great one-eyed warrior's face said more than any words ever could. *Pemetosusk* reached for him and they embraced each other in silent anguish.

CHAPTER VIII ... THE
CURTAIN DROPS

T he *HA-sah-pah-pe* (Black Men) were grateful beyond words to the *Choptanks* for their new found freedom on the western shores of the Bay. Being forest people from the Dark Continent untrained and unaccustomed to harvesting the waters, once they established a semblance of a settlement, they began to explore inland. Excellent trackers and attuned to the voices of the land, they gleaned its bounty and continued to grow stronger and more confident day by day. As they expanded their new homeland it was inevitable that they would come face-to-face with its indigenous population. Three Native tribes, the *Patuxent, Potopaco* and *Yaocomaco,* had occupied the nearby forests and waterways for generations and knew about the arrival of the *TOK-cha oh-YAH-teh* (strange people) long before the Africans knew they were under observation.

Interestingly, the color **black** was considered sacred, and when the *HA-sah-pah-pe* eventually initiated contact with the Native villages they were approached with great respect and honor. These holy men were 'beautiful' in the eyes of the Indians and were accepted with open arms into their families. That perfect blending of races is noticeable even unto today.

———

The *Chicamacomico* Nation never matured into a vibrant and growing community. Despite Queen *Wicompo's* dreams of empire the new reality was too overpowering. Finding the lost tribal members and bringing them back was an impossible task because of time and geography.

The two English seamen, Theodore Brooks-Hughes and Jonas Profit, were able to return to the village with the slaves they had bartered for with the *Nanticoke* tribe. The women had been in captivity for so many years there was no sense of *Te-YAH-dah* (home) as they followed the Englishmen into the pleasant glen. *Wicompo,* in an effort to glean something from their efforts to find survivors claimed them as her slaves despite the contentious responses from her daughter *Cahonke* and her daughter's friend *Cah-cookos.* In reality, the lives of the two women had a slim hope at best of improvement.

The older withered and disheveled man suffered from the rigors of the return trip, but his determination to find his home kept him putting one foot before the other. When the party left the dense forest and emerged into the open area where the village had been rebuilt, he fell to his knees and began to weep uncontrollably. Clearly the return brought painful memories from deep within his soul. He wandered to a mostly destroyed *wig-wam* that had not been rebuilt and with a profound sense of hopelessness peered through the darkened doorway. Of course it was empty and had been for many years. Turning and looking blankly at the Englishmen his body posture clearly expressed his disappointment, and his outstretched arms said simply, "Now what?"

The younger man covered with scars from countless floggings stood by impassively. His miserable life had left him devoid of any emotions except hate. It was apparent that this change in his situation was not going to be met with any sense of relief or gratitude. He may have been a *Chicamacomico* in his distant past, but now he was basically a homeless renegade. As the others tried to find a place for him in the community, he was reticent to help or to be productive without being prodded or ordered. He never volunteered for anything nor gave his best effort at his tasks. *Wicompo's* maid servant, *Scoseweto,* took a special interest in his welfare, but he could not return the kindness. Not unexpectedly, after a short stay in the village, he began to secretly stash away food and weapons; and one spring morning … he was gone.

The trade pathways that had once been main thoroughfares of commerce through the *Chicamacomico* settlement had long been abandoned and forgotten as the brush and undergrowth reclaimed the land. This did protect the elopers from the searching *Choptanks,* but other Native groups had found easier routes between their villages and had utilized them for many years. The beautiful offspring from the union between the English boys and *Choptank* girls grew into robust and handsome men eager to explore and to find new homes and start their own families. Even unto today, the young ones of all families eventually leave home and relish their new-found independence. These marvelous boys from the *Chicamacomico* village were taller, lighter skinned and stronger than their Native counterparts, so wherever they roamed they stood out as worthy mates.

History does not divulge what happened to the village or its beautiful setting. A study of the current map of the state of Maryland's eastern shore displays a small river called the *Chicamacomico* flowing south and westward

into the Chesapeake at Fishing Bay. Some years later the
Chicamacomico were noted as an indigenous group on Cape
Hatteras in what is now North Carolina. Whether or not
there was any connection to the Maryland group of the 1500's
and 1600's has never been determined.

———————

As if the cruel voice of Fate murmured "never again" the
story of the *Choptank* people was destined to be lost among
the countless pages in the book of "Time."

The beautiful village was never rebuilt. The wretched
souls of the lost men, women and children wailed pitifully in
the cold, unforgiving winds that walked across the headland
bringing tears to the eyes of the survivors as they surveyed
the heartbreaking vestiges of their homes. A sense of dread
and foreboding seemed to grasp their throats as if the dead
were screaming in rage because of the injustice. The shattered
and uprooted trees added to the sense that this would be for
hundreds of years ... a cemetery

The numbed Indians who had fled to the protective arms
of the English fort, as well as the hunting party camping well
inland when the storm struck, were the sad remnants of the
once proud and powerful *Choptank* nation. As they chanted
the names of the lost during their moon phase of mourning,
among the missing was Captain Gabriell Coverdale who
had wandered to and from the edges of the world until he
found his home and became the gentle *AH-ban-nah Chon-
TEH*. Partially buried in the remains of the village was an
amazing relic. Captain Coverdale had saved his sword and
scabbard as a memory of his past. The Natives recognized it
from the early contact with their *Ha-KAH-sha-nah* brothers
and cherished it as a truly Holy Icon. With great respect and
deference they constructed a pyramid shaped cairn with

sea worn rocks and interred it with wailing songs of grief. Hundreds of years later, beach combers found some rusting metallic shards among the rocks and sand and the mystery was never resolved.

The *Choptank's* remarkable water craft, the envy of all the tribes who resided along the Bay, were completely destroyed part and parcel and the Mother of All Waters greedily took the shards and pieces to her breast. She had jealously tried to claim them over the years with her storms and angry waters, but the canoes were too well built to succumb to her efforts. In the sacred canoe construction lodge a new craft was partially completed. The marvelous eagle-carved bow peered plaintively through the limbs and branches of the smashed and shattered oak trees. The total demise of the boat builder clan took the secrets of their ages-old time tested skills and artistry to the grave, never to be duplicated again. Equally heartbreaking, in the blink of an eye countless generations of effort building and harvesting the salt cairns along the north shore of the headlands were lost forever. The ravaging hurricane deposited a mountain of sand and debris well into the bay taking everything of value with it. In recent years an archeology team was able to excavate a partial wall of carefully stacked stones with accompanying salt crystals near the coast line west of Bellevue, Maryland. They determined it was some sort of "Pre-Columbian" stone-aged structure and noted it for future exploration.

Unable to continue the traditions of a proud water-people, the hapless *Choptanks* had to rely on the abilities of the gatherer clan and the hunters. Sadly they would eventually wander aimlessly away from the seashore over the ensuing years for survival and sustenance. Their namesake still marks the geography of Maryland's eastern shore. The powerful Choptank River for all eternity will flow into the arms of the Mother of All Waters. History's last mention of the once-powerful *Choptank* people was a simple, almost forgotten, entry in a 1720's property title transaction. A Native identified as a *Choptank* received payment from an English family for a small land parcel.

APPENDIX

I ... Native Vocabulary –
Choptank to English

AH-bah-nah Gentle

Ah-NOP-tah Stop

CHA-pah Beaver

Chicamacomico Neighboring tribe

Chon-TEH Heart

Chop-tah-nk Native name for local tribe. The Englishmen thought it was the name of the elderly Medicine Woman and called her that throughout the story.

DAH-ku-oh-WAH-s'een Everything

Doh-WON deh hon-YEH-du Tonight we sing

Ha-HON-nah Wo-e-YUK-she-cha Tomorrow we can be sorrowful

Dook-SHIN-cha Mink

Eesh-DE-mah Sleep

E-EH-ched-gah-gah The Imitator (Satan)

E-H'DU-ska-pe won-KEH-yah Sweat bath lodge

E-NAH Mother

E-TON-chon Master

e-YEH ne He is alive

Ha-KAH-sha-nah Groundhog. Became the generic name for the Englishmen

Hay-YU-ha-ha Ground up antlers used as an aphrodisiac

He-YAH No

Hin-TOON Hairy

Hok-SHE-oh-pah Child

Ho-KU-wah-s'ah The clan that harvested the sea's bounty

Ho! Le-ci-YAH ni-CO-pi Choptank welcoming song

Ho! Le-ci-YAH ni-CO-pi

Hoo-HA-pe skeletons

Ho-SAH-pah Bass fish

Ke-WE-dah-yah Gather around

Ke-WE-dah-yah-s'ah The clan that gathered roots, herbs and medicinals.

Ko-DAH Friend

Koh-DEE Transparent

Kon-HE Raven

Mah-GAH All kinds of geese

Mah-GAH-k'see-cha All kinds of ducks

Mah-KAH-ze Sulfur

MAH-ne To Walk

Mah-TOH Bear

M'ne-SKOO-yah Salt

Nah-DON-pe TOH-kah Choptank victory song Charged the foe,

WEEN-yon KAH-gah-pe But I made a woman of him

Oh-WAH-s'ee-nah Te-WAH-hay "All my relations." The comment said when exiting the sweat lodge

Oh-YAH-teh People

OON-she-kah Poor or Destitute

Oonk-CHAY Animal or human excrement

Ozinies Neighboring tribe

PAH-pah Generic term for all jerky meat

Pe-DAH-mah-yeh Thank you

Peh-ZHU-tah Medicine

Shoon-HE-nah Red fox

Shoong-TOK-cha Wolf

SHO-tah smoke

Sin-TEH-h'dah Rattlesnake

Ska White

Soon-KAH Little Brother

Susquehannock Raiding Indians from the north bay area

TAH-cha Deer

Tah-ee-vah Nah-mah-Eeyoni Nanticoke healing song

Tzeh-ee-hoot-zittoo

Nah-mah-Eeyoni

Tah-TEH Wind

Te-YAH-dah Home

To-bac Tobacco

Toh The color blue

Toh Ho-KU-wah The ferocious blue fish and talisman of the
fishing clan

Toh We-CHOSH-tah The blue man

Wah-KON-kon-s'ah Magicians. Also the clan that carved the
canoes and harvested the salt cairns.

Wah-M'NAH-eh-zah Indian corn

Wah-K'TEH-s'ah Killer

Wah-PEH-pe Leaves (Indian name for peppermint and other
leafy herbs)

Wah-KO<u>N</u>-kon Magic

Wah-TOH-toh We-CHOSH-tah-pe Green Men

Wah-ZE-yah-tah Wok-PAH The North River. *Nanticoke* for the
Choptank River

Wash-TEH-cha-kah Friendly

Wash-TEH TOH-ke-yo-peh-yah Good Trade

Wah-YAH-kah-pe Slaves

Wak-KON-ton-kah God

We-CHA Raccoon

We-CHOSH-tah Man

WE-h'ne-s'ah Hunter

Wig-ah-wum Home or house

Win-CHIN-yon-nah Girl

WIN-yon we-CHOSH-tah Holy man (displays some feminine
    qualities)

WO-dah Eat

Wom-BLEE Eagle

Won-YAH-kah See or Look

WO-oh-ke-yeh Peace

Yu-HOM-ne Turn around

Yu-TOH-kon Get a move on!

Zoo-YAH-we-CHOSH-tah Warrior

II … Native Vocabulary – English to *Choptank*

All My Relations *Oh-WAH-s'ee nah Te-WAH-hay*

(Said While Exiting Sweat Lodge)

Aphrodisiac (made of *Hay-YU-ha-ha*

ground up antlers)

Bass Fish *Ho-SAH-pah*

Bear *Mah-TOH*

Beaver *CHA-pah*

Blue Color *Toh*

Blue Fish *Toh Ho-KU-wah*

The Blue Man *Toh WE-CHOSH-tah*

Brother (Younger) *Soon-KAH*

Child *Hok-SHE-oh-pah*

Deer *TAH-cha*

Duck (all kinds) *Mah-GAH-k'see-cha*

Eagle *Wom-BLEE*

Eat *WO-dah*

Everything *DAH-ku-oh-WAH-s'een*

Excrement *Oonk-CHAY*

Fishermen *Ho-KU-wah-s'ah*

Friend *Ko-DAH*

Friendly *Wash-TEH-cha-kah*

Gather (or Come Nigh) *Ke-WE-dah-yah*

Gatherers *Ke-WE-dah-yah s'ah*

Geese *Mah-GAH*

Gentle *AH-bah-nah*

Girl *Win-CHIN-yon-nah*

God *Wak-KON-ton-kah*

Good Trade *Wash-TEH TOH-ke-yo-peh-yah*

Groundhog (also generic *Ha-KAH-sha-nah*

name for Englishmen)

Hairy *Hin-TOON*

Heart *Chon-TEH*

He lives *e-YEH ne*

Home *Te-YAH-dah*

House (or home) *Wig-ah-wum*

Hunter *WE-h'ne-s'ah*

Jerky meat (all kinds) *PAH-pah*

Killer *Wah-K'TEH-s'ah*

Leaves (Peppermint) *Wah-PEH-pe*

Lodge *Won-KEH-yah*

Magic *Wah-KO<u>N</u>-ko<u>n</u>*

Magicians *Wah-KO<u>N</u>-ko<u>n</u>-s'ah*

Man *We-CHOSH-tah*

Master *E-TON-chon*

Medicine *Peh-ZHU-tah*

Mink *Dook-SHIN-cha*

Mother *E-NAH*

Move It! *Yu-TOH-kon*

No *He-YAH*

Peace *WO-oh-ke-yeh*

People *Oh-YAH-teh*

Poor *OON-she-kah*

Raccoon *we-CHA*

Rattlesnake *Sin-TEH-h'dah*

Raven *Kon̲-HE*

Red fox *Shoon-HE-nah*

Salt *M'ne-SKOO-yah*

Satan (the Imitator) *E-EH-ched-gah-gah*

See (or Look) *Won̲-YAH-kah*

Skeletons *Hoo-HA-pe*

Slaves *Wah-YAH-kah-pe*

Sleep *Eesh-DE-mah*

Smoke *SHO-tah*

Stop *Ah-NOP-tah*

Sulfur *Mah-KAH-ze*

Sweat Lodge *E-H'DU-ska-pe won-KEH-yah*

Tea leaves *Wah-PEH*

Thank You *Pe-DAH-mah-yeh*

Tobacco *To-bac*

Transparent *Koh-DEE*

Turn Around *Yu-HOM-ne*

Choptank Victory Song *Nah-DON-pe TOH-kah WEEN-yon KAH-gah-pe*

Walk (to step forward) *MAH-ne*

Warrior *Zoo-YAH-we-CHOSH-tah*

White *Ska*

Wind *Tah-TEH*

Wolf *Shoong-TOK-cha*

III … Noteworthy *Choptank* Indians – The Children of the Bluefish

AH-ban-nah Chon-TEH – "Gentle Heart." *Choptank* name for reborn Captain Garbriell Coverdale.

Asquash – The Chief Hunter of the *Choptank* Tribe and member of the Tribal Council. Later named *"Won-ZE e-SH'DAH-su"* which translates to "One Eyeball" as a result of the battle with the *Susquehannock* renegades.

Cah-cookos – Daughter of *Pacowassamuck* and *Pencookos*.

Cahonke – Daughter of *Weesanusks* and *Wicompo*

Chop-tah-nk – Elderly woman who first met the White Men. Later known as the leading Tribe's Medicine Woman.

Ho-KU-wah-s'ah – The 'sea harvester clan." Their totem was *Toh Ho-KU-wah* – The Blue Fish. They wore a fish-shaped mother of pearl talisman to identify themselves. Lesser chief *Weesanusks* was a clan member until his suicide.

Ke-WE-dah-yah-s'ah – The "gatherer clan." Their totem was *TAH-cha* – The Deer. All medicine men and women were in this clan. Lesser chiefs *Tattowin* and *Weanchum* were members of this clan.

Mah-TOH Wah K'TEH-s'ah – "Bear Slayer." *Choptank* name for Seaman Jonas Profit.

Nehatuckwis – Guide for the Upriver Mapping Crew

Pacowassamuck – Lesser Chief and husband of *Pencookos*. Father of *Cah-cookos*

Pemetosusk – Head Chief and husband of *Watsawasoo*.

Pencookos – Wife of *Pacowassamuck*. Mother of *Cah-cookos*

Tattowin and *Weanchum* – Twin Holy Men of the Tribe

Wah-KON-kon-s'ah – The clan that produces salt and build boats. Their totem is *Wom-BLEE* – The Eagle. They are the only group allowed to wear feathers. Head chief *Pemetosusk* and lesser chief *Pacowassamuck* are members of this clan

Watsawasoo – *Pemetosusk's* wife and member of *Chicamacomico* Tribe

Weesanusks – Life-long friend of *Pemetosusk* and Lesser Chief who had a special affinity for "grog." Husband of *Wicompo*.

WE-h'ne-s'ah – The hunter and warrior clan. Their totem is *Mah-TOH* – The Bear. They identify themselves by wearing necklaces made of bear claws and teeth. They were the only clan without membership on the tribal leadership council until *Asquash* was selected after the death of *Weesanusks*. They normally never participated in 'politics'.

Wicompo – *Weesanusks'* wife and also member of *Chicamacomico* Tribe

IV ... The African *HA-sah-pah-pe*

Ajali – Died while being brought ashore by the Dutch slavers. His name translates as "Destiny."

Akida Khalfani – Formerly the most important chief of his clan of the Swahili tribe. He emerges as the leader of the *HA-sah-pah* (Black Man) as they recover from the ordeal with the Dutch slavers and resume their lives on the mainland.

Anga – The most quiet and discerning member of the former slave group. He was able to survive the Dutch mistreatment by having the power to flow his consciousness in and out of the dream world. His name means "Sky."

Betoto – The oldest of the survivors. His wisdom and ability to listen proved extremely valuable to the future course of the former slaves. His name means "Owl."

Bin – The last living member of *Akida Kalfani's* family and also the last of his many sons. Logically, his name translates as "Son."

Fumo – The most fierce and aggressive of the Swahili survivors. He was a famous and feared warrior of his tribe, and vowed vengeance on everyone who had brought pain to his people and himself. As he grew in strength he also grew in ego. His name means "Spear."

Sabra – The saddest and most damaged of the survivors. He never did fully recover his strength, and this proved to be a burden on all the survivors in their future pursuits.

He was given this name by the others. It means "patient or enduring."

Zuberi – He was a captured Zulu tribesman, taller and more spiritual than the other survivors. He, too, was a great warrior for his people who were traditional enemies of the Swahili. Eventually, there would be a major conflict with *Fumo*. Both were unable to forget the past as they grew more able to assert themselves. His name means "strong."

V. Ship's Compliment of the *Phyllis Redoubtable* upon Departure from Jamestown

London Company Employees

Master Edward M. Wingfield - Duly appointed President of the Virginia Colony
Cuthbert Guilford – Magistrate
William Love – Tailor
Captain Gabriell Coverdale
Master Robert Hunt – Preacher
John Martin
George Martin
William Cassen
George Cassen
Thomas Cassen
Thomas Couper – Barber
Ustis Clovill
Kellan Throgmorton
Francis Midwinter
Edward Pising – Carpenter
John Capper – Carpenter
William Wickinson – Surgeon

Fusilier Detachment

Sergeant Bartholomew Lusby – Commander
Private James Dixon – Fusilier
Private Kenneth Quinby – Fusilier

Ship's Crew

Edwin Marian – Ship's Officer
Oscar Johnson – Ship's Cook
Eldred Parksley – Able-bodied Seaman
Obadiah Withams – Navigator
Jonas Profit – Able-bodied Seaman
Matthew Tasley – Able-bodied Seaman
Percy Exum – Able-bodied Seaman
Theodore Brooks-Hughes – Able-bodied Seaman
Jerald Pennyfeather-Grayson – Able-bodied Seaman

ABOUT THE AUTHOR

Stan E. Hughes, aka Ha-Gue-A-Dees-Sas, is an artist and retired public school administrator who consulted for an Indian Education Center in Spokane, Washington, and has been an advocate for Indian education. He lived in the Chesapeake Bay region for several years and often visits Kent Island in Maryland. This is his ninth book.

Printed in the United States
by Bookmasters

Printed in the United States
By Bookmasters